Enemy Mine

**Also by Lindsay McKenna
in Large Print:**

Sister of Fortune
Hunter's Woman
Man of Passion
Hunter's Pride
The Untamed Hunter
Destiny's Woman
An Honorable Woman
First Born
A Man Alone
Man with a Mission
Heart Lost (Published in Spanish as
    Corazón perdido)

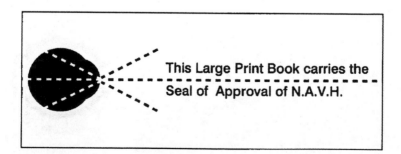

This Large Print Book carries the
Seal of Approval of N.A.V.H.

Enemy Mine

Lindsay McKenna

Thorndike Press • Waterville, Maine

Published in 2006 by arrangement with Harlequin Books S.A.

Thorndike Press® Large Print Romance.

The tree indicium is a trademark of Thorndike Press.

The text of this Large Print edition is unabridged.
Other aspects of the book may vary from the original edition.

Set in 16 pt. Plantin by Ramona Watson.

Printed in the United States on permanent paper.

Library of Congress Cataloging-in-Publication Data

McKenna, Lindsay, 1946–
    Enemy mine / by Lindsay McKenna. — Large print ed.
       p. cm. — (Thorndike Press large print Thorndike
romance)
    ISBN 0-7862-8272-X (lg. print : hc : alk. paper)
    1. Drug dealers — Fiction.   2. Drug traffic — Fiction.
3. Helicopter pilots — Fiction.   4. Women soldiers —
Fiction.   5. Large type books.   I. Title.   II. Thorndike
Press large print romance series.
PS3563.C37525E54 2006
    813´.54—dc22
                                                    2005027965

To: Stacie Albee
and her grade school class.
A wonderful teacher, a great reader
and an inspiration to her children.
Thank you for being who you are.

As the Founder/CEO of NAVH, the only national health agency solely devoted to those who, although not totally blind, have an eye disease which could lead to serious visual impairment, I am pleased to recognize Thorndike Press* as one of the leading publishers in the large print field.

Founded in 1954 in San Francisco to prepare large print textbooks for partially seeing children, NAVH became the pioneer and standard setting agency in the preparation of large type.

Today, those publishers who meet our standards carry the prestigious "Seal of Approval" indicating high quality large print. We are delighted that Thorndike Press is one of the publishers whose titles meet these standards. We are also pleased to recognize the significant contribution Thorndike Press is making in this important and growing field.

Lorraine H. Marchi, L.H.D.
Founder/CEO
NAVH

* Thorndike Press encompasses the following imprints: Thorndike, Wheeler, Walker and Large Print Press.

Chapter One

Kathy Trayhern knew she was going to die. The only thing left to wonder was when and how. She knew *who* was going to kill her: Carlos Garcia. Hands tightening on the wheel of her red Toyota MR2 sports car, the wind tugging at her loose blond hair, Kathy took in a deep, ragged breath.

She was driving through the majestic Rocky Mountains, familiar friends to her, as she'd grown up here. At least she'd spent from age eight onward in the Montana Rockies. Before that . . . At the memory, her mouth pursed in pain — a raw pain that never healed. Before that she'd lived in Washington, D.C. Her father, Morgan Trayhern, had thought he and his family were safe from retaliation by the drug lords of South America because of the power he brokered in the capital. He'd made a near-fatal error in that assumption. Kathy had watched her family — both her parents, the twins, Pete and Kelly, and her older brother Jason — begin a death spiral of slow deterioration after they'd been kidnapped by her father's enemies.

Kathy touched her dark aviator glasses, a nervous habit whenever she thought about that terrifying time. The treacherous act had been engineered by Guillermo Garcia, Carlos's father. . . . She lost herself in the memories, no longer smelling the fresh pine scent along the two-lane asphalt highway that wound through the forested mountains. Nor did she notice the fluffy white clouds accumulating — rain clouds that soon would shed water upon the thirsty land. No, her heart, her soul were focused on the obsessive rage she felt, a desire for revenge that gnawed at her gut. She couldn't forget the kidnapping.

Tunneling her fingers through her wind-tossed mane, Kathy followed the twisting curves of the road. The June sun was high overhead. It was noon, and she should have been hungry, but her carefully planned mission of reprisal had robbed her of an appetite. Whether her parents guessed it or not, she was coming home to say goodbye to them. Because what she had decided to do — get even with the Garcia drug family, would kill her.

Grimly, Kathy stared unseeing at the road before her. There was no regret in her; after all, she'd lived twenty-seven years

— long enough to witness the ongoing effects the kidnapping had had on her parents and Jason. After they were rescued, they lived in hell, struggling every day to overcome the terrible, tragic wounds of their trauma.

Who could *ever* forget a rape? Her mother, Laura Trayhern, certainly couldn't. And Kathy's father, who was larger than life in her eyes, had been drugged and tortured. He'd nearly died at the hands of his captors, who had beaten him three times a day with their fists, chains and boots. No one could get over such abuse.

With the atrocities he'd committed on her parents and Jason, Guillermo Garcia had stolen Kathy's loving family from her. For they'd changed, all of them. From the kidnapping day onward, Kathy had lost the happy parents she'd adored.

Over the years, guilt had eaten at her because she'd been spared as a child, she'd known something was terribly wrong with her family, but was too young to understand what or why. In her teens, she'd grasped the truth and wondered why the kidnappers hadn't taken her, too. Why had she been left behind? Kathy knew drug lords in South America felt sons were important, especially the firstborn. Women counted for nothing, except to be mothers of a man's children. Maybe that was why they'd left her behind and taken Jason, instead.

Her thoughts lingered on her brother, firstborn son of her generation of the proud Trayhern dynasty, with its two-hundred-year tradition of military service to the nation. Jason had been kidnapped by another drug family, in Maui, Hawaii, and kept a captive there. They'd tried to win him over with candy but when he'd balked and fought back, they'd beaten six-year-old Jason, taunted him endlessly, slapped him and made a cowering dog out of him. Kathy remembered her extroverted, assertive older brother. After his rescue, he'd come home a different person, a stranger to her. He'd become so withdrawn, so unresponsive that Kathy felt she'd lost her brother, too.

As a small girl, she had cried nightly about this loss, sobbing quietly into her pillow so no one could hear her. She didn't want to waken her parents, who were still reeling from the shock of their imprisonment. Kathy had understood even at that age that she couldn't run to her mother or father when she was scared or needed to be held. Not anymore.

Life had spared her from the brutal kidnappers. Yet now, many years later, Kathy was well aware of the message those cretins had wanted to convey to her family. They'd warned Morgan's supersecret agency, Perseus, to stop trying to halt the drug trade in the Caribbean and South America . . . or else.

When her father refused to halt his secret missions, the drug lords had gotten even. Guillermo Garcia had planned his retaliation perfectly. Morgan's arrogant belief that his family was immune to the drug lords' treachery had been off the mark entirely. What better way to even a score than with a man's family? In South America, the family unit was everything, and that was where they struck at Morgan. With his family.

A slow, simmering anger stirred in Kathy as she braked gently for a curve around a black granite cliff. Patches of wildflowers clung to pockets of yellow soil on the vertical incline.

The time was *now.* She'd just gotten back from a yearlong black ops flying a Seahawk helicopter with insertion teams in South America. She'd worked with the CIA, Navy SEALs and Recon Marines. As a pilot, she'd experienced plenty of action

11

and some near misses on her own life. After seeing firsthand what drug lords did to many families in Colombia, Kathy had a gutful of rage. Witnessing others' horror had triggered violent feelings from her family's past, and it fed her need for revenge.

And, as if to seal her quest, the drug dealers had killed the man she loved: Lieutenant Curt Shields, a U.S. Navy SEAL who had gotten into a lethal firefight with a group of them on a jungle-clad hill. She'd met Curt shortly after starting the black ops mission. He had been an incredible man — a good friend, a wonderful lover. Under the shadow of danger, daily, they'd planned out the rest of their lives together. There was no doubt that Curt's murder played prominently in her obsession to bring down those monsters.

For whatever reason, Kathy couldn't let her father off the hook, either. The family's kidnapping was partly his fault. When he was rescued and returned home to Washington to pick up the pieces of their shattered life, Morgan had made amends very quickly. He'd immediately left D.C. for Phillipsburg, Montana, a little fishing and hunting town in the Rockies. He'd brought his family here to this sheltered, secluded place to live and, hopefully, to recover.

At first, Morgan swore he would quit the rescue business he'd created. He'd spent years developing Perseus, with the help of his well-trained mercenaries, mostly ex-military types. Morgan had used Perseus to help people in need around the world. But in less than two years after their move, Kathy had seen him slowly go stir-crazy, with too little to do. All her father knew was the military and assisting others in need. It was in his blood, in his genes. After all, he'd been raised in a military family, and was used to carrying a great deal of responsibility on his broad shoulders.

Finally, her father resurrected Perseus, which this time was absorbed into the CIA for even deeper cover. Morgan had talked it over with Laura, and she'd agreed he needed to revive his company. He hadn't consulted Jason or Kathy — much as they would have liked him to. The gesture would have been so healing. But Morgan no longer was as close to his older children as he'd been before the kidnapping, or what Kathy called "BTK."

Her father had happily dived back into his work, with a heavy layer of camouflage to protect his family from another possible attack. It had worked, thus far. And with fraternal twins being born three years later, Pete and Kelly, the family became one, once more.

Kathy had watched and listened at the doorway of her father's office as he'd sketched out the details on making Perseus look like a tourist center — with condominiums to rent to fishermen during the summertime and to hunters in the fall. In actuality, the main office was a three-story Victorian house that functioned as just that: a tourist facility. Below ground, however, deep in the earth, was the heart and soul of Perseus. Her father literally went underground in an effort to save his family from danger.

Abruptly, Kathy stopped the flow of memories. Ahead was the dirt road that led to the cedar home where she'd been raised. Her heart beat harder. No stranger to adrenaline, she didn't allow it to affect her reflexes, her focus or her thinking. Turning right, she directed her little red sports car up the hill, toward the large, two-story house embraced by Douglas firs. The trees had always reminded her of soldiers standing at attention, guarding the family.

The porch was wide and long, built in an L-shape around the front of the house.

Thanks to her mother's green thumb, large pots of red, white and pink geraniums adorned the porch. The bright blooms looked so beautiful to Kathy, and the fierce love she felt for her mother nearly overwhelmed her.

Laura Trayhern was the light of the family, whose combined souls had been darkened, tortured, twisted and almost destroyed. Despite being raped and drugged, and nearly beaten to death one night, her mother had rallied and pulled the frayed fabric of their disintegrating family back into place. Kathy stood in awe of her mom's steel backbone, her ability to overcome what seemed to be insurmountable circumstances. Maybe because Laura had been adopted, she'd acquired a special spiritual strength. It had helped keep their family from completely self-destructing after the kidnapping ordeal. . . .

No one knew Kathy was coming home. That's the way she wanted it. Her family couldn't suspect the real reason for her surprise visit. If they did, Morgan would stop her, and Kathy wasn't about to let that happen. Her father was privy to the most supersecret activities going on inside the U.S. government. If he caught wind of what she'd planned, he'd dismantle it in the blink of an eye.

Morgan was so protective of the women in his family. He was a throwback to another era, Kathy thought, as she turned off the engine and opened her car door. At the same time, he respected women's strengths and abilities. He always paired up a man and a woman on Perseus missions, teams he sent around the world to help people in distress. His pledge was to help others out of hell. Morgan had been put there himself, the victim of an underhanded plot deep within the CIA decades ago. He'd sworn, once he cleared his name, that he'd never let it happen to someone else. And so Perseus was born.

The breeze was soft and pine scented. Kathy breathed in deeply, to steady nerves jangled by the flush of adrenaline pumping through her bloodstream. Mounting the stairs slowly, she saw that the main door was open, the screen door in place. As she neared the entrance, she heard the pleasant strains of classical music. Beethoven. Her mother loved the classics, and as a result, Kathy did, too. Instead of rock, she loved Wagner, Bach and the rest of the classical composers.

Kathy opened the screen door and stepped inside. Running her fingers through her blond, slightly curly hair, she looked across the carpeted foyer. Nothing had changed since her last visit, a year ago. She usually spent her thirty-day leaves at home.

A lush, leafy philodendron hung in the golden-toned cedar foyer. Her mother had living greenery in every nook and cranny of the house. Kathy smiled fondly. If Laura Trayhern could drag the forest inside her home and make it grow, she'd do it.

Because it was mid-June, her mother was probably out back, doing her daily weeding in the huge vegetable garden, which was fenced in to keep the deer at bay. For Laura, weeding was like a meditation. Kathy hated weeding, but understood her mom's love of it. *Better her than me,* she thought with a smile.

She felt a new awareness as she ambled through the spacious, airy house. The place was dazzling, with many windows looking out into the forest, and she absorbed its warmth and beauty deeply into her heart. This was the last time she would walk these rooms and halls. The realization cut like a knife.

Anyone who toured her home would notice how her mother loved light and hated darkness. Funny, so did Kathy. Smiling again, she checked the large kitchen. Nope, no one there, although she did see a pot on the stove. She went over to it and, lifting the lid, inhaled the familiar fragrance of her mom's tomato-based gazpacho soup. It smelled delicious, the fresh herbs obvious. After settling the lid back on the pot, Kathy went through the back door that led to the yard and the large, rectangular garden.

Yep, there she was. Kathy stood quietly on the steps. Dressed in a light pink blouse and dark red shorts, her mom was weeding the rows of carrots. She wore a worn, floppy straw hat with a wide brim that protected her face, neck and shoulders from the sun. Warmth — soft and haunting — flowed through Kathy.

She hadn't seen her mother in nearly a year. Laura was now in her middle forties and yet looked so much younger — despite having endured so much. Kathy thought of her being repeatedly raped, and her gut twisted into knots of rage. Laura was short, five foot five compared to her own five foot eleven inches.

Laura had her back turned and, absorbed in her activities, didn't see her daughter standing there watching her. Kathy recalled her father telling her that when he'd met Laura on one fateful day at the Reagan Airport in Washington, D.C., at first glance she'd reminded him of a swan — so graceful and beautiful.

Kathy held out her arm and realized that she was not small-boned like her mother, but more like her dad. While Laura had a model's body, Kathy was more statuesque and curvy. She was glad she shared her mother's sun-streaked hair, with some strands golden, others wheat colored and still others a dark caramel.

Because she was in the Marine Corps and flew the SH-60 Seahawk helicopter, she was encouraged to have short hair. Instead, she wrapped her shoulder-length locks up in a twist beneath her helmet. Some things she wouldn't give up — such as her femininity or her long hair. Regulations said to keep it off her collar, and she did that. But that was all.

"Mom?" Kathy's husky voice cut through the noontime buzz of insects and the songs of birds.

Instantly, Laura jerked upright, a bunch of weeds in her right hand as she whirled around.

"Kathy! Honey, what are you doing here?" She smiled widely and hurried across the garden.

"I thought I'd drop in without warning. I wanted to surprise you. . . ."

19

"Well," Laura laughed breathlessly, coming up the steps onto the back stoop, "you sure did!" Holding out her arms, she hugged her tall, lean daughter. "Oh! It's so good to see you, Pet!"

Kathy wrapped her arms around her mother and pressed her face into her loose, sun-warmed hair. Pet. That was what her parents had always called her. The nickname was short for Petunia, a flower Kathy had loved to pick as a little girl, sucking out the sweet honey. Laura had showed her how to do that when she was three years old, and Kathy had gone on a hunt to find every blooming petunia she could, to steal its sweetness. The story had become a family legend and her relatives often reminded her how every year she would find a way to pluck every single flower until there were none left in Laura's garden.

After giving her mother a gentle squeeze, Kathy released her. "I've got about five days before I go on a new assignment, and I thought I'd see you all before I left. Normally, I get thirty days of leave, but this OPs has allowed me less time than usual."

Laura dropped the weeds into a nearby can and pushed a strand of hair from her face. "I'm glad you have. Are you hungry?

I haven't eaten lunch yet. It's been so hot here, nearly a hundred last week. I thought I'd make a pot of gazpacho soup and chill it for dinner. Want some now? It's just done."

Opening the door, Kathy followed her mother into the service porch, where she shed her garden shoes and padded barefoot across the gleaming reddish-gold cedar floor. "Yeah, I took a whiff of it before I came out here. I'd love a bowl."

Looking over her shoulder, Laura smiled. "You bet. Come on, let's get some and go sit out on the front porch. There's a bit of breeze out there and I need to cool down." She grinned and wiped her perspiring forehead with the back of her dirt-stained glove.

Kathy nodded and followed. Her mother was a true child of nature. If Laura didn't have to wear shoes or socks or nylons, she didn't, but went barefoot. She went braless whenever possible, as well. Kathy liked that streak of wild woman in her mother. She'd acquired that trait, too. Big time. They called her "Amazon" in her squadron, and she'd earned the handle.

In the kitchen, Kathy brought down the white china soup bowls while her mother took the lid off the pot and set it aside.

"So, you're on a new assignment? South America again? More insertion and extraction stuff?"

"Yeah," Kathy said, setting the bowls next to the stove. That was what she did: insert Navy SEAL and Marine Recon teams into hotspots in South America, hang around in the jungle, then pick them up at a specific time and place, after they'd done their damage. The work was interesting to Kathy. She liked the element of danger that always went with the missions. They never went anywhere quiet or safe. Truth be known, she grooved on the edginess of those ops. More than a few bullets had creased the fuselage of her Seahawk, although she kept that knowledge to herself because she didn't want her parents to worry about her.

Laura filled the first bowl. Kathy didn't want to lie to her mother, or at least lie as little as possible, so she didn't go into detail about this new mission. She just let her mom think it was the same type assignment as before. She wouldn't divulge her true intentions, unless pushed beyond her limit. She knew her father would want to know everything, and that was going to be tricky ground to tread with him.

Chuckling, Laura pulled out a loaf of

freshly made sourdough bread from the refrigerator, as well as the butter dish. "Talk about new assignments. You know what my summer mission is?"

Kathy slathered butter on thick slices of bread. "No, what?" Her heart expanded. Just being with her mother lifted her spirits. Laura's large, intelligent blue eyes shone with happiness. Kathy wished she could feel that elation. How many years had it taken her mom to finally climb out of the hell she'd suffered and get to this point? Two decades. Two decades of her precious life lost to those bastards. Kathy's anger began to kick up again and she had to fight to shove it way down inside her.

"Well, since the birth of little Alexander Morgan Trayhern to Jason and Annie, I got to thinking that this family has photo albums, but the children, individually, don't have one. Do you realize their little one is one-and-a-half years old already? Gosh, time flies by!" She beamed and handed Kathy her soup, and then two buttered slices of sourdough. "I've just gotten Jason's photo album finished and I'm almost through yours. It was going to be a Christmas gift to each of you. Rachel, Morgan's mother, had given each of her children an album, and I'm using hers as a template for all of yours. Come on, let's go sit in the porch swing and eat."

They didn't rock much in the swing as they supped their lukewarm soup. That was okay with Kathy. She loved moments like this with her mother, remembering how much Laura loved rocking chairs in general, and that almost every chair in their home rocked. Bread on one knee, the soup bowl in her left hand, Kathy spooned the thick, tasty gazpacho into her mouth.

Between sips, she said to her mother, "You took an awful lot of photos of us growing up. There's gotta be a godzillion to choose from. You aren't putting *every* photo in our albums, are you?" Hers would weigh forty pounds. Even now, every time she turned around, her mom had a camera in her hand. Perhaps this project meant so much to her because she had never known her own parents, had never had photos of herself growing up.

"Heavens, no!" Laura chortled. "I've been choosy!" She set her soup dish on a wooden table next to the swing. "But I spent January through March chronicling your life up to this point, like a life line."

"Oh . . ." Kathy frowned and swallowed the bite of bread she'd been chewing. It jammed in her throat. "Then you're in-

24

cluding the . . . kidnapping?" Even the word stuck in her throat. No longer hungry, Kathy dropped the rest of her bread into her empty soup bowl on the table. Silently berating herself for sounding so emotional, she stole a quick look at her mother.

Laura's dark blue eyes were warm with love as she reached out and settled her hand on her daughter's thigh. "Pet, life is made up of happy moments and sad ones. I gave that a lot of thought, but you know what? The kidnapping is a part of our family saga now. It's history in a way. Not happy history, certainly, but it happened to us and affected *all* of us. I think I would be less than honest if I avoided that part of your life, don't you?"

Her mother's softly spoken words sent an ache through her. Kathy leaned back, closed her eyes and rested her head against the striped green-and-white cushion. When Laura removed her hand, Kathy whispered, "I guess. . . ."

"Honey, I'm forty-seven years old and you're half my age. I've found that with time — and greater perspective — the horrible times evolve and take on a different aspect. If you don't want me to include those years, I won't."

Opening her eyes, Kathy rolled her head to the right and gazed at her mother, who looked young and untouched by life. Oh, Laura had lines around her mouth and a few across her brow, but other than that, she looked so vibrant and alive. Kathy herself felt raw inside. She had since the kidnapping. And at the same time, she felt like a robot, going through the motions of living, but never connecting fully with the passion of life. Since the kidnapping, she'd felt empty and devoid of emotions. Thanks to the Garcias.

But she would get even. She would hurt Carlos Garcia as much as his father had hurt her entire family. Kathy knew she'd be successful but felt due to tight security around Carlos Garcia that she'd be shot in the aftermath.

"Pet?"

"What? Oh, I'm sorry. I want you to be happy, Mom. You've always been creative and I wouldn't dream of telling you how to do something like this." Kathy forced a smile she didn't feel. "Besides, this is *your* project. Your passion. I don't want to be a wet blanket." *Liar.* Oh, God, she *was* lying, and it hurt her in a way she hadn't expected. Kathy absently rubbed her chest as if to ease the ache in her heart.

This wasn't going to be easy at all. What made her think it would be? Maybe she'd hoped for an effortless goodbye, but now that she was home, everything was sharply poignant. And hurting her inside because this was the last time she'd be here. No more hearing her mother laugh. Or seeing that mischievous sparkle in her blue eyes. Or smelling the pine. Or inhaling the odor of the leather couches and chairs in the living room. So many little things that suddenly meant a lot to Kathy . . .

"Are you *sure?*" Laura dug into her daughter's sky-blue eyes. She must have seen the dark shadows there as Kathy lowered her lashes.

"Yeah, Mom, I'm sure." Again, Kathy forced herself to play a part she hated. "In fact, I'd be unhappy about it. You're right — life has lots of ups and downs." *Life and death.* Her death, shortly. She suddenly felt a pang of anxiety. And a wave of grief that nearly was her undoing. Yet no matter how she felt, her need for revenge against Guillermo Garcia's son and his family overrode it. The anticipation of vengeance soothed some of her panic.

"Good! Listen, we need to call Jason and Annie. I'll invite them down for supper tonight. You must see little Alex! He's so

cute, learning to walk! And such an adorable, loving child. But Jas and Annie are
like that, so why shouldn't their baby be,
too? Have you seen your father yet? Does
he know you're here?"

"Uh, no. I drove straight here, Mom."

"Pete and Kelly just graduated from the
Naval Academy, as you know. We were so
proud of them, Pet. I wish you could have
been at the ceremony."

"Me, too," Kathy murmured. Her younger
sister and brother, fraternal twins and
twenty-two years old, had graduated from
the Naval Academy less than two weeks ago.
She'd still been on her black ops assignment in Colombia and unable to attend.

"Well, the good news is they are supposed to be here tomorrow! They're both
taking their thirty-day leaves with us! Oh,
this is so wonderful! The *whole* family is
going to be home."

When Kathy saw tears begin to shimmer
in her mother's eyes, she felt the merciless
grip of an icy fist around her heart. Laura
loved her children so deeply and unabash-
edly. Kathy would miss that. Horribly.

Laura lived to make their lives better
than her own had been. She wanted them
to know that a *real* family was supportive
through thick and thin. Bowing her head,

28

Kathy forced back hot tears that pricked at her eyes. Pretending to be hungry she cleared her throat, and picked up her slice of bread and took a bite.

"That's great, Mom," she said when she'd managed to swallow it. "The whole gang will be here. Like old times."

Clasping her hands, Laura sighed and smiled, her gaze on the fluffy white clouds floating above the canopy of firs in front of their home. Along the white picket fence grew smiling white Shasta daisies with yellow centers, fragrant clumps of lavender and bright red-and-yellow gallardia waving in the breeze. The flowers reflected Laura in every way. "Never in my wildest dreams did I think you could be here for this, Pet. Now everything is *perfect.* Perfect! Morgan is going to be thrilled to death!"

Sitting there with her mother, pushing the swing idly back and forth with one toe, Kathy nodded and choked down the rest of the bread without tasting it. She had a fierce, uncompromising love for her brothers and sisters; they all got along, unlike many other families, with their war stories of sibling rivalry. Not so with the Trayherns. Their bonds were strong and resilient. What ate at her was that she had to stick to her lie with all of them. She'd never lied to anyone before. Kathy drew a silent breath. She knew she was all screwed up inside, thanks to the kidnapping. . . .

Gazing upward, she watched the clouds drift overhead, casting a cooling shadow across the front of the house. What was wrong with *this* picture? She laughed inwardly, but it wasn't a cheery laugh; it was one filled with derision — and hatred toward Guillermo Garcia. One way or another, Kathy was going to make his family pay the same heavy price that hers had paid for the act of terror he had waged against them.

Chapter Two

Kathy tried to steel herself for her father's return from his office. She was helping her mother set the table in the dining room when she heard the screen door open and shut. It was 5:00 p.m., and unless all hell was breaking loose on a mission, her father quit at that time. Tonight must be one of those rare, quiet nights.

As she laid each shining white china plate on the reddish-gold cedar table, she mused over how her father had changed his work schedule since the kidnapping. Before that he had worked until all hours, sometimes coming home long after she was in bed, sound asleep. Kathy recalled having an absentee father before the kidnapping. After that, Morgan's attitude and focus had changed dramatically in favor of the family.

"I'm home!" he called, dropping his briefcase in his home office and making his way to the kitchen. He sniffed appreciatively as he peeked into the room, but saw no one.

"We're in the dining room, dear," Laura called, "and you'll never believe who's come home?"

Raising his brows, Morgan halted at the entrance to the spacious room. "Kathy?"

It took everything she had to force a smile she didn't feel. Standing at the end of the table, she struggled with unexpected grief and couldn't find her breath for a moment. "Hi, Dad," she whispered and nervously placed the plate on the red woven placemat. Moving around the table, she lifted her arms upward in genuine welcome. Though choking back a tidal wave of emotion, Kathy sank into her father's hug. She knew this visit would be the last time she would see him. Her heart contracted violently with raw, overwhelming pain. She pressed her cheek against the gray pinstripe woolen fabric of his suit and felt her father's arms tighten gently around her waist.

Since the kidnapping, Morgan had been far more effusive about showing how he felt toward his children, and Kathy hungrily absorbed his embrace and the kiss he placed on her hair. She didn't want the hug to end, but felt his arms slipping away — just as she would slip away from him forever.

"What a nice surprise," Morgan declared, easing her away from him, his hands sliding down to cup her elbows. "It's wonderful to see you! Why didn't you let us know you'd be dropping in for a visit?"

After squeezing her father's hands, Kathy stepped away. "I'm going on an unexpected black ops assignment in seven days so I begged my commander to give me five days leave. He did, and that's why I came home."

Morgan Trayhern was a living legend in the military and spy community. Tall, proud, strong, to Kathy he symbolized everything noble about their family's military heritage. The vertical scar that ran from his temple to his chin on the right side of his face reminded everyone of the price he'd paid during the Vietnam War when he was a captain in the U.S. Marine Corps.

Brows dipping, Morgan removed his suit coat, loosened his tie and unbuttoned the shirt at his throat. "Oh? A new mission so soon after the last one? That's unusual." He hung the suit coat over the back of a chair at the dinner table. Laura stopped and gave him a kiss on the cheek. He smiled at his wife and touched the small of her back as she moved quickly back toward the kitchen.

As her mother left them alone for a few moments, Kathy reminded herself to be careful with her father. Morgan knew intimately how the military worked. The very fact that she was going on this mission so soon after the last would raise red flags for him. Her father had Q clearance, which meant he knew most of the secret missions going on within the government. But not all of them. Not hers.

As he pulled his dark blue tie from around his neck, he watched her. She knew what he was thinking: why hadn't the mission ops commander let him know what was happening with one of his children? They always had before. It was an unspoken rule between Morgan and those who worked with his kids. He had enough clout behind the scenes to get that kind of info. His children might be adults, but they were in the military, Morgan's turf. And Kathy knew without a doubt her dad kept a keen eye on all their missions and assignments. In one way, this knowledge was a comfort. This time it wasn't. If he got wind of what she was going to do, he'd scuttle the mission and all hell would break loose.

"Yeah, black ops . . . I can't talk about it, Dad. You know how it is."

Morgan scowled and picked up his suit

coat again, draping it across his arm. With his tie in hand, he said, "Let's talk about this over supper, shall we? I'm going upstairs to change. Be down in a little bit."

Quelling the butterflies in her stomach, Kathy said in a far more confident voice than she felt, "No problem, Dad." She went back to setting the table.

Just then Kamaria, the fifth Trayhern child, now four years old, came running breathlessly in from the backyard. She had been adopted when she was less than a year old by Laura and Morgan. After a terrifying earthquake in Los Angeles, a team of marines had found her trapped beside her dead mother in a collapsed apartment complex. Kamaria, an African name, meant 'beautiful like the moon,' was tall and skinny for her age.

"Kat!" she called from the entrance. "Come quick! I found a *huge worm* on Mommy's cabbage! Quick! Hurry before it leaves!"

Grinning, Kathy was relieved to escape. She silently thanked her little sister as she placed the last of the flatware on the table and turned to Kamaria. The little girl's long black hair was gathered into haphazard pigtails on each side of her head. Wearing dark green cotton coveralls and a pink tank top, she stood restlessly, her blue-gray eyes shining with excitement.

"If Mom catches you in here with those muddy shoes, Kammie . . ."

"Ohhh, I know! Hurry, Kathy!" She quickly glanced around the edge of the dining room door as if to see if Laura was in sight. Then, grabbing her older sister's hand, she yanked on it eagerly and dived for the rear screen door.

Laughing softly, Kathy allowed her baby sister to haul her along like a piece of heavy cargo. Once out the back door, they bounded down the steps and across the lawn to the garden.

"Hurry! She was movin' fast! I wanna know what it is! I don't wanna lose her!" Kammie released Kathy's hand, ran to the gate and quickly opened it. The garden, nearly an acre in size, was enclosed by an eight-foot-tall fence, so that deer couldn't jump it and eat the vegetables.

Kathy shut the gate behind them and watched Kammie race along the long row of cabbages. Halfway down, the girl bent over, her butt in the air like that of an ostrich sticking its head in the sand. There was a milkweed sticking up between the cabbage. Laughing to herself, Kathy followed, careful not to muddy her tennis shoes.

"Oh! Here she is! Here's the worm!" Kammie hunkered down on her knees in the mud. With her short, thin fingers she deftly curled back the milkweed leaf. "Look! What is it?"

Kathy came and squatted down between the cabbages. She took delight at her sister's joy and awe. Looking down between Kammie's muddy fingers, she saw a fat black-white-and-yellow-striped caterpillar inching along. "Hmm, looks like a caterpillar to me, Kammie." She smiled into her sister's wide eyes. "If you keep it in a jar and let it eat some milkweed leaves, it will spin a cocoon sooner or later."

"Yeah? And then what? What will happen?" Kammie watched the caterpillar progress across the leaf, heading toward her fingers. As if to muster courage, the child sucked in her breath when the creature stopped and daintily tested her fingertip.

"Magic will happen. It will turn from a worm into a beautiful Monarch butterfly, Kammie," Kathy murmured, watching the wonder in her sister's shining eyes as the caterpillar touched the girl's fingers. It must have decided that they weren't a tasty leaf, for it turned around and wriggled across the cabbage.

"Oh, oh! She felt so soft, Kathy!" Kammie gasped, looking up at her sister. "She touched me! It didn't hurt! That was cool!"

"Most caterpillars don't bite." Kathy ruffled Kammie's hair. "Do you want to keep it and watch it turn into a butterfly?"

"Yeah! Oh, yeah!"

"Then pull off several milkweed leaves — carefully — and bring it to the garage. I'll find you a jar big enough for it to live in. All it will do is eat and eat and eat until it's ready to spin its cocoon. You'll have to poke holes in the lid so the caterpillar can breathe. It has to have air, Kammie, just like you and me. And you'll have to feed it a fresh leaf every day until it spins its cocoon."

Kammie's brows squeezed together as she leaned over and very carefully tore a leaf off the milkweed then held it steady until the caterpillar crawled onto it. With Kathy's help, she got to her feet. "Wow, this is so cool! I'm going to name her Pretty! She's so pretty!"

Chuckling, Kathy steered Kamaria ahead of her, and together they walked back to the gate. "Let's get to the garage. You can tell Mom that you've pulled a dastardly weed out of her garden."

★ ★ ★

"Where are the girls?" Laura asked as she put the bowl of salad greens on the table.

Morgan brought in the sourdough bread, which sat on a pine cutting board. "I never saw Kamaria. Kathy was here setting the table earlier." He looked out the large picture window at the backyard and garden.

"Kammie just got home from vacation Bible school a few minutes ago. She ran upstairs and changed and was supposed to be pulling her ten minutes' worth of weeds a day out in the garden."

"Nobody in sight," Morgan murmured. "They're up to something. I can feel it." He walked back to the kitchen with his wife, who frowned at him. After slicing the roast beef, he followed Laura back out to the dining room. She placed a bowl of gravy near the platter of meat.

"Hmm, you're right. Those two are up to something," Laura said with a shake of her head. "I'll get the veggies. Why don't you go down to the garage? I got a feeling they're in there."

"One of your hunches?" Morgan teased.

"Yep. Hot fudge sundae says I'm right."

Grinning, Morgan held up his hands. "I

39

learned a long time ago that your instincts are always right."

Giving him an I-told-you-so smile, Laura chuckled. "Darn, I just missed out on a hot fudge sundae. Just make sure Kamaria is *not* wearing muddy shoes or clothes at the dinner table, okay?"

"I'll do my best," he promised.

Morgan found them in the garage, giggling, their heads bent together over a jar. They were busy doing something. What, he wasn't sure. The main door was open to allow in the breeze. Kathy was just handing Kamaria a gallon-size, wide-mouth glass jar when he arrived.

"Okay, caught you red-handed," Morgan called.

"Daddy, look!" Kamaria ran across the concrete to where he stood. "It's a butterfly! Well, it will be," she said breathlessly, lifting the huge jar up for her father to see.

Morgan took the container and saw the caterpillar happily munching on leaves. "My, my, Kammie. You've got a real nice caterpillar in there, and it's a weed, I see." He squatted down to Kammie's eye level. He loved his adopted daughter fiercely. If anything, she had breathed new life into him.

He glanced up and saw Kathy leaning against the wooden jigsaw bench, arms crossed and a grin hovering on her lips. Pain struck at Morgan. He'd never played with Kathy as he did with Kamaria. At that stage in his life, he had been an absentee parent. Unfortunately, Jason and Kathy had been his training-wheels children — the ones who bore the brunt of his mistakes. Pete and Kelly, their fraternal twins, had had it easier, and now smiling Kamaria, her blue-gray eyes bright with delight, would be blessed with all his experience. He wouldn't hurt her as he'd hurt them.

"She's got a new friend," Kathy said, easing away from the bench. "I think it's a monarch caterpillar, but I can't be sure." For her, there was a painful synchronicity in Kammie's finding the caterpillar. Kathy believed in symbolism and fate. Butterflies were significant to her because they meant transformation. The caterpillar would live for a while in a rigid cocoon, a prisoner within. Hadn't she been a prisoner in this whole kidnapping tragedy? Guilt and revenge had been her lifelong cocoon. Like the butterfly, she was going to morph and change, fueled by the power of her desire to get even. Yes, this butterfly-to-be was just like her. Pretty soon, she was going to change from Kathy Trayhern into an impostor. She would go undercover and become something else — a beautiful, deadly butterfly who could extract her revenge and balance the scales so that her family could finally be free.

Morgan gave his oldest daughter a look of pride. "By golly, I think you're right, Pet." She was a Marine Corps aviator, a Seahawk helicopter pilot and every inch a proud, confident woman in his eyes, but he still called her Pet. He always would. Kathy was the spitting image of Laura, his wife, except she was taller and larger boned. She had her mother's blue eyes and was just as beautiful.

"Daddy, can I keep Pretty? Kat says she has to stay in my room, out of the sunlight. I have to feed her a new milkweed leaf a day until she spins her cocoon."

Morgan carefully handed the jar back to his excited little daughter. "I don't think Mommy is going to be real happy to hear you're going to pull milkweeds from her garden."

"Aww, Daddy, it's only *one* leaf." Kammie tilted her head and pouted. She wrapped her arms around the jar and stood there, pleading silently.

Chuckling, Kathy came over and patted Kammie's small shoulders. "Let's convince her over dinner, okay?"

"First," Morgan said, raising an eyebrow at his youngest, "I think you'd better head up to your room and change. Your knees and shoes are muddy. Mommy won't be happy to see you arrive dirty at the dinner table. Okay?"

"Oh." Kamaria laughed after looking down and examining herself. "Okay! I'll be right down!" She whirled around with her jar, ran across the garage and flew up the steps into the house.

"Boy," Morgan said, straightening up to his full height and brushing off his jeans, "I sure wish I had one-fourth of her energy."

"You did," Kathy said, following him into the house, "when you were her age."

Morgan chuckled. Within minutes, everyone had sat down at the dinner table.

"So, what's this sudden black ops popping up on your radar screen, Pet?" Morgan asked a few minutes later, as he spooned gravy over the mashed potatoes on his plate. Sitting at the head of the oval table, with his daughters at his elbows and Laura at the other end, he gave Kathy an inquiring look. He saw her cheeks turn a faint pink as she pushed a piece of roast

43

beef around on her plate. Otherwise she looked totally relaxed.

"I can't say much about it, Dad."

"Hmm," he murmured.

"You're flying the Seahawk as part of an insert-extract mission?" Laura asked.

Nodding, Kathy felt her stomach tense like a fist. She had to pull this off! One thing in her favor was that no matter how fearful she felt, how awkward or unsure, she never allowed any of these things to broadcast on her face or seep into her body language. No, she'd learned to hide her emotions when she was a very young child. Crying had become something she'd done alone, in her closet if her family was around, her hand over her mouth so no sound would escape.

Her father, whom she'd idolized, wasn't always there, and when he was, he'd been preoccupied with the mercenary teams he sent out around the world to do good for others. He hadn't had time for his daughter or for his eldest son, Jason. Kathy couldn't count the many times she'd ached for her dad to come and hold her, to say he loved her. After the kidnapping, he'd tried to be there for her, but by that time the damage had been done. Kathy had learned not to show emotions on her face or allow her body or voice to betray her real feelings. Now she was glad of that, because this time it was essential.

"Yeah, I'll be piloting my helo, Mom."

"South America?" Morgan asked.

Kathy nodded. "That much I can say."

"The country?" Morgan pressed.

"No, Dad. I can't. . . ." She held his narrowed gray eyes, which made her feel as if he could look into her mind and read the truth. Her heart beat hard in her chest. Kathy forced herself to take slow, deep breaths and chew her food, even though she didn't taste a shred of it. Where she was going, the ability to play a part was paramount. It would keep her alive until . . .

"Hmm," Morgan said, slicing more of the beef. "I'm just surprised I haven't been made aware of it, is all."

"It's come up in a hurry, and it's a changing mission ops, Dad, that's why. It might be different by the time I arrive at the base."

Laura groaned and rolled her eyes. "One of *them.*"

Kathy at least had her mother fooled. She wasn't so sure about her dad. He still regarded her with a strange glint in his eyes, which alarmed her. Still, Kathy reminded herself, if she was scared of

Morgan Trayhern finding her out, she'd better be far more worried about Carlos Garcia discovering who she was and why she was there.

"Daddy, you said you wouldn't talk job at the table," Kammie reminded him, tapping him on the elbow.

"Uh-oh, so I did, Kammie."

"That's right," Laura said apologetically. "And I'm just as guilty."

Kathy smiled across the table at her sister. "Why don't you tell Mom about your butterfly in the making?" Anything to divert her parents' focus from her. Kathy felt bad about using Kammie that way, but she had to do something to distract them.

On other missions, she had been able to tell them more. Usually, what she couldn't say, Morgan found out anyway, because he worked so closely with the Pentagon and other military and security networks. Crossing her fingers mentally, Kathy hoped that Commander Patrick O'Conner of her SEAL team would keep this mission compartmentalized on a need-to-know basis only.

While forcing herself to slowly chew and swallow her food, she vaguely listened to Kammie's exciting account of finding the caterpillar. If Kathy didn't finish her meal,

Morgan would know something was wrong, and that was the last thing she wanted. The food sat like a lead ball in her stomach.

"You know, Kelly and Pete will be here tomorrow," Laura said as they ate their dessert of freshly made apple pie and vanilla ice cream.

Kathy lifted her head. "Yes, you said they'd be coming home." She saw the joy shining in her mother's eyes, as well as her father's continued scrutiny, which set her nerves on edge yet again. Stomach clenching, Kathy had a feeling he wasn't about to let go of the topic of her black ops mission. Damn! She'd have to call Patrick and make sure that it stayed under wraps. She decided to do so at the first opportunity.

Giving the excuse that she'd eaten too much and was going to hike the wildflower trail behind their home, Kathy slipped away after dessert. Kammie was dragging their parents to her room to look at the captured caterpillar, so it was an opportune moment. Dressed in her hiking boots, a pair of jeans and a dark blue tank top, Kathy borrowed one of the many knapsacks from the garage, put a water bottle in it and took off for the woods.

Hoping that her cell phone would work from the top of the ridge, Kathy stood facing the west, toward the setting sun. Above her, through the dark branches of the stately evergreens, the evening sky was turning an apricot color.

"Commander O'Conner speaking."

"Hey, Pat, this is Kathy Trayhern."

"You're coming in scratchy. Where you callin' from, Kathy?"

Turning slightly, Kathy waited. "How's this? Can you hear me better now?"

"Yeah, a little. What's up? You've still got four days on your R and R."

Hearing his chuckle, Kathy smiled slightly and pressed the cell phone to her ear. "I'm counting them, trust me. Listen, I *really* need to give you a heads-up on our mission. My father is giving me the fish eye, which means he intends to find out about what we're doing."

"Don't worry, Kathy, I've got that covered. There's no way he can get to it. Relax, okay?"

Relief sheeted through her. Kathy closed her eyes for a moment and felt her stomach begin to relax. "Good . . . good."

"Listen, the ops has changed. I was going to call you, so you musta been reading my mind."

48

"Oh?" Her heart pounded.

"Yeah, we just got a KNR — a kidnapping and ransom call — from the State Department. Carlos Garcia just kidnapped Sophie, a little girl from an oil executive down in Lima, Peru. She's an American citizen. The kid is only seven years old, blond-haired, blue-eyed, and was abducted from her parents' apartment in the Mira Flores district, the wealthy area in that city. They probably kidnapped her for either political gain or for a ransom. This isn't the first time Garcia has kidnapped. It's part of his profile."

"You're kidding me."

"No, I'm not. So that doubles the ante on getting you in place, in Garcia's good graces. You're going to be looking for that little girl while you're insinuating yourself into his command structure. She becomes our top priority now. And this lends credence to your mission. Before, we were standing on shaky ground, trying to snatch the child of a drug lord. Now, with this girl being kidnapped, we're a bona fide mission."

Rubbing her brow, Kathy stared at the darkening woods surrounding her. "This complicates things, Pat." She was counting on hurting the Garcias just as much as they'd hurt her family, by kidnapping Carlos's only child, a little girl named Tiki Garcia, age six. If the American girl was there, the mission would involve two children, not one. That made it even more tricky to carry off. And Pat was telling her that if she had to make a choice between the children, Sophie, the American child, would have to be the one she spirited away. After all, the U.S. wasn't in the kidnapping business — at least not officially — and Kathy knew her mission would put Patrick into a lot of hot water if it was discovered by higher-ups. For him, this mission had just gotten a blessing. For her, it had become more complex.

"Yeah, it does complicate things. But you knew from the get-go that this ops was an evolving one, like a pissed-off snake twisting around, trying to bite."

Grimacing, Kathy nodded. "You're right. Okay, no problem. Then the time frame is the same?"

"Yeah, stay where you are. There's no sense in changing the schedule. If you dropped in on Garcia early, he might suspect something. This way, it'll be at least four to five days after the KNR."

"Right." That made sense. Patrick O'Conner was one of the oldest SEALs in the business, but one of the smartest and foxiest when it came to strat and tact — strategy and tactics. That's why Kathy had gone to him in the first place. It would take a mastermind to draw up a mission that Carlos Garcia wouldn't suspect. "Okay, then I'll be there as scheduled."

"You bet, Kat. See you soon. Out."

Standing there, watching the apricot sky deepening to gold overhead, Kathy pushed the cell phone back into her pocket.

Damn. Not one child to steal from beneath Garcia's nose, but two. An innocent American child was now part of the mix. Already Kathy felt dread. She shook it off, and the thirst for revenge that had lived liked a good friend in her all these years resurfaced. She allowed her rage to burn off whatever doubts she had. Anger, if directed and focused properly, could become a powerful ally, and that was exactly what Kathy wanted.

Hiking slowly back down the mountain, across pine needles brown and slick beneath her boots, she tried to clear her mind of the new twist on her mission. Far below she could see the two-story home bright with lights. With life. A terrible sadness cloaked Kathy as she continued her descent on the well-worn path. She knew her mother often came up this trail, which ran through a flower-filled meadow on the side of the mountain. Laura would trek the mile to gather wildflowers, arranging them in vases throughout the house — colorful reminders of nature, which she loved so much.

Well, at least Kathy would get to see the twins tomorrow, as well as Jason, Annie and their new baby. A series of goodbyes, she reminded herself grimly, and felt new grief edging through the hatred and rage that the Garcias brought out in her. It was going to be a tough role to play. She wanted to cry, because she knew she was going to die. This would be the last time she'd ever see her brothers and sisters. *Oh, God, help me pull off this charade. Please. . . .*

Chapter Three

How was she going to say goodbye to her family? Kathy lay in bed, the morning sunlight slanting across the familiar pink rose wallpaper. Her bed faced the window and she gazed out at the pines, hands behind her head, mulling over the situation.

Today was going to be a heady day of celebration for the Trayhern family. Jason and his wife, Annie, were coming for brunch, driving from their mountain cabin, twenty miles away. Kathy would get to see their baby, little Alexander. This afternoon, Kelly and Pete were flying into Anaconda on a commuter flight from Annapolis, Maryland, where they'd just graduated. Both were choosing to go into the Marine Corps, following in their father's footsteps, as she had.

Sighing, Kathy shut her eyes. For her, it was going to be a day of exquisite, silent anguish. How could she tell each of them goodbye without revealing that they'd never see her again? She ran over this point again and again in her mind. Already immersed in grief, Kathy didn't even try to banish the heavy feeling wrapped around her heart. At no point, however, did she reconsider her choice to go after the Garcia drug cartel, to try to hurt Carlos's family as much as his father had hurt theirs. Not once.

She turned on her side and pressed her face into the soft feather pillow. Outside the open window she heard a robin trilling its long, beautiful song, along with a cardinal vying for territorial rights.

Looking at her watch, she saw it was 0600. Hearing no sounds in the house, Kathy knew the rest of the family must still be asleep. She threw off the sheet and placed her feet on the cool cedar floor, rubbing her face and pushing her thick blond hair over her shoulders. What to do?

The answer came as she showered, scrubbing her hair with a light jasmine-scented shampoo and contemplating the dilemma. After completing her toilette and climbing into jeans and a pink tank top, she sat at her desk in the corner. Over the next two hours, Kathy penned a letter to each member of her family. Sealing them in envelopes, she painstakingly printed the name of each of her loved ones on the outside.

Kathy saved the most painful for last: Alex Morgan Trayhern, the newest member of their clan. Frowning, she pulled another pink linen sheet from the drawer beside her and scrawled the date in the upper right-hand corner.

To Alexander Morgan Trayhern

Dearest Alex, You and I don't know each other so well just yet, but I already feel close to you. I have to go away for a while, but before I leave, I have a few things to say.

I want you to know that your dad, my brother Jason, loves you very, very much. And your mom, Annie, thinks the world of you. There are so many children around the globe that would love to have what you have: two loving parents who think you are the most wonderful little boy in the world.

I remember flying home on special leave when Grandma Laura called to say that you were about to be born. I remember sitting on that plane, wondering what you would look like, thinking about how we would watch the miracle of your birth and how it would impact us in the most wonderful of ways. I was truly looking forward to meeting you.

Well, as things would have it, you decided to come *early!* When I arrived, Annie and you were at home, where a midwife had helped deliver you. Your mom doesn't like hospitals! I found out that your dad had helped with your birth, too. And of course, your grandma was there with the video camera. So I got to see your whole birth on film, which was great.

When we first met, you had long, black hair, and I marveled at how thick a head of hair you had for such a new baby! Your mom said it was the Apache blood in you. When she let me hold you for the first time, I felt such a thrill, Alex. You were a big baby — ten pounds!

As I sat there in the rocking chair, holding you like the fragile gift you were, I marveled at all your little fingers, how perfectly formed they were, and how innocent you looked in sleep. I rocked you for nearly half an hour, and as I did so the world seemed to stop, and my heart opened.

I found myself wondering what kind of life you would have. What would you be interested in? What kind of a career would call to you? What kind of woman would eventually capture your heart? How many kids would you have? Would life treat you kindly or roughly? I had all these questions, as I'm sure your parents did, and no answers. I do know that I loved you and will continue to do so until I draw my last breath.

What is so great is that you are half Apache and half Anglo. Of course, I know Grandma Laura will fill you in on our proud Welsh history. You've come into a great family with great traditions, great honor, and a calling to help the world in large and small ways. Your mother, Annie, is an Apache medicine woman with wisdom far beyond her years, and I know she will teach you the ways of her people. You will be the first child in the Trayhern family to be half Native American blood. You should be proud of that. I'm sure we will all learn more about your mother's side and her warrior people. Already, I can see your mom's way of living making a better life for my brother Jason. Your dad was very gravely wounded during the war in Afghanistan, and he nearly died. If not for what your mom knew about healing his spirit and heart, he might not have made it. Your mother is a powerful, heart-centered woman, and I know she will bring good things into your life that will help you surmount challenges and obstacles.

Alex, this is a hello and goodbye letter to you. As the oldest daughter of my generation, I feel it's my duty to right a grave wrong. Someday you will know about the awful kidnapping that took place, where your dad, Grandpa Morgan and Grandma Laura were all captured and made to suffer gravely at a drug lord's hands. I have seen the damage this has done and I feel it my duty to square things with the Garcia drug cartel, which is responsible for this heinous act against our family.

I know that what I must do will cost me my life. I know that I'll never get to see you grow up. That makes me ache with a pain that I can never ignore. Just know that what I have done is for the family's honor.

Please know I love you with all my heart. That I got to hold you the day after you were born, to rock you in my arms, to smile down at you, to touch your tiny, perfect little fingers . . . and that I'll always love you. Kathy Alyssa Trayhern, your aunt.

★ ★ ★

Tears burned in Kathy's eyes, blurring the letter as she carefully folded it in half and slipped it inside the envelope. She heard the family stirring to life outside her door. Wiping the tears away with the back of her hand, she sniffed and wrote Alex's name on the envelope. She set it aside and pulled a tissue from the box. After blotting her eyes and blowing her nose, Kathy got up and looked around her room. One side held nothing but books, because she'd been a voracious reader as a child growing up. How many times had her mother read to her and her siblings at bedtime? Oh, how Kathy had looked forward to that! All that had been missing from those nightly readings was her father. Rubbing the area above her heart, Kathy told herself she'd better get used to the pain there. It was the pain of goodbye.

Where to put the letters so they wouldn't get discovered? She knew her mother had a housekeeper, Sally, who came twice a week to clean. Where to put the letters . . .

"Hey, Kat!" Jason called as he entered the living room. "How are you?"

Kathy grinned and walked over to her older brother. He was dressed in a pair of jeans, a short-sleeved white cotton shirt and loafers. His blue eyes were alive with joy as he hauled her against him and gave her a fierce hug of greeting. For just a moment, Kathy allowed herself to be crunched against him. He was slightly taller than her, slightly huskier, and now, three years after his near fatal head wound, was looking much more like his old self. His lopsided grin was there once more.

The air rushed out of her lungs and she hugged him back. "Hi, Jas." Kathy pulled away and smiled up at him. It always pained her to see the jagged scar that ran along the right side of his face. He'd gotten that wound when flying shrapnel landed in the tent where he had been sleeping at the Kandahar air base in Afghanistan. He and Annie were the only two survivors of the horrifying experience.

"Hey, this is great, Kat. Dad said you came in unexpectedly."

"Yeah, I wrangled some time off before a black ops." At least that wasn't a lie. Kathy looked around Jason to see Annie carrying her son into the house on her left hip. "Hi, Annie."

"You're a sight for sore eyes, Kathy. Welcome home," Annie said, laughing. She held up Alex, who was dressed in a blue romper and tiny white tennis shoes. "You know, I think our son is very psychic. The day before you came home, he kept going to the screen door and looking out of it." She hefted Alex into Kathy's awaiting hands. "He started walking six months ago, and now he has a fixed routine of where he toddles. But that day he went straight to the door, put his hands on the screen and looked out. He kept saying *'Ninya.'*"

Holding Alex in her arms, Kathy noticed his thick black hair was short and neatly cut. She looked down into his wide blue eyes and grinned, her heart expanding with love for this precious little one. "Ninya is the name he gave me."

Jason chuckled and slid his arm over Kathy's shoulder. "Yeah, that's his name for Aunt Kathy."

"So," she whispered, placing several soft kisses across Alex's broad little forehead, "you knew I was coming home, didn't you?"

"Ninya . . ." Alex cooed and grabbed a lock of her blond hair.

Laughter erupted and Kathy smiled at Annie, who stood at Jason's side. She was a full-blood Apache, her copper skin and nearly waist-long braids proclaiming her proud heritage.

"Watch it," she warned. "Alexander has taken to yanking on my hair, so you're liable to lose some of yours if you aren't careful." She picked up one of her braids and grinned. "I learned a long time ago to keep my hair away from this little guy."

Kathy reached down and gently removed the lock from his greedy little hand. The baby smiled up at her and her heart broke. She cuddled him for a long moment and then, reluctantly, set him down. Once his feet touched the gleaming cedar floor, he was off, darting one way and then another. Kathy followed, making sure he didn't lose his balance and hit the coffee table between the leather couches.

"He's like a tank in high gear with no driver," Jason called, chuckling as he settled his hands on his narrow hips.

Kathy laughed. "No kidding! Is Alex always in this much of a hurry?"

Annie walked around the living room and stood at the opposite corner, where her son was heading. "Sometimes. I think he smells the cookies Grandma made and he's making a beeline for the kitchen —" she hooked a thumb over her shoulder "— which is directly thatta way."

"And he knows that?" Kathy was amazed as she watched the toddler maneuver between the couch and coffee table. The boy confronted his mother, who stood between him and the cookies in the kitchen.

"He's not dumb," Jason said. "In fact, he's probably too smart. He's very visual."

"The eyes of a wolf, the ears of a bat," Annie murmured with a smile, taking her son's hand and walking with him toward the kitchen and those cookies.

"Wow," Kathy said as Jas came up and stood near her. "That's amazing. He's only one and a half and in this big house he knows exactly where the cookie jar is. I don't think we learned that until we were around four."

Grinning, Jason rubbed his chin. "Yeah, compared to him, we were slow on the draw. This little guy of ours is special." He held up his hand. "I know, I know, every parent says that about their child. But Alexander really is unique."

Watching Annie and Alex disappear around the corner, Kathy said, "I believe it." She looked up at her older brother. Since his traumatic brain injury Jason had recovered at home as well as going to the Veterans Hospital in Anaconda for additional medical treatments. His skin was ruddy with good health and he'd gained back all the weight he'd lost. His eyes burned with a fierce passion for life that Kathy knew existed because of his love for Annie and his new son.

"He gives his babysitter hell, let me tell you," Jason chuckled. "He's got her figured out and gives her a run for her money."

Giggling, Kathy said, "I feel for her, then."

"This little guy is going places. I don't know where yet, but he's definitely got a mission in life."

Kathy noted the catch in Jason's voice and saw worry in his dark blue eyes. "We all have a date with destiny, Jas." She said the words quietly, and when she saw him nod his head, his gaze fixed on the empty doorway to the kitchen, she knew he would replay this conversation someday and take her words in a different light. She hoped Jas wouldn't blame himself for not picking up on the double entendre.

"Hey," she said, mustering a playfulness that she knew was the "old" Kathy, "how's work with Dad going? Are you enjoying learning the ropes at Perseus?"

Groaning, Jas sat down on the couch and stretched out his long legs. "Yeah, I empty the wastebaskets, sweep the floors, dust the cobwebs out of the corners of the offices — you know, things like that."

Laughing softly, Kathy sat on the couch opposite him. "Oh, come on! It can't be that bad. Dad said he wanted you to join Perseus and to learn it from the ground up."

"He meant every word, Kathy." Her brother smiled wryly. "I'm lucky he doesn't have me on my hands and knees waxing the floors."

"Mom said you were working with Mike Houston, learning mission planning. Sounds interesting."

Losing his smile, he sat up and rested his elbows on his knees. "Yeah, it is. I've only really been working at Perseus for six months. Before that, you know, the head recovery thing . . ." He pointed to his skull.

"And the baby. You were a little busy, Jas. I'm glad Dad gave you time off to be with Alex."

"Yeah. And I'm discovering he's quite the handful."

"Oh, he's a curious little boy, Jas. I'm sure Mom told you about your own growing up years? Remember how you used to get into *everything?* Mom told me you drove her crazy when you were going through your terrible twos." She laughed.

"Guilty as charged." Jason sobered. "Hey, what's this newest black ops about?"

"Oh," Kathy lied, "same old thing. I've been flying Marine Corps helo support for Navy SEAL missions for over a year. This is just another one. It's no big deal."

She could see Jason's concern etched on his face. He knew she'd loved Curt Shields and that he'd died in combat. Kathy hadn't come home after that, but had buried her grief and shock in her work. No one in her family knew of the rage she carried over his death. He'd been a good man trying to right wrongs in the world. And right or wrong, she felt she could never love another man. There was only one Curt and he was gone forever.

"Usually you come home for thirty days once a year, not between missions," Jason said, giving her a worried look. "Is there something different about this one? More dangerous? Longer time out in enemy country?"

Her stomach knotted. She and Jason were two years apart in age, and in some ways he knew her better than anyone. They'd been the ones to suffer through the kidnapping. It had bonded them in a way that few children experienced, and that tie was strong and supportive.

Lifting her hands, Kathy said, "No more dangerous than any other, Jas. I missed the twins' graduation at Annapolis, and I knew they were coming home now, so I thought I'd do a post-grad celebration here and congratulate them." Kathy was hoping he'd buy that explanation. She was amazed at how well she lied, and she didn't like doing so. Seeing Jason's worry dissolve and a grin replace it, she drew a deep breath of relief.

"Oh hey, that's great, then. Mom is sure planning a nice shindig for them. I hear we get beef Wellington tonight for dinner, with all the trimmings." He rubbed his hands together. "My favorite meal, and she only makes it once or twice a year."

"That's why you're here so early!" Kathy exclaimed.

"Caught red-handed! And my son is already into the cookie jar!"

For the next few hours, Kathy planned to savor every moment with Jason, Annie and Alex. She had to tuck a lifetime's worth of memories into one day. And her heart tugged with sadness as well as joy when she anticipated the twins returning home that afternoon. The house would ring with rare happiness, and Kathy was so glad to be a part of it. The perfect farewell.

Chapter Four

Sophie Taylor Langford tore through the Peruvian jungle, racing just as fast as her seven-year-old legs would take her. She was barefoot, dressed in a long white night-gown. Sobbing for breath, she held her hands up to protect her face from branches as she raced down a narrow animal path outside the villa, from which she'd just escaped. The morning was drizzly, with drops of water dripping on her as she ran. The sky was a dull gray where she could see bits of it peeking through the lush, thick jungle canopy.

She heard heavy footfalls behind her. Soldiers! Oh! She had to get away! But she had no idea where she was! She'd awakened two days ago to find she'd been kidnapped, taken from her home in Lima. Frightened now, she cried out as she heard a man screaming at her in Spanish. He was so close! Lungs burning from her exertion, Sophie darted down the vine-entangled, muddy trail. She had to get away from him!

Her bare feet flew over the slippery red clay. The earth was soggy and tree roots crisscrossed the trail as if trying to trip her. Leaves of bushes slapped at her repeatedly.

"Stop or I'll shoot!"

Fear jolted through Sophie. Having lived for two years in Peru, she knew Spanish. She shrieked in terror and ran even harder.

Just as she rounded a turn, a huge root caught her left foot, and Sophie cried out. She flew end over end and landed at the side of the trail, nearly lost in the thick underbrush. Gasping for breath, she rolled over, her white nightgown catching between her legs as she tried to scramble up again.

"No you don't, you little bitch!"

A man's hand grabbed at her long, blond hair, which was now damp and coated with crimson mud. Dressed in green khakis and holding a rifle in his left hand, the soldier grabbed Sophie and hauled her out of the bushes onto the trail.

Her scalp burned as he lifted her to her feet by her hair. Sophie screamed, her hands flying to her scalp.

"You little brat!" he roared in her face. "I'm gonna kill you and get this over with. You aren't worth kidnapping!" He shoved her to the ground again.

Sophie landed hard on her back, the wind knocked out of her. Her blue eyes grew huge as the giant soldier raised his rifle and pointed it at her heaving chest. She saw him grin. His teeth were yellow and one of the front ones was missing.

"I'll kill you and they'll never know the difference." He placed his finger on the trigger.

Giving a little cry, Sophie raised her hand, vainly trying to protect herself. She saw the rage in the man's brown eyes. What had she done to make him hate her?

Just then, she saw another man, come running up behind the soldier.

"Ernesto! No!" the man growled, and jerked the rifle upward.

Sophie screamed as the gun discharged. The sound of the shot was instantly muted, swallowed up by the thick jungle around them. She saw the white man wrestle with her captor. Who was he? With two quick movements, he disarmed the soldier and knocked him off his feet, onto the muddy path.

"What do you think you're doing?" he yelled at Ernesto. Mac Coulter breathed hard. He held the Peruvian soldier's AK-47 in his left hand as he glared down at the

70

man. "You don't shoot children!" he snarled. Wiping his mouth, Mac turned to the little girl, who lay on the trail. His heart pounding in his chest, he crouched down and held out his hand to her.

"Sophie, I'm Mac. Mac Coulter. I need you to reach for my hand. Can you do that? You're safe now. Come on. . . ." He saw the blond girl's huge blue eyes well with tears. She was a muddy mess, her thin gold hair covered with clay. The white cotton nightgown was stained a reddish-brown color. She seemed so little compared to him. Mac stilled his rage. He couldn't blow his cover with Carlos Garcia. Not now. But he couldn't let these soldiers, who would rather rape and kill any female, child or adult, get hold of Garcia's latest victim.

"It's okay," he said soothingly, hearing Ernesto get to his feet behind him.

Sophie was watching the soldier with fear etched in her eyes. She was a beautiful child, Mac realized. He'd caught a glimpse of her yesterday in the villa, here at Garcia's headquarters in the mountains near Agua Caliente. Mac had flown in a bunch of underworld leaders for a meeting at the drug lord's estate near Machu Picchu, considered the national treasure of Peru. Too bad Garcia had built a huge villa, invisible from the air, only ten miles away from the beautiful Incan temple complex.

"I — I want my mommy!" Sophie wailed, pulling away from his proffered hand.

Mac's heart contracted. He didn't trust Ernesto. The soldier had syphilis and was crazy as hell from the disease eating away at what little brain cells he had left. Straightening to his full height, Mac turned and faced the heavily muscled soldier.

"Here," he said, throwing the AK-47 back at him. "Get the hell out of here. Go back to the villa and tell the *patrón* I have the girl. I'll bring her back myself. Now go!" He saw Ernesto's chocolate-brown eyes narrow. The soldier held the rifle in his hands and stroked it.

"Don't even go there," Mac snarled, and he pulled the 9 mm Beretta out of the holster at his side. It was loaded and the safety was off. In the drug business no one ever went without a round in the chamber.

"Humph! *Norteamericano* trash!" Ernesto yelled. "I don't know why Patrón Garcia keeps you on the payroll."

Grinning savagely, Mac said, "Because I fly, shithead. I fly any of his helos. Now get out of here and return to the villa. Call off the manhunt for the girl. I'll bring her back myself."

Lifting his lip, Ernesto barked, "This is not over, gringo."

"It never is between you and me, *compadre.*"

After spitting vehemently, Ernesto turned and stomped back up the trail.

Relief flooded through Mac as he returned his attention to Sophie, who sobbed her heart out. His own heart wrenched. Sometimes being an ATF mole in this godforsaken green hell was too much for him to bear. It was enough that working undercover for the U.S. Bureau of Alcohol, Tobacco and Firearms, Mac had to transport soldiers, drugs, plus Garcia and his spoiled wife, Paloma, around South America.

As he studied the muddy little child, he wanted to put a bullet into Garcia's temple. The man was a sick bastard. But if Mac did that, he'd blow his cover — which had taken more than a year to develop — and could no longer feed information to the ATF. His main goal was to stay undercover long enough to identify all of Garcia's drug ties and find out where the other drug lords lived. He would then give all that information to the ATF and the CIA so that an international sting operation could be coordinated to bring Garcia and his buddies down for good.

As Mac reached out for Sophie, he wanted to chuck the whole thing. He hated the fact that Garcia regularly kidnapped people; that was a way of life and a source of earnings for many people down here, including drug lords. But when it came to harmless, innocent children like Sophie, Mac could barely hang on to his composure.

"Come on, Sophie. It's all right. I won't hurt you. My name is Mac. Can we be friends?" He crouched down because he knew his size would intimidate her. He wore a shoulder holster as well as a sidearm over his dark green flight suit. Mac knew he looked scary to the child. She sat there and scrubbed her eyes with her dirty hands, making messy red circles around them. With a very slow movement, Mac opened the Velcro fastening of the pocket on his right thigh and pulled out a white linen handkerchief.

"Hey, I'd say you need a little cleaning up here." He handed her the handkerchief. She hesitantly took it and then scrubbed her mud-streaked face. Behind him, Mac could hear the shouts dying down. Sophie hadn't gone far from the fortresslike villa hidden in the jungle.

"I want my mommy. . . ."

"I know you do. We're working on that, Sophie. In the meantime, you have to come back to the villa with me. Can I carry you? Look at your toe. It's bleeding. I think you stubbed it while running." Her left big toe was bruised, swollen and purple, and Mac thought she might have broken it.

"Oh . . ." she whimpered.

"It's okay, Sophie," Mac said in English to her. "Will you let me take my other handkerchief and wrap it around your foot? We'll get you cleaned up back at the villa. I'll make sure your toe gets taken care of. Can you move it, honey?" He kept his voice low and soft. Little by little, Sophie responded. She held up her leg and wriggled all her toes. Grinning, Mac said, "Hey, that's terrific, Sophie. Looks like you just stubbed it. Let me lift you up and take you back to the villa? I'll get Señora Renaldo to clean it up for you. Okay?"

Renaldo was the latest nanny hired by Garcia to tend his only child, six-year-old Tiki, a beautiful black-haired little girl. Mac knew that the reason Sophie had been kidnapped was because Tiki was lonely, and she had a *norteamericano* doll with white skin, blond hair and blue eyes. Tiki had said she wanted a real doll matching that description. Garcia had put out a call to find a child around Tiki's age, and poor little Sophie had been targeted.

"Where's my mommy?" Sophie asked, sniffing.

"She's at home in Lima," Mac explained. He slowly eased up on one knee and held out his hands toward her. At first she cringed away, but then changed her mind and moved into his arms. When she wrapped her own slim arms around Mac's neck, he nearly cried. Sophie clung to him as if desperate for protection.

"It's going to be okay, Sophie," he told her as he lifted her gently and got to his feet. Sophie buried her head against his neck and sobbed once. Mac could feel her trembling with fear as he turned and began to walk back to the villa. Mac purposely kept to a snail's pace in order to give Sophie time to settle down.

"My daddy smells like you," she muffled against his neck. "He always smells of lime."

Mac smiled, watching his footing. The many woody vines were a precarious trap for anyone following the animal trails around the villa. "Well, I was running pretty hard to find you, so I don't think I smell all that good right now."

Out in this humid jungle, everyone sweated profusely, and he was no exception. On any given day, as he flew to and from the mountain retreat to cool, dry Cuzco, which sat at nearly thirteen thousand feet, the underarms of his flight suit were dark with sweat.

"Is . . . is Daddy looking for me? What happened? Where am I?"

Holding his large hand against the small of her back, Mac patted her soothingly. "Sophie, you've been taken from your home, but I know your mother and father are looking for you. I'm sure they will do everything to get you back home." Soon, he hoped, but from what he'd heard from the housecleaning staff at the villa, Garcia had taken Sophie as a permanent playmate for Tiki. That meant that the American child would become a virtual prisoner to Garcia's family, with no hope of escape. His heart broke.

His mind churned over ways he might get her home, but none of the plans he'd come up with would work. No, if he tried to get Sophie out of here, he'd blow his cover, and then all of his work would be for nothing. How could he reconcile one child's life against bringing down a drug empire? Was it really worth it? Sophie was innocent. One more helpless victim in the global drug war.

Mac knew the protocol for South American KNRs. The Press would be kept out of it. Everything would be handled behind the scene. As Mac walked along the trail, moving up the steep incline toward the green-painted stucco villa, his hatred for Garcia mounted. And that kept him going, kept him focused on his mission.

As he entered the villa, Mac heard Garcia screaming. He halted just inside the foyer of the main house, which the heavily armed soldiers at the door allowed him to enter. After scraping his muddy boots on the woven rug, an Incan design of red, yellow and orange, Mac waited. He knew this villa like the back of his hand and had sent off a carefully sketched diagram of it to his Washington contacts many months ago.

The screaming continued, and Mac could tell it came from Tiki's playroom. Garcia was shrieking at the nanny, Señora Renaldo.

"You stupid bitch! You let her escape! Who do you think you are? You were supposed to watch Sophie! She's Tiki's playmate! And what do you do? You let her out of your sight!" Then he slapped her.

Mac placed his free hand over Sophie's ear to keep the girl from hearing Paulino Renaldo's shriek of outrage. Damn, he'd like to get Sophie away from this, but at this point there was no place to go.

"I'm tired of you! Antonio, take her out and get rid of her. Permanently. I'm gonna get someone in here who knows what she's doing!"

Mac heard the nanny put up a fight. After all, she was trained in the martial arts. He knew that Antonio, one of many guards in charge of protecting the child, would handcuff the older woman outside and taken under heavy security to a remote location where he'd put a bullet in her head. Then they'd dump her body in the nearby Urubamba River, and her lifeless form would be swallowed up by the restless, angry water, never to be seen again by her family in Lima.

As Paulino's angered curses echoed off the walls, Mac moved into the spacious living room. He then crept quickly into the kitchen, which distanced them from the woman's piteous screams.

Within minutes, the villa became quiet

again. Mac continued to hold Sophie safely in his arms near the kitchen counter. The kitchen staff, their eyes wide with fear, had backed off and left Mac with the girl.

"Where is my golden-haired child?"

Cringing inwardly, Mac heard Garcia's voice. His stomach clenched. He hated himself, because now he would have to hand Sophie over to the bastard. This child was playing hell on every emotion he had. Under any other circumstances, Mac would have gotten her back to her worried, grieving parents. Swallowing bile, he moved out of the kitchen, meeting Carlos Garcia in the living room. His boss was casually dressed in a white peasant shirt, jeans and sneakers. It was Garcia's black eyes, narrowed and glittering, that made Mac halt with Sophie in his arms.

"Is she all right, Coulter? You found her, yes?"

Mac wanted to pull away as Garcia reached out with his strong, athletic hand to touch the little girl's back. The moment he did, the little girl cried out and clung even more securely to Mac.

"She's okay, *Patrón.* Ernesto found her. I told him I'd carry her back to the villa. Look, she's stubbed her toe pretty badly. Can I take her over to the dispensary so

Dr. Macedo can treat her? In this jungle, infection can set in and become deadly. I think she tripped over a vine on the trail."

"Oh, of course, of course," Garcia patted Sophie's small shoulder. "She's wet, too. That damn nanny! I'm tired of her whining and excuses. Now I must look for another one."

"I'd get someone with a military background this time," Mac said. "You've had trouble with nannies since I started working here." Señora Renaldo was the second one to be dispensed in such a way. All it took was for the spoiled Tiki to complain to her daddy about her mean nanny, and the woman disappeared — for good.

"Perhaps you are right." Garcia lit a cigarette and inhaled deeply. He motioned for Coulter to walk toward the door. "*Sí,* take her to the doctor. I will accompany you. Therese is with Tiki, now. Poor little *nena,* baby. She is crying because she misses her Sophie here."

Gritting his teeth, Mac nodded his head. He shifted Sophie to his left side so that Garcia couldn't keep reaching out to pet her as if she was were a dog. "I'm sure Tiki is upset."

Tiki was spoiled as hell, like Garcia's twenty-four-year-old drug addict wife,

81

Paloma. The woman was either high on heroin or drinking tequila until she passed out in a stupor. Paloma had a body that wouldn't quit, which was why Garcia had decided to marry her. How Tiki ever got born was something Mac didn't understand, because the woman was clearly an addict bent on dying from an overdose.

"I like your idea, Mac. Perhaps I should be looking for a nanny with a military background. Perhaps that is where I made my mistake."

Mac knew that Garcia had already lured three or four South American women trained in child care to his compound and put them through a life-and-death test to see if they passed muster. Of course, not many lived to tell about it. The few that did survive suddenly found themselves in Garcia's employment with no way to escape. In essence, the surviving nanny with martial arts and weapons skills was as much a prisoner of Garcia as was Sophie. Only they didn't know that was going to happen. Once in the employ of a drug lord, one never left unless in a body bag.

"Hmm," Carlos murmured as he walked through the open door and out into the parking area, "perhaps I need to expand my search, for a different kind of nanny."

He turned and waited for Mac to catch up. Together they headed for a single-story dark green stucco building against the north wall of the complex.

"So far, you've chosen all Spanish women. I know England is renowned for its trained nannies." Mac was making small talk. He knew next to nothing about child care.

The sky above was still gray, with low-hanging humid clouds, but at this time of morning it was always like that. Around noon the clouds lifted, burning off in the powerful equatorial sunlight. The sky would turn a hazy blue — just right for flying. Mac would give anything to be flying right now, just to escape being around this bastard.

"I know!" Carlos snapped his fingers and turned toward him. "I hate the English! They're so arrogant. They think they are a superior species compared to the rest of the world. But what do you think about a Canadian nanny? Perhaps a woman with a military background? Canadians aren't pretentious. I don't want a supercilious snob looking after my little Tiki."

Shrugging, Mac let the guard stationed at the dispensary open the door for them. Carlos walked through first. "Sounds okay to me." Mac felt sorry for whomever Garcia would find. His field operatives would put out feelers, lure the poor women down here.

Carlos hailed Dr. Pablo Macedo as they walked into one of the examination rooms. Mac gently set Sophie down on the gurney. As he smoothed her straight, dirty hair back from her face, he smiled down at her.

"Sophie, the doctor will help your toe. He's a good man and he won't hurt you." Mac kept his hand cupped around her small shoulder.

Sophie gave a quick glance at Garcia, who stood near the door, smoking his cigarette. A feral look blazed in her huge blue eyes. All Mac could do was pat her back and try to give her some form of solace. He knew children had a strong sixth sense. They were like primal animals and reacted instinctively to danger. There was no question that Garcia was a danger to Sophie.

"She seems taken with you, Mac," Garcia said, studying him intently through the haze of cigarette smoke. "I'll tell you what. I am going to take you off the flight roster. I want you to temporarily be Tiki and Sophie's bodyguard for me. I know, I know, you're not a nanny, but I want this little one to know she has a friend at the villa until she can make friends with Tiki. Yes?"

Mac stood there, thunderstruck. One part of him thought it was a great idea because he could protect Sophie and try to help her adjust to her imprisonment. The other part — dealing with spoiled Tiki and drunken Paloma — didn't sit well with him. Still, little Sophie looked so forlorn. He might not be able to rescue her from this ugly situation, but he could provide her some badly needed care and comfort.

"Well . . . I . . ."

"Look how she adores you, *compadre*." Carlos grinned and flipped his manicured hand toward Sophie. "Right now what I need is for her to befriend my beloved Tiki. I'll get a babysitter within twenty-four hours. You're too valuable a pilot to remain on the ground for long."

"I'm not real good with kids, *Patrón*. All I know how to do is fly." That was a lie, but Mac could never let the drug lord know the full scope of his skills. Not yet.

"I understand that. And I do not expect you to be a bodyguard for too long."

"And if Tiki goes crying to you, are you going to take me out in the bush like you did the nannies?" Mac grinned, but he wasn't kidding.

85

Carlos's eyes lit up with amusement. "No, no, do not worry about that. You are my best pilot! I don't get rid of people who do their job right. And if Tiki cries, we will deal with those situations as they arise? I'm sure my contacts in Canada will find qualified nannies in a week or two. This is only temporary, I assure you."

Because of the way Sophie clung to the front of his damp flight suit , the look of sheer terror in her eyes, Mac gave in and nodded. As if on cue, Macedo, the doctor, entered the room with his nurse and wife, Luisa. "Yeah, okay, Boss. I guess I can babysit for a while."

"*Bueno!* Good. Well, then that's settled. Bring Sophie over to Tiki's playroom when she's done here. She needs a bath and change of clothes. You'll see to that, *sí?*"

Nodding, Mac kept the grimness he felt out of his voice. *"No problema, Patrón."* As he moved aside for the doctor, Mac hoped that the next nanny would be found very shortly and pass the harrowing tests. He was already desperate to be taken off this unexpected assignment.

Chapter Five

Kathy hoped like hell the sweat trickling down her rib cage wasn't staining the pink blouse she wore beneath her conservative business suit. She sat in a skyscraper in downtown Lima, Peru, and peered nervously out the window. The dreary clouds that blanketed the city six months out of the year seemed depressing and ominous to her.

Two weeks. God, two long, torturous weeks to get this far! She sat in the plastic red chair outside the office of Señora Marita Olivares. To her knowledge, this woman was a "front" for Garcia's empire, involved with hiring employees. She handled personnel work in his legal businesses, which were fronts for his illegal activities.

As she waited, Kathy mentally went over how she must appear to others. She'd taken great pains to research what a British nanny would look like. Thus, she'd chosen her neatly tailored gray suit, a no-nonsense blouse and plain black, low-heeled leather shoes. Nothing fancy. To complete her prim appearance, Kathy had woven her blond hair into a braid down the back of her head. A few errant strands fell across her brow. Well, she wasn't perfect.

From Calgary, Alberta, to here, she'd been "shepherded" by a man who pretended to be employed by Señora Olivares. But Kathy felt sure he was one of Garcia's goons. Not wanting to appear anxious, Kathy forced herself to relax, although that was the last thing she wanted to do. Being a kidnapper and now a spy to help Sophie. That was the toughest thing she'd ever done, aside from lying to her family. Her lack of official training could put her in jeopardy, and this fact compounded her anxiety. While Commander O'Conner had helped her set up this mission, Kathy had to ensure that her fake life history was tacked down to a gnat's ass via a paper trail. This way Garcia wouldn't find out she was a spy. Still, she worried. What if she slipped up? Forgot a name? A place? A school? It would be so easy to do. Ordinarily, she was one brazen, confident pilot, but this situation had pitfalls she'd never encountered before.

The door opened. An elegant, short and thin woman with black hair wrapped up in a French twist stepped into the office. She was dressed in a tasteful silk burgundy suit, which embellished her mature beauty. The gold wire-frame bifocal glasses dipped down on her aquiline nose and emphasized her narrow features. But it was the woman's eyes, gravely serious and chocolate brown, that sent Kathy's heart skittering.

"Ms. Lincoln? I'm Marita Olivares. Welcome." She shook Kathy's hand. Smiling, she said, "Please come in for your interview."

"Yes, of course. It's nice to meet you," Kathy said, and released her warm, bejeweled hand. She noticed the woman had a British accent, and this surprised her. Ms. Olivares was not what she appeared, and that put Kathy even more on alert as she rose and walked confidently into the woman's office.

Señora Olivares's office was constructed completely of expensive mahogany, from the walls of bookshelves to her massive rectangular desk, behind which she settled herself. Kathy sat down in a green wing chair, her knees together, hands clasped in her lap. She watched as Señora Olivares quickly opened her file.

"So . . . you are from Calgary? In Canada, Ms. Lincoln?" She peered over her bifocals at Kathy.

"Yes, born and raised there, ma'am." Another trickle of sweat started down her ribs. The gray blazer hid her perspiration, thank God.

"Your accent, if you do not mind me saying so, sounds very Americanized, Ms. Lincoln. Not Canadian." Her arched, thick brows rose in question.

"My mother was American, my father Canadian. He met her on a business trip to the States. They fell in love and the rest is history. I was born in Calgary and have dual citizenship as a result." Kathy allowed a slight smile. "So, if my English sounds flawed, that is why." She saw Señora Olivares's mouth twitch. Was that a good or bad sign?

"I see here that you have been trained in early childhood education at the British Nanny Institute in Toronto. Two years of training and you were an A student."

"Yes, ma'am."

"What kind of employment are you looking for, Ms. Lincoln?"

Taken aback, Kathy quickly said, "Permanent only, ma'am. I want to fit into the family and work with the little ones."

"I see . . ."

This was torture.

"I thoroughly checked all your credentials last week, Ms. Lincoln."

Kathy's heart thudded in her chest. She kept her face carefully composed. Having sent her résumé two weeks ago, she expected to have her references verified. But still, as she watched Señora Olivares tap her bloodred polished nails over the personnel file, arched brows drawn downward, Kathy's fears mounted. What the hell did that look mean? Had they found her out? Had her cover been blown? A hundred other worries floated in her head. Kathy saw no guards in the office, but she was sure the goon that had escorted her was out in the hall. Out of sight, but close enough to shoot her or bury her if Señora Olivares gave the order.

"Do you prefer working with a particular gender, Ms. Lincoln?"

Shrugging, Kathy said, "I love all children, no matter what their age or gender, Señora Olivares."

"I see. Well, I am fascinated with your other livelihood before you took child care training. You were in the CAF? The Canadian Armed Forces? Isn't that a bit of a change in career paths?"

Kathy didn't know how to read the woman's inscrutable look. Her brown eyes were flat and reminded her of a snake eyeing its next meal. "I suppose it is, ma'am, but when I was eighteen I had a lot of wild oats to sow. My parents felt it best that I spend three years in the CAF, enlisted ranks, to get over that."

"And you agreed with their plan?"

"I thought it would be interesting work. I'm very physical by nature and I wanted a job that would test me."

"I see you worked in security?"

"Yes, ma'am. In the civilian world my career would be that of a police officer."

"I see. . . ." More tapping on the file with her claws. Another inscrutable look.

Kathy sat very still, unable to gauge the woman. Her instincts told her to stay quiet.

"And so, you took many police courses while in the CAF? Such as karate? Firing weapons of all kinds? Or were you in the office typing?"

Kathy smiled slightly. "I was a field operative in security. I was cross-trained in hand-to-hand combat, and I am proficient in all the weapons I listed on my résumé. I did not sit in an office."

"Excellent. Well . . ." Señora Olivares raised her head ". . . the family I represent is looking for a bodyguard *and* a nanny, Ms. Lincoln. And they want someone who desires long-term employment. They pay handsomely, and you will travel the world with them."

"That sounds exactly what I'm looking for," Kathy said. She noticed that throughout the two weeks she'd spent getting to this point, no one had ever mentioned the family's name, which she knew was Garcia.

"Before you meet my employer, he insists upon a small test to see if you can meet the requirements for this position. He needs assurance that you are highly competent and skilled in these areas."

"Okay." What tests? Kathy had taken a ream of written tests last week. They were all psychologically oriented and examined by a male psychiatrist in Garcia's employ. She'd bluffed her way through the paper chase and past the shrink, who had reminded her of Freud in more ways than one. More tests? What kind now? She was sick of them. Seeing Señora Olivares smile for the first time, her hands folded over the file, Kathy got a bad feeling. Her smile never reached her eyes, which remained curiously flat yet very probing.

"My employer wants a young woman with a background like yours. Because he is very rich, he worries for his daughter's safety and the possibility that she could be kidnapped. My employer desires someone who, at an instant's notice, can take his child to safety wherever they are, be it in the jungle or the city."

Kathy nodded, unsure of where this conversation was headed. In all the research on Garcia, no mention had ever been made of these "tests." There was a growing coldness in the pit of her stomach. Forcing herself to remain relaxed and attentive, she said, "Of course. I'll take the tests. I'm aware that very wealthy families in South America are at risk for kidnapping and that kidnappers try to take a child first."

"Exactly," Señora Olivares murmured. She closed the file with finality. "I will ask Teres to take you to the Lima airport, where you will be flown by helicopter to my employer's villa, near Agua Caliente. It is his favorite country home. Someone at the villa will give you the instructions for these tests. Once you pass them, you will then meet your employer, Ms. Lincoln."

What was she getting into? For a moment, panic hit Kathy. And then she settled down. *Focus.* Focus on what was important: getting into Garcia's villa, getting close enough that she could kidnap his child and make him suffer as her family had. Kathy compressed her lips and said with confidence, "That's fine, *señora*. I'm more than ready for any tests."

Mac Coulter was getting desperate. He'd more or less volunteered some of his rare "free time" to check in on Sophie. It tore him up daily to see what the child was going through — alone. Never had he felt so damn helpless. He couldn't rescue her without showing his hand. And his handler didn't have any ideas how to get Sophie out of there, either. To ease his guilty conscience, Mac dropped in often to visit her.

He sat in the playroom with Sophie in his lap and Tiki rocking on her beloved, much-used wooden rocking horse over in the corner. For the past two weeks, Sophie had clung to him, and Mac knew that he represented safety in a world gone mad around her. The child cried herself to sleep every night, and this tore him up. During the day, Sophie was glum and refused to play with Tiki, who was thrilled her new, living "doll" had been delivered to her. Keeping Tiki otherwise busy with her hundreds of toys was the real challenge.

Repeatedly, Garcia's daughter would come over, pull on Sophie's hair and scream at her to play. Mac would then get up, patiently remove Tiki's fingers one at a time from Sophie's long blond hair and tell her that she couldn't do that. Oh, the temper tantrums. And Tiki, who had been raised by a series of nannies, had her reactions down pat. His ears ached from her high-pitched, endless shrieks. What Mac wanted to do and what he could do to reprimand Tiki was a real walk on the edge of a sword. Tiki was utterly spoiled. No one dared to discipline her, not even her teacher or himself. Sophie, who was grieving over the loss of her parents, had retreated deep inside herself, so no matter what Tiki did to her, she wouldn't respond.

Mac looked out the window. From the second-floor nursery and playroom area, he could see the helicopter landing pad, a slab of concrete colored green to match the surrounding jungle. Garcia had told him last night that a potential nanny and bodyguard had been found.

When Señorita Adelina Martinez, the British educated Brazilian teacher, entered, he hoisted Sophie into her arms. Adelina, a fifty-year-old spinster with gray hair pulled severely into a chignon, gave him a look of surprise. Her thick glasses made her watery brown eyes seem buglike to Mac. Yet she must have the patience of Job, because she'd been hired by Garcia when Tiki was three years old. Somehow, the woman persevered with the petulant child.

Out of desperation, and a need to get out of there, Mac decided to assert some authority. "Can you take care of them for a few hours, *señorita?* I have to fly the chopper in a little while. I'll be back, of course."

"Certainly, Mr. Coulter." She gave him a slight smile. "I'm sure the babysitter could use a rest."

The knowing glint in her kind eyes made Mac grin. "Yeah, something like that, *señorita.*" He patted Sophie's shoulder. The girl had come to trust the teacher, as well. "She's not eaten her breakfast yet."

"Poor child." Adelina twittered and she touched Sophie's cheek gently. "I'll see what I can do while you are gone, Señor Coulter."

"Yeah, fine. Tiki threw oatmeal at Sophie earlier. I had to clean her up and get her a set of fresh clothes."

"Tsk, tsk, that wasn't right, now was it?" Adelina held Sophie away far enough to look at the little girl's pale face. "Well! We must remedy this, young lady. And I'll make sure our sweet Tiki doesn't throw any more food at you, either."

Go for it, Mac thought as he left. Adelina, because of her British training and therefore the best, in Garcia's eyes, had a cool, calm manner when dealing with the truculent Tiki — one that garnered a fair measure of success. Her elevated status in the household was evident, for she was just about the only one of the staff who could manage the uncontrollable and lonely Tiki. What Mac would like to do was swat Tiki on the rear and make her behave, but if he did that, all hell would break loose. No one ever laid a hand on the child.

Hurrying out of the villa, Mac saw Carlos Garcia near the dispensary. The morning was gray, the clouds hanging low over the jungle, as always. The temperature was climbing already, the humidity high and making him sweat.

Carlos saw him and stopped. "Tiki is with Adelina?"

"Yes, sir, she is." Mac halted and pointed toward the Bell helicopter sitting on the pad. "I need some flight time, Señor Garcia. I've only flown twice in the last two weeks and that doesn't help keep my flight skills sharp. I understand you've got a nanny to pick up in Lima this morning? I'd like to have that mission." Mac stated it as a fact, leaving no room for Garcia to say no.

Shrugging, the man said, "Of course. Do what you like. This is the third nanny I've seen in a week. I'm giving up hope of ever finding a woman who can be good with a child *and* be a bodyguard."

"Yes, sir." Mac was going to change the odds on this one. He was going to get out of this babysitting gig one way or another.

"Her name is Katherine Lincoln. She's Canadian. Señora Olivares said she has had CAF police training, so I'm hopeful her survival skills are superior to the other two."

I do, too. Mac nodded and said nothing.

Brightening, Garcia said, "And do you know what? This is *amazing,* Mac! The color photo Señora Olivares sent me of this young nanny shows that she has blond hair, blue eyes and, of course, white skin. Isn't that something? I do hope she can pass the tests, because I'm sure Tiki would dote on her. She's an even bigger doll than our little Sophie, who sulks and refuses to play with my Tiki."

"I see," Mac said. Tiki was enamored with blond hair, blue eyes and white skin. The child had coffee-colored skin, impish sable-brown eyes and thick, straight black hair.

Looking at his watch, Garcia said, "Teres is with our employment prospect in Lima. I will have my secretary call him and tell him to meet you at the Lima airport shortly."

"Will Teres be coming back with us?" Mac hoped not.

"No. He has other business to attend to down there. You will fly Miss Lincoln here, and I will have one of my guards meet her here at the landing pad."

"Very well." Mac mentally rubbed his hands together. This was turning out better than he expected. Now, if only Miss Lincoln wasn't a wimp, he could get out of babysitting mode and back into the air to continue his undercover work.

Kathy tried to keep her surprise to herself when she climbed into the copilot's seat of the Bell helicopter at the Jorge Chávez Airport in Lima. Her surprise was that the man sitting behind the controls on the right side was an American. Teres had shuffled her into the seat, thrown her luggage in the rear and slid the door shut. As he backed off, the ground crew slid the chocks away from the helo's three wheels. Teres looked as if he wanted to get rid of her once and for all.

100

"I'm Mac Coulter," the pilot said, turning and giving her his hand. There wasn't anything he didn't like about this woman. To his surprise, she was nearly six feet tall! And he could see she was no wimp. Her extended hand was medium-boned and had calluses built up on her knuckles, which meant she knew more than a little karate. A nanny with muscle.

"Katherine Lincoln, Mr. Coulter." Kathy tried to ignore the firm warmth of his hand as she shook it. She liked his low, modulated voice. He wore aviator sunglasses so she couldn't see his eyes, but his mouth drew her female attention. It was sensually shaped, with a boyish smile. What a kissable mouth! Snorting silently to herself, Katherine figured this was the wrong place and time to be drawn to a man. *Any* man.

Mac liked her firm but gentle grip. Just touching her hand sent an unexpected ache through him. It had been a long time since he'd touched a woman. And this was one he *wanted* to touch. *Not today, dude.* Releasing her hand, Mac busied himself with the controls, switching on the engines and waiting for the crewmen to clear the helo so he could engage the blades.

"I assume you're here for the job of nanny?"

"Yes, I'm applying for the position," Kathy said, trying not to look too interested in the cockpit display. She had to pretend she didn't know a thing about helicopters. It was a tough act.

"Great to hear." He flipped a salute to the man who stood on the asphalt twirling his finger above his head. That meant engage rotors, and Mac did. The Bell helo began to sway and vibrate as the blades moved, sluggishly at first and then faster. Soon, Mac saw they were up to the rpms necessary for liftoff, and he called the tower over his headset for clearance. Lima sat close to sea level, very near the Pacific Ocean. Where they were going — up to thirteen thousand feet and then back down across the Inca Trail system to Agua Caliente, situated in the jungle at sixty-five hundred feet — would test the helo's abilities.

Before lifting off, he pulled a pair of earphones off a hook above him and handed them to the woman. He liked her flawless turquoise eyes framed with thick blond lashes. In his estimation, the black ring around her irises gave her a look more of a hunter than a nanny. That and those callused knuckles. This was no city chick, that was for sure. Yet she was elegant in her trim gray suit and pale pink blouse. The white pearl earrings and necklace she wore emphasized her femininity.

"Put these on," he yelled over the roar of the rotor. She nodded, took them and smoothly settled them over her head, positioning the microphone close to her full lips.

Mac hesitated fractionally. Her movements were unexpected. Out of place, maybe. She handled the earphones and mike as if she'd put a set on a thousand times before. Was she ex-military, maybe? That would fit. He was burning to ask her, but they didn't have much time and he damn well wanted her to survive the tests. One way or another, Tiki was getting this provocative and interesting new nanny, so he wouldn't have to shadow Sophie so much. He had had so little time to himself that he was suffering from a lack of sleep. And to be a spy and stay on top of the game, sleep was essential. Still, little Sophie deserved his protection — as much as he could give her under these terrible circumstances.

Chapter Six

Kathy reminded herself that Mac Coulter was in bed with a drug dealer. He was being paid by Garcia, and she bet he was running drugs for him. As the bird lifted off and broke connection with the earth, she grudgingly admitted Coulter had a nice touch with the helicopter. His actions were competent and smooth. As she glanced down, she saw his muscles move beneath the dark hair covering his left arm. Why was she so attracted to him? Frowning, Kathy looked out the window. He was a stranger. A drug runner. No matter how good-looking he was, she could not get involved with him.

Gripping her hands in her lap, Kathy forced herself to refrain from shifting into helo pilot mode. She had to remember that she didn't know how to fly one. God, it was tough to hold herself back! Flying was like breathing for her. The sky was where she found peace from the world below.

As the aircraft moved forward down the runway, Kathy gazed at the surrounding mountains, bare and brown in the distance. Coulter kept the helo just below the somber blanket of clouds along the seacoast, she noticed. This bird did not have the advanced avionics equipment to fly through such stuff and not hit a mountain in the process.

As they left Lima behind, she saw the mighty blue-and-white Andes on the distant horizon. Below her, the land stretched, brown, undulating and barren.

Mac glanced over at the woman. Her profile tugged at him. She had flawless skin, a broad brow, soft full lips and a stubborn-looking nose. Attractive but not a raving beauty. Mac smiled to himself. Going undercover, he'd left his personal life behind. Not that there'd been much of one before that. No, just a divorce two years ago and raw heartbreak. Frowning, he forced himself to concentrate on the present.

"You American?" he asked. He absorbed the shuddering vibrations of the helo. It felt good to be flying again! Comforting. The sky was always his place of refuge and healing. Mac removed his aviator glasses to take a really good look at her.

"Er, no, I'm Canadian. From Calgary."

"Hmm, you sound American."

Kathy cringed inwardly. "My mother was American, my father Canadian. I have dual citizenship." Would he buy it? She saw curiosity burning in his sharply intelligent gray eyes as he turned and gave her a half smile.

"I see. . . ."

Squirming beneath his scrutiny, Kathy remained silent. Those big gray eyes of his with their huge black pupils made her feel as if he had X-ray vision. Plus Coulter was an easy man to look at. Dammit, her body was responding like a yo-yo to every glance he gave her, to the deep, personal tone of his voice, and it drove her crazy. With his deeply suntanned, square face, thick black brows and full mouth, he could have been someone she knew back home, and she didn't feel at all threatened by him. Still, the pistol strapped to his right thigh reminded her that he was a drug dealer, pure and simple. No matter how she responded to him, he was a bad guy and in cahoots with Garcia, her enemy.

"You were in the military?" Mac asked, sliding his sunglasses back on. He guided the helicopter to an ever higher altitude.

Her stomach clenched. Kathy pursed her mouth. She had to play along. It would do no good to lie. She'd lied enough already to Señora Olivares in Lima. "Does it show?"

Shrugging, Mac said, "The way you handled the earphones and mike."

"Oh." *Damn!* Her heart thudded once. The cloud cover was beginning to break up a bit, the farther east they flew. Gulping, Kathy said, "I was in the CAF for a while. I was in security."

That made a lot of sense. "You musta flown in some planes then?" Mac smiled over at her. Yes, he definitely liked what he saw. There was a challenging look in her eyes and the way she set her jaw. And yet Mac felt panic deep inside him. Kathy Lincoln would be in danger. Real danger. And very shortly.

"Uh, sometimes, yes."

"Canadian MP?"

"Something like that, yes."

"I can see why the *patrón* would be interested in you as a nanny for Tiki, his little girl."

"Oh?" Glancing to her right, Kathy studied his rugged profile. She tore her gaze away and decided Mac Coulter was too addictive. Up ahead, tentative streaks of weak sunlight were creeping through the dense clouds.

"He'd mentioned he wanted to hire

someone to be both bodyguard and nanny."

"I see." That was what Señora Olivares had told her. "You must know the *patrón* pretty well?" Kathy asked.

"Carlos Garcia. I'm the family pilot. When they need to be shuttled to and from his villas here in Peru, I do the flying."

"And you're an American?" Why would someone who looked as nice and clean-cut as Coulter become a drug dealer? Kathy just couldn't understand it. Yet he was. And it sounded as though Coulter was very close to the drug lord's family. Elation soared through her, because with Coulter, she'd hit an unexpected gold mine of information.

"Yes, I am. Born in Idaho." Well, that was his cover story. Mac found himself wishing he didn't have to lie to her, but he had no choice.

"What led you to become a private pilot down here?"

He grinned. The chopper's controls — the cyclic and collective — felt good in his hands. It was a good thing that his helo was not bugged as so many other places were around Garcia's estate. "What led you to become employed as a nanny down here?"

Kathy managed a tight smile. He wasn't going to answer her question. "I love to travel." Well, that, at least, wasn't a lie.

"If you get hired by the *patrón,* you'll certainly get your fair share of that."

Looking down at her fingers, Kathy stated, "Señora Olivares back in Lima said something about tests. Do you know anything about them? What they are? She didn't say."

Mac frowned and looked around the empty sky. Ahead, the dark brown foothills began to rise from the flat coastal plain, and he started their climb to thirteen thousand feet, which would take them over Cuzco, once the center of the Incan Empire. "She didn't?"

"No. I'm a little worried, to tell you the truth. I *really* want this job, and I'd like to know what I'm facing so I can pass the tests."

Mac wanted her to know, too. "Listen, I'm going to level with you, Ms. Lincoln. And the deal is you can't tell anyone what I'm going to share with you. Okay?" Mac looked at her for a long, pregnant moment to emphasize his words. She had such huge, beautiful blue eyes. He could drown in them, but told himself to not go there.

"Sure. That's a promise." Kathy forced a

little laugh. "I can use all the help I can get."

Nodding, Mac said, "What I'm going to tell you is going to sound like something out of a science fiction book, but you have to believe me and know it's for real."

Heart pounding briefly, Kathy wondered what the hell he was talking about. "I'm all ears."

"Carlos Garcia doesn't want just a nanny. He wants a bodyguard, first and foremost. He's very sensitive about his wife and daughter being kidnapped. I think you know that kidnapping is a way of life here in South America?" Mac turned again to glance at her. If he expected Ms. Lincoln to look pale, he was disappointed. Seeing the set of her mouth, Mac realized she wasn't quite the cream puff he'd first thought. Further, her eyes had narrowed, and damned if she didn't remind him of a hawk hunting its prey. Again, her reaction was unexpected.

"Yes, that's what Señora Olivares told me. She seemed very pleased I had a military background."

"No kidding. Patrón Garcia needs to have his family well protected. And toward that end, he wants to make sure that whomever he hires is going to be able to

110

make the grade should something happen. Your military background will be a plus."

For many reasons.

Kathy wanted to ask what had happened to the last nanny, but decided it wasn't the time or place. "I feel I can be a bodyguard, no problem."

"Well, there's more to this than you realize," Mac said, not wanting to tell her the truth and send her screaming in the other direction.

"What don't I realize, Mr. Coulter?"

"The tests that Patrón Garcia will put you through. You have to be prepared ahead of time or you'll probably never make it out alive." He glanced at her to make sure she heard him correctly. Mac saw her face finally drain of color and her lovely lips part. She got the message.

"What are you talking about?" She stared at Coulter, who gave her a very grim look.

"When I land at his villa near Agua Caliente, the *patrón* is going to put you through three physical tests. In the first you'll have to demonstrate your ability to fend off an attacker. Garcia will put you in his recreational hall, the gym where he works out. You will have to deal with three of his soldiers attacking you all at once. If you disarm and disable them, then you go for test number two." Searching her taut face, he saw her eyes glint. "You've got calluses on your knuckles. I'm assuming you do karate?"

"I'm a black belt."

She said it with a steely coolness that made Mac smile inwardly. Ms. Lincoln certainly was no easy mark, even if she looked it, dressed in that prim suit of hers. "Good, because when these guys rush you, pull out all the stops. Don't run, don't scream, stand your ground and do some major damage to them before they do it to you. Patrón Garcia will be there, watching you every second, from a window you can't see through. If you don't disable those men, you've lost your chance for employment. And don't be nice." Mac glanced at her. "Draw blood, because I can guarantee you the three guys intend to do just that. Draw *your* blood."

Flexing her hands, Kathy muttered, "I can see why most nannies seeking employment with this guy don't make the grade."

Mac nodded. "Just remember that this man knows his family can be kidnapped, held for ransom or murdered. He loves them with his life and he wants to make sure their new nanny and bodyguard will be able to prevent that. Or at least make a difference should such an occasion arise."

"I got it," Kathy said, her mind spinning. She hadn't expected this at all. Her black belt in karate had always been for fun, not to kill, though she had been trained to take someone down. All her exercises with her Japanese master had been to use karate as a defense and to delve into the deep spiritual nature of the art, which appealed to her strongly. Now she was going to have to use it on three goons who were going to try and incapacitate her.

"It would be nice if he sent only one man against me."

Mac shook his head, and his gaze ranged across the control panel. The clouds were breaking up more as they climbed up over the dry hills to five thousand feet. Ahead he could see the peerless Andes, dark blue giants topped with a white frosting of snow. "You have to put yourself into his head," he told her. "If someone is going to kidnap his little girl, they'll send more than one man to do the job. They always work in teams of two or three. That's why he's going to throw three big soldiers at you. And these guys are mercenaries hired from around the world. The best in their business, Ms. Lincoln. Patrón Garcia wants complete assurance you can handle such an attack."

"Okay. If I manage to take them all out, what's the next test?"

"The firing range. He'll want to know you can handle an assortment of weapons. His armorer will take you there and you'll have to demonstrate your knowledge of different pistols and rifles. You'll be asked to shoot at close range, as well as two, three, four hundred yards."

"That sounds easy compared to the first test," Kathy muttered.

"Don't get too cocky just yet. After the trial with pistols and rifles, you get to show them how good you are with a knife."

Eyebrows raised, Kathy said, "I've had knife training."

"Figured you did, but at least you'll know going in what to expect. And the guy you have to fight is an expert."

"You mean he's going to come after me to try and kill me?"

"That's the idea, Ms. Lincoln. I think you're getting it."

Trying to tamp down her fear, Kathy swam in her own sweat. Never had she thought getting to Garcia was going to be this hard! Her assumption that being his child's nanny would be easy had been a huge tactical error on her part. Of course, the only other way she could have come to him was as a pilot. And Kathy didn't really think Garcia would swallow the story of an American woman running drugs for him. Glancing over at Mac, she decided that maybe she should have gone that route instead. Garcia trusted Coulter. Why not her? But then, macho South American men didn't like strong women, so she probably wouldn't have been able to get in that door, anyway. Better to be a nanny.

"You still with me?" Mac demanded. She looked pale and overwhelmed.

"Yes. You said there was a third test if I survive this knife fight. What's it about?"

"The worst and hardest of them all," Mac warned. As he eased the helo up to seven thousand feet, the Andes looked more and more beautiful. Cuzco lay on a high plateau near twelve thousand feet in a bowl-like valley surrounded by naked brown mountains.

"I can't even begin to imagine what it would be." And she couldn't.

"The *patrón* will have you flown fifty miles away from his villa. This is a survival test, Ms. Lincoln. He'll give you nothing except a pair of good hiking boots and the clothes on your back. You'll be dropped

115

across the Urubamba River, which you'll have to figure out how to cross, and then find your way back to the villa through the jungle."

"Do I get a compass?"

"No."

"Water?"

"No. Nothing."

"A weapon?"

"No."

She gave him a frustrated look. "What's the *point* of this test?"

"Simple. The *patrón* knows that if his villa is attacked by kidnappers, that the nanny must grab his daughter and head into the jungle. He has three hideouts, which he will reveal to you after you've passed the tests. You would take his child there for safekeeping. He figures that if they are attacked, you will only have time enough to grab Tiki and make a run for it. Under those circumstances, you wouldn't have water, a weapon, a compass or anything else. He needs to be assured that you can get clear of the villa and head for one of these jungle strongholds, where he will come pick you up later, when the coast is clear."

"Good God . . ."

Searching her face, Mac saw frustration

and concern in her sharpened blue eyes. Her mouth was thin and set. "I told you this would sound like science fiction, didn't I?"

"Yes, you did," Kathy admitted, rubbing her damp hands against her thighs.

"You've had survival training, I assume?"

"Yes. Desert and jungle."

"Good, because you're going to need it."

"Right now, the easiest test looks like this little fifty-mile hike."

"Be careful," Mac cautioned. Up ahead, he saw the clouds finally break and bright shafts of sunshine pour down through the holes. "There's something else you need to know."

Kathy looked over at him and raised her brows.

"Jaguars live in the jungles of Peru. After you cross the river, you'll be traversing one particular jaguar's territory. This animal was raised by the *patrón* from the time it was a kitten. The mother had been shot by a farmer, and they brought a male kitten to Garcia's villa five years ago. This jaguar," Mac warned her gravely, "was set loose in that area."

"Okay, so he's had contact with humans."

"Yes, but not how you think."

Kathy frowned.

117

"The jaguar has a fondness for human flesh." He saw his words sink in. Again her lips parted, and then she snapped them shut.

"So what you're saying is that once I cross the river, this jaguar will be lying in wait for me? Because he likes human meat?"

"Exactly."

"Just how many nannies have died trying to pass this man's tests?"

"You don't want to know."

Anger and fear warred in Kathy. "My God. I never expected this."

"None of them do," he told her softly. He looked around and eased the helo up to eight thousand feet. The climb up to Cuzco was sharp and sudden. Luckily, this helo could manage the high altitudes of the Andes, but not many could.

"This is *ridiculous!*"

"I know."

As she gazed out at the mountains below, Kathy felt fear eating at her. She was angry, because any one of these tests could claim her life before she even got near enough to Garcia to take his daughter.

"I mean, I'm *not* the Terminator, for God's sake!"

"You have some advantages," Mac said.

She eyed him. "Like what?"

"I'm telling you ahead of time. The other nannies didn't have a clue. Further, if you pass those first two tests, I'll make sure I'm the one flying you to that survival area. I'll give you a Swiss Army knife and a compass so that you can make it back in one piece, alive."

"A Swiss Army knife against a jaguar?"

"I know it's not much, but it's more than the others had."

She sat there in fear. A part of her wanted to scream, *Turn this helo around and get me out of here.* The other part said, *No friggin' way. I can do this. I can handle these situations. Keep your eye on the ball, Trayhern. Remember why you're here. Stay the course.*

Getting a grip on her escalating feelings, her fear, she glared at Coulter.

"I guess the question begs to be asked — why are you telling me this?"

Chapter Seven

Mac stared at her. He could sense something wasn't right here. But what the hell was it? One moment, Katherine Lincoln was a docile young woman, the perfect nanny. The next, she looked like an honest-to-God hawk ready to attack him. It was in her eyes and her voice. Carefully, he said, "Look, the *patrón*'s little kid needs some stability in her life. I'd like to see you pass the tests."

Yeah, right. Kathy gazed into his shadowed gray eyes. He wasn't telling the whole truth, she knew it. But he was a drug dealer, so what did she expect? Being undercover without training made her feel incredibly vulnerable. When she realized she was in military attack mode, her posture assertive, Kathy forced herself to sit back, prim and proper, her hands folded in her lap.

"I see," she said. Glancing at the altimeter, she realized they were at eleven thousand feet and still climbing. The helo labored upward in the thinning air, the chopping blades vibrating her entire body. Below them stretched brown, lifeless mountains. And straight ahead rose the mighty Andes, topped with snow — the awesome lords of the region. And highly dangerous to fly over, due to the sudden up- and downdrafts they caused. Where was Cuzco? Kathy wondered. The gray, flat ceiling of clouds had turned into white puffy ones scattered like sheeps' fleece across the dark blue sky.

"I mean . . ." Mac waved his hand ". . . Tiki really deserves to have a steady adult in her life. I like the little kid a lot. I just want to see her happy." He glanced over at Katherine Lincoln's wary expression. Tendrils of blond hair emphasized the clean lines of her face. She wore no makeup save for some pale pink gloss on her lips, which were a helluva lure to him. Her cheeks were naturally pink, that clear peaches-and-cream complexion that all women lusted after, he supposed.

"I understand." And she did. More than Coulter would ever realize. Her mind spun and churned with a hundred questions. "How much longer before we land?"

"We're an hour from our final destination." He pointed out the cockpit window. "Cuzco is about fifteen minutes away. We have to climb to thirteen thousand feet and then turn and head down to Agua Caliente, which sits at half that elevation, in the jungle."

"Can you give me any more information on the first test, with those soldiers?"

"They're mercenaries. One is German, named Otto. Frank is from the French Foreign Legion — he's Belgian. The third dude is North African. His name is Turban. At least that's what they call him. I'm sure it's not his real name."

"And are they skilled in karate?"

"No. Just the hand-to-hand combat training you get in the military."

"And they're big guys?"

"Frank is small, built like a rat terrier, but he's fast. Turban is two-hundred-and-fifty pounds and all muscle. The one you have to look out for is Otto. He fights dirty. He'll do whatever it takes to win."

"And you say the last nanny managed to nail these dudes?" Kathy was skeptical.

"Yes, she did." He smiled slightly. "She was a karate expert, like you. She also had a black belt."

Kathy felt a tiny wave of relief. "Well, that's hopeful."

"These guys are bar-room brawlers. They don't play fair. They'll pick up a handful of dust and throw it in your eyes if they can. I told you this would feel like science fiction."

"You did."

Mac took a breath. "If you want to pull out of this, they'll give you the chance. Once you land at the estate, they'll inform you of what tests you have to pass. The only thing they won't mention is the jaguar. They never tell anyone about that."

"And previous nannies managed to survive the cat?"

Mac nodded. "Yes." Most applicants did not, but he wasn't going to tell her that. "The most important thing is that if the jaguar does show up, do *not* look him in the eyes, okay?"

Frowning, Kathy asked, "Why not?"

"Because jaguars freeze their prey that way. Peruvian medicine people down here will tell you that a jaguar has the ability to pull the spirit out of a person's body, and when that happens, you can't move. You're paralyzed. And then the jaguar leaps on you and kills you. He doesn't have to chase you because you're frozen."

Rolling her eyes, Kathy said, "That is so far-fetched!"

"But true," Mac cautioned. "Please." He lowered his voice. "Please believe me on this one thing. That cat can freeze its quarry.

Animal or human, it doesn't matter."

Flexing her fingers again, she stared down at them. "That's if I pass the first two tests."

"I feel you will, Ms. Lincoln. You might look like a cream puff, but under that soft veneer, I think, is a woman warrior." He smiled.

Kathy didn't want to feel the warmth of his smile, but she did. She saw crow's-feet form at the corners of his eyes. She couldn't see his eyes very well behind his sunglasses, but she didn't need to. Unexpected heat raced through her. When this guy gave her that ten-thousand-megawatt smile, she felt like melting. That was a first! Kathy sternly reminded herself that he was a drug dealer. The scum of the earth.

"I'll survive," she muttered defiantly, "however I have to."

Mac banked the Bell helicopter, and the first sight of the mighty Incan city of Cuzco came into view. He dropped the helo into the circular valley in the rolling mountains. "My money's on you, Ms. Lincoln."

If she hadn't been so worried about dying in the first test with the three goons, Kathy might have appreciated Cuzco. It had been built by the Incas, she knew —

the cradle of their far-flung civilization, which had spread north to Ecuador and down south to Chile. Cuzco was where the emperor and empress had stayed.

As the helicopter lost altitude, she saw many stone Catholic churches set in rectangular plazas, with three- to five-story stone buildings in between. The city was a growing metropolis, buzzing with cars, diesel-fueled buses, that left clouds of dark fumes in their wake, and swift-moving taxies weaving in and out of the other traffic. And yet, Cuzco was surrounded by brown, barren mountains. How did anything grow here? Kathy wondered.

Uneasy because of the coming tests, she felt adrenaline leak into her bloodstream, making her antsy. As Coulter guided the helicopter to the south, through a narrow pass and into a much more verdant-looking valley, Kathy took a deep, ragged breath. Could she survive? Oh, how had she gotten herself into this mess? Why hadn't she done more thorough research?

The answer was obvious: Garcia would never reveal this information to the world. No, his tactics, like his drug dealing, were kept secret from the press and public.

Gulping a couple of times, Kathy tried to steady her screaming nerves. Would she make it? Or was she going to die ignominiously here, without being able to kidnap Garcia's child? It would be a shameful death, certainly not what she'd expected. Somehow, some way, she must prevail. . . .

Kathy swallowed her shock when a tall, beautiful and stylish South American woman met her on the landing pad near the well-hidden villa complex. Mac Coulter was at her side, his fingers cupping her elbow and guiding her toward the woman.

"Welcome, Señorita Lincoln. I am Therese Osoro, your hostess. Welcome to the Pink Orchid Villa, which is owned by Patrón Garcia and his wife, Paloma." The woman stepped forward, her black eyes shining with genuine warmth, her hand extended.

Replying in Spanish, Kathy gripped the woman's hand, which was surprisingly strong. Mac had warned her not to divulge any of their cockpit conversation to Garcia's personal secretary.

Therese released her hand. "Well! There is much to do, Señorita Lincoln. Señor Coulter, thank you for bringing her to us. Patrón Garcia has a flight that he needs undertaken immediately. My assistant in the office, Sarita, has the mission briefing for you."

Mac bit back his immediate reaction. He wanted to stay nearby as Katherine Lincoln went through the tests. Hiding his expression, because he knew Therese was more than just a loyal worker to Garcia, he said, "Of course. I'll go up to the office and get the info." He turned to Katherine, whose own expression was unreadable. "It was a pleasure meeting you, Ms. Lincoln."

"Likewise," Kathy said. She kept her voice purposefully cool.

"Come with me. You must be hungry. Some tea, perhaps? Let us go to my office and I'll fill you in on some information, Señorita Lincoln."

Yeah, right. Information, hell. Therese was going to set her up for the tests. When Coulter turned and sauntered toward the first large green stucco villa, she panicked inside. Whether she wanted to admit it or not, Mac Coulter represented stability, a friend in an enemy land. Her heart pounding with fear, Kathy wrestled with the panic deep inside her.

Without a word, she followed the assistant down a concrete walk to a smaller building that was attached to the first one by an enclosed walkway. If she hadn't been so scared, she'd have scanned the compound closely. As it was, she saw a few soldiers in military garb here and there, heavily armed, walking the perimeter of the ten-foot-tall stucco wall that surrounded the massive estate. There was nowhere to run. No way to escape. She was committed more than ever now. With her life . . .

"Are you ready, *señorita?*" Therese called. She stood at one end of the huge gymnasium with its spotless, waxed pine floor. The building housed an Olympic-size swimming pool and a full-size basketball court.

Kathy wore gray sweatpants, tennis shoes and a light gray tank top, perfect attire for the ordeal ahead. Throughout lunch at Therese's office, the woman had talked about the trials that Kathy had to undertake. In her husky voice, the assistant had asked if Kathy was willing to be tested. She'd assured her that, if she didn't want to, she would immediately be flown back to Lima and put on a flight home to Canada. Kathy had said in a strained tone that she'd try to pass the tests. Therese seemed relieved and very pleased with her decision, praising her courage.

As she stood on the thin tumbling pads spread across the gym floor, Kathy waited to see the three goons, whom she was sure would arrive any minute now. It was nearly 1400, and the humidity outside was heavy. Fortunately, the gym was air-conditioned, and the coolness revived her somewhat. But it didn't stop her from sweating.

Kathy grimly noticed the video cameras at all four corners of the gym, no doubt videotaping her test. She wondered if Garcia would be watching. This thought made her sharpen her resolve. She took that anger and fed it through herself. It wiped out some but not all of the fear clattering through her body like a runaway freight train.

Kathy didn't have long to wait. Therese, who stood at the door to watch, had warned her the men would be armed and would come at her all at once. This, she told her, would be to simulate a kidnapping attack. Kathy must be ready to defend Garcia's daughter, Tiki, with her life. *Yeah, right.* Therese left out the fact that her boss was a drug lord and that other powermongers would love to take him down and kill his family, to become kingpins in his place. Swallowing hard, Kathy saw the three men enter and walk past Therese, whom they acknowledged with deferential nods. And then their gazes swung to her.

Steeling herself, Kathy silently thanked Coulter for the information he'd shared. He'd described them flawlessly. The German, Otto, was a pale milky man, whose shaved head shone like a cue ball. His blue eyes narrowed upon her. Frank, the Belgian, grinned at her, revealing that his front three teeth were missing. Her attention swung to the last one, Turban, whose ebony skin glistened with perspiration. His head was shaved also and his beady chocolate eyes were set close together.

Otto and Turban had bands of ammunition draped across their massive chests. All had weapons in their hands, AK-47s, the snub noses aimed at her. And all had knives in their belts or strapped to their lower legs. Her skin crawling with terror, Kathy crouched and took a steadying breath, feet slightly apart for balance.

Once they reached the mats, fifty feet away from her, they attacked. Fanning out, they came toward her from three different directions. Kathy had no time to think, only to react. Otto raised his rifle butt to club her. She instantly lashed out with her right foot and caught the German squarely in the chest. The powerful impact jarred her, but she kept her balance.

"Oomph!"

Otto went down, the rifle he carried flying into the air. Kathy caught it and spun around as Frank charged her. She saw the surprise in his eyes when she swung the rifle, smashing the stock against his upraised hands, which held his own weapon. Then she balled up her right fist and slammed it into his face. Pain from the punishing crunch ran all the way up her arm to her shoulder, but Frank went down, unconscious, his weapon hurtling to the floor.

Kathy had no time to notice how her knuckles burned. Instantly, she felt the air exploding inches from her head. Turban had raised his weapon and brought it down, thinking to catch her from behind and split her skull open.

Breathing hard, she leaped away. The rifle smashed into the mat at her feet. Frank and Otto were still down, so she had to contend with Turban, who was grinning and showing his yellow teeth. Crouching again, Kathy let him come at her. This time he jabbed his rifle toward her chest. Deftly moving to one side, like a fencer parrying a blade, Kathy went for the man's eyes. In seconds, she was jabbing his eye sockets with her fingers.

With a roar of pain and surprise, Turban jerked back, dropping the AK-47. His hands covering his eyes, he peddled backward, off balance, arms flailing like a windmill. His screams filled the hall.

Whipping around to her right, Kathy saw Otto start to get to his hands and knees. Mouth open and breathing hard, Kathy attacked him. The toe of her tennis shoe caught him beneath the jaw, and she heard a terrible crunching sound. She'd broken it. Otto cried out and slumped unconscious to the mat.

Turning, she eyed Frank. He was still flat on his back, and groaning.

"Enough!" Therese trilled. "You have won this contest, Señorita Lincoln! Congratulations! Come, you must leave for the shooting range." The woman hovered by the door and waved for Kathy to join her.

Stepping past the three goons, Kathy felt no exhilaration, only relief that she'd been able to disarm them. Her right hand hurt and she looked down at it. Her knuckles were bruised and turning a bluish-purple color. She was sure she'd broken a vein, but pumped up with adrenaline as she was, she felt little pain. After hurrying by the soldiers, Kathy jogged to Therese's side. As they walked out the door, the hot, humid air hit her like a hand slap. Kathy brushed back her hair from her face and saw a tough-looking hombre in military fatigues standing near a dark green jeep.

"You will now go with Capitán Jules Quintana. He will oversee your shooting test, and the knife fight with Renaldo afterward." Therese clapped Kathy on her shoulder. "I have never seen anyone take down those three soldiers so fast. You are truly a prize, *señorita.* Good luck on test two. I will be awaiting your triumphant return to my office. *Adios.*"

Kathy nodded and said nothing. She wasn't feeling as positive as Therese was. Gazing into the captain's dark eyes, she realized with horror that they were a killer's eyes. The fact made her blood run cold.

"Climb in, *señorita.*"

As Kathy slid into the frayed canvas passenger seat of the jeep, she looked over at the helicopter landing pad. At some point, Coulter had lifted off, and she hadn't even heard the noise. As the captain drove through the main gates of the estate, Kathy gripped her hands together in her lap, feeling terribly alone without Coulter's protective presence. Could she survive the next test?

Chapter Eight

Was Katherine Lincoln dead or alive at this point? After landing back at the villa, Mac tried to appear his easygoing, nonchalant self as he disembarked from the Bell helicopter. Garcia had had him run an errand into Cuzco — pick up a passenger who Mac knew was part of the Colombian drug cartel, and bring him here. Mac had been gone two hours and was champing at the bit to return.

Was it the nanny's lush curves making him react like this? Mac couldn't recall a woman ever impacting him like this with her essence, her spirit. Never had one interrupted his mission focus, either. Not until now. Damn, what was he going to do? What *was* it about Katherine Lincoln that was dismantling him minute by minute? Making him feel like a teenager driven by hormones and not by his head? Mac didn't fool himself: he harbored a hot, sexual need for her — and that was dangerous ground to be on. One look from those stunning blue eyes and all he could think about was slowly undressing her, mapping her body with his tongue, hands and lips. What kind of power did she hold over him? Mac shook his head, frustrated with his unexpected reaction to Katherine Lincoln. No matter what he did, he couldn't stop caring about her, or being worried for her.

Mac looked around, but didn't see Therese, who always shepherded unsuspecting applicants through this disgusting series of tests. The driveway was filled with expensive cars — Mercedes, BMWs and Jaguars. Garcia was having another cartel meeting, no doubt. Standing near the concrete landing pad while the ground crew took care of the Bell, Mac placed his hands on his hips.

Had Katherine survived the first test? How badly he'd wanted to stay and find out. Inwardly, Mac pictured her tall, proud body and the way her full breasts filled out that blazer she wore. The curviness of her hips were just right for a man to grip, bring her under him and — He had to stop thinking like this! Was he going loco? Too long without a woman, and now he was paying the price for it? Mac wasn't sure, and he couldn't stop feeling edgy.

Where was Therese? He craned his neck and looked around, finding the answer almost immediately when the door to the dispensary at the left of the main villa opened. Out trooped all three soldiers, swathed in various bandages. Curbing a grin, Mac watched them limp toward the barracks, which was at the rear, well hidden by the tall green stucco wall. Then Therese emerged, looking like a runway model strutting her stuff in the middle of this godforsaken, humid jungle.

Walking over to her, Mac said, "Well, how's your nanny doing?" Inwardly, he held his breath and tried to steel himself for bad news.

Therese laughed. "Just fine, Mac." She gestured to the three soldiers who had just left. "I think the *patrón* is going to be *very* pleased with her."

"She's finished both tests?" Relief flooded through Mac. Katherine Lincoln was alive! A soaring sense of elation swept through him and he wrestled to keep that emotion hidden from Therese, who never missed a thing.

"Yes." She frowned. "Though in the knife fight, unfortunately, Señorita Lincoln got cut."

His heart dropped. "Oh? How bad?" His throat tightened with worry.

"Minor, really. What she did to Renaldo

— well, let's just say he's going to be on crutches for a while! She takes no prisoners, this one, but I think that is good! The *patrón* has been looking for a woman who can truly handle any situation thrown at her. If Señorita Lincoln passes the last test, then she will have her interview with the boss."

Therese gave Mac a flirtatious look, but he was completely immune to her. The woman was a tease and had gotten more than one soldier here in trouble with Garcia. She was having a flagrant, ongoing affair with the *patrón,* right under the nose of his wife.

"With your permission, Therese, I'd like to drop Ms. Lincoln off at the starting point for the last test. Any problem with that? I'm feeling rusty on my flying skills since I've been grounded the last two weeks, taking care of Tiki. I'd like any airtime I can get."

Giving him a long, appreciative look, Therese said, "But of course. Jules should be bringing her back here any moment now."

Hearing the chug of the jeep coming up the hill, Mac stepped away from Therese. The woman had moved closer, like a sinuous cat, her hand now resting on his upper arm. There was no way Mac wanted the *patrón* to see her hanging all over him with her vapid, come-hither looks. Garcia was a jealous bastard, and any man who valued his family jewels knew to stay away from Therese.

"Here they come," he muttered.

"*Sí.* Do *me* a favor, Mac?" Therese glanced at the elegant watch she wore on her thin, golden wrist. "Take Señorita Lincoln to the dispensary. Then get her over to the guest quarters, have the kitchen prepare whatever she wants to eat and then let her rest, okay? Tell her that tomorrow at 0500 you will fly her out to the jungle for her final test."

Thrilled with the opportunity, Mac kept his face carefully neutral. "Sure, Therese, not a problem."

"*Bueno.* I'm off! The office begs for my presence. So many calls to return! *Adios!*" She turned and walked quickly up the brick walk toward the main villa.

Drawing in a deep breath, Mac felt relieved that he had permission to fly Katherine out for her last test. He waited impatiently for Jules to drive into the compound. The moment the jeep entered the gateway, Mac's eyes found Katherine Lincoln. She wore a body-hugging gray, thin-

138

strapped camisole top and gray sweatpants, both damp with her perspiration. At the sight of blood on her upper arm, of her other hand clamped over the injured area, Mac scowled. Jules didn't look very happy, either, as he braked the jeep in front of him.

"I'll take her to the dispensary," Mac told him. "Therese asked me to do it."

"*Sí,*" Jules said, nodding curtly.

As Mac offered his hand to Katherine, he saw the dark look in her blue eyes, her lips pursed. She ignored his hand and climbed out of the jeep herself. After giving Jules a glare, she turned to Mac.

Kathy meant to keep the strain out of her voice, but Mac Coulter's unexpected presence tore at the wall she'd erected to keep her rollicking emotions in check. Without his aviator glasses as cover, she felt the full impact of his large gray eyes upon her. Damned if she didn't see genuine concern for her burning in them. And something else. Unsure, Kathy licked her lower lip. She'd swear she spotted tenderness lurking in their depths. "I need a doctor," she stated.

"Come with me," Mac said. He kept the rage out of his tone. He wanted to kill Renaldo himself for even touching Katherine, not to mention making her bleed. Automatically, Mac placed his hand beneath her elbow. "Therese asked me to take you to our dispensary. Just relax. The worst is over, okay?" He said it quietly as Jules backed the jeep up and took off for his mountain barracks.

Legs wobbly, Kathy forced herself to walk in a straight line, albeit stiffly. She didn't want to trust Coulter, but just his nearness steadied the churning, adrenaline-driven sensations that raced through her. "I've never had to really hurt someone with a knife," she whispered unsteadily. Grateful he'd shown up, she cast a glance at him. His profile was grim, his mouth pursed. And then she felt trembling deep in the pit of her stomach. She'd come so close to death . . . so close. . . .

"They play for keeps here," Mac said apologetically. "You passed the tests. I just saw what you did to those three soldiers." He smiled at her. "Nice work. They weren't prepared for your karate skills."

"Thank God," Kathy whispered. She felt as if she was going to faint. "I — I need to sit down — soon. Something's wrong. . . ." She touched her brow. Sounds began to fade away, and she felt nearly disembodied. Kathy continued to focus on Coulter's strong body next to hers, his hand around her elbow.

Seeing her go pale, Mac panicked. Her eyes seemed confused, helpless looking. He quickly opened the dispensary door. "A few more steps and you can rest. Come into this examination room." He led her through the first door to the right. After helping her sit on the gurney, he made sure she was all right, then went to find Dr. Macedo.

Sitting in the cool room, Kathy dragged in several deep, ragged breaths. The faintness began to lift, and she felt as if she was coming back into her body once more. Pain drifted up her left arm where that son of a bitch Renaldo had sliced into her. Soon, Kathy heard voices drifting down the hall and the sound of approaching footsteps. Mac was coming back. That stabilized her as nothing else could. He represented a quiet, deep, healing harbor in this unbelievable storm. Straightening up, Kathy tightened her hand over her wound, trying to stanch the continuing bleeding.

In the half hour that followed, Kathy was glad Mac remained in the room. He stood beside her, neither too close nor too far away. When she managed to steal a look in his direction, his smoky-gray eyes met hers with an intensity that sent her soul skittering. That raw look of undeniable interest made Kathy's breath hitch. An ache began, sharp and deep in her heart and lower body. It was completely unexpected and disconcerting.

Dr. Macedo cleaned her wound, closed the cut with ten stitches and finished with a hefty shot of antibiotics. Her wound wasn't deep, thank God, just long, a fact Kathy could live with.

"You'll be fine, *señorita.* Señor Coulter will take you to your quarters now, and I suggest you eat and rest. I've placed a special protective dressing over your wound so you can take a shower. It will remain dry. Tomorrow morning before you leave for your final test, I will change the dressing."

The third test. Kathy was almost too tired to respond. "Don't worry, I will do as you say, Doctor. Thank you." She slid off the gurney. Her legs were stronger now, the adrenaline no longer racing through her bloodstream. But she was groggy, utterly fatigued and wanting desperately to sleep. This whole experience was a nightmare. One she wasn't at all prepared for.

Mac nodded his thanks to the kindly doctor and led Katherine Lincoln out of the examination room. "Come on, we've got nice digs waiting for you, Ms. Lincoln."

On the way down the brick walk lined with colorful orchids, Kathy saw a small, two-story caseta directly ahead of them. It stood to the right of the main villa.

"How are you feeling?" Mac asked as he opened the door.

Kathy stepped into the teak-wood foyer. It was an incredibly beautiful villa, plushly decorated beyond her wildest expectations. Looking around in awe, she murmured, "Tired."

"Hungry?"

"Starving to death."

"What do you like to eat?"

"Right now, I could eat a three pound T-bone steak."

Chuckling, Mac said, "A meat-and-potatoes kind of woman?"

Turning around on the highly polished wooden floor, Kathy looked at him as he stood in the doorway. Mac Coulter was too easy to like. She didn't know whether his generosity toward her was genuine or a decoy to catch her off guard. He could well be a spy for Garcia. And if he wasn't, why was he helping her? It just didn't add up, but Kathy was far too tired to go anywhere with her suspicions. "Yes, meat and potatoes. And a lot of bread and butter with it? Sour cream on the side?" She might as well ask for everything she was fantasizing about.

"You got it. I'll notify the kitchen staff and they'll whip you up something in a jiffy."

"Wait!"

Mac halted, his hand on the door. "Yes?"

"Are you leaving?"

"Yes. Is there something else you need?"

Looking toward the airy interior, Kathy said, "I guess not." She didn't want to admit she needed his quiet and stabilizing presence. Unused to looking to a man for anything, Kathy felt a yearning deep within. "What's up for tomorrow?" she asked.

Mac gave her a slight smile. "How about I drop by later this evening and we can talk? I've got some maintenance to handle with my ground crew at the hangar right now."

Disappointed, but trying to not show it, Kathy nodded. "Yes, that would be fine, Mr. Coulter."

"Call me Mac."

"Okay, Mac. Thanks for everything." And she meant it. Their gazes met and locked. Again, her heart was suffused with an incredible warmth that made her feel safe and cared for. What was *with* this guy? With *her?* Stymied, Kathy gave a slight shake of her head.

"See you around 2100." Mac reluctantly closed the door. More than anything, he wanted to stay with her. Katherine Lincoln looked frail and needy right now, and he was a sucker for a woman in trouble. Always had been and always would be.

As he headed for the kitchen at the rear of the main villa, Mac looked up at the light blue sky flecked with wisps of white clouds. It was early afternoon and he had a lot to do between now and then. Still, unaccountably, his heart lifted when he thought of going back to see Katherine this evening. The woman was a magnet tugging at his heart and body. No one had ever affected him so profoundly before. No one.

Kathy rubbed the sleep from her puffy eyes as the knocking continued on the heavy wooden door of the villa. Shuffling to the foyer, wiping her eyes one more time, she opened it. Mac Coulter stood there, dressed in clean clothes. Despite her sleepiness and being awakened by the knocking, she thought he looked strikingly handsome in his white cotton short-

145

sleeved shirt, dark blue chinos and polished brown leather boots. He had shaved and his hair looked damp, as if he'd just come from a shower. Her heart twinged when his mouth curved in a confident, all-male smile.

"Come in. I was asleep on the couch," she said, stepping aside. Tugging self-consciously at the yellow beach towel that she'd wrapped around her body after her shower, Kathy shuffled back into the oval living room. She remembered how, after eating the delicious dinner, she'd taken a shower, come out to the living room and fallen on the brightly upholstered sofa. How long had she slept? She looked at her watch. A good four hours. Maybe she was going to live, after all.

"Sorry, I didn't mean to awaken you," Mac said. Never had he expected Katherine to answer the door dressed only in a towel. The yellow color emphasized her blond hair, which lay across her shoulders in mild disarray. She had obviously not bothered to comb out the strands before falling asleep, such was the state of her exhaustion. Mac didn't blame her.

Nervous because she was barely clothed, Kathy saw the glimmer in his narrowed gaze as it slowly moved up her body, scalding her. First, heat swept across her hips and abdomen, then her breasts tensed hotly beneath his penetrating stare. When he lifted his eyes to her lips, she felt like a deer caught in headlights. Never had a man looked at her so hungrily, stripping her to her flesh. My God. Her lips tingled as his smoldering glance lingered there. "That's all right. Just give me a minute?"

Clearing his throat, entranced by her soft, shapely mouth, Mac replied, "Sure. I'll wait here in the living room." What kind of spell was she weaving over him?

Kathy saw he had a small brown paper bag in his hand. She almost asked about its contents, but her need to get dressed won out. She turned and dashed to the bedroom, located at the end of the long hall. Glad to escape Mac's smoldering, appreciative inspection, Kathy discovered the walk-in closet full of clothes. Her heart pounded, as she tried to concentrate on what to wear. The man looked at her and she melted! Kathy didn't melt. But she did with him. Shaking her head, she muttered an expletive.

She discovered her luggage in the closet and dragged it out. Opting to wear some of her own clothes, she pulled out a pink tank top and a pair of comfortable trousers. Still groggy, she didn't bother to put on a bra, which she hated wearing, anyway. She grabbed her comb and brush from the bathroom, then frantically slipped on a pair of socks and her sensible brown oxfords. Mystified by her eagerness to see Mac Coulter again, Kathy slowed her pace. Why was she acting like a smitten teenager? Those years had long since passed her by.

Mac stood up when Katherine emerged from the hall. As she came to the sofa, he gave her a slight smile. When she managed a smile in return, he felt ten feet tall. After sitting down, she drew a brush through her hair. He couldn't help admiring those blond strands, her lush and curvy body. Before her beauty could overwhelm him, he sat down once more.

"How are you feeling?" Mac sank back in the flowery, overstuffed chair. A teak coffee table with a huge vase filled with white-and-purple dendrobium orchids provided a barrier between them.

"I feel like death warmed over," Kathy said sleepily as she brushed her hair. When she started to raise her left arm, she flinched and bit back a moan. White-hot pain shot up her arm.

"Sore?"

"No kidding."

"The doc said for you to take some aspirin. Did you find it in the medicine cabinet in the bathroom?" Mac watched as she lowered her arm, her soft lower lip tensed with pain.

"No, I didn't. I was too hungry, and then after I ate, I took a hot shower and dropped dead on the sofa. I just wasn't thinking very clearly at that time." Of course, once she got around Mac, all her wits went out the window, anyway. Men had never affected her this way. Oh, she'd heard of some of her girlfriends being smitten like this, and she'd laughed. How could it be possible that one human could so elementally affect another? She wasn't laughing now.

"You have a high tolerance for pain, then."

He didn't know the half of it. Kathy gave Mac a wry look and continued to brush her hair. "I've been told I do." Managing the left side of her head was a little tricky, but she finally did. Now her hair, which was slightly wavy, hung in gold sheets around her shoulders and halfway down to her breasts. She saw his shadowed face in the lighting provided by the one lamp she'd turned on. His eyes glittered and her skin responded, tingling. Feeling vulnerable, Kathy set the brush on the coffee table.

"What do you have in that sack?" She flinched inwardly because her tone sounded snappish even to her.

"Oh . . ." Mac opened it up. "Some arnica cream." He motioned to her right hand. "I saw the black-and-blue bruises you had on your knuckles. This is a homeopathic ointment that's great for taking out soreness. I thought you might like to try some. All you do is rub a little across the area. You'll get fast relief, I think." Mac got up and handed her the tube across the coffee table. Their fingers briefly touched, and the sensation was electric to Mac. Unexpected. Nice. It stirred memories of a woman touching his body. He hadn't been with a woman in over a year, not with his deep undercover work. And he sure as hell wasn't interested in Therese, who was always teasing and flirting with him.

"Thanks." Kathy felt warmth, a tender ribbon, flow from her heart toward him. She tried to ignore the sensation Mac's fingers caused by touching hers. A sizzling feeling of fire ignited within her lower body, a yearning that took her completely by surprise. There was no question that Mac Coulter was someone she could easily fall for. The fact that he worked for a drug dealer splashed ice-cold water on her ridiculous attraction. Opening the tube, Kathy carefully spread ointment across her discolored knuckles.

"I thought I'd broken my hand on that one dude," she confided.

"Looking at the three of them, I'd say they got the worst of it."

Her mouth quirked. After capping the ointment, she laid it on the table. "That was thoughtful of you, Mr. Coulter. Thanks."

"Call me Mac. Remember?" God help him, he wanted to move over to her and kiss her pain away.

"Okay." Kathy curled up on the sofa, resting her left arm against her body. The cut area ached and she knew she should take some aspirin to dull the pain. The way Mac looked at her, that hungry look, made her uneasy. Two lonely people stuck out in the middle of the jungle . . . Both of them Americans . . . That was it: loneliness was the reason for her crazy reactions to Mac. She forced herself to meet his gaze. "You came here for a reason?"

Nodding, Mac could see she was going to be all-business. That was fine with him, although a tiny part of his heart wished that she was as attracted to him as he was to her. He knew this was dangerous for him and his cover, so he quickly squashed those feelings. "I'd like to take you for a late evening walk around the villa. It's very beautiful this time of day." Mac sat up and smoothed his hands on his thighs.

Kathy frowned as she saw him nod his head toward the lamp near the end of the couch. What was he doing?

"I really don't feel up to a walk. . . ." she said, tilting her head and giving him a questioning look.

"I think you'll feel better if you limber up, Ms. Lincoln." Again, he flicked his gaze discreetly toward the lamp. He wanted to alert her to the fact that there was a listening device in it. Garcia had almost every area of the compound bugged. He had a team of men who constantly monitored and taped conversations to spy on his employees and guests. What Mac wanted to tell Kathy would be in direct violation of his orders, and Garcia would have him shot in the head for it. Would she realize what he was trying to tell her? Mac saw the confusion clear and her eyes sharpen.

Kathy had been slow to realize it because she was wiped out from the day's events.

Somehow, Mac was trying to tell her something. What? Who was he, really? Standing, she said, "Maybe you're right. The more I sit around, the stiffer I'll get. A walk would do me good. Thanks for suggesting it."

They were on a narrow jungle trail of red coleche clay, which led down the mountain, at least half a mile from the estate. The sun had set and the day was dying, but there was still ample light to see where they were going. Around them, the jungle was alive with insects singing, frogs chirping and monkeys howling.

Mac spoke to her for the first time, in a hushed tone. He had walked at her right elbow until now. Stopping, he turned and drew close enough so that their arms nearly brushed.

"Your villa is bugged," he informed her. Mac saw her go pale, her eyes growing huge with shock. "The *patrón* listens to all of us. He has men constantly monitoring nearly all buildings and the people who live in them."

"That doesn't seem right." Kathy searched Mac's stern countenance and saw honesty mirrored in his gray gaze. She could feel his heat and found herself absorbing his protectiveness.

Shrugging, he said carefully, "It's his way." *Garcia is a drug lord and he's paranoid, so that's why he has bugs.* Of course, Mac couldn't say that to her, nor would he want to right then. The stunned look in her eyes told him she wasn't a spy. She had beautiful, soul-stealing eyes. A man could spend his entire life mapping out her face and losing himself in her sea-blue gaze. It took a huge effort to restrain himself and keep to the point of their talk.

"And that's why we're out here? You wanted to talk to me but you knew we were being taped?" To escape Mac's steady look, Kathy glanced away and pretended to gauge the trail. It curved steeply downward, and she didn't feel like taking it. Mac stood less than a foot from her, his hands resting languidly on his narrow hips, his brows bunched.

"Yeah, that's right. We have some privacy here." Mac had excellent hearing, and if someone was coming up the path, he'd know it. But to be sure, he dropped his voice to a bare whisper. "You need to listen to me, Katherine." It was the first time he'd used her first name. She hadn't given him permission, but the driving fear overrode his normal social skills. "I'm supposed to drop you at the jungle test point at 0500 tomorrow. I told you that they give you nothing and you'll likely run into that jaguar on the way back. You have to survive that encounter."

Nodding, Kathy leaned her head forward so that his lips were almost brushing her hair. Fear zigzagged through her. More and more, Mac Coulter was looking like a guardian angel to her. "Go on." The unexpected desire to simply take one step and lean her head against his broad shoulder was nearly Kathy's undoing. His ability to draw her to him was mind-blowing. He had powerful male charisma, and it was working overtime on all her senses. Kathy told herself it was the danger of her situation that was making her over-react to him. After all, Mac was the only person in this nest of snakes who was trying to help her survive.

"It's a short flight across the Urubamba, so I won't have time to tell you what you need to know before I drop you off. That's why we're standing here right now. You have to know the river is turbulent — fast, deep and dangerous. But one mile upstream is a rope bridge that the locals use. You can't cross safely any other way. A lot of women have lost their lives trying to cross where they were dropped. Just hike a mile upriver." His nostrils flared, and he unintentionally inhaled the subtle, sweet scent of ginger from her recently washed hair. His fingers positively itched to tunnel through the thick, gold strands.

"Okay, I will."

Mac studied her shadowed face, her narrowed eyes. She was a hundred percent focused, just like a combat pilot ready to destroy a target. Again he couldn't shake the feeling that there were two very different sides to this woman — one the meek and mild facade he saw most of the time, and then this one, the warrior woman.

"On the other side of the river you have two choices. The jungle is so thick you can't penetrate it without a machete and a helluva lot of hacking. For hundreds of years the Peruvian people have been using paths created by the wild animals that traverse the rain forest. Wild pigs have carved most of them out, but there are paths that the jaguars have made."

Kathy glanced up at him. Mac was so close she could feel the palpable energy of his masculine strength. The evening was humid and she was perspiring. She gulped unsteadily and tried to stay focused on what he was saying. "Okay, so which trail do I take once you insert — er, I mean, drop me off?" Fear racked her. She'd nearly used the military term *insertion*. A civilian wouldn't use that word. For a moment, he lifted his chin and studied her. Had she corrected herself in time? Or had she just blown her cover? It was hell standing there beneath his scrutiny. His eyes glimmered with some unknown emotion she couldn't decipher.

"After you cross that rope bridge, you'll see a trail going off into the jungle. That's the one you'll take. But it's the jaguar's path, too. And it will lead you directly through his territory."

"Where will I meet him?"

"There's no way to know. A jaguar has a large territory. If you get lucky, he'll be sleeping during the day. Unless they're really hungry, jags sleep in the day and hunt at night."

"You said this was a fifty-mile stroll."

"Yeah, it is. The most you can walk in a day's time, providing you're up to it, is maybe thirty miles on foot."

Nodding, Kathy said, "You're right. When does my employer expect me back here?"

"They give you four days to pass this test, so that's not an issue. Your problem is the cat. That whole path from beginning to end is his territory."

"How am I going to survive, then? I have to sleep at night. What should I do?"

She was asking all the right questions. "I'm going to stow some gear for you. Once I drop you, you'll have a pack containing a lightweight hammock, beef jerky, a compass, a tube of antibiotic ointment, extra dressings for your arm and a knife."

"What about water?" Every moment spent with Coulter was like a rich, unexpected dessert to Kathy. She saw the ruddiness in his cheeks, absorbed the warm intimacy of his husky voice. When he lifted his hands, she stared at their shape and wondered what it would be like to feel those long, strong fingers caress her. Closing her eyes, she touched her brow. Somehow, she had to get a handle on her desire for this man.

Mac barely controlled his desire to reach out and touch her cheek. The look in her eyes told him that she wanted him as much as he wanted her. Struggling not to be so drawn to Katherine, he managed a slight, disarming smile. "That's the easy part. You'll see a lot of wooden vines no matter where you walk — lianas. All you have to do is snap them off and pull them into your mouth. They're filled with water, and will quench your thirst."

It felt as if she were standing with him

outside of time, just the two of them. Her breathing seemed to be in sync with the slow rise and fall of his broad chest. With a strangled whisper, Kathy said, "Then it sounds like I'm set."

Mac hesitated. He saw the burning look in her eyes, its meaning unmistakable. He drew in a deep, ragged breath. "Almost. At dusk, lay up for the night. Find a nice big tree and climb up into it. Suspend your hammock between two stout branches. Jags hunt the trail at night. And yes, they're tree climbers, but if you're suspended high up, he isn't going to spot you. His attention will focus on anything moving on the ground. And you do *not* want to be sleeping at ground level or he'll find you for sure."

"So being in a tree minimizes my chances of the jag finding me?"

"Yes, but it doesn't guarantee he won't. You are going to have a restless sleep, and there's no way around it. But it cuts the chances of him finding you." Mac wanted to touch her cheek. What did her skin feel like? Was it soft and firm as he suspected? His fingers ached to find out.

"And a pocketknife as a weapon isn't going to do me any good." She felt Mac's burning gaze linger on her face, then slowly move down the column of her neck. Oh, God, it felt as if he was actually touching her. Her body responded, her skin tingling wildly in the wake of his intimate inspection.

Mac shook his head. "No, it won't. That cat is big, strong, built low to the ground and pure muscle. Remember, do *not* look him in the eyes. Avert your gaze. If he does go after you, do what you can to escape. If he corners you, stand your ground, don't make a sound and don't move. If you make noise, he'll leap. If you run, he will sure as hell come after you. The only way you can out-macho this jaguar is to stand your ground but avoid his gaze. Okay?" Mac dug into her eyes and at the same time slid his fingers across her proud shoulder. He felt the warmth of her flesh, the firm muscles. Her eyes turned soft, an almost haunting look as he kept his hand in place, his heart thundering in response to her unexpected expression. She *wanted* his touch, as much as he wanted to touch her. Heat bolted jaggedly through his lower body and twisted like a writhing snake. Mac ached to make hot, swift love with her. It was the craziest idea in the world, coming totally out of the blue. There was something special about Katherine Lincoln that overrode every guarded wall he'd ever put up between himself and women. She blew through every one of them as if they weren't there.

Kathy tensed beneath his exploring fingers as they moved tenderly across her shoulder. The contact was startling. Heated. Necessary. She felt her breasts tighten, her nipples contracting sharply at his touch. The look in his hooded eyes told her he wanted her — badly. Mouth dry, her heart banging away in her throat, she made the mistake of gazing at his mouth. The overriding desire to kiss Mac was nearly her undoing.

Panicked, Kathy stepped back, more afraid of herself than him. She managed to choke out, "Sounds good. Thanks for all of this." She nervously searched his shadowed face as he stood on the trail. He'd dropped his hands back on his hips. His stormy eyes were flecked with concern. "I don't know why you're doing this. You're running some serious risks here to help me." She tried to read his expression. What wasn't he telling her?

Katherine Lincoln didn't have a clue as to how serious the risks were. "Yeah, the *patrón* runs a tight ship and he doesn't like to be fooled like this. Whatever you do, protect me on this, okay? Don't ever mention to him what I gave you for the test, or anything else. Otherwise, well, I'm in deep trouble."

Mac saw a new glint in Katherine's eyes. A slight smile pulled at the corners of her mouth. "What you've told me right now will go to my grave, Mac. I promise you that. . . ."

Chapter Nine

"Be careful out there," Mac told Katherine as they approached the dark ribbon of the Urubamba River far below. It was barely light on the horizon, the jungle black beneath them. Katherine Lincoln sat in the left seat, gripping the dark green canvas knapsack that he'd stowed away last night when no one was looking. He'd given it to her once they were in the air.

"I will be," Kathy said tightly, the headphones on, the mike close to her lips. Today, she wore a long-sleeved dark green blouse, olive-green nylon pants and a good pair of heavy-tread hiking boots. That was all Therese had brought to her villa the evening before. The woman had also given her a bottle of antibiotics to take along, too, which was damn nice, in Kathy's opinion.

"You're clear on everything we talked about last night?"

Kathy nodded and felt the shudder of the helo change as he eased the bird to the opposite side of the river. She could see crests of white water leaping upward. "Yes, I've memorized every word, believe me."

"The reason they drop you here is so you won't be able to see the rope bridge a mile upstream. They do this on purpose. So, when I hover a little off the rocks here, you know to head north, correct?" Mac could not look at her since he was too busy flying. He had to concentrate extra hard since he hadn't slept a wink last night. All his mind and body would do was recall how silken and firm Katherine's skin had felt beneath his hungry inspection. He'd so badly wanted to kiss her. Why hadn't he just leaned over, cupped her shoulder and drawn her toward him? Mac had seen that she wanted to kiss him, too. God, it'd been so close. So damn close. All night he'd wondered what her mouth would feel like beneath his.

"Yes." As the helo slowly sank downward, she saw Mac switch on the landing lights. The strong, brilliant beams shot from beneath the carriage of the helicopter, revealing the gray and black rocks below. The terrain from river to jungle wall was a carpet of rocks ranging in size from a person's fist to large boulders. She understood now why he wasn't going to land; it would be impossible to do so. Wiping her mouth nervously, Kathy glanced over at Mac. The green light from the cockpit bathed his face and showed the grimness of his profile. His mouth, usually relaxed and ready to smile, was tense.

Adrenaline thrummed through her. This was dangerous. Maybe even more so than her other tests. Even though the cockpit was air-conditioned, a sheen of perspiration beaded Mac's broad brow. Was he worried for her? Or for himself? After all, he'd told her a lot of things he apparently shouldn't have. Kathy had a tough time believing it was all because he wanted to get out of babysitting Tiki. Maybe Mac had other feelings for her. Maybe he wanted her to succeed. Her heart expanded for just a moment and she felt powerfully drawn to him. No! That couldn't happen. Not now, not ever. Yes, he'd been "nice" to her, but he also had his own selfish reasons for that, too, she reminded herself. And he'd nearly kissed her out on that jungle path. . . . Oh, she knew she could have taken the lead, stepped up to him and pressed her mouth against his, but she was frightened — for a lot of reasons. Part of her was glad they hadn't kissed, but another part, her silly heart, ached for his touch and yearned to complete something that had been left undone on that trail.

"Okay, in about a minute I'll be as close to those rocks as I want to get," Mac told her, his eyes on the boulders below them. "You'll have to be careful jumping out. One wrong leap and you'll twist your ankle or bust your leg. It's happened before." Mac was unable to look over at Katherine just then, but he could feel her presence. And in the last moments together, she was making an indelible impression on him. She had pulled her blond, thick, shoulder-length hair into a ponytail at the back of her head. In the gear she wore, she looked like a military combat soldier, not a civilian. But more than anything, the expression glinting in her eyes, or maybe the way she carried herself with an unconscious confidence that few women radiated, convinced him she could make it back. Mac tried to release his mixed feelings toward her. He told himself he was concerned for her for all the right reasons: Tiki was going to get a damn good bodyguard and nanny. But his heart said otherwise. Unwilling to examine those reasons, Mac said, "Okay, get ready, Katherine. And remember, I'll try to hang around the villa on the third and fourth day. You won't make it back before the third day, I don't think. And if I'm not there, just walk into the villa and go straight to Therese's office."

"I got it." Kathy reached out spontaneously, her hand settling on his broad shoulder. She could feel the muscles beneath his red polo shirt tense at her unexpected touch. "Thanks, Mac, for everything. You're my hero."

Kathy wondered where the hell all this had come from. Just as quickly, she withdrew her hand.

"Honey, I'm no one's hero, believe me," Mac said, his voice gritty. "Just get home safe and sound? I'll try to be there to meet you, unless the *patrón* has me flying a lot of unscheduled missions in the next few days. Take care of yourself, bright angel. . . ."

Bright angel. The endearment was beautiful. Unexpected. Heart-rending. Mac's voice had dropped to a husky whisper, the emotions clear behind his whispered words. And that was what it was — an endearment.

Kathy stared at him one last time. Mac didn't look at her, since his focus was needed to keep the bird steady as she leaped to the rocks below. Suddenly, she turned around and twisted the door

167

handle. The door opened, the wind instantly buffeting her. After shoving it open with brute force, Kathy held the door in place with her body. The punishing wind caused by the turning blades slapped violently against her. In her left hand, she clutched the precious knapsack. As she eyed the rocks below, she chose the spot where she wanted to land. Mac was more than skilled at holding the bird steady for her.

Kathy leaped out of the helicopter as it hovered a foot from the rocky shore of the raging, splashing Urubamba River. It was 0530, with the sky still dark, a bare gray line hinting at the coming day. Her feet landed with force and she quickly fought for balance, swinging her arms wide to keep herself steady. Then she moved away from the hovering Bell. If he so much as tipped the bird a little, one of those blades could potentially slice her in half. It wasn't wise to stand beneath a helicopter.

As soon as Kathy landed and stepped away from the blades, Mac pulled the helo upward. The backwash buffeted her like a boxer, and she crouched down against the rocks until the he moved away. Standing up, Kathy pulled on the knapsack and watched as the Bell headed back across the river. Fear stabbed her. Mac was gone. He could no longer help her. Or protect her. She was totally alone, in a jungle that was her enemy.

Wiping her mouth once more, Kathy felt the humidity bathe her body. As she considered her next steps, the roar of the Urubamba beside her was like continuous, unending thunder. When Coulter had told her this was a powerful river, he hadn't been kidding. Many foolish kayakers, mostly young men in their twenties, thought they could tame this river, and ended up dead, smashed against the rocks at terrific rates of speed. The emerald-green water tunneling down the canyon, he'd said, came directly out of the towering Andes. Furthermore, it was near freezing in temperature, and if she should fall into it, hypothermia would kill her very quickly even if she managed to avoid the thousands of boulders she'd be swept over.

Kathy felt panic as the helo disappeared into the grayness of the coming dawn, and sternly ordered herself to settle down. She pulled the compass out of her pocket and read it, getting her bearings. As a helo pilot herself, she was used to working with one. After shoving it back in and zipping her pocket closed, she slowly began the trek upriver to locate the rope bridge. Every step was a potential ankle turner among the tumbled rocks. There was no solid, steady ground. Her boots slid again and again on the smooth, worn surfaces of the boulders. All Kathy could do was move slowly, choose her path and keep her arms outstretched to stay balanced.

Dawn came as a vague yellow-gray color hidden behind the thick, slowly moving mist above the jungle. In a reasonably short time, Kathy found the rope bridge, though it didn't seem all that sturdy. The Peruvians had built two rock towers with thick posts stuck in the tops. From these posts two thick rope cables were strung across the river. The rope bridge was hand-tied beneath the two cables.

Even climbing up the rock tower was going to be precarious and challenging. Kathy reached down and found some wet sand beneath some stones. She rubbed the sand into her hands so that it would give her purchase on the smooth granite. As she hoisted herself up the twenty-foot rock tower, Kathy felt her left arm twinge painfully. Her stitches pulled, and the pain increased. She climbed, anyway, her leg muscles tightening as she found one niche for the toe of her boot and then another.

A flock of dark green and red parrots flew over her to the other side of the river, and she heard the shrieks and screams of monkeys welcoming the coming day. The world was waking up. Sweat ran off her brow and trickled down her temples as she continued her upward climb. Once she reached the top, Kathy stood with her legs apart for maximum balance and carefully examined the cable ties.

The bridge, if one could call it that, was a make-shift affair of baling wire and ropes knotted around the posts. She wondered if she'd find bubble gum, too. Kathy pushed on the wooden posts and found them solid and unmoving. It appeared the builders had stood the logs on end on the ground and then built the stone towers around them, which would make sense. Otherwise, how could anyone traverse this flimsy-looking bridge and not pull the stakes out in the process? Kathy remembered as she moved to the footholds, the thick, horizontal woven ropes, that the Incans were some of the finest engineers in the world. Well, she was about to find out. . . .

"Tiki! My beautiful little Tiki! Come here! Come to Papa!" Carlos Garcia held out his arms to his six-year-old daughter, whom Therese had brought into his office. Every morning before he began the day, he wanted to hold his black-haired, dancing-eyed daughter. Today, Tiki was dressed in blue cotton coveralls and a short-sleeved pink shirt. Her long, straight hair had been drawn into two cute little pigtails, one on each side of her head.

"Papa!" Tiki shrieked and ran forward, her arms wide. She slipped momentarily on the Oriental rug, but then got up and laughed. Scrambling around the huge mahogany desk, she launched herself into her father's arms, yelping with joy as he blew raspberries against her cheek and neck. Writhing in his arms, shrieking, she tried to dodge the noisy kisses. This was a morning ritual, one that Tiki loved.

Laughing heartily, Carlos brought his squirming daughter back into his arms. She continued to giggle and threw her tiny arms around his neck. Patting her lovingly on the back, he whispered in a deep, playful growling tone, "And what are you up to today, my little pastry?"

Therese ambled into the room, smiling. "Today, I take her to the dentist in Cuzco. Dr. Sedano has promised her a lollipop when he gets done examining her."

"Oooh," Carlos said, holding his daughter

172

on his lap and gently smoothing her hair off her forehead. "You will see Dr. Sedano, eh?"

"Papa, come with me?" Tiki held out her hands toward him.

"Oh, little pastry, I cannot. But, hey, Therese will be with you. Does she not care for you and love you as much as I do? Eh?" He drew his daughter close, embraced her tenderly and placed a kiss on her shiny hair.

Pouting, Tiki sniffed. "I want you, Papa! Please?"

"I can't, little one, but I promise when you return, we will go down to the fish pond, eh? You always like to look at the colorful fishies. We will work on your counting. You can show me how Señora Fields has taught you to count. All right?" Carlos looked into his daughter's wide, liquid brown eyes. There were tears in them. Oh, that look hurt him! Carlos fiercely loved his only daughter. She was his life, the reason he wanted to ruthlessly expand his empire. Someday, she would run his organization. True, it wasn't a woman's place, but Paloma had had a girl, not a boy. At first, Carlos had been highly disappointed, but after one look at the little bright-eyed baby girl in pink blankets, his heart was forever smitten.

"Okay, Papa. The fishies?"

"*Sí,* my little one. Let Therese take you to Dr. Sedano in Cuzco, and this afternoon, when you return, we will walk to the fish pond." He pressed another soft kiss on her brow and set her down. Therese gave him a crooked smile of understanding, took Tiki's hand and led her around the desk.

"We will be back," the woman called liltingly at the door, lifting her hand in farewell.

Carlos nodded as the door shut quietly. Once alone, he frowned and walked over to the wide wall of windows that overlooked the grounds below. Hands on his hips, he glanced to the right, where the helicopter pad was located. Two hours ago Coulter had come in from dropping off Señorita Lincoln for her final test. Carlos pulled a cigarette from his gold case, tapped it and then slid it into his mouth. After lighting up, he inhaled deeply. The white smoke curled lazily around him as he thought about the Canadian nanny.

It looked as if this woman might be the answer to his dreams. None of the other nannies had ever done as well as this one had in the first two tests. Hope grew within Carlos's chest as he stood thinking and smoking. If only this woman would pass the last test. So few had. Did she have the smarts? The moxie? The intuition it would take to deal with the jaguar whose territory she would have to cross? Carlos wasn't sure. People were funny. Some of them seemed strong and confident, and yet they failed. Others looked like wimps, incapable of anything, and yet they survived. Which was Señorita Lincoln?

Mac tried to stop worrying about Katherine. As he stood in the airport at Cuzco waiting for Therese to return with Tiki from the dentist's office, he glanced at his watch for the hundredth time. It was now noon. He knew Therese would take Tiki to lunch at their favorite restaurant, La Retama, which was located on Soldier's Plaza.

His stomach growled. Maybe he should eat, but since dropping Katherine off at the river, his stomach had been tied in knots. He'd never had such a reaction to a woman before. What the hell was going on? Scratching his head, he climbed the stairs to the second level of the terminal. Cuzco had the second largest airport in Peru, and today it was exceptionally busy. Mac made his way through the milling crowds of tourists and dark-haired Peruvians. The noise level was high, the place packed. Cigarette smoke filled the building. There were no nonsmoking laws down here, unfortunately.

Thanks to Garcia, Mac had privileges at the airline club. At least there he'd escape the throngs and get a little peace and quiet. His mind turned back to Katherine. He'd called her bright angel. Where had *that* come from? Coulter didn't have a friggin' clue. The words had just flown out of his mouth, without planning or thought.

When he sat down at one of the small, round, linencovered tables, a waiter in a black-and-white uniform quickly approached to take his order. The club was nearly empty and Mac was glad. He ordered coffee and a sandwich. What he really wanted was a good shot of Kentucky bourbon to clear his head and heart of this Canadian nanny. He didn't like acting like a love-struck teenager.

At all costs, he couldn't reveal to her that he was a mole for the ATF. Katherine had no idea what she'd be getting into, working for Garcia, and as much as Mac wanted to tell her, he couldn't. If he did, she might inadvertently blow his cover. Could she keep a secret? There was no telling, and in Mac's business, he could trust no one. For all he knew, Lincoln herself could be a spy — for Garcia. She might be there to test Mac's allegiance to the drug lord. Garcia was known for doing this. The *patrón* was paranoid and often put his employees to the test to make sure they were faithful to him. No, Mac couldn't say anything more to Ms. Lincoln. He'd already revealed too much.

The coffee came in a white china cup and saucer. After thanking the waiter, Mac took a sip, relishing the smooth espresso coffee. Katherine Lincoln's face refused to leave him. She was intelligent, confident and, God help him, damn good-looking. Oh, he'd seen her legs that first day, in that prim, conservative little gray suit she wore, not to mention when she was wrapped in that towel. She had fabulous limbs that were firm from daily workouts. They seemed to go on forever. Legs he wanted to slide his hands over, feel their warm, firm quality and follow upward . . .

What was wrong with him? Disgusted, Mac sipped the espresso again and burned his mouth. Scowling, he set the cup down with a clatter. He wiped his mouth with the crisp, white linen napkin and looked around. Classical music played in the background. Aside from himself and two business executives, who sat at a larger table near the window, the club was empty.

He wrestled with his feelings, which he always had to contain and control. But Mac found himself unable to stop thinking of Katherine and how she was coping in the jungle. She had such arresting blue eyes, with that black ring around the iris. It was a sign of a hunter, of a combat warrior. And yet she worked as a nanny. It just didn't make sense. He'd spent years undercover as an ATF agent, and one of his skills was reading people's faces and body language with a high degree of accuracy. Her eyes *were* those of a hunter.

And her mouth. Groaning softly, Mac covered his own eyes with his hand as he pictured her lips softly parted, full and beckoning. Too many times he'd wondered what it would be like to press his mouth against hers. Would her lips be as bold and caressing as he thought? What would she taste like? All women had their own unique taste. And would her response be as bold as her eyes? Christ, he had to stop this! It was driving him loco.

"Your lunch, Señor Coulter," the waiter

said in stilted English. He set down the platter holding a club sandwich, dill pickle and french fries.

"*Bueno.* Thank you," Mac muttered, pulling the napkin across his lap. *Better focus on the food and eat, you dumb bastard. You're letting your horny body override your brain, and it's going to get you into a lot of trouble if you don't stop right now. Having a fling with one of Garcia's employees is the wrong thing to do.*

Okay, so he was drawn to Katherine Lincoln. There, he'd admitted it. Mac slathered mayonnaise across the turkey and placed the whole-wheat bread back on top. He was smitten by a blond nanny with the eyes of a hunter, eyes the color of the sky he so loved to fly in. Katherine Lincoln was part warrior, all woman, and drew him like one of the sirens who lured sailors to their death.

He bit into his sandwich, but didn't taste it. Okay, more admissions: he was worried sick about Katherine out there all alone. Leaving her without his support, without his protection, had been the hardest thing he'd done in a long time.

As he slowly ate his sandwich, he began to realize that he wanted to protect her. It was an old pattern of his, one he thought he'd crushed completely in his work as an undercover agent. But no, his need to protect seemed alive and well.

Damn. What was he going to do? Would Katherine survive the test? Would the jaguar leave her alone or challenge her? What would he do if she died? Mac scowled and salted the french fries. As with everything he saw, all he could do was send the name and what happened to his handler in Lima, and that was the end of it. He couldn't retrieve a body, bury it or send it home. That was the pisser about being undercover. He could do nothing honorable for a person, or for the family who had lost that individual. Not a damn thing.

Well, she'd better survive. That's all there is to it. And then what? Mac shook his head, not wanting to explore the possibilities. But he sure hoped to be there for Katherine when she came back to the villa. If she came back at all . . .

Chapter Ten

As dusk fell, it began raining . . . again. Kathy blew out a sigh of frustration. Judging by the small pedometer that Mac had thoughtfully given to her, she'd walked twenty miles today. Shortly after she'd made her way across the treacherous rope bridge, it had started to rain. And early in the afternoon, the first of a series of thunderstorms began to roll over the thick, impenetrable jungle. If Mac hadn't put a plastic poncho in her knapsack, she'd be soaked to the skin.

She was, anyway, from her own perspiration in the high humidity. The baseball cap she wore protected her eyes from the slashing rain. Thunder caromed across the jungle, the sound quickly swallowed up by the thick vegetation. Her legs ached from the brutal punishment of the continuous uphill climb out of the river basin. Her boots were waterproof, so her feet were still dry.

She would need to stop soon. Wiping her face, Kathy began to look for a tree where she could hang the lightweight nylon hammock for the night.

All day, she'd been on edge about meeting the jaguar. The only animals she'd seen were startled monkeys skittering across the tree canopy above her. They'd follow her at a distance, screaming out a warning that she was an intruder, and to beware. The only good part about today were the gorgeous, colorful orchids and bromeliads that hung on moss-covered limbs above her. Their fragrance lifted her spirits and made her a bit less pessimistic about what she was doing here.

Unlike her previous jungle survival test, which had taken place in Kauai, Hawaii, years ago, this jungle was impenetrable, a solid wall no one could cross without a machete and hours of work. Coulter was right: one followed the trails animals had created. Most of the paths were narrow, but the jaguar path was wide enough for her to walk with some comfort. Kathy almost chuckled at the irony.

Because the trail was muddy, she slipped for the hundredth time. Tree roots routinely blocked the way, so that if she didn't pay strict attention, she would fall belly first in the red goo. She'd done so several times already. Luckily, the rain had washed most of the clay off her poncho.

As she rounded a bend in the trail, Kathy spotted a huge, tall rubber tree. It had to be very old because its smooth, spreading arms were numerous and reminded her of an octopus. The climb would be easy, so she chose it as her "bed" for the night.

There was no way to get completely off the trail so as to avoid the jaguar's nightly foray. Kathy worried about that as she hoisted herself, limb by limb, toward the top of the tree. The huge, leathery leaves provided some protection from the rain. About fifty feet up, she tied one end of the hammock to a sturdy branch near the main trunk. For the other end she chose a limb that she hoped would allow the hammock to hang level.

As rain ran off her face, she held on to another branch above her and set her butt in her new bed, testing it gingerly several times before trusting it with her full weight. Everything held, although the hammock sank deeply, almost brushing the thick limb just below her.

As quickly as the storm had rolled in, it left. Kathy stayed wrapped in her poncho, figuring it would be pointless to pull it off because, sure as hell, sometime during the night it would rain again. She opened her knapsack and pulled out another protein bar. This would be dinner. She'd taken her fill of water from a liana vine earlier.

Looking down, Kathy saw that she'd suspended the hammock directly over the narrow trail. Could a jaguar leap fifty feet into the air? She didn't know, but the thought unnerved her. Coulter had said jaguars climbed trees, slept in them and regularly lay on a branch overhanging a trail, so they could easily drop onto unsuspecting prey.

Did the jaguar use *this* tree as an ambush? Coulter had told her to look for scratch marks on the base of the tree, where the cat would sink its claws to haul itself upward. She'd inspected the trunk of the rubber tree and found no such markings. From time to time today, however, Kathy had run into the powerful odor of jaguar urine, where he must have sprayed a tree trunk to mark his territory. She'd smelled cougar urine before while hiking in the Rocky Mountains and was able to easily identify the odor. The smell was so strong that it made her eyes water, and she'd held her breath as she hurried past.

Night fell amid the cacophony of crickets, screaming monkeys and hooting

184

of owls. Exhausted, Kathy tucked the knapsack beneath her knees for support, wrapped her arms around herself and closed her eyes. Her adrenaline had been pumping all day in anticipation of meeting the jaguar, and she felt nakedly vulnerable. A pocketknife was no match against a fierce, muscular cat, the lord of this jungle. As added protection, Kathy had picked up a limb the size of a baseball bat and carried it with her all day. It rested beside her in the hammock, poking uncomfortably against her ribs and hip, but she didn't care. If the cat climbed, her only defense would be to swing the branch like a club and try to hit the animal in the face. She knew from training that hitting any animal in the nose was a surefire deterrent. The flashlight, small though it was, was tucked in her left pocket, beneath the poncho. If she needed it, she could grab it in a hurry.

Her mind refused to shut down, although her aching, fatigued body screamed for her to fall asleep. Soon the darkness was complete. There would be no moon tonight, Mac had told her. It was the dark of the moon, or what Peruvians called the Jaguar Moon, a time of magic, danger and possibility.

Scrunching her eyes shut, Kathy sighed.

The distant rumble of thunder caught her attention for a moment. The monkeys never stopped chattering or screaming, near or faraway. Didn't they *ever* sleep? The jungle was not the quiet place Kathy thought it would be. She kept swatting at mosquitoes and God knew what other kind of creepie-crawlies wandering along her skin.

Her mind veered for the hundredth time toward Mac Coulter. He'd done all he could to help her survive this test. He'd warned her to hide the pack about five miles from the villa, so no one could ever discover what he'd done for her. Kathy was glad to have the pedometer, which she wore around her waist. Why had he done this? Why? The question whirled in her mind.

Her heart gave her the answer: Mac was drawn to her, as she was drawn to him. *Impossible.* They'd just met. Kathy had never been drawn to a man like this before. Even her love of Curt Shields, the U.S. Navy SEAL officer who'd been her fiancé, had not had the heat or crazy yearning she felt toward Coulter. She supposed she'd felt a quiet love for Curt — not that she was an expert on romance. When Curt had died in an ambush a year ago, Kathy had stopped living. Maybe she was coming back to life? Maybe Mac was just reawakening her hormones? Hell, she didn't know for sure. She blew out an exasperated breath. Coulter was different. Her body sure knew it. And so did her heart. She wondered who he was — the man, not the helo pilot in the employ of her enemy.

Kathy rubbed her face and pulled the poncho hood as low as she could to discourage the hungry, buzzing mosquitoes. The scent of vanilla wafted toward her. It was from an orchid, she was sure, and the fragrance relaxed her.

Her mind swung to her family. She'd been gone more than two weeks now. On other black ops she had never contacted the family. But if her father got worried, he'd start making noise and sending out his feelers to find out more about her present mission. Her dad was highly instinctive. She'd had the good luck to inherit that gene, but if Morgan became worried about her, he could blow holes in the cover Patrick had put into place. And that would not bode well for her or her objective.

Sleep finally came to Kathy as she thought about her mother. Laura always gave her a sense of safety in a world gone mad. . . .

The piercing shriek of a wild pig woke Kathy with a jerk, and she nearly fell out of the hammock. The night was black. Seeing nothing, disoriented, Kathy fumbled and the hammock swung dangerously. As the pig shrilled right below her tree, she heard a cat growling — a low, menacing sound. The hair on the back of her neck stood up.

What time was it? What was happening? For precious moments, Kathy was flummoxed. Her sleep-drugged mind refused to work. The grunts, screams and sounds of struggle shot adrenaline back into her bloodstream. Heart pounding, Kathy sat upright, her legs dangling outside the swaying hammock. She dug for her bat and the flashlight at the same time.

The screams of the wild pig were hideous and it sounded like a young child being mauled and bitten by a dog. Switching on the light, Kathy shone it downward. Gasping, she saw a male jaguar, his gold coat spotted with black crescents. A huge hundred-pound boar struggled in its massive jaws. The cat had seized the pig by the throat and blood spurted everywhere. Watching in horror, Kathy saw the jaguar's tail switching from side to side. For an instant, he lifted his head and his large yellow eyes rested directly on *her.*

Oh, God! Snapping off the light, breathing raggedly, Kathy gripped the stick at her side and brought it up — just in case she had to hit the animal. Her mind whirled. She was trapped! The pig's squeals became fainter and fainter as it stopped struggling. Finally, there was silence. *Real* silence.

Then Kathy heard the cat's gruff breathing. Mac had told her that jaguars were the only members of the cat family that never roared. They would growl sometimes, but that was it. The cat's breathing was labored and quick. What was it going to do? Crouch there and eat the pig? *God, what should I do?* Biting her lower lip, Kathy looked around, and found the night was as black as a cave. She couldn't see her hand in front of her face, but she could see the radium dial on the watch she wore. Holding it close to her eyes, she saw it was 0300 hours.

The silence of the jungle amazed her. Nothing croaked, screamed, twitted or howled. Nothing. It was as if all creatures knew that the jaguar had killed, and didn't want to become its next victim. Shaking with fear, Kathy tried to take several calming, deep breaths. If the cat had food, it wasn't going to come after her — or was it? Unsure, she keyed her hearing to the ground below. The crunching of bone and flesh sent shivers through her. Feeling sorry for the pig, Kathy wondered how the drama had played out before she'd been rudely awakened. The thought that the cat had been sitting under her tree, waiting for its quarry, sent renewed fear zigzagging through her.

Gulping several times, her mouth dry, she waited in silence. Could the cat smell her? He'd seen her when she'd flashed the light on him — a stupid thing to do, she realized belatedly. She'd given away her hiding place to the jaguar. Would he think her an even bigger prize, leave the hapless, dead boar, climb the tree and come after her? Her mind whirling with questions and no answers, Kathy sat unmoving, breathing through her mouth and trying not to draw the attention of the jaguar, which was devouring his kill just fifty feet below.

After a while, the sounds of eating convinced Kathy that she was safe. Well, as safe as she could be under the circumstances. If the cat had his fill of wild pig, he wasn't going to be hungry for her. Exhaustion from the brutal trials she'd undergone began to seep into her being. Leaning back in the hammock, her legs still dangling over the edge, she closed her eyes. Without meaning to, she immediately fell asleep, the stick of wood gripped in her hand.

The shrill screech of a monkey made Kathy jump into a sitting position. The animal had apparently come to the old rubber tree, seen her and cried an alarm. Jerking upward, Kathy gasped and saw the furry gray mammal disappearing into a nearby tree.

The jaguar!

Breathing hard, her sleep-ridden mind barely functional, Kathy looked below her. Nothing. She saw no sign of the jaguar or the wild boar on the muddy, vine encrusted trail. All that remained was a dark pool of blood that had soaked into the soil. Blinking several times, Kathy scrubbed her eyes. She must have fallen asleep. God, that hadn't been smart! What was wrong with her? What if the jaguar had decided to climb the tree and go after her? She'd have been a sitting duck. Fear sizzled through her and the surge of adrenaline made her wake up in a rush.

What time was it? Looking at her watch, she saw it was 0700. Time to get up and get going. Cottony clouds lay atop the tallest trees above her. The drip, drip, drip of water falling off the leaves was constant. Wiping her face, Kathy decided she'd better eat another protein bar before she climbed out of the tree.

Where was the jaguar? Where was his lair? Had he dragged the pig off while she slept? He must have. Was he sated and sleeping now? Would that mean the trail was safe? She wanted to make another twenty miles today. Quickly digging into the pack, she found a raspberry granola bar and consumed it with unaccustomed pleasure. If she made it through this hellish test, she promised to buy Mac Coulter a steak dinner in Cuzco and thank him properly. Without him, she knew she would not have lasted. She owed him her life. . . .

Two and a half days and still no sign of her. Mac tried to curb his worry over Katherine Lincoln. It was noon on the third day and he'd just landed at the villa, after taking several drug lords from the Caribbean back to Cuzco to catch their flight to Lima and onward. After the blades stopped turning, the two-man ground crew quickly scurried up to the Bell helicopter to place chocks around the wheels. As Mac shut down the helo, he saw

Carlos Garcia strolling toward him.

Today was a rare day, weatherwise. There had been no low-hanging clouds this morning. The sun had risen full and bright over the jungle. Taking off his sunglasses and sliding them into the pocket of his light blue, short-sleeved shirt, Mac disembarked. His boss was dressed in casual dark brown slacks, his white silk shirt open at the collar to show off the many gold necklaces he wore. One that evoked Coulter's disgust had a huge gold crucifix hanging from it — outside his shirt. *Yeah, right. A real Christian, this bastard.* Swallowing his rage and keeping his face unreadable, Mac met the *patrón* at the skirt of the landing pad.

"Nice day for flying?" Garcia said, gesturing to the cloudless blue sky above them.

"It is," Mac agreed as he came to a halt. Garcia wanted something. It wasn't like the man to come meet him like this.

A few gardeners were in the background, picking up fallen branches from the thunderstorms that regularly hammered the jungle this time of year. They, too, had confused looks on their faces. Therese wasn't in sight, she must be in her office, running the place as usual, Mac decide

He had learned early on that the beautiful Peruvian woman was Carlos's personal assistant par excellence. She kept his bed warm, kept him happy and had the steel-trap mind of a military strategist. Truth be known, Therese was the power behind Garcia's throne, and in some ways, Mac believed the *patrón* knew that.

"What do you think, *compadre?*"

"About what?" Mac asked, on guard.

"Señorita Lincoln."

His heart thudded. Carefully, Mac said, "What about her?"

Carlos pulled out his gold cigarette case and opened it. He delicately took a cigarette and snapped the case shut. "Well, today is the day? If she has passed the test, should she not show up soon? Do you figure twenty miles a day?"

Mac wondered if Garcia was fishing. Had they found Lincoln's body with the knapsack on it? Fear thrummed through him as he tried to appear casual. "Yeah, if she's in good physical shape she might make twenty a day. Why?" He watched Garcia light his cigarette and take several puffs before removing it from his thin lips.

"Just curious. Do you think she'll do it?"

"I don't know, *patrón.*"

"Therese says she will. You know,

194

woman's intuition . . ." Garcia chuckled indulgently as he looked toward the gate in the compound's wall.

"She has good instincts," Mac agreed.

"What do *you* think?"

Uneasy, Mac said, "I hope she'll make it. I think she'd make a great nanny for Tiki. From the looks of things, she has the right amount of defensive skills to keep your daughter safe, *patrón.* I haven't seen her personnel file, of course, so I'm talking through my hat on this."

Nodding, Carlos puffed away. "*Sí,* you do not have all the information, that's true. But you were in the military at one time until your dishonorable discharge. You were in combat in Afghanistan, so you have good gut instincts, too. I was just wondering what you thought."

Maybe Garcia was genuinely hoping that Katherine Lincoln would make it home today. That would be a first. Carlos didn't usually bother with a nanny's test results, leaving those things to Therese.

"Well, if she does make it, she'll either show up today or tomorrow, I would guess," Mac said.

Grunting, Garcia nodded. Sticking the cigarette in the corner of his mouth, he clapped Mac on the shoulder. "If you see her, let Therese know immediately."

"Of course," Mac said, and watched the drug lord turn and amble down the brick sidewalk toward the main villa. What had that been all about?

Yesterday, an unmarked black Apache helicopter had been spotted less than ten miles from the villa. Mac knew that there was a secret U.S. Army black ops base near Machu Picchu, hidden away in a huge lava cave. The mountains in the area looked like huge loaves of French bread turned on end and covered with greenery. They had been created from lava millions of years ago, and many had cave complexes running through them.

It wasn't a secret to Garcia or his men. They knew that the U.S. Army had put a fleet of combat Apache helicopters down here, with the approval of the Peruvian government. The Apache pilots tried to stop him and other drug lords from flying cocaine out of Peru to surrounding countries. Yesterday, an Apache had flown very close to the villa, which had been unusual and had sent jitters through the community. Mac had heard about it from distressed soldiers who thought for sure the black helo was going to attack them. It never had before, but Mac suspected that the Apache pilots operating out of that cavern knew exactly where Garcia was — at all times.

He himself had never been harassed in the air by the phantom Apaches. Of course, his flights were to Cuzco and back, not considered a drug flight route. Maybe that's what had Garcia spooked. Had the black ops helo spotted Katherine on the trail within range of his villa? Was that why they'd come so close?

"What the hell is *that?*" Chief Warrant Officer 2 Jessica Merrill demanded into her head set. She was talking to her copilot and friend, Vickey Mabrey, who was serving as weapons officer on this mission. Grasping the controls, Jessica urged the Apache into a slight starboard bank at five thousand feet above the Peruvian jungle. "You got your infrared on, Snake?"

The Boeing Apache helicopter was one of the most advanced in the world for combat. It not only carried live television pictures back to their HUDs, or heads-up display units, it also had an infrared scanner so precise it could detect the heat of a single human. Sitting in the lower cockpit, Jessica frowned and kept her feet steady on the rudders while she gripped the collective and cyclic with her hands.

"Hold on a sec, I'm switching modes," Snake muttered. "I'm looking . . . Yeah, there it is! A definite heat signature source down there." She grinned crookedly. "My, what good eyes you have, Wild Woman." Jessica had gotten her handle because she dyed a thick strand of her blond hair red, and generally raised hell like a good ol' Montana gal should, even if she was in the ultraconservative U.S. Army.

Wild Woman snorted, "I'm bored to death. There's not a druggie in the sky." It was midday and they were trolling along a known drug route about twenty miles from the temple complex of Machu Picchu. Of course, they were under strict orders by Major Maya Stevenson, commanding officer of the Black Jaguar Squadron, never to expose themselves to *turistas*. That was a huge no-no in their game book. As a black ops outfit, they weren't supposed to be seen, photographed or identified by outsiders — especially camera-happy tourists who snapped anything that moved.

Wild Woman grinned wickedly. The black Apache might show up in a camera frame and be called a condor because the tourist wouldn't know what else it could be.

Everyone in the BJS knew that Carlos

Garcia, the chief drug lord in Peru, had a villa very close to the known drug routes. Today, for some intuitive reason, Wild Woman had decided to fly over this area. Garcia usually had his drug flights originate elsewhere, and she knew why. He didn't want to draw the lethal capabilities of the Apache arsenal down upon his head.

As combat pilots, Wild Woman and Snake were under strict orders not to fire on any ground structures — only on airplanes or helicopters whose fuselage numbers could be checked by computer and verified as known druggies who flew cocaine out of the country.

Snake frowned. She pushed up her visor and squinted into the HUD in front of her. "Yeah, this is a human, Wild Woman. One person. Doesn't look armed or dangerous."

"Probably a villager on the path," she agreed.

Snake looked up. She sat in the upper cockpit, above the flight commander. "The target is heading toward Garcia's villa."

"Drug carrier, then?"

Shrugging, Snake tweaked the HUD. "I dunno. He's carrying something on his back."

"Let's take a closer look, shall we?"

Snake glanced up to her right. "Remember the flight restrictions. We can't get too close to Garcia's villa or the major will have our ass, not to mention our rank. I'm up for CWO3 and I don't want to lose it on a wild-goose chase."

"Yeah, yeah, I know, I know." Wild Woman headed down, aiming the nose of the dinosaurlike Apache toward the thin strip of trail. The air was smooth this morning, the sky a bright blue. Blinding rays of sunshine shot through the cockpit, but the air-conditioning kept her cool in her Nomex fire retardant black flight suit.

The only identification either pilot wore was a BJS patch attached with Velcro on her upper right arm. It showed the head and shoulders of a snarling black jaguar on a red-white-and-blue backdrop. Otherwise, no one would know they were Americans, because their aircraft bore no fuselage numbers or flag.

Snake craned her neck toward the cockpit Plexiglas. "Hey, I see him!" The chopper trolled slowly, following the muddy ribbon in the thick jungle about a thousand feet below. The rotor wash made the top leaves shake and shimmy as the aircraft passed.

"Naw," Snake said after studying the person through binoculars, "that ain't no native carrying cocaine. It's a *hiker!* One of those stupid white women who probably didn't get her fill of excitement on the Inca Trail, so she's trying this one out. Fool that she is . . ."

"Dumb, if you ask me. She's hiking straight for Garcia's villa. I wonder if she knows where she's headed? She'd be the first one that did." Lost hikers weren't uncommon around Machu Picchu.

Shrugging, Snake put the binoculars down. "She looks free, white and twenty-ish to me. Nothin' we can do. She's a legitimate hiker here in the wilds of Peru."

"Let's take a photo of her, just in case. Another mug shot for the major's files."

"Roger that," Snake muttered, flicking a switch. "Candid Camera time, honey. Hey! She's looking up at us! Isn't that cool, dude?"

"Just snap the photo, will you, Snake?"

"Smile! You're on Candid Camera!" Snake pressed a button that would capture the hiker's image on a digital card. "Now she's indelibly printed in our BJS files of who's who, Wild Woman. Are you satisfied?"

"Hell yes! I'm bored. Let's go see if we can scare up some druggies south of here, shall we? This is our last month down here before we go to new assignments. Let's make the most of it."

Snake broke out in song. *" 'Fly me to the moon. . . .' "*

Quirking her mouth, Wild Woman eased the Apache back toward the known drug routes. She guided the helicopter upward, the gravity pressing her back into the seat, the harness biting slightly into her shoulders. "Gawd, Snake! Stop yowling! You sound like a damn Siamese cat with its tail stuck in the door! Give my ears a rest, dude!"

With the weather so clear today, Major Stevenson had anticipated a lot of druggies wanting to make a run to the border of Bolivia, and she'd put every available helicopter and flight team into the air to stop them. Jessica and Vickey had other fish to fry and couldn't waste time checking out a lone hiker. Sometimes, though, drug dealers paid Indians in the surrounding villages to carry the goods. BJS pilots would use infrared to find a dozen or so of them with huge sacks of cocaine on their backs, walking to Bolivia or other drop-off points. Not the case today.

"Hey, I thought you liked my singing!"

Snickering, Wild Woman said, "Yeah, when I'm drunk on pisco and sittin' at a bar in Cuzco, drownin' my sorrows."

"Let's go find some druggies, Wild Woman. I'm hungry for a kill. . . ."

Chapter Eleven

It was 1500 in the hot, humid afternoon when Mac heard Esau, one of the guards, sing out in an excited voice, "She's coming! She's coming!"

Mac had been sitting in the helo, doing some weekly safety checks on the bird. He twisted around to see for himself. Sure enough, Katherine Lincoln had just come through the archway in the outer wall. Relief, sharp and sweet, sheeted through him.

Her hair was matted and uncombed, obviously dampened from the humidity and her exertion. He could tell she'd slipped and fallen many times because her clothes were covered in red mud. She held her head high and her shoulders square as she marched confidently into the stronghold. The look in her eyes was one of fearlessness, of self-assurance. Even the two soldiers on guard duty at the gate grinned and hailed her like a conquering heroine.

Mac knew that Therese was asleep. Mid-afternoon was siesta time in South America, and only gringos like himself worked through it. Guards, however, had no choice. They were on duty around the estate 24/7. Therese had given him instructions to take care of Ms. Lincoln should she show up. Mac remembered the wolfish smile Therese had given him and the glimmer in her large, intelligent eyes. She was sure Katherine would make it back. And she had.

As he slid out of the Bell, Mac wiped his hands. He closed the door and walked briskly so that he could intercept her before she went to Therese's office. Several other gardeners, all older men who used to be farmers in the region at one time, clapped as Katherine passed by. She had a weary smile for all of them.

God help him, but she was beautiful, mud and all. It was the look in her blue eyes that made Mac realize all over again how much of a warrior she was. When Katherine saw him her mouth pulled into a dazzling smile of unparalleled beauty. Heat burned through Mac as he returned her smile of greeting. He drew to a halt six feet away, because if he didn't keep a safe distance, he would sweep her into his arms and kiss her until they melted together. Every night she was gone, his dreams of kissing Katherine had been torrid and too real.

"Welcome back, Ms. Lincoln."

"Thank you, Mac. Call me Kathy." She drowned in his stormy gray eyes, unable to tear her gaze from his face. Mac stood relaxed, hands resting languidly on his hips, that boyish smile dissolving her defenses. Suddenly, her body simmered with a throbbing need that only he could soothe, a need that caught her completely off guard. Since Curt's sudden, shocking death, she thought her heart had died.

"Not Katherine?"

"No, that's my official name. My friends and family call me Kathy."

Friends and family, eh? Well, okay, he definitely wanted to be friends with her. Much more than that, Mac realized. As Kathy pushed her bedraggled blond hair off her face, he grinned. "There's a nice swimming hole in back of the villa." He lowered his voice. "Away from prying ears and eyes. Everyone is sleeping right now because it's siesta time. They won't start stirring for another two hours. Therese wanted me to take care of your needs if you came in during this time. What will it be? Swimming hole or a hot shower in your villa?"

Gazing up at his warm, intimate expression, Kathy felt her heart contract.

"I'm a nature girl. I'll take the swimming hole." Besides, she could be alone with him — the man who had called her bright angel. The endearment had never left Kathy. When she'd felt scared on the trail, she would replay that sweet name and the husky tone with which Mac had said it. It had calmed her frayed nerves many times. She didn't want to divulge that to him, though. If he knew how much power he had over her . . . Well, she was barely able to keep her hands to herself. All Kathy wanted to do was kiss him and sink into his strong arms and cherish him as she was sure he would cherish her.

Mac gestured between the two main buildings. "Follow me. I have some towels, shampoo and soap waiting down there."

"You're really on top of things," Kathy said with a low laugh. She fell into step with Mac and realized he was cutting his stride back to match hers. Though her legs were aching and tired, Kathy felt amazingly alert. When they were well past the buildings, she looked around to make sure no one was near. "I ditched the knapsack five miles away from the estate. They'll never find it if they go looking for it. That's why I was late. I dug a hole for it in a dense grove of trees well off the path."

"That was quite a job," Mac said. He was relieved she'd taken such care to hide the knapsack, because if it were ever found, he would be fingered, and a bullet to the brain would be the next order of business.

Shrugging, Kathy pushed the hair off her face. She felt gritty, dirty, sweaty and longed for a cooling bath. The brick path curved downward at a much sharper angle now and she could hear a waterfall below them. Surrounding them on all sides was the jungle, but it had been thinned out here at the compound. Large-leaved plants swatted gently against them as they walked.

"I fixed up a lunch pail with some food, too. You're probably starving to death, after subsisting on protein bars for a couple of days."

Laughing softly, Kathy said, "Just like that jaguar." She told him the story as they went down to the pool. Just as she finished relaying her adventure, they found themselves at a twenty-foot waterfall, which flowed over black lava rocks to an oval pool below. The open water created a hole in the thick jungle cover. Kathy appreciated seeing the hazy blue sky and bright sunlight that poured through the opening.

"Wow, this place looks like Shangri-La," she exclaimed. Spotting two pink, fluffy beach towels on a flat rock near the pool, she quickly unlaced her wet, muddy boots and took off the damp socks.

"Yeah, Therese said that the *patrón* had this place created for his wife, Paloma." Mac decided not to say too much more about her. Kathy would find out soon enough about this sordid family. He walked over to a nearby fallen log. "I'll sit here with my back to you while you strip down and jump in. You can tell me about the rest of your adventures." Mac knew he should leave, but he caved in to his need to remain with her.

"Thanks." Kathy quickly shed her damp, filthy clothes, stepped gingerly into the soft wooden chips at the edge of the water and stuck her toes into the clear turquoise pool. It was deliciously cool and terribly inviting. Grabbing the washcloth and soap, she waded across the sandy bottom until the water was up to her waist.

Mac stared up the path as Kathy washed herself and shampooed her hair. No one ever used this pool, to his knowledge. At least not now. Paloma, ever addicted and in a heroin haze, lay in her sumptuous bedroom suite on the second floor of the main villa. Mac had heard that she used to come down here daily to bathe and swim, but now preferred heroin to natural highs.

Another reason to bring Kathy here was that it was one of the few places that wasn't bugged. He could hear her splashing happily behind him. Every once in a while she would groan with delight. He liked that husky sound, and his imagination was going wild, wondering how she looked without her clothes.

"You know," Kathy called as she waded deeper into the water, "I saw something very unusual in the sky."

"Oh?"

"Yesterday afternoon I saw a black helicopter hover above me, where I was walking on the jaguar path. It was pretty close." She tried to sound casual and matter-of-fact. Kathy figured a civilian couldn't distinguish one helo from another, but she knew damn well it was an Apache combat helicopter that had swooped down to above where she'd been walking on the trail. Since it was an Apache, she guessed it was either owned by the Peruvian government, or there was a U.S.-backed black ops going on down here that she wasn't aware of. Would Mac know anything?

"A black helicopter?" Frowning, Mac realized the Apache that had given everyone at the villa the jitters must have been the same one she'd seen.

"Yeah. Black and evil looking. It was carrying what looked like a lot of weapons." Kathy could name them off, but that would be a dead giveaway. She stared at Mac's wide, strong back. She wondered what he was thinking, because he was quiet for a moment.

"There are a lot of helicopters in this area," Mac said, pretending not to be that interested. He knew exactly who'd been piloting that helo. He'd been briefed on the Black Jaguar Squadron before he'd gone undercover. "Probably a *turista* flight from an outfit in Cuzco. They fly out here all the time. Tourists like seeing the Machu Picchu area from above."

Kathy turned and started wading out of the water. "Oh. It didn't look very civilian." She hoped Mac would say something else. He didn't, much to her consternation.

After getting out of the pool, Kathy quickly toweled off. Mac had thoughtfully left a pink cotton, knee-length shift for her to wear. Eyeing her muddy clothes, she was more than happy to slip into the simple gown. "Okay, I'm dressed. You can turn around," she called. To her delight, Mac had brought a comb and brush, too, which she picked up. She walked over to the log and sat down a few feet away from him, facing the pool.

"I'm beginning to feel human," she said. "Thank you . . . for everything. I owe you — big time."

Mac turned and faced her, sitting with his thighs parted, elbows resting on them. "Yes, you do, bright angel." He saw her cheeks suddenly redden, and he held his breath. Why had he used the endearment? He couldn't get involved with this woman! He simply couldn't. Yet he sat there frozen, waiting for her reaction.

Feeling the heat in her cheeks, Kathy knew she was blushing over his calling her bright angel. His voice had turned so damn personal and husky, flowing across her as if he were using his fingers to graze her flesh once again. "That's a beautiful name."

"You like it?"

Kathy gently worked through the snarls in her hair with the comb. Once again she saw the warmth in his gray eyes as he held her gaze. "Yes, I do. But it's making me feel kind of awkward." She saw his brows dip. "I'm not even hired here yet and there's something . . . between us." God, the *last* thing she'd ever expected in an undercover mission was to be irresistibly drawn to a drug dealer! And her heart was winning the battle. Kathy knew she had to put a stop to Mac's obvious interest in her, but how? Seeing the disappointment in his expression, she whispered, "I just didn't expect, well, to meet a man I was attracted to. Not here. . . ."

"I wasn't looking for a relationship, either. It's just sort of happened." His heart beat hard to underscore the truth of his words. So he'd roast in hell at night, wondering over and over what it would be like to kiss that beautiful mouth of hers. Judging from the yearning and confusion he saw in her eyes, Mac sensed that she liked him, too. A lot more than she was willing to admit. That was okay; he could live with it. He had a lot of patience when it came to courting someone he liked.

She managed a slight, nervous smile. "Can we take this one day at a time, Mac? I have a job to do and I don't want to disappoint the *patrón.* But I want to take you to dinner in Cuzco later if I get this job. That's the least I can do to repay you."

Barely able to handle the burning look in

his eyes and the way the corners of his mouth quirked, Kathy felt her desire for him triple. Mac had done nothing but help her. Ever since they'd met — was it only four days ago? — he'd been there for her. Kathy was torn up inside, especially when she thought about what she'd come to Peru to accomplish. She would just have to take it a minute at a time. An hour at a time. It was so easy to pretend Mac was just a man, not a drug dealer. Did undercover agents ever get involved on a mission? Kathy didn't know, but it was happening to her right now.

"That would be nice. I haven't been taken to dinner by a woman in a long time." Mac met her laughter-filled eyes. Kathy Lincoln sure cleaned up nice. He could smell the faint scent of the jasmine shampoo she'd used on her hair. The blond strands, though darker when wet, still shone like old gold as she patiently worked the strands free of snarls. Her cheeks were glowing with good health, and when his gaze fell to her parted lips, he groaned inwardly. Too many times he'd thought of what it would be like to kiss her, to feel the strength and softness of her as a woman.

Chuckling, Kathy said, "I promised myself if I made it back, I'd buy you a steak dinner in Cuzco. I'm good for my word."

"You're on, then," Mac said. Dinner with her would be a gift. An unexpected one, that was for sure. He was going to have to figure out how to look but not touch.

"Can you tell me what's next on my agenda here, Mac? Do I finally get an interview with the *patrón?* Do I find out now if I have the job or not?" What did Mac Coulter want in payment? Those words begged to be asked, but Kathy didn't go there.

In no time her hair hung free around her shoulders, drying in the sun. Holding the comb and brush in her hands, she assessed his reaction to her questions.

Keeping his voice almost a whisper, Mac said, "My guess is you'll be debriefed by Therese in a couple of hours, after siesta. Tell her everything except about the knapsack. And don't say anything about your run-in with the jaguar. If she asks, just say you didn't see one. Play dumb."

"Of course," Kathy said. She saw darkness enter his eyes. He started to scowl as he looked out across the pool.

"I'm sure Therese will give the *patrón* the debrief of your test tonight or tomorrow morning."

"Then I get to meet him?" Kathy's stomach knotted and she held the brush more tightly in her hand. Finally, she'd get to meet the son of the man who had so grievously wounded her family. Would she be able to keep her cool? Not allow her hatred or rage to show? To conduct herself calmly and attentively, so that Garcia would never know her real intentions? So much of what had happened already had thrown her off course, unbalanced her. Kathy knew now, more than ever, that she had to be careful to not blow her cover. Garcia could never suspect her. Not once.

"Well, I think Therese will wait to hear from him. When he says it's okay, she'll take you to meet his daughter. Tiki has to approve of you." Mac glanced over at Kathy, who had a faraway look in her eyes. He wished he could read what was behind those large blue eyes of hers, but he couldn't.

"Wouldn't that be something? Go through three life-and-death tests only to be jettisoned by the daughter?" Kathy laughed ruefully at the thought, but it wasn't funny. To be so close to her goals and then have them yanked away from her . . . She could barely conceive of such a thing.

"Yeah, that would be a helluva note, wouldn't it?" Mac didn't tell her that it had happened before. No sense in setting her up for failure. "I think Tiki will take to you."

"Really?" Kathy turned and studied his grave features. Coulter had the most masculine, delicious looking mouth she'd ever come across. His lips were full, well-sculpted, strong and the corners tipped slightly upward in a natural slant to tell her that he laughed a lot. The crow's-feet at the corners of his eyes were a tell-tale sign that he was an aviator. He had a trustworthy face. Mac represented safety to her, whether Kathy wanted to admit it or not. He was a drug dealer and yet she could feel herself gravitate to him, look to him for help and information. It was disconcerting to her.

"Yeah, Tiki has this thing, this obsession, for blond hair." Mac gestured toward her drying locks. "She's a quick little girl, very smart like her father, very curious and always asking questions." He smiled slightly. "She also has temper tantrums."

"Oh? Why?"

Shrugging, he said, "I don't know. She's spoiled, that's for sure. She's the apple of her father's eye and he refuses her *nothing.*" Not even a real live playmate — Sophie — whom he'd kidnapped to entertain his little girl. Mac wondered how Garcia was going to handle the topic with Kathy if he hired her. He wouldn't tell her Sophie was kidnapped.

Once again Mac racked his brains for a solution to the heartbreaking problem. But he always came back to the same dilemma: if he tried to steal Sophie away, he'd blow the cover he'd worked so long to create. If he called his contact and they sent someone up here to get Sophie, Garcia would find out who'd let out the secret. Mac had seen people double-cross his boss before, and every time, Garcia found them out — and murdered them on the spot.

"I guess I'll deal with that after I get the seal of approval from Tiki and her father," Kathy was saying.

Grimacing, Mac said, "Be careful on reprimanding Tiki. I saw one nanny fired for smacking her on the butt. The *patrón* doesn't allow Tiki to be physically reprimanded."

"Thanks for letting me know that." Kathy crossed her legs and looked idly at the blisters on her bare feet. She'd soak them later. "Sounds like it will be a chess game of minds, then."

"That's it. And my money's on you to figure her out and get her straightened out."

"I'll sure try." Kathy smiled briefly. No one could know that she was here to steal Tiki.

Mac pulled the lunch pail over and handed it to her. "Some food. Unless you want to go back to the villa? The fridge is stocked with everything you'd ever want to eat."

Shaking her head, Kathy took the proffered lunch box. "Thanks, but knowing the place is bugged leaves me a little gun-shy, if you know what I mean." Kathy gestured to the pool. "Unless someone is in the bushes listening to us, we have the freedom to talk out here."

"No one comes down here. Only the gardeners, in the early morning, to clean the pool and pick up branches that might have fallen overnight. It's a safe place to talk."

Kathy opened the lunch box and found a sandwich of shaved roast beef, crisp lettuce and sliced tomatoes, slathered with mustard. As she unwrapped it quickly, her stomach growled. She was starved for some real meat! As she bit into it, she groaned. "This is wonderful, Mac. Thanks so much!" She spontaneously reached out and briefly touched his arm. When she did, Kathy saw his eyes narrow. After telling him she wanted to take their relationship a step at a time, she'd broken a cardinal rule and touched him. Kathy realized she was giving him mixed signals. Damn her heart — and her brain for being in neutral.

Mac tried to recover gracefully from her touch. "You're welcome. You looked like a hot 'n' spicy kind of gal, so I added the mustard instead of bland mayonnaise." Her featherlight touch had sent prickles up and down his arm. Mac tried to control his surprise at her gesture. Her eyes shone with such gratitude that it reached inside him and grabbed his heart. No, he didn't think she was playing games. Kathy was a warm and sharing person. She knew how to make him feel good in a very ugly situation.

"You're right, I love spicy food. Especially mango chutney and curry." Kathy sighed. "I love Indian, Thai and Mexican food." She munched happily on the sandwich and it disappeared in record time. Giving Mac a teasing look, she asked, "How could you know that I like spicy foods?" She picked up a fresh cinnamon roll lavishly slathered with white frosting and took a huge bite. She desperately craved the sugar it would provide her starving body. After the euphoria of passing the final test, Kathy was beginning to feel tired and knew she would sleep soundly after this sumptuous meal.

"I didn't know. Just a lucky guess," he said. But of course, he survived by reading people and their faces. And Katherine Lincoln was no wimp. Underneath, she was a wild woman, and in his experience, wild women liked wild spices. As her hair dried, the strands curled, framing her beautiful face. There wasn't anything about Kathy that *wasn't* beautiful, he decided unhappily.

Why had Garcia chosen someone so damn comely and desirable? Mac started to worry. Wasn't Therese enough of a woman for the *patrón*'s bed? As far as Mac knew, Garcia did not have other women. No, one thing he'd give the man was that he'd stuck with Therese through thick and thin, even though he was married to Paloma, who spurned all his advances.

Mac worried that Kathy might become more than just a nanny, and he now had another unexpected dilemma. She had no idea that Garcia would murder in the blink of an eye. Mac had seen him do it. If she rebuffed *any* of Garcia's advances, he'd kill her. Swallowing hard, Mac hoped he was wrong. Thus far, Therese seemed to satisfy Garcia. The two appeared happy together, or as happy as they could be. Being a Catholic, Garcia would never divorce Paloma, so he couldn't marry Therese. If his assistant was unhappy about this, she never showed it. Tiki loved her and they got along fine, which was good for all of them in this quasi nuclear family. Mac supposed that was as good as it got under the circumstances.

"That was a fabulous meal!" Kathy exclaimed, wiping her fingers on the paper napkin. "I love cinnamon rolls. I keep thinking you've read a file on me from somewhere and seen my list of fave foods." She grinned wickedly at him. After shutting the lunch box, she stood up. "Listen, I'm heading back to my villa. I'm bushed. I need to sleep."

Rising, he smoothed the light brown chino slacks he wore. "I bet you do. I don't think Therese will wake you. I'll put a note on her desk about you coming back. That will make her happy."

Kathy went over to her muddy clothes, threw the two towels across them, bundled them up and tucked the parcel beneath her arm. Mac retrieved her boots and the lunch pail. Walking up the hill with him,

Kathy said, "And what about you? What are you off to do now?"

"Helo maintenance," he said wryly. The last thing he wanted to do. He wished he could spend time with her, get to know a bit more about her. Somehow, he had to stop pining for that. There would be opportunities in the future.

"There's a lot to it," Kathy said, before catching herself. She saw confusion etched on Mac's face. "Well, I mean, I'm sure there's lots involved in taking care of a helicopter. I wouldn't know, but it looks pretty complicated." Would he believe her? She began to sweat. God, she was terrible at this spy business!

"Yeah, it is complicated." Again, Coulter had the feeling that she knew a helluva lot more than she was letting on. How could that be? He shrugged off his suspicions and slowed his steps as they started to crest the hill. In the distance, he could see the green stucco walls of the villas. "Listen, Kathy, there's one more thing before we go back." He turned to her. Seeing the startled expression in her eyes, Mac decided she was very readable.

"What?" Her heart pounded in dread. Had Mac found her out? She gripped the bundle in her arms more tightly.

"About Carlos Garcia. Your employer." Mac's black brows drew together, his eyes becoming very serious. "Look, if Tiki likes you, and I'm sure she will, you'll interview with him. You need a certain, well, demeanor in front of him. He's a very rich and powerful person and you need to be aware of that."

"Are you suggesting I be humble?" She smiled a little. She could see Mac was worried. "Say 'Yes, sir'? 'No, sir'? Don't speak unless spoken to? Don't argue? Just sit and listen?"

"Yeah, something like that. Just be careful and never, ever cross him. If he gives you orders, follow them without thinking. And don't argue with him. He's the boss. He'll expect you to follow his orders blindly." Looking up, Mac scoured the area to make sure no one was nearby. At this time of day, few were up and about. Even the dogs and cats were asleep. "He has a very short, violent temper. I'm telling you this because you seem to be a person who speaks her mind, and he isn't necessarily going to appreciate that about you."

"I see. . . ." Kathy stared down at her bare feet. The coolness of the brick felt good on her warm, blistered soles. "Thanks for letting me know, Mac. Play dumb. Roll over and pretend I'm dead. Be a beta wolf in reaction to the alpha one. Right?" She wanted to be very clear in her understanding with Mac. He was giving her a huge amount of information on how best to conduct herself. For that, Kathy was more than grateful once again. At first she'd wondered why he was helping her. Now that he'd admitted his attraction to her, she could understand his motivation.

"Yes, you got it, Kathy." He liked the way her name rolled off his tongue. Seeing her eyes dance, Mac wanted to reach out, slide his hand across her smooth cheek and plant a very hot, molten kiss on that delectable mouth of hers. *Whoa, pardner. Not now. Take your time. . . .* Mac censored himself as his body responded to the unbidden desire.

"I owe you once again, Mac. Don't worry, I'll conduct myself like the professional nanny I am. We were taught to be discreet, to listen without interrupting and always to carry out the employer's wishes without argument."

"Good," Mac murmured, turning and walking beside her again. "Because Señor Garcia can be a very genial, generous man to those who work with him."

He wanted to come clean with Kathy,

but didn't dare. She might not deliberately blow his cover, but he couldn't afford to have her speak offhandedly of this conversation to anyone. As they approached the buildings, he put his hand out and stopped her. "Whatever you do, never breathe a word of this conversation to a living soul, okay?"

Kathy nodded and saw the hard glint in his gray eyes. It was more than a warning. "You have my promise," she whispered huskily. "It goes nowhere. I'll die with it." And she would. Sooner or later.

Chapter Twelve

Kathy's stomach twisted into a Gordian knot as she slowly walked toward Tiki's playroom. It was nearly noon and she'd had a good night's sleep. At nine that morning, Therese had awakened her and informed her that it was time to meet Tiki. She'd told her to be at her office at 10:00 a.m. sharp.

Kathy had dressed in pale gray linen slacks and a plain white silk blouse, wanting to project a conservative air. Her instincts told her to keep her hair down today instead of up in a tasteful French roll. The golden strands were clean, slightly curled and hung around her shoulders, loose and free. Kathy knew it didn't look prim and proper, but she never ignored her intuition.

Today was the day. The interview with Therese had gone well, and there had been no trick questions. Therese's secretary had transcribed their conversation onto the computer from the recording that had been made. Kathy was sure the transcript would instantly go to Garcia.

After the interview, Therese took her to Tiki's quarters. The little girl had three rooms at her disposal on the second floor of the main villa — enough space, in Kathy's opinion, for ten people. Therese had shown her two children's bedrooms, located at the back of the villa, across the sidewalk from where Kathy would live. Kathy noticed the windows on each bedroom were well protected with vertical black, wrought-iron rods. No intruder was going to break into this fortress, that was for sure.

Now came the next test. As they walked down the highly polished teakwood hall, Kathy tried to appear relaxed. If Tiki didn't like her, all of this was for nothing. Therese said that she'd immediately be flown back to Cuzco, and then she could take a commercial flight to Lima, with a one-way, first class ticket in hand to Calgary. Kathy wanted to ask how many nannies Tiki had refused, but thought better of it.

"Here we are, Señorita Lincoln." Therese opened the bright blue-and-red door that led to Tiki's playroom. "Go on in. We have a camera in the room for security reasons. The *patrón* is worried about kidnapping, and he has guards who watch this tape twenty-four hours a day. I will go to the guards' office and watch how you interact with Tiki from there. I'll come and get you at the appropriate time." She smiled a little. "Good luck, *señorita.*"

Good luck, indeed. Kathy nodded and smiled back. "Sounds fine to me." She entered the room and quietly shut the door. Tiki Garcia rocked away on her rocking horse in the corner. Dressed in pale pink coveralls, a bright red T-shirt festooned with cartoon characters, her hair in two braids, she seemed like a happy child.

Kathy smiled and lifted her hand. "Hi, Tiki. My name is Katherine."

Tiki let out a squeal that rang through the toy-filled room. At first, Kathy didn't know what to do. She froze. Her ears buzzed from the child's unexpected shriek. What was wrong? Was this her way of expressing dislike?

The little girl slid off the horse and screamed joyfully, "Dolly! Dolly! You're my dolly!"

When Tiki came barreling toward her, pointing excitedly at her head, Kathy instinctively knelt down on one knee and opened her arms to the child. Tiki came crashing into her like a wiggling puppy.

In that instant, Kathy forgot she was

there to kidnap the little girl. Tiki's eager hands wrapped around her long, blond hair. She tugged on it several times, which hurt Kathy. Scalp tingling, she smiled down at her and patiently removed Tiki's searching hands from her hair.

"Dolly! You're my dolly!" Tiki reached for her hair again.

"Tiki, you can touch my hair, but don't pull it, okay? It hurts me, little one," Kathy said, holding out her arm so that the girl couldn't yank on her hair again.

Tiki seemed to accept this, so Kathy picked her up and walked back over to her rocking horse. The child constantly touched Kathy's hair, stroked it and admired it.

How could she take this adorable child away from her parents? Gulping, Kathy stared down at Tiki. She hadn't expected her to be so beautiful, more like a porcelain doll than an ordinary child. The happiness in the girl's eyes made mush of Kathy and her kidnapping plans.

After sitting down on a small wooden stool next to the horse, Kathy balanced the child on her right thigh. Tiki was still happily engaged in playing with her hair. Mac Coulter had been right about her obsession with blond hair. Again, Kathy mentally thanked him for his information.

"So," she said, grinning, "you obviously like blond hair, eh?" She couldn't forget that many Canadians put an "eh" at the end of some sentences. And since she was supposedly from Canada, she decided now was a good time to reinforce her cover.

"Dolly has sun hair," Tiki gushed as she looked up at Kathy. Pointing to her eyes, she said, "Sky eyes! Sky eyes, too! You're my Dolly?"

Chuckling, Kathy said, "Sure, I can be your dolly." Instantly, Tiki's round little face broke into such a radiant smile that it stole her heart. The child was beautiful, with her coppery skin, shining eyes and bow-shaped mouth.

In Kathy's estimation, Tiki was short for a six-year-old and obviously underweight for her age. She compared Tiki's size with that of her little sister, Kamaria, who was two years younger. Kathy could feel Tiki's ribs as she ran her hand along the child's back. How odd, she thought. This kid had a father who obviously gave her everything she'd ever want. Why was she underweight? Intent on her exploration of Tiki, she saw the child wore little white tennis shoes on her feet. Kathy reached down to make sure they fit right. Tiki's toes were pressing against the end of the shoes, which meant she needed a larger size.

Quietly examining Tiki as she played happily with her hair, Kathy made a mental list of things to discuss with Therese. Because the child was happy, Kathy allowed her to sit and play in her lap. There was no need to move or entertain her. Being watched by the camera made Kathy feel highly uncomfortable. If she were employed here, every word and action would be recorded and, she was sure, would get back to Garcia. She remembered Mac's warning about never hitting Tiki in any way, shape or form.

"Dolly," the girl breathed joyfully. "You're my Dolly!" Her little index finger traced one of Kathy's blond eyebrows.

Kathy laughed and patted Tiki gently, her other hand around the child's waist to keep her balanced on her thigh.

The door opened, and Therese poked her head in. She was smiling. "Tiki, darling, Señorita Katherine must come with me for a little while."

"No!" Tiki shrilled, immediately starting to pout.

Shocked at the girl's response, Kathy hurriedly tried to calm her. "Hey, little one, it's okay," she crooned to her in

Spanish. "I'll be right back."

Huge tears welled up in Tiki's large eyes as she looked up at Kathy. The kid was a helluva manipulator. Despite the girl's tears, Kathy got up and placed Tiki on the saddle of her stuffed rocking horse. The black fur that had once covered the toy animal was just about gone, the fabric telling Kathy that the child loved her horsey and spent a lot of time on it.

"Dolly go away," Tiki wailed, rubbing her tear-filled eyes with her fists.

"Not for long." Kathy smiled and placed a kiss on Tiki's hair. Patting her gently, she picked up the well-used leather reins of the horse. "Here, rock on your horsey for a while. You can show me how well you ride when I get back, okay?"

Somewhat mollified, Tiki took the reins from her. "Dolly come back?"

"That's a promise," Kathy whispered, settling her hand on the child's thin shoulder. Oh, God, how was she going to rip this little girl away from her parents, now that she'd met her? Kathy turned and walked across the immaculate room.

Outside in the hall, Kathy pulled the door closed. Two sentries on their rounds, stared at her. Gulping, she wondered if she'd been found out.

"These are some of Tiki's guards, Señorita Lincoln. Antonio and Andres," Therese said. "They will always be making rounds on this floor. Two other guards, Julio and Mario, take the twelve-hour shift at night. They always guard Tiki's floor. Come with me?"

Heart pounding, Kathy barely acknowledged the two soldiers in jungle fatigues. Talk about guards! They had every conceivable weapon on them — rifles, knives, two pistols slung low on their massive thighs, and a belt of bullets crisscrossing their sizable chests. Edging past them, Kathy followed Therese to her office.

"Sit down, please," the woman said, gesturing to the red leather high-backed chair in front of her mahogany desk. In the corner, Sarita, her secretary, a Peruvian woman with graying hair up in a bun on the top of her head, sat alert with her hands resting on the laptop.

Kathy settled into her chair and waited. She knew Tiki liked her, but what did Therese think? Unsure, she watched the woman as she slowly flipped her thick, wavy dark hair over her proud shoulders.

"Well, I am impressed, Señorita Lincoln! Tiki had a surprising reaction to you."

"I thought so, too," Kathy said. A breath

of relief started to trickle through her. Maybe she was going to get the job. She wrestled with her hatred for Garcia, but managed to rein it in.

"What you didn't know is that our little Tiki has an interest in fair-haired Anglos." Chuckling, Therese sat back in her black leather chair. "She's got an entire collection of Barbie dolls. You know, the blond-haired, blue-eyed type?"

"Yes, ma'am, I'm familiar with them." Better to keep up the sirs and ma'ams. Kathy understood she was an employee and Therese was the queen of the villa, being Garcia's mistress. Placing her hands in her lap, she said, "Do you think that's why she was so taken with me? Because of my coloring?"

"Absolutely. Tiki has never had an Anglo nanny before." Therese looked at her through narrowed eyes. "The *patrón* always wanted South American nannies, but I persuaded him to consider other nationalities. I told him that I wanted a Barbie-type of woman who could speak flawless Spanish and be a bodyguard, as well. Tiki loves her Barbie dolls with blond hair. I felt we could find someone like that." Therese buffed her nails on the sleeve of her emerald-green silk jacket, seeming very pleased with herself.

"He didn't think such a woman existed, but I knew she did." Therese smiled at Kathy. "I've got good instincts. They told me that, of the three women we interviewed this time, you were the one. I *knew* you could survive the tests." The elegant woman sipped delicately from her white, gold-trimmed china cup, then set it down.

"There is one more hurdle to leap, Señorita Lincoln. I must show the *patrón* the videotape of Tiki responding to you, as well as give him your last test report."

"Of course," Kathy murmured, forcing herself to look down with humility she really didn't feel.

"For the rest of the day, I want you to just take it easy. The *patrón* may or may not see you, so please stay near the villa. If his secretary, Señora Elena Maronas, calls you, then come to my office and I will escort you to Señor Carlos Garcia's office."

Kathy nodded. "No problem. I'm still tired from that jungle trek, so I'll be glad for the time off."

Laughing politely, Therese said, "I'm sure you are. You may leave, Señorita Lincoln." She lifted her hand and gestured toward the door.

So much for a royal dismissal. There was no doubt in Kathy's mind that Therese considered herself queen of Garcia's castle. But she rose and nodded politely. "Yes, ma'am." Feeling a sense of absolute relief, she quickly left the office and hurried back to her little villa.

So far, so good. Now all she had to do was roll over and play dead with Garcia. Would she be able to handle herself correctly when she saw the bastard for the first time? Hatred flowed through her and choked off her breathing as she walked down the hall. And yet guilt warred with her desire for revenge. Kathy hadn't expected Tiki to be so cute or to remind her so sharply of Kamaria, her little sister.

At the other end of the hall a guard stood, heavily armed and alert. No matter where she went in this villa, there was a soldier on duty. Kidnapping Tiki was not going to be easy at all.

It was time. Kathy had been called to meet Therese at her office at 1700, shortly after siesta. She nervously rubbed her hands down her thighs as they walked to the east side of the villa, where Garcia's office was located. Kathy wasn't surprised to see two heavily armed guards at the massive mahogany door, which was elaborately carved and embossed with gold, showing the sun rising over the jungle. The artistry was breathtaking, but at the moment it was lost on her. All she could do was force herself to breathe evenly and keep her expression carefully neutral.

Therese knocked on the door.

"Enter!"

Just hearing Garcia's voice through the intercom sent a shiver of hatred through Kathy. *Keep calm. Keep cool. Don't look at him too much. Don't show anything except humility.* Mac's directions echoed through her and she kept reiterating them as a mental litany.

Therese opened the door and entered as if she were royalty. Kathy discreetly walked in after her, trying to look humble and unassuming. Her gaze swung to the center of the magnificent office. Carlos Garcia sat at a huge mahogany desk that had a golden sun emblazoned on the front, echoing the carved artistry of the door. *Of course.* The Inca, the emperor in times past, had been called the Sun God. And it wasn't lost on her that Garcia had taken that ancient symbol and had it stamped on his desk and on his door. Obviously, he considered himself an emperor. *The bastard.*

"Here she is," Therese announced with a flourish as Kathy approached his desk.

"Señorita Katherine Lincoln." She turned, smiling at Kathy. "And this is your employer, Señor Carlos Garcia. Please greet him." She stepped aside with a dramatic sweep of her arm.

Swallowing acid that rose instantly into her throat, Kathy forced herself to move forward, her hand extended across the desk. Garcia was dressed casually but elegantly. He had on a long sleeved, cream silk shirt, which was open at the collar to expose his darkly haired chest and three heavy gold necklaces. Disgusted, Kathy kept the friendly smile affixed to her face.

"Good to meet you, sir." *Liar!* Kathy saw the man's narrow face light up with what looked like genuine pleasure. He had been smoking a slim, long cigar and placed it in a heavy leaded-glass ashtray. When he stood and extended his hand, she noticed several gold and diamond rings on his slender fingers. The watch he wore was a gold Rolex. Garcia obviously liked to show off his wealth.

"Ah, Señorita Katherine! Believe me when I say it is a pleasure! Welcome to my humble abode. We are most glad that you have come to us." He gripped her hand and shook it heartily.

Nausea overwhelmed Kathy. Just the

touch of the man's soft, manicured hand made her want to vomit. *No! Don't you dare! Keep smiling. Keep the look in your eyes that shows you're really glad you're here.* The words she spoke were like tearing flesh off her body. "A pleasure, *patrón.* I'm happy to be here, thank you."

Releasing her hand, Carlos grinned hugely. "Well! This calls for a celebration! Therese, my little dove, will you have Veronica serve us high tea?"

Gulping, Kathy stood there at attention, her hands at her sides. The hand Garcia had touched tingled, and she wanted to wash it to get rid of his energy. Garcia was short, maybe five foot seven inches, if that. Lean and athletic, in her estimation. His hair, black and shining beneath the lights from above, was carefully lacquered.

So this was the son of the man who had hurt her family. Barely able to breathe, Kathy wrestled with her hatred. Her hands itched to throw a couple of deadly karate chops at the son of a bitch and get it over with. But she stopped herself. She roughly reminded herself that her mission was to kidnap Tiki and make him suffer as much as her family had. A quick, easy death wasn't in the cards for him. No way. He was going to twist in the wind like they had. . . .

In that moment, Kathy's hatred was so pure and powerful that her hesitation to kidnap beautiful little Tiki disappeared. The hatred consumed her, so strong she could taste it in her mouth. There was no question that it was worth going through the motions of meeting Garcia. She was so close to avenging her family. Finally.

"Of course, *mi patrón*," Therese said, gesturing to a maid who stood attentively at the door with a silver tea service in hand.

"Sit, sit," Carlos said to Kathy, smiling broadly, and gesturing to the dark green leather, high-backed chair in front of his desk. Turning, he looked at Therese. "Will you join us?"

"No, *patrón*. I have some details to take care of in my office. Will you forgive me?"

"But of course," Carlos murmured, picking up his cigar and puffing on it. The maid hurried in, set the tea service on a cart and rolled it up to his desk.

After Therese left, Kathy sat at attention in the chair, her hands feeling like lead weights in her lap. The maid, her almond eyes darting from her to Garcia, expertly poured the fragrant Earl Grey tea into a china cup.

"Gracias," Kathy said after the woman

handed her a cup of the fragrant brew. "Thank you."

"*Sí*, Señorita Lincoln."

So, did everyone know her name already? Kathy sat with the tea in hand as the maid brought over a three-tiered lazy Susan adorned with chocolates, an assortment of English shortbreads, scones and finger sandwiches.

"Thank you," Garcia told the maid. "You may go now."

Bowing deferentially, the servant hurried out of the room and quietly closed the door.

"Look at this! Surely in Canada, Señorita Katherine, you have high tea?" He waved his hand at the highly polished silver lazy Susan that sat between them.

"Yes, sir, high tea is widely practiced where I come from."

"Well," he said, seeming pleased as he crushed out the cigar and set it aside, "I had this especially created for you!"

Kathy couldn't hide her surprise. "Sir?" Her fingers gripped the white saucer so hard she had to force herself to relax so that she didn't break it. Heart pounding, she could barely look at Garcia's animated, pleased face as he inspected the goodies on display.

"Therese thought it would be an appropriate way to honor you and your country, as well as your training as a nanny, to have high tea. We must celebrate your employment with me and my darling little Tiki. Look!" He nudged several of the crustless white sandwiches. "You see? We have taste in Sudamerica, no? There are cucumber sandwiches. Egg sandwiches. Watercress sandwiches. Please, please, help yourself." He handed her another, larger plate.

Taken aback by his obvious joy and pleasure in surprising her, Kathy nodded. "Thank you, sir. But I just ate. I'm still on North American time. You know? We eat dinner between 5:00 and 6:00 p.m." Kathy knew that in South America, the schedule was very different. Dinner could occur between 8:00 p.m. and midnight. People slept late and had *desanuno,* or breakfast, around 11:00 a.m. Lunch, came around 3:00 p.m., after siesta.

"Oh . . ." Garcia said, disappointment evident in his voice.

Kathy decided to take a couple of the sandwiches, anyway. She couldn't afford to make him angry or deny his efforts to please her.

"They look very good," she said, taking one of each type. "I can't resist." She forced a slight smile and looked directly at him, which was a mistake. As soon as she peered into those black eyes, narrow and alert, Kathy was reminded that Garcia was a murdering son of a bitch just like his father. At first glance, he seemed more like an athletic gym teacher than a drug lord. Everything about Garcia was subdued and refined, from the way he used his hand with a flourish, to his gentle way of speaking. She had expected a hard muscle-bound killer. Garcia belied the labels.

As she considered her enemy, Kathy did not taste the cucumber sandwich she stuffed into her mouth. Garcia's crestfallen look changed to one of radiant pleasure. He quickly filled his plate with at least half-a-dozen sandwiches and sat back to savor each one with gusto. *Go ahead and enjoy yourself, you bastard, because pretty soon you're going to suffer.*

"I forget sometimes that *norteamericanos* eat at the strangest hours," Garcia said.

"Yes, sir, we do." No sense in arguing with him. Kathy repeatedly told herself to relax.

"There are scones here, too. Look! My chef went to great pains to call the British Culinary Institute in London this morning to find the perfect recipe for scones. Surely you must try at least one?"

Kathy reached for a warm, triangular shaped scone filled with raisins and other dried fruit. "It looks wonderful, sir."

"Call me *Patrón*," he said with a quick smile. Reaching for three small containers on the second level of the lazy Susan, he said, "Here, I just had these flown in from Lima. They arrived this morning — clotted cream, lemon custard and strawberry jam from Britain. The real thing, *señorita*, for high tea. Please, please, take some."

She felt like a pig stuffing herself on command. The whole thing seemed like an absurd, distorted Salvador Dalí nightmare to Kathy. Her stomach was knotted. Jamming the scone slathered with a bit of the thick cream into her mouth almost made her gag. Her heart never stopped pounding. She slugged down several sips of Earl Grey tea to dislodge the lump building in her throat. As the tea soothed her nerves, Kathy breathed a small sigh of relief. She wasn't going to completely lose it.

Garcia sat back, eating each finger sandwich with relish. "You see, *señorita*, since you are in my employ now, you will have high tea every day, just like in Canada. We will try the best we can to anticipate your every need. My chef is already preparing smoked salmon and other Canadian delicacies for your dinners to come. We want you to be happy here. If you want a certain type of wardrobe, certain designers, all you need do is talk to Therese and she will see that you get it."

He was like a Santa Claus without end, Kathy thought. As if to stall her response to his generosity, she took another sip of tea.

"Well, that is very, very kind of you, sir, not to mention generous, eh? But I really have all the clothes I need." *Because I won't be staying long enough to need any others, you bastard.*

"Oh, but I'm afraid you will, Señorita Katherine. You see, my little Tiki often accompanies me in my jet when we go for visits around the world. As her nanny, you must, of course, be properly dressed." He raised his brows to emphasize his point.

Nausea rose again in her throat. "Of course, sir, whatever you say."

"*Bueno!* Therese already has several designers picked out and she has a wardrobe in mind for you. Of course, you must like it."

"I'm sure I will," Kathy murmured. "Really, all I want to do, *Patrón,* is care for your daughter. I'm not one for the limelight." Or the photographers who might put her at risk of having her family see a picture of her in a newspaper or magazine. That would be disaster for Kathy, since her whole mission would be scuttled.

"I'm a very wealthy man," Garcia said, "and I'm afraid the press of the world follows me. But I do not want my baby daughter exposed to their prying eyes, so you need not worry about being set upon by the paparazzi."

"Good. I don't feel a child should be subjected to that sort of thing. Tiki needs a fixed, stable environment to grow up in," she said. Had she overstepped her bounds? She saw Garcia tilt his head and his eyes narrow speculatively upon her.

"*Sí,* yes, I agree with you, *señorita.* What else do you see about my little pastry? I would value your insights about her."

Little pastry? She realized it was Garcia's endearment for Tiki. Every father had a pet name for his child. Her own dad still called her Pet. Why wouldn't Garcia have one for his daughter? Somehow, Kathy hadn't envisioned a murdering drug lord being so human and caring.

Setting the cup and saucer on the edge of his desk, she wiped her mouth with the linen napkin and then gripped it in her lap. She had to be careful here.

"Well, sir, I hope you don't think I'm being forward, but Tiki seems underweight and small for her age. I could feel her ribs beneath the clothes she wore. Perhaps she's been sick, or something else caused this, eh? Something I'm not aware of?"

Garcia's face seemed anguished for a moment. Again the emotion was real. Kathy hadn't thought Garcia capable of human feelings. She was wrong, again.

"Well, it's complicated, *señorita.*" Waving his hand, he said, "My little pastry is a very picky eater. But it goes beyond that." His voice grew sad. "Her mother, Paloma, is very sick and rarely sees her. She is here at the villa, under a doctor's care, of course — twenty-four hours a day. My daughter pines away for her mother, but she is incapable of being there for her." Shrugging, he gave her a weary smile. "So I try to be both parents to her, knowing full well I can never replace her beautiful, darling *mamacita.* Tiki loses her appetite as a result. You can understand this, of course?"

Kathy didn't want to be touched by the

information, but she was. Tiki was such a bright, active child and Kathy ached for the girl's pain. "Yes, sir, I certainly can."

"Anything else you noticed about my little pastry?"

"Only that she's outgrown the shoes she has on, *Patrón.* I think she needs a new pair."

"I am pleased that you have already noted these things." He snorted and bit into a scone. "The last nanny was not as alert as you are." Brushing his hands after consuming it, he said, his mouth full, "I would be deeply indebted to you if you could find a way to help my daughter grow and gain weight. I've hired nutritionists, but none of them have been able to help. The psychiatrist's recommendations haven't aided her. The only other person she truly responds to is her teacher, Señorita Adelina Fields, but that only goes so far, too. I would give all the money in the world to see my daughter flourish once more."

Deeply moved by his pleading tone, Kathy said, "With your permission, sir, I'll try. Maybe in a couple of weeks, after I get to know her and her tastes better, I might work with someone in your kitchen?"

Brightening, Garcia said, "But of course! I'm very pleased you care about this, *señorita.*" He beamed at her. "Truly, as Therese has already said, you are an angel from God himself for my little pastry."

Choking down the bile, Kathy demurely lowered her eyes and kept her voice soft. "I hope only to make her happy, *Patrón.*"

"Well, you must know that Tiki has a little American friend named Sophie who is staying with her presently. She has the other, smaller bedroom. You will meet her soon." Garcia leaned back in his chair and waved his hand. "She is a friend of the family. Her parents have left her here with us as they travel the world. When you meet Sophie, I'm sure she will tell you many stories."

"Oh?" Kathy kept her voice even. She knew Sophie had been kidnapped, and she was wondering how Garcia was going to handle this topic.

He smiled briefly. "Sophie is, well, how do I say this? She is very unhappy here. Of course, she'd rather be with her family and is very angry they have left her in our care. I'm afraid you'll find that she will tell you lies, *señorita.* She would do anything to leave." He chuckled indulgently. "Her latest tall tale is that she was kidnapped by us. So you must not play into her lies, and understand that she is simply an unhappy child for the present. You will be caring for her, also."

"That's not a problem, *Patrón*." Amazed at how Garcia spun his story, Kathy cautioned herself to remain on guard around the bastard. If she didn't already know Sophie had been kidnapped, she'd have believed him.

Chapter Thirteen

"I don't like that!" Tiki jabbed her index finger at the breakfast plate that the waiter had just brought her from the kitchen.

So much for her first day of work. Kathy hadn't been here an hour and Tiki was already in rebellion. She sat with the child at a small table in the rear of her playroom, where she ate her meals. Kathy had spent the short amount of time she'd been there acquainting herself with the little girl, her habits, her likes and dislikes.

Where was Sophie? Kathy hadn't had time to look for her, and suspected she was probably back in the bedroom area.

Looking at the uninspiring scrambled eggs and thinly sliced bacon with some french-fried potatoes, Kathy didn't blame her for her disinterest.

"Is there anything you do like there, Tiki?" She pointed to the plate in front of the child.

Poking at the rubbery bacon, she said, "This. I like this." Tiki quickly grabbed a strip and started to eat it.

"Whoa, kiddo. This is knife-and-fork time. . . ." Kathy took the meat out of her hands. Smiling patiently, she wiped off the girl's mouth and fingers. "Now, I know your other nanny taught you manners. You're a young lady and you need to use good table manners." She picked up the fork and placed it in Tiki's hand, the knife in the other. The girl scowled. Getting up, Kathy positioned herself behind the child and guided her to cut up her meat. Tiki seemed mollified by this attention and mimicked her directions.

Though worried when Tiki still ate only a few ounces of meat, and drank only soda pop, not milk, Kathy gave up on coaxing her to eat more. She thanked Mateo, the nervous-looking servant, who whisked away the uneaten portions.

She was still sitting with Tiki at the table when she heard a child crying softly. It had to be Sophie. Frowning, Kathy turned and cocked her ear toward the faint sounds.

"Tiki? Do you hear that? Who's crying?" she asked as she patted the little girl's bow mouth with a napkin.

"Oh, that's Sophie. She cries all the time."

"Really? Can you show me where Sophie's bedroom is?"

Tiki scooted off her chair and over to a door on the other side of the room. "Sure!"

Kathy followed, keeping her expression neutral.

"Sophie's here," she said, stretching and pushing open the door. Tiki then ran across the hall and stood proudly in front of another door.

"This is *my* room!" The girl bounded inside.

Peeking in, Kathy smiled and said, "Yes, it is. And a very nice room it is." It was a simple room with a twin bed, one window with iron bars across it and lots of toys, especially blond-haired Barbie dolls scattered helterskelter across the freshly made bed. Kathy made a mental note to teach Tiki about taking responsibility for her bedroom.

In Kathy's opinion, the room was nondescript. Tiki didn't have personal identification with her room. What did she like? What were her favorite colors? Tucking those questions away, Kathy turned and walked back across the hall to the door where the crying was coming from. At the end of the short corridor was another camera high on the ceiling.

"Let's knock gently on Sophie's door, shall we?" she asked.

"Sure!" Tiki moved to the door. "She's always sad." She knocked politely on the door. The sobbing continued.

"Really?" Kathy didn't dare let on she knew about the kidnapping. "Why is that, Tiki?" Kathy opened the door to Sophie's room.

Tiki moved inside, looking worried. "They took her away from her mama and papa."

"Oh?" Kathy feigned surprise as she walked into the room. There, on a twin bed near the window, sat little blond-haired Sophie. She was dressed in a crumpled white nightgown, her long hair uncombed and hanging in snarls about her shoulders. Instantly, Kathy's heart went out to the child whose eyes were red and swollen from crying.

"Get out!" Sophie shrilled at them. She raised her hands and made a dismissing motion. "Go away! I don't want you in here, Tiki!"

Crouching down, Kathy brought Tiki into her arms. "Do you want to go rock on your horsey for a while? Let me get Sophie dressed. I'll join you in a few minutes. Okay?"

Nodding, Tiki looked worriedly at Sophie. "She cries all the time, Dolly."

Kathy knew that to Tiki she would always be Dolly. That was fine. Smiling gently, she smoothed some of Tiki's dark bangs away from her scrunched up brows. "Let me talk with Sophie and let's see if we can help her. It's always good to try and help others, Tiki."

"Okay." Tiki moved out of her arms and went back to her play area.

Kathy scanned the room and saw another damnable video camera. She would have to be careful how she spoke to Sophie. Slowly rising to her full height and wiping her damp palms against her slacks, Kathy moved toward the bed and halted a few feet away from the child.

"Hi, Sophie. My name is Katherine Lincoln. I take care of Tiki. Is there anything I can do to help you?"

Sophie glared up at her and wiped her cheeks with quick, angry swipes. "No! I hate you! I hate all of you!"

Kathy saw the fear and deep sadness in the child's blue eyes. "Do you mind if I sit here for a moment, Sophie?" She patted the end of her unmade bed. Sophie must have awakened earlier, but stayed in her room, crying. That broke Kathy's heart.

"I don't care," Sophie muttered defiantly.

Kathy sat down on the bed. "It's 10:00 a.m., Sophie. Would you like me to help you get dressed for the day? Or do you like wearing your nightgown all the time?"

Looking down, Sophie touched the wrinkled white material. "I don't care . . . I don't care. . . ."

"If I choose something from your dresser over there, can I help you get changed?" Kathy pointed to the beautiful antique dresser made out of burnished teak.

Shrugging, Sophie whispered, "I don't care. . . ."

Kathy eased off the bed and walked over to the dresser. From the drawers she chose a pair of denim coveralls and a bright yellow T-shirt. Kathy found a pair of orange socks and white tennis shoes and came back over to the bed.

"Do you want to dress by yourself, Sophie? Or do you want me to help you?" Her heart bled for the girl, who was obviously suffering deeply from the kidnapping. Was this how her older brother, Jason, had felt? Sophie was depressed, her hair unkempt, her face swollen from constant crying. Had Jason pined away like this in that villa in Hawaii? Had he cried endlessly like Sophie? He rarely talked about that time in his life, and now Kathy was having her eyes opened as to what he'd endured.

"I can do it," Sophie muttered, and pulled the clothes from her hand. "My mommy taught me how to dress."

"Good," Kathy said. She watched as Sophie got rid of the nightgown. Alarmed at how thin the girl was, with every rib pronounced, Kathy gulped. She kept her tone reasonable and soft. "Are you hungry, Sophie?"

"No." She quickly put on the T-shirt, shimmied into the coveralls and pulled the ankle socks on her feet.

Kathy handed her each small tennis shoe, which she diligently put on. She even tied the strings into a nice, neat little bow.

"Would you like me to fix your hair?" Kathy asked. She got a brush from the bathroom.

Shrugging, Sophie sat on the edge of the bed, her long legs dangling over it. "I don't care."

Seeing just a glimmer of light in the child's blue eyes, Kathy smiled and gently sat down next to her. "Well, I think you're a very beautiful young girl and if you'll let me, I'll put your hair into braids." Sophie had long, fine blond hair.

"Tiki always pulls my hair. And it hurts."

Kathy carefully began to brush out the

snarls in Sophie's hair. "She does?"

"Yes, she likes my blond hair. She keeps trying to pull it out and put it on her own head. I keep telling her she'll never have my color of hair."

"I see," Kathy said. Little by little, Sophie was warming up to her. "Maybe she's just trying to make friends with you."

"But she hurts me. That's why I stay in here. I don't want her pulling my hair." Sniffing, Sophie wailed, "I want to go home. I miss my mommy and daddy. Why won't they let me go home?" The child buried her face in her small hands and sobbed.

Heart breaking, Kathy brought Sophie into her arms and rocked her back and forth. She couldn't say anything that would give away her mission and she was afraid the guards might see the contempt in her expression. Closing her eyes, Kathy held the sobbing girl until she calmed down. Once she'd dried Sophie's tears, she continued to work on her hair until it was straight and unsnarled. She set the brush aside and made a single braid down the back of her head. Then she arranged it on top of her head with a barrette.

"There, I think we have your hair up," Kathy said with a slight laugh. "Go over to the mirror and look, Sophie. Tell me what you think."

Sliding off the bed, the girl dejectedly did as requested. She looked at herself in the mirror and shrugged. "It looks okay. Thanks."

Kathy got off the bed and went over to her. "Are you ready for an adventure, Sophie?"

"Adventure?" she asked, looking up at her.

"Sure. I have an idea, but I need you and Tiki to help me with it. Are you game? Do you want to play?"

"Well, Tiki will pull my hair and it hurts."

"No, she won't," Kathy promised with a smile. "I won't let her, okay?"

Standing there, Sophie looked around. She held on to Kathy's hand a little more tightly. "You're different."

"Oh?" Kathy saw hope suddenly burn in Sophie's eyes, the sadness replaced.

"The other lady didn't care if I sat in here all day. She just left me alone. A man would bring in the meals, but I didn't feel like eating."

"I see," Kathy murmured. "Well, that's over now. Come on. Let's pick up Tiki and go on our adventure, okay?" She saw the

259

girl's blue eyes clear of the ever-present tears. As she slowly drew Sophie out of the bedroom and down the hall, Kathy felt her heart wrench with anger and sadness over the child's abduction. Compressing her lips, she dipped her head to hide her expression. This mission wasn't turning out anything like she'd planned. It was out of her control and heading in directions she'd never thought possible.

When Kathy appeared in the immaculate kitchen, the head chef, a Frenchman by the name of Denis Franchot, hurried up to her. He had a look of stunned disbelief and wariness written across his thin, narrow face.

"Mademoiselle?" he queried. "How may I or my staff help you?" Distrustfully, he eyed Tiki, who stood at Kathy's side.

Thankful for her years of studying French, Kathy introduced herself and the two girls in the chef's native tongue. "Chef Franchot, I need your help with my two charges. I would like to go through your refrigerators with them and find out what kinds of food they like or don't like."

"But you speak flawless French!" the chef declared.

"Thank you," Kathy said, smiling.

"You're very kind to say so." She looked at the girls. "Chef Franchot, I'm sure you know they aren't eating much, but I have an idea of how to get them to eat more, with your help, of course."

She saw the chef's eyes light up with joy. "*Oui,* but of course, *mademoiselle!* I, too, am worried about them. I have tried everything, but they have turned it away." He gave a very French shrug, but seemed genuinely concerned.

Kathy knew the French felt their cooking was the best in the world. "I'm sure you have done everything you could. I've tasted your cooking and I've loved it."

The chef glowed over her compliment and bowed his head. "Thank you, *mademoiselle.* Those are words that make my heart sing. I live to create beautiful food that makes people joyous to consume it."

"May we sit at one of the tables where you chop up your veggies?"

"But of course!" Chef Franchot snapped his fingers. Instantly, servants hurried over to find three chairs for them. In moments, Kathy had the girls positioned at the wooden table. The sous-chefs moved to another part of the kitchen, where they prepared lunch and the evening meal. Once they had the space to themselves,

Kathy opened one of the walk-in refrigerators and retrieved some vegetables.

"Okay, girls," she told them, "this is our adventure." She spread at least ten different vegetables in front of them. "Now, since I'm new here, I need to know what you do and don't like. Tiki, you first. You take the veggies that you like and put them in front of you."

Grinning, Tiki quickly grabbed a few. "I like this game!"

"I do, too." Kathy turned to Sophie. "Your turn."

Sophie glumly chose five other vegetables.

Kathy wrote down all the information in a small notebook she carried in her pocket. After asking the servants to return the veggies to the refrigerator, Kathy went and retrieved several kinds of fresh fruit. She laid them out on the table. This time, Tiki didn't wait. She quickly lined up four of them in front of her and gave Kathy a glowing look of triumph. "These are mine! I like these!"

"Very good," Kathy exclaimed, writing them down. "Your turn, Sophie."

Sophie nodded and delicately picked out her favorites.

By the end of a half hour, Kathy had all the staff in the kitchen assisting her with smiles and laughter. The two little girls, who were the stars of this adventure, loved the attention from the staff. Even Chef Franchot came over with an armload of spices and joined them. Kathy praised him for his idea and Franchot glowed.

Kathy had each girl open a spice jar and smell it. If they liked the fragrance, they kept it in front of them. If they didn't, they placed the bottle in the center of the table. Further inspired by the fun, one of the sous-chefs, a Frenchman named Philippe, brought over a large tray filled with different garnishes. Tiki squealed with delight over the rainbow of colors on the plate. Sophie even took some interest as the sous-chef placed it with dramatic grace on the table between them. Both girls eagerly picked their favorites from the plate, and Kathy recorded the information.

Next came drinks. Kathy instructed the servants to bring over small paper cups filled with a beverage, so each girl could sip and choose. Tiki giggled nonstop, completely wrapped up in the adventure. Sophie gave Kathy a hopeful smile, which made her day.

"No one has ever done this before," the chef confided excitedly to Kathy after she'd helped the children off the chairs.

"These girls need to eat more," she told him.

"*Oui,* this is true. And it has been a great concern to all of us, especially the *patrón.*"

Kathy could read between the lines on that one. She was sure the chef was worried that, one day, Garcia would kill him if he didn't get Tiki to eat. "I think I have a way to get them to eat, sir, but I'll need your help." Kathy smiled. "I hope my idea will inspire the girls to *want* to eat their meals."

"Ohh," Franchot whispered, "if you can perform such a miracle, *mademoiselle,* I will thank you endlessly from the bottom of my heart."

Kathy was sure he would. "Once I get the girls back to the playroom, I'll come show you what to fix for their dinner tonight."

For the evening meal, as well as the others, Kathy knew that the girls ate in their part of the villa, while the adults supped in another part. It was 8:00 p.m., the day nearly gone, as she worked with the kitchen staff. After finding out Tiki's favorite colors, Kathy had gone in search of a seamstress earlier today to create a brightly colored tablecloth for the table. The orange, red and yellow were bright, happy colors. Tiki, particularly, was excited about the upcoming meal because Kathy had bet both girls that they would want to eat all the food on their plates.

Once Tiki and Sophie were seated, with white linen napkins in their laps, Kathy signaled for Mateo, their server, to bring in the meals. Grinning, the male staffer pushed the dinner cart to the table. Two huge silver hoods covered the plates, which increased the level of anticipation. Kathy chuckled as she witnessed both girls growing impatient.

"Quick!" Tiki said, pointing to the cart. "Let me see!"

Kathy nodded her thanks to Mateo, took the plate and set it in front of the girl. "Okay, here you go. One of your favorite meals — spaghetti!" Kathy lifted off the silver hood with a flourish.

Tiki gasped and clapped. She instantly grabbed her fork and dug in to her meal. The chef had created a round hamburger patty with red marinara sauce. To add some fun, he had placed two green olives for eyes and a strand of spaghetti for a smile. For hair, the chef had used more spaghetti. The effect was cute and dramatic.

Kathy brought Sophie's dinner to her

and lifted the hood. The sad little girl perked up.

"Wow! This is cool!" Sophie picked up her own fork. Kathy had learned that she hated hamburger but loved roast beef. The sous-chef had created a horse head of sliced beef, kernels of yellow corn for the forelock and mane, a black olive for an eye and a ring of mashed potatoes with red pimentos as a flower wreath around the horse's neck.

The staffer and Kathy smiled at each other as they placed the hoods back on the cart.

"Would you go ahead and serve their milk, Mateo?" Kathy asked him.

Kathy knew that neither girl liked milk. And of course, growing children needed calcium for strong bones. She'd consulted with Philippe, the sous-chef, and he had made chocolate milk with a bit of whipped cream and a cherry on top. When Mateo set the drinks in front of them, both girls grabbed their glasses and started drinking.

Kathy watched them and felt a deep contentment. "Well?" she said to Tiki. "What do you think? Did Chef Franchot do good or what?" Tiki looked, her mouth full, and tried to talk. Kathy smiled. "It's okay, Tiki, one doesn't speak with food in their mouth. Just say yes or no." Tiki nodded dramatically.

The server seemed stunned as the girls rapidly gulped down their food.

"Please tell Chef Franchot and his staff that they did well," Kathy said.

"Oh, I will, Señorita Lincoln. I will! This is wonderful!"

"And you'll bring dessert, Mateo?"

"Of course, Señorita Lincoln. Right away." He wheeled the cart out of the room.

Pleased, Kathy watched as the children scarfed down every last morsel on their plates. She breathed a sigh of relief that Sophie had eaten. Careful not to lavish more attention on her than Tiki, Kathy operated like an airport control tower between them, training each in the use of cutlery.

When dessert arrived, something healthy instead of junk food, Kathy crossed her fingers that the girls would like her idea. She'd had the dessert sous-chef, Gregoire, create a parfait made of fresh guava and whipped cream. On top of each flute was a thin slice of kiwi fruit with two eyes made from half a cherry and a smile created with tiny chocolate sprinkles. Kathy wasn't going to deny Tiki junk food completely, but she sure was going to control her intake of it!

On Sophie's dessert, the "face" on top of the parfait was half a slice of orange with red cherry eyes and white chocolate sprinkles for a smile. Sophie smiled — again — and looked up at Kathy. There was such gratitude in the girl's expression that Kathy felt her heart tug in her chest. Thank God. Kathy swore she would try to make Sophie's time here as easy as possible.

Within ten minutes, the girls had consumed their desserts and their milk.

"This is *fun!* What will I have tomorrow for breakfast, Dolly?" Tiki burped and happily laughed.

"Oh," Kathy chortled, "that's a surprise, Tiki!" She sat there, a warm glow in her heart for these two little girls. There was such an affectionate look shared between them with Kathy that she felt an incredible pride in both girls who deserved to be unequivocally loved.

Chapter Fourteen

"In the four months you have been with us, Señorita Kathy, you have been a miracle worker," Carlos Garcia gushed as he pulled out the leather chair for her.

Kathy sat down. She hadn't expected to spend four months infiltrating this place, but that's exactly what it had taken. She'd discovered Garcia and Therese were like wolves — always wary of outsiders. And she'd needed the four months to break down those barriers and get them to accept her. She felt they had, but maybe she was wrong. It was unusual that Garcia would call her in like this unexpectedly. Sweat began to form on her brow.

"Excuse me, sir? How have I helped?" Instantly, Kathy went on guard, hoping her cover hadn't been blown. After situating himself behind his desk, Garcia snipped the end of his Cuban cigar, then lit it. He took a few puffs, pulled it out from between his lips and gave Kathy a glittering smile. "My darling Tiki is fifteen pounds heavier and has grown a full inch! Her pediatric doctor in Cuzco just called me with this news. He is very happy, and I am ecstatic! For so long we've taken her to specialists, the best in the world, and they all said her problem was genetic. Bah!" He waved his hand, anger in his tone. "And you come here and feed her 'funny food' as she calls it. She has gained weight and now is considered within the normal range for her age group. I am very pleased with you, *señorita.* You have surpassed all my expectations."

Well, at least he didn't know she was a mole. Relief flowed through Kathy. "Thank you, *Patrón,*" she said as she looked down at her tightly clasped hands.

She had to restrain herself with regard to Sophie's plight. Having seen too many examples of Garcia's manic-depressive states with others, Kathy avoided him as much as possible. She knew his routine by now. Every night at bedtime he visited Tiki's room and read her a chapter from her favorite books, Harry Potter's adventures. There was no question in Kathy's mind that Garcia loved his daughter. He would pop in from time to time during the day, spend five or ten minutes with her before he had to rush off to an appointment — with another drug lord, she was sure.

"I want to reward you, *señorita.* I reward people who do well," Garcia said now.

Kathy sat up a little straighter. "Sir?"

"Therese speaks highly of you," he said with a flourish of his hand and a contented puff of his cigar. "Therese told me that you do little things for her to help out in the office. She's very appreciative that you are something of a computer geek." He grinned, flashing his perfect white teeth. "She knows PCs. The secretary ordered a Macintosh, so she is at her wit's end, as you can imagine. Your knowledge of Macs has relieved her greatly."

If he only knew she was gathering information about his drug operation! And Therese's office was the only place in the villa that did not have a damnable video camera, insofar as Kathy could tell. "My family has a work ethic, *Patrón.* Many times when Tiki is napping in the afternoon I have nothing else to do. I once saw Señorita Therese in tears in front of her Mac, so I thought I'd ask if I could help her out."

Kathy had used her skill to find certain files, but they were protected with a password. Nevertheless, she was determined to bring down Garcia in any way possible. Some nights, when everyone was asleep, she would sneak back to Therese's office with her key. She would run passwords, but so far had had no luck breaking in. It was only a matter of time. . . .

"*Sí*, you are very helpful, *señorita*, and that is why I am going to reward you!" Garcia leaned back and rocked in his burgundy leather chair. "Therese will look after Tiki for the next twenty-four hours. I have ordered Señor Coulter to fly you to Cuzco. There is a reservation at the five-star Liberator Hotel for you — in their presidential suite. When you go there, you will want for nothing. I have the finest of champagne waiting for you." He grinned and sat up straight.

"I have given Señor Coulter instructions to take you to the finest, most expensive stores in Cuzco to buy yourself something you've always wanted but could never afford. And be willing to buy your dream, *señorita*. If you love diamonds and have always hungered for a diamond bracelet that cost fifty thousand soles, then buy it! Whatever you desire, it is yours. Do not be afraid to spend the money." He chuckled. "My Therese does it all the time. She wears the finest designer clothes. Señor Coulter knows where these shops are located because he flies her to and from

Cuzco for shopping sprees."

"Well, why, sir . . ." She was stunned by his generosity, but then, it was dirty money. Money gotten from drug addicts. "I really am not a clotheshorse, *Patrón.*"

"No? Then jewelry?"

"Well . . ." Kathy opened her hands and gave him a forced smile, "I come from a poor family, *Patrón.* I am happy with my life and I'm certainly happy with what you pay me for a salary."

"Humph! You are beautiful! You should be dressed in beautiful fabrics! Men should be swooning at your feet! Here in South America, romance is alive and flourishing! Well, enough of this," he muttered, standing. "Come! I have had your servant pack you an overnight bag with only the essentials. You must buy yourself some new clothes. I have ordered Señor Coulter to take you to the finest of restaurants tonight, and then you two can dance the night away."

Speechless, Kathy stood up. At all costs, she wanted to avoid Garcia's outstretched hand, so she moved quickly to the door and opened it. His hand came to rest on the small of her back, which made her flesh turn cold. *Never* did she want Garcia to touch her! It took everything she had to let herself be escorted by him to the foyer. Her mood lifted, however, when she heard the Bell helicopter warming up outside.

"Enjoy your reward, *señorita*. Therese will look after the girls while you are away, so do not worry about them. We will see you here tomorrow, at this time." He waved goodbye to her as the servant picked up her small suitcase and ushered her to the helicopter.

As she left, Carlos leaned back and smiled, very pleased with himself. Yes, Therese was correct: it was time Mac Coulter had romance in his life. And why not Kathy Lincoln? After all, they both worked for him. A little matchmaking to bring them together had been Therese's idea, and it was a brilliant stroke of genius. Carlos didn't like to see Mac, someone he liked, being alone. No, a man needed a woman. And Katherine Lincoln was certainly comely. Carlos had more than once seen Mac steal discreet glances in her direction.

Rubbing his hands together, Garcia chuckled indulgently. Maybe he was an incurable romantic, but he'd rather be that than the opposite: cold and uncaring. In South America, a man had to have a woman to take care of him, love him and support his goals. Mac Coulter needed such a woman.

From the frying pan into the fire. Kathy battled nausea stemming from the overwhelming desire to strike Garcia in the face with a killing blow. She could have done it, but death would be too quick and easy. No, she wanted to take Tiki from him. The girl was his Achilles' Heel and the thought of kidnapping her calmed some of Kathy's bloodlust. Or did it? Not a day went by when she didn't feel conflicted about her intention to kidnap Tiki. Her conscience ate at her. How could she hurt an innocent child? She would be just as heinous as those who had stolen Jason from his family. Right now, Kathy wasn't sure about anything and felt suspended in a hellish kind of limbo.

As she walked toward the landing pad, her heart began to pound. A servant opened the door on the left side of the helicopter and Kathy climbed in. In the last four months she hadn't seen much of Mac Coulter except when work brought them together. But when she bumped into him she saw the longing for her in his eyes even though he kept his distance, much to her relief.

Of course, Kathy still thought about Mac, still felt the pull of her silly heart toward him. And now she was being thrown into his arms by Garcia! She shook her head and wondered what twisted karma had placed Mac on her path. Of all the things she could have anticipated happening, romance wasn't one of them.

Oh, there were times when Kathy longed to be with Mac. Even though he worked for a drug dealer, he was an American like her. They were both far from home and living on the edge. She tried to convince herself that their attraction was nothing more than needing a friend to talk with. *Yeah, right.*

Mac adjusted his earphones and mike, then nodded curtly in her direction. Because he had on his aviator sunglasses, she couldn't read the expression in his eyes. Did he still want her? Was he angry that he had to take this special trip with her?

Kathy nodded back to Mac and climbed into the harness. He handed her the other set of earphones, and she slipped them on. Once the servant put the bag in the back and slid the door shut, Kathy couldn't help but sense the finality in the moment. It was as if she were in a prison. Well, wasn't she? From the cockpit window, she watched as the mechanic, a Quero Indian, held up his hands in a signal for Mac to take off. The chocks had been removed. The Bell powered up, shaking and vibrating around her.

"Well, you're Cinderella for twenty-four hours," Mac said wryly as he lifted the bird off the concrete landing pad and up over the jungle. He tried to sound professional and unemotional about their journey. He didn't know whether to be thrilled or depressed that Garcia had hinted broadly that Kathy should become his lover during their stay in Cuzco. Mac's loco heart jumped up and down for joy over the idea, but he tried to remain low-key about it. He'd never been able to erase Kathy from his heart or his feelings no matter how hard he tried. Now Garcia had thrown them together like some imperial matchmaker. *Damn.* How was Mac going to keep his distance from her? "Patrón Garcia has ordered me to entertain you for a day and a night in Cuzco. Congratulations."

His smile was sincere even if she couldn't see his eyes. Just being this close to Mac made her heart race, and it wasn't due to panic. Except that she couldn't develop a relationship in the middle of this spy game, which made her sweat every day she was here. One mistake could get her killed before she met her objective.

"Thanks, I think. I'm stunned, to tell you the truth, eh?" From time to time, Kathy made damn sure she added that little Canadian expression to ensure her cover. "And I'm sorry you got thrown into this."

"I'm not." To hell with it, Mac was going to be honest with her whether she liked it or not.

Great. Kathy compressed her lips and hoped to escape the tension by looking out over the green, rolling jungle. Above them the usual morning blanket of gray, thick clouds stretched across the sky. Rain began to fall, pelting the helicopter as Mac headed toward the mountain range in the distance.

She enjoyed the shaking and shuddering of the helicopter. How much she missed flying! There were so many times when she yearned to walk out to that helipad, climb into the chopper and take off. Gazing at the sky gave her clarity of thought, and being up in it made her feel safe.

"I imagine this is a day off for you and that's why you're not completely un-happy about the assignment?" Kathy ner-vously brushed back strands of hair that had dipped across her brow. She settled the microphone more closely to her lips, and sneaked a peek at Mac's profile as he flew. He still had that cockeyed grin. What was so funny?

"From the way Tiki was coming around, I figured the *patrón* would reward you lavishly sooner or later. You've done some nice work with that little kid. And Sophie's happier, too. You deserve this, so enjoy your day away," Mac said as his heart wrenched hard in his chest. He'd already contacted his handler in Lima about recovering Sophie, but nothing could be done. Not one breath of Sophie's whereabouts, even the fact that she was alive, could be divulged to the parents. Mac hated that verdict because he could only imagine what torture her parents were suffering — the grief, the wretchedness of losing a child — and she was alive. He tried to think of another way to get Sophie out of the villa, but struck out. It always came back to the same thing: any rescue attempt would blow his cover. And he was getting too close to Garcia to jeopardize his mission. All he needed were a couple more months and then, maybe, he could blow the joint with the information the DEA needed to bust Garcia once and for all . . . and Sophie would escape with him.

"I don't want to spend Señor Garcia's money," Kathy said fretfully, rubbing her brow.

Mac glanced to his left and saw the stormy look in her eyes. She looked like a winsome college girl, given her choice of clothing. Her only jewelry was the small pearl earrings in her delicate lobes. "Why not? You've earned it."

"Because." Kathy didn't dare say another word. Mac was in league with the devil. Yet being this close to the guy made her melt into a puddle. He had that damnable boyish smile that made her happy whenever he bestowed it upon her. And she liked the intimate, husky quality of his voice.

At least once a month, he had flown her to Cuzco with Tiki to visit a dentist or doctor or to buy the little girl some clothes. That was about all the contact she'd had with him. Oh, he was busy, that was for sure. On a daily basis, Coulter ferried men in expensive Italian suits from Cuzco to see Garcia at the villa. And Kathy knew they were all drug dealers. She had finally found a list of their names on Therese's computer, had made a disk and had it hidden in Tiki's playroom where no one would find it — she hoped.

"I like days like this," Mac murmured, looking around for other air traffic. There were two helicopter services near Machu Picchu that flew tourists up for a grand view of the area. "This is what I call a 'play day.'" He glanced at Kathy, who was frowning deeply. "You do like to play, don't you?" He grinned wickedly.

"I don't like taking the *patrón's* money," Kathy choked out. She gripped her hands so hard that her knuckles whitened. This time alone with Mac was *not* going to be easy.

"He's a generous man to some," Mac said, resuming scanning the sky. "You're on his good list, so enjoy the status."

Kathy snorted. "Yeah, I've seen him with people on the other list."

"Umm, yeah, I know what you mean. He can lose his temper pretty easily."

"He's manic-depressive."

"Yes, he is. I think I heard Therese say that one time. I'm not a doctor, but I've flown for him for over a year and have probably seen most of his moods."

This was the most Coulter had ever divulged to her. Whose side was he on? Giving him a quick, sharp glance, Kathy said nothing. Usually, no one at the villa breathed a word about Garcia for fear he'd kill them or at the least have a monumental temper tantrum, strike them across the face and humiliate them in front of everyone. Kathy lived in dread of having that happen to her. But she wouldn't take it lying down. She'd fight back, even if by doing so, she'd blow her cover.

"Well, you can drop me off at the hotel and be on your way," she told him grimly. "I'm not shopping for clothes, jewels or anything else."

"I see."

She heard the humor in his tone. Giving him a different look she said, "This isn't funny, Mr. Coulter. I'm *not* taking his money!"

"Calm down, Kathy. I have a plan you just might agree to," Mac said gently.

"What are you talking about?" Kathy was breathing hard, her feelings raw. This man bedeviled her!

"I happen to know of a little Catholic orphanage known as Santa Maria's Home for the Poor on the edge of Cuzco. They're always appreciative of receiving food, clothes, shoes and things like that for the children." He smiled, turned and held her mutinous blue gaze. "Wouldn't you like to spend a small fortune on them? We could buy these kids things they need, including school supplies. The sisters are school-teachers and always need paper, pencils, crayons and other stuff. I happen to know the shops where we can get them. We could have it all delivered to the nuns who run it. How does that sound?"

"I can't figure you out. Are you a devil or an angel, Coulter?"

Laughing, Mac shrugged. "Hey, I'm just trying to make you happy. That's what the *patrón* ordered me to do. He didn't specify *how*, only that you should come back to the villa tomorrow morning with a smile on your face."

"I see." Kathy rubbed her brow. "Will he be pissed off if I buy things for the orphanage?"

"I doubt it. He's Peruvian. He donates a lot of money to his favorite charities in Lima, so he would understand your inclinations. Probably expects it of you." Mac smiled again.

"He doesn't know me *that* well."

"The *patrón* is a man who lives or dies by knowing the company he keeps." Mac bit back the rest. It was too easy to confide in Kathy Lincoln. There was just something special about her that opened his soul and made him want to trust her. But he shouldn't do that.

Groaning, Kathy threw up her hands. "Okay, okay, I can certainly spend his money for kids who have nothing."

"Great," Mac exclaimed. "We've got a deal, then." He picked up his cell phone and punched the automatic redial. After taking off his earphones, he made a call to Cuzco.

Kathy couldn't hear him because of the earphones she wore. Plus, the noise in the cabin was so high that even if she'd taken them off, it would have done no good. But just looking at the dazzling smile on Mac's face as he talked, the ruddiness coming to his recently shaved cheeks, made her think that whoever he was talking to was someone he liked a great deal. Maybe he was calling a girlfriend in town? After all, he might have to escort Kathy around, but he wasn't sharing the suite with her. He'd have to go somewhere else for the night. Kathy didn't like the jealous feeling that flowed through her as he talked on the phone.

Of course he has a woman, you dolt. He's a damn good-looking man. Respectful of women. Says all the right things to them. He's engaging. Has a great sense of humor. Isn't stuck on himself.

Yeah, Mac Coulter was definitely a catch. This guy seemed perfect, if not for the fact he knowingly worked for a drug lord. Still, as Kathy rubbed the area of her heart with her fingers, she felt the acid sensation of jealousy eating at her. Her attraction to him had just tripled.

Mac flipped the lid down and tucked the cell phone back in his pocket. Once he put on his headphones, he adjusted the mike close to his lips. "Okay, it's settled."

"What's settled?" The date with his girlfriend? A bed to lie in? Making love to a woman who was undoubtedly Latin, hot, sensuous and stunningly beautiful?

"The French nuns who run this orphanage. I was talking to Sister Bridget. She's in her sixties," he said. "I told her we're flying in and to start expecting truckloads of stuff rolling up to their doors by late this afternoon. I asked her what they really needed and she said shoes."

"Oh . . ." Kathy felt mortified. So much for the green-eyed monster in her! Mac's voice was buoyant with joy. She saw it in the curve of his beautiful male mouth, which now beckoned so much more strongly to her. "I thought . . . well, if you want the truth, I thought you were calling your significant other."

Mac glanced over at her. They were climbing to thirteen thousand feet now, the helicopter straining as the blades searched for oxygen. "There's no one in my life right now," he told her, his tone serious. He thought he'd made that clear right after she'd returned from her trip through the jungle. Now the look in her eyes was a surprise to him. She seemed absolutely thrilled to hear that he was single. Why?

And then Mac realized that even though four months had passed, she was still just as drawn to him as he was to her. That wasn't good news and he knew it. But the smoky gaze she turned on him was clearly decipherable: Kathy liked him.

She was forbidden fruit to him. Off-limits. As an undercover agent, he didn't want any serious relationship with a woman. No way. And yet, as he drowned in those china-blue eyes of hers, Mac could feel the walls of his resolve crumbling. He was in big trouble. . . .

Chapter Fifteen

"Well, are you pleased with your shopping spree so far?" Mac asked as their chauffeur drove them away from the orphanage. The Quero driver, Luis, turned onto a side street and headed toward the Liberator Hotel.

Kathy pushed several strands of her hair off her brow and smiled. "Very pleased. I'm afraid I'm not one of those women who enjoys shopping till she drops." She sat back and relaxed on the soft burgundy leather seat of their sumptuous black Mercedes. They zoomed across the city to the Plaza de Armas, the central square of Cuzco. The hotel was located a couple of blocks away from the busy center.

It was nearly dusk and Cuzco, a city of cobblestone streets and stone buildings created by the hands of the Incas, glowed in the rosy light of the setting sun. Ancient gray monuments, mostly temples, stood alongside more modern buildings. This was a place of Catholic churches as well, their spires rising higher than anything else in the city.

Mac absorbed the look on Kathy's face. When they'd landed this morning, he'd had Luis take them to several children's stores in the city. Kathy rung up a whopping ten thousand dollar bill on shoes, clothes and school supplies by the time she was done. She'd obviously attacked this project with a fierce passion.

"You're really good with kids," he said. "I don't know who liked you more — them or the nuns who run the orphanage." Kathy still looked radiant. Children made her laugh and smile, and this was the first time Mac had had this kind of one-on-one with her since her arrival four months ago. The experience was exhilarating for him and made it obvious to him how lonely he was without a vibrant woman like Kathy in his life. Yet he had to resist her.

"Thanks. I love kids." She studied her hands as she splayed them out in front of her. "Phew, I'm looking forward to a hot bath. I'm grimy!"

The orphanage was huge, with too few nuns to manage the numbers of children. They came off the streets of Cuzco, everything from day-old babies to teenagers. The building was an old Inca structure with beautifully carved stone walls, but it was drafty and dust constantly filtered in from the city.

"You'll have a whirlpool bath in your suite. I think you'll like your digs at the hotel," Mac said with a knowing grin. He watched as she took out a linen handkerchief from her leather purse and wiped off the worst of the offending dust from her hands. Beautiful, long hands.

Mac wondered what it would feel like if she touched his body in heated exploration. All day long as he'd shopped with Kathy for the orphanage, he couldn't get her out of his mind — or heart. She was like a child with the children, and now he understood why Tiki and Sophie both gravitated to her, why they'd flourished in her warm care. The word *nurturing* had been invented for her, Mac thought. And it all seemed to come naturally to her.

One of the many drawbacks to his undercover work was that he found himself starving for a woman's genuine attention. It had been over a year since he'd had female companionship. Not that he wanted one-night stands. No, he wasn't cut out for that emotionally, he knew. What he craved was a real relationship — someone he could confide in, hold, and in his darkest hours of suffering, someone who would hold him.

Kathy Lincoln represented all those possibilities to him. Mac knew that, more than ever, he had to be careful. Above all, he couldn't risk getting involved with anyone at the estate or in Garcia's employ, even though the *patrón* had just given him the green light to do just that: pursue her.

Mac wondered again if she was a mole, someone planted by Garcia to check on the rest of the employees and report back to him.

Yet, when he looked into her eyes, he saw innocence. He wondered how he could suspect her at all. Coulter knew that the best spies in the business appeared exactly like Kathy — above suspicion. Their looks belied their real purpose. And somewhere in his deepest instincts, he sensed Kathy Lincoln had an ulterior motive for being at the villa. She hadn't shown up here by accident. So what was her real reason for coming to Garcia's villa?

Luis pulled the Mercedes up to the stone lobby of the Liberator Hotel, where flags of many nations waved in the breeze. Mac got out and held out his hand to Kathy. She gave him a warm smile and reached for it. He was delighted as her long fingers slid into his. Her hand was strong, nourishing his starved heart with even this brief contact. A rush of desire flowed hotly through him as he helped her out of the car. The doorman, dressed in a green uniform with gold braid and a garrison cap, nodded and opened the doors for them. Mac reluctantly released Kathy's hand and ushered her inside the huge, airy lobby.

Kathy was instantly taken with the Incan architecture within the hotel, not to mention the brightly colored orchids and bromeliads. At the center of the lobby was a huge silver samovar to serve coca leaf tea to arriving visitors. Incans had chewed the leaves for thousands of years to stop altitude sickness. With Cuzco so high in the Andes, people not yet acclimated to the elevation always got some form of the sickness unless they drank the tea.

Mac went over and poured her some, handing her the cup. "It's good and it will stop you from coming down with high-altitude symptoms," he told her. "You stay here and I'll get you checked in." He motioned to the plush, expensive leather couches that lined either side of the tea service.

The coca leaf tea tasted somewhat bland, Kathy found, but not unpleasant. Her gaze never left Mac, who moved like a military pilot. Well, hadn't he been? She could spot her own type anywhere. She had a thousand questions for him. Maybe tonight, over dinner, she could ask some of them.

Every time she looked at Mac, she had to remember to paste the label Drug Dealer all over him. It was tough to do, especially after today. If Mac Coulter was the bad guy Kathy kept telling herself he was, why had he detoured her shopping spree to children in need? That showed he had a heart. And it was obvious to Kathy that the nuns at the orphanage loved Mac. The children all called him "Papacita" and hung around him for a touch, a hug, a kiss on the noggin or a quick wrestling match. He even gave "horsey rides" to the youngest children, neighing and galloping around the room. How could she not like this guy?

In desperate turmoil, Kathy sipped her tea and watched well-heeled tourists enter the hotel. It was the only one like it in Cuzco and she heard German, Italian, French and British English as visitors strolled through the magnificent architecture of the lobby.

She turned her gaze back to Mac as he walked toward her, key in hand. He was definitely eye candy. His shoulders were broad and thrown back with confidence.

And his gray eyes, alive and dancing with warmth, made her heart beat heavily in her chest. Plus that mouth of his! God, would she ever get over it? Its seductive shape and that careless little-boy smile melted her resolve even more. Groaning internally, Kathy stood and placed the empty cup back on the tea service table.

"Okay, Cinderella, your palace awaits." Mac cupped her elbow and walked her toward a bank of elevators at the rear of the hotel.

"I don't need a palace," Kathy protested. His hand was comforting on her elbow as they both strode out of the lobby. He was a little taller and that sense of protection radiated from him.

"Well, tonight enjoy the good things life gives you, bright angel." Mac caught himself. *Damn!* He'd slipped — again! What was wrong with him? He gave her a quick glance out the corner of his eye and saw her blue eyes widen. Then Kathy flushed. *Great.* He'd just embarrassed her.

"Sorry, I get carried away at times," he murmured, guiding her to the right and down a highly polished stone hall toward the elevators.

"Do you call all women by that name?" Kathy asked a little breathlessly. Panic rifled through her because he'd kept his distance until now. Kathy was more afraid of her responding to Mac than vice versa. All day she'd fought his nearness, the wild desire to reach out and touch him, to bathe in his sunlit smile. She carefully pulled out of his grasp as they waited for the next elevator.

"No, not really," Mac said, running his fingers through his dark hair. "It must be high altitude sickness getting to me." He gave her a sheepish grin that he hoped she would take as an apology.

"Yeah, right. You're so full of it, Coulter," Kathy muttered.

Chuckling, he held up his hands in surrender. "Guilty on all counts, Ms. Lincoln. Will you forgive me?"

Kathy eyed him warily and tried to fight against her heart. "Yeah, I'll forgive you this one time." She headed into the elevator as it opened, and he followed at her heels. Turning around, she stared at the highly polished brass doors as they whooshed closed.

Mac smiled. "Thank you." As they sailed upward, he decided to move to a much safer topic. "The presidential suite is on the top of the hotel," he informed her. "A penthouse. Patrón Garcia uses it when he comes here."

"I see. Where will you be?" Kathy gave him a scalding look that spoke volumes: she'd be spending the night alone in the suite.

"Down on the third floor. Room 301. That's my assigned room when I have to stay here overnight and fly people from Cuzco up to the *patrón*'s villa. Because of the morning fog and hazardous mountain conditions, airlines usually fly in to Cuzco only in the afternoon."

"So you spend your fair share of time here?"

Shrugging, Mac said, "It's a place to sleep. Usually, I'm over at the orphanage helping out anytime I've got an hour or two to kill before a flight."

"I see. . . ." The doors opened and Kathy escaped down a sumptuous carpeted hall with colorful Peruvian rugs hanging on the walls. Mac moved ahead of her and opened the double white doors.

"You're home," he said and stepped aside. The hotel staff had already brought up her luggage, one suitcase. Mac quietly closed the doors as Kathy entered the palatial suite of rooms. In the foyer was a gleaming pink Italian marble table. An expensive burgundy hand-blown vase, filled to overflowing with a variety of tropical flowers, mostly vibrant and exotic orchid species, sat on the table and brightened her suite. The room smelled like spicy vanilla because of the orchids.

Gulping, Kathy looked around. The place was decorated in Italian renaissance, with filmy white drapes across the windows that showed off all of Cuzco. The small city sat in a cuplike valley surrounded by craggy brown mountains.

Kathy glanced over at a bottle of champagne cooling in a polished silver bowl filled with ice. Two fluted crystal glasses sat on the inlaid table.

"Wow . . ." she said.

"Impressive, isn't it?" Mac murmured, coming to her side. Kathy turned around, her eyes huge as she surveyed the lavish penthouse. And then Mac saw her frown.

"Not happy with the place? It's not bugged, by the way."

"Well . . ." Kathy whispered, running her fingers across the inlaid wood of the table to her right. "This is such a waste of money. When you look at those children in the orphanage and all those poor kids in rags on the streets of Cuzco, and then you look at this place . . ."

"Yeah," Mac said ruefully, "I know."

His eyes revealed something she'd not

seen before. What *was* that look? Anger? Frustration? Bitterness? She studied Mac in the quiet, which was broken by the splashing of a fountain in the corner.

"Do you know *who* you're working for?" Kathy demanded. Then she tensed. The words had exploded out of her mouth before her brain could censor them. *Oh, God!* The look of surprise on Mac's face disappeared quickly.

"Sure I do — a very rich Peruvian employer," he told her smoothly. Mac began to wonder who the hell Kathy really was, especially when he saw the shock in her eyes after she'd asked the question. What kind of game was she playing? "Do you know something I don't?" he asked playfully, while analyzing her facial expression. Obviously upset, she frowned and then brushed a few blond strands away from her cheek. He was glad that to his knowledge this suite was not bugged. If it had of been, she could be in a heap of trouble with Garcia. Kathy knew more about the *patrón* than she was letting on. And this was dangerous.

"Uh, no." What a fool she'd been! Her instinct told her Mac knew Garcia was a drug lord. That look he'd given her, one of sudden suspicion, made her feel as if she were on unsafe ground with him. *Oh, damn!* Why had she let her guard down? She was so incompetent at keeping up a facade! Why had she ever thought she could pull this off? Somehow, Kathy had to scramble to fix it so that Coulter didn't go back to Garcia and squeal on her.

Sure as hell, gossip was alive and well at the villa. Everyone watched everyone else. Any unusual infraction was reported to Therese, who then took the story to Garcia. Kathy had seen a number of people suddenly disappear — there one day and gone the next — because of some innocuous thing they had said or done.

"I meant . . ." Kathy paused, lifting her hands, ". . . all this money being spent on this when I could see it going to the orphanage instead . . . or to all those young children we saw on the streets. It just breaks my heart, Mac." When she said his name in her husky voice his eyes widened and then narrowed again. This guy was *not* what he seemed. She felt it in her gut. Her intuition screamed at her that he was a survival expert with unknown abilities. Who *was* he? Unable to ask and completely frustrated, Kathy smiled into his eyes. Might as well use her woman's wiles to advantage here, shouldn't she?

Mac melted a little beneath her smile. But it hadn't reached her eyes. Who was fooling who, here? The errant thought that Kathy might be an undercover DEA agent suddenly struck him. No, that was impossible. His ATF handler would have mentioned that to him. As far as Mac knew, he was the only U.S. government agent on this case and inside the Garcia drug empire at this level. Still, he wondered. . . .

"Listen, after I have a bath, how about we find a place to eat? I'm starving!" That was a big lie. Kathy wanted to just sit and hide in here for the night and sweat it out. Somehow, she had to persuade Mac that she wasn't a threat to the Garcia empire. One slip — just one — and she'd done it. Angry at herself and uncertain exactly how to repair it other than to suddenly leave the villa, which she wasn't going to do, Kathy stared at Mac and waited for his response.

"Sure. I know just the place. It's a family-owned restaurant, La Troucha, that serves the best Peruvian food." He looked at his watch. "How about I come knocking at your door in about two hours?"

"Great," Kathy stated, relieved he seemed enthused over her unexpected invitation.

"I'll show myself out," he said, and left.

Standing there alone, Kathy gazed around the suite. Automatically, she looked for cameras. There didn't seem to be any. And then her heart pounded. What if the place was bugged? Had her question been recorded? Mac had said it wasn't. But could she believe him? Perspiration flooded her. Hands damp, she nervously wiped them against her jeans. If her question was recorded the tape would be taken to Garcia immediately. And what then? Her nerves jangled, Kathy turned and went to find the bathroom. Once more she'd proved that she wasn't undercover material.

It was nearly midnight. The restaurant, La Troucha, was filled with happy revelers from all over Cuzco. Husky sounding pan flutes, a melodic, lively accordion and deep kettle-type drums hammered out soul-stirring Incan music. As Kathy had discovered, this restaurant was a local hangout and not a tourist spot. She could see why it was Mac's favorite restaurant. The warmth of the Quero family who owned the place was infectious.

Mac had escorted her to the quieter outdoor area of the single-story restaurant. The carefully manicured terrace garden had a fountain, and tiny lights on the brick path allowed visitors to walk on the flat stones without tripping. The night was cool and Kathy had a lavender alpaca shawl over her fuschia dress. These two garments had been her only purchase for herself.

Over the ensuing hours and after consuming part of a bottle of burgundy wine, much of Kathy's trepidation dissolved. The drinks had soothed her screaming nerves and anesthetized her worry over her faux pas. And Mac was a charming dinner companion. He had showered, shaved and changed his clothes. Dressed in an open collared white cotton shirt, a blue blazer and tan chinos, he looked to Kathy like a suntanned Hollywood star. Maybe it was the wine, because she had had a few glasses. Maybe too many. Their meal was flavorful — freshly caught trout with lime juice, along with some of the most delicious Peruvian potatoes she'd ever encountered.

"This is like a dream," Kathy said, glancing at the large three-tiered fountain. The fountain was the center of the private garden. The water fell with a musical splash, and she looked up at the night sky. In the jungle she couldn't see the stars

301

most of the time due to the high humidity, but Cuzco, which was much drier, was a natural observatory at this altitude. The sky was clear, the stars twinkling boldly and so close she felt as if she could reach out and touch them.

"Yeah, there's a mystical quality to Peru," Mac murmured, standing behind her. Kathy was more than pretty tonight. She was beautiful. Those thick blond locks lay around her shoulders and glinted like Incan gold in the soft lights of the restaurant. The perfume she wore enticed him.

Her jewelry was simple but elegant. White pearls in her earlobes and a single strand around her throat showed off the elegant length of her neck. She stood with the soft, fuzzy lavender shawl curved around her proud shoulders, her hands holding the ends together over her heart.

To hell with it.

For once, Mac was going to break protocol. Kathy Lincoln had been the perfect companion tonight. She'd danced with laughter and delight to the inspiring Incan music after dinner. Her body had moved against Mac's when the slow tunes were played. She had melted against his frame with a boldness that caught him by surprise in the most delicious of ways.

Mac took a huge risk. He settled his hand on her shoulder and gently turned Kathy toward him. Her face lifted toward his, her eyes wide and vulnerable looking. Blue smoke. Their color reminded him of the sinuous, magical wisps of clouds that silently moved over the jungle at the villa. She was like that, Mac realized as he settled his other hand on her shoulder and brought Kathy against him. Her hands remained between her breasts, softly touching his chest. Would she push away? Scold him for not keeping his distance? Mac didn't care and was willing to take the chance. His heart was beating powerfully, short-circuiting his normal mindset of not getting involved. Maybe it was the high altitude making him loco. Maybe it was her. Or a combination. Right now, he didn't care.

"You're magical, you know that?" Mac said in a low voice. He lightly grazed Kathy's hair, the strands soft against his palm as he followed them down to her shoulder. If she pulled away, if she said no, he would stop. But she didn't.

Emboldened, Mac said, "Do you know how long I've wanted to kiss you?"

An arc of pleasure shot through Kathy.

Her brain screamed for her to resist. But her heart . . . oh, her damnable heart wasn't listening at all! Was she doing this to seal Mac's lips so he wouldn't repeat what she had said earlier? Kathy had found out through some manipulation of conversation earlier that Garcia did not have the penthouse bugged. So Mac was the only person who could take her words back to Garcia and undo everything she'd been working to set up for the last four months. But did she want to kiss him as a trade-off for his silence? Or did she want to kiss him out of her own desire?

Unsure, Kathy slid her hands beneath the front of Mac's blazer. She felt him tense and take a deep, shuddering breath. His eyes turned stormy and narrowed upon her. He was going to kiss her, and that was okay with her heart.

"You've been magic for me, too," Kathy whispered, her voice off-key and husky. As Mac settled his hands upon her face, framing it and easing her mouth toward his, Kathy closed her eyes.

For one moment out of this dangerous dance she was playing, Kathy wanted to forget it all. Just forget for just a few moments . . .

With the first brush of his lips against

hers, Kathy drew in a sharp breath. His mouth was masterful, beguiling and coaxing as he caressed her parting lips. Oh! His ability to kiss was so much more than Kathy had hoped for. Her fingers dug convulsively into his shirt as he moved his mouth more boldly against hers. He was taking it one step at a time, leaving her hungry and craving more. Much more! His hands tightened as he angled her head slightly to take advantage of her opening lips. The moment his tongue moved across hers, a silvery heat threaded from her breasts to her needy core.

Groaning, Mac felt Kathy sway against him, as if finally surrendering to him. Tensing, he took her full weight and felt her long fingers sliding provocatively across his chest, his neck and then around his shoulders. Mouth hungry and bold, he met her surprising onslaught. For just a minute or two he wanted to forget the life-and-death game he played.

Her mouth tasted of sweet chocolate as he moved his tongue slowly, worshiping each corner. Mac felt her smile against him. He smiled in return. Her arms tightening behind his neck, her body moving softly and teasingly against his, were nearly his undoing. Her lips were soft, pliable, pleasing. She was bold, too, and it fueled a fire that nearly set him aflame. Through a haze of pleasure, Mac again wondered about her being a nanny. Her fiery passion, her wantonness surprised him.

Reluctantly, he ended the kiss. As their lips slowly drew apart, wet and heated, he opened his eyes and drowned in her blue gaze. They were both breathing hard and he could feel her heart skittering wildly against his chest. He savored the sensuous strength of her body. Tunneling his fingers through her hair, he watched as her lashes fluttered and her eyes closed. *I have to stop. I have to stop. . . .* But God help him, he didn't want to.

Groaning, Mac whispered near her ear, "You're like the clouds around these jungle mountains, bright angel. You're here and not here. Holding you is like holding one of those soft, moving clouds between my hands. You're part mystery, part something I can't put into words. . . ." Mac forced himself to ease his fingers from her hair. Seeing the disappointment in her smoky eyes, he gave her an apologetic smile.

The huskily spoken words spilled through Kathy like a cascade. Her body screamed to be satiated. How long had it been since a man so inspired her like this?

306

A long time. Not since Curt . . . She was thirsty for Mac Coulter. Was her attraction based upon emerging from a year's worth of grief over losing Curt? Just hormones on the rampage because she'd had no sex during that period? Or was it something more?

As Kathy gazed with confusion into his hooded, stormy eyes, she found herself spiraling helplessly into a cauldron of need for him alone. The rueful smile on those perfect male lips sent a keen ache through her. No, her attraction to Mac didn't stem from that long tunnel of grief. It was him. And that scared the hell out of her.

Wordlessly, she eased her hands from around his shoulders. Mac was strong and capable. And yet surprisingly gentle. Unlike a lot of men, he hadn't hurt her or gotten selfish with her. Instead, he'd courted her with that life-altering kiss. Mac knew how to pleasure a woman, no doubt. Her lips were still tingling in the wake of his masterful onslaught. All she could do was stare up at him, lost in the heated lightning reflected in his eyes.

Knees weakening, Kathy didn't know what to do. No other man had ever made her feel this way. Not even Curt. The night air was cool. Mac made her feel warm and safe. But nothing was safe in her world. Nothing was to be trusted. And yet Kathy had capitulated and kissed him. She'd wanted this as much as Mac, she discovered. It simply couldn't be. Not now. Not when she was so close to springing her trap to send Garcia's world into hell.

Chapter Sixteen

"Morgan, do we have a mission going down in Peru that I don't know about?" Major Mike Houston sauntered into Morgan Trayhern's office on a Friday morning, cup of steaming black coffee in hand.

"What?" Morgan lifted his head. He had been looking over two new missions that Mike and his team had sent for his approval. "Peru?"

"Yeah, look at this. Jenny just handed it to me. A top secret fax to us."

Scowling, Morgan took the paper. "It's from the ATF."

"Yeah. We don't work with them," Mike said, leaning against his desk and sipping his coffee. "At least, not that I know of."

Snorting, Morgan took a bite of a Krispy Kreme doughnut, his morning ritual. "We have no ties to them. This is the head of the ATF, asking us if we have an agent in place down in Peru."

"Yeah. Apparently they've got a mole there sending this inquiry back through his handler."

Morgan read the fax and his scowl deepened. "A female operative?"

"We work in teams of two, a man and woman. So it can't be one of ours."

"Right." Something bothered Morgan. Setting the fax down, he murmured, "I think I'll have Jenny get this ATF guy on a secure phone line. I want to know more."

Raising his brows, Mike asked, "Got a hunch?"

"Yeah . . . maybe," Morgan barked, reaching for the red phone on his desk. It was a secure satellite line that could put him in touch with any government around the world.

"Would you let me know what you find out?" Mike said over his shoulder. "I'm kind of curious, too."

Morgan nodded and asked Jenny Wright, his assistant, to make a connection to Mort Houseman's office. Mort was the head honcho of ATF and the man who'd sent him the fax.

"Mort speaking."

"Mort, this is Morgan Trayhern from Perseus. How are you this morning?"

"Fine, Mr. Trayhern. You got my fax, I see?"

"Yes. Whoever this operative is, it's not one of our people. I'm usually privy to such operations and this one has caught me off guard. With a Q clearance, I thought I had all of them in my sights."

Chuckling, Mort said, "This is ATF territory, Mr. Trayhern. I'm familiar with Perseus, but you work more with the FBI, DEA and CIA, as I understand it."

"That's correct, although we do many interagency missions, with anyone who needs our assistance or assets."

"Oh . . . I see."

Morgan smiled wryly. "We met briefly at a closed senate hearing about a year ago, but there was a lot going down at that time and you may not recall me." Morgan remembered that Mort Houseman possessed a bean-counter personality. And he looked like it, too — tall, thin, balding, with spectacles and a pallid complexion. He also zealously controlled the ATF to the exclusion of everyone else. Of course, after 9/11, he was forced to begin sharing information, but in Morgan's opinion, the man hedged his bets, just as he was doing now.

"That's possible," Mort said. "Well, look, if this operative isn't one of yours, I'll go to some of the other agencies and find out who inserted her down there."

A thin thread of alarm slithered through Morgan's gut. "Do you have a name? A de-

scription from your agent?" He held his
breath. Houseman could refuse to say anything. Morgan heard a rustling of papers
over the line.

"Just a moment . . . yes, here it is. Our
agent says she's a Canadian-American
woman by the name of Katherine Lincoln.
She's working as a nanny for Carlos
Garcia, at his villa near Agua Caliente."

That rang no bells for Morgan. Still, his
gut niggled him. Something was out of
place here. What was it? Racking his brain,
he finally asked, "Is there a physical description of her?"

"Yes, but Mr. Trayhern, I think I've
given you quite enough information, especially since you know it isn't one of your
field agents."

Bastard. Morgan nodded and kept his
voice smooth. "I understand, Mort. Well,
listen, I appreciate what you did give me. If
I can ever help you out, let me know." *That
will be a cold day in hell.*

After getting off the phone, Morgan sat
there thinking. Katherine Lincoln. Kathy
Trayhern. Canadian-American? Over the
last few months, he had grown increasingly
worried about Kathy. She'd gone undercover to South America. That was all the
information she'd given him, and he'd

been stonewalled by the Pentagon on her mission a couple of months ago. He still hadn't heard anything from her. These types of operations could take up to a year to complete, but he didn't like the idea of his oldest daughter undercover for such a long time.

Laura had nightmares from time to time about Kathy being in danger. Morgan would get up, hold his wife and reassure her. He didn't admit he was worried, too. Oh, Kathy was capable, there was no question. But it was his daughter, dammit, and he didn't like being shut out of a mission that involved her.

Something had to be done. But what? Drumming his fingers on his desk for a moment, he finally decided what to do. He picked up the secure phone and asked Jenny to get Major Maya Stevenson of the Black Jaguar Squadron on the line. Her black ops was situated fifty miles from Agua Caliente, hidden in a massive cave complex.

Yes, Maya might know something. And she might be willing to cough up his daughter's whereabouts. Morgan had helped refinance Maya's all-woman Apache combat helicopter squadron, which had gone down there to halt cocaine shipments out of

Peru. Within four years, they had stopped sixty percent of the drug flights from leaving the country. They never shot them down, just intimidated the hell out of them, when necessary throwing rockets or cannon fire across the nose of the drug runner, who got the message and turned back.

Morgan waited impatiently. He knew Maya had a full squadron of Apaches and they plied that territory twenty-four hours a day. Frequently she would send him information on drugs being moved by land, by truck or by ship, and he would pass the info to the DEA and FBI or CIA.

No question, the drug trade in Peru was being seriously hurt by the women who flew those helicopters. Despite their brilliant success, the U.S. Army had been planning to pull the plug on Major Stevenson's brainchild, until Morgan pumped life-sustaining money and support into it.

He was glad for his contribution, because now more than ever the legendary Black Jaguar Squadron was riding roughshod over the drug network, even creating incredible pressure on the biggest drug lord of them all, Carlos Garcia, the son of the man who had kidnapped his family. It gave Morgan particular satisfaction to be putting the screws to the son, even if the father was dead.

If Garcia couldn't get his drugs out of Peru, other drug lords would encroach on his markets and topple him. This placed Garcia in a dangerous position, and Morgan knew the pressure on the bastard had to be tremendous — thanks to Maya Stevenson and her group of gung ho women pilots.

The phone rang.

"Maya?"

"Hi, Morgan. What's up?"

He smiled. He liked the no-nonsense Brazilian-American woman. She had been one of the first females to graduate from Fort Rucker and fly the powerful Apache combat helicopter.

"I have a question for you."

"Shoot."

Laughing, he said, "I just got an interesting fax and then followed it up with a phone call to the ATF back in D.C. Mort Houseman, the head honcho, was asking if we had a woman operative undercover at Garcia's villa near Agua Caliente."

"Okay . . ."

"He gave me her name and nationality. I asked for more info and he refused me. He can, of course. It's his undercover black ops."

"Where do we fit into this?"

"Well, I know your pilots frequently take photos of drug carriers, on foot hiking through the jungle, in trucks, on bicycles or whatever. You send that info to me and I pass it on to others. I was just wondering if in the last four months you've taken any photos of a woman at Carlos Garcia's villa near Agua Caliente."

"Hmm, I don't know. Let me get my executive officer, Lieutenant Dallas Klein, on this, Morgan. She looks through all the photos, sorts them out and sends them on."

"Maybe some of your combat pilots took photos near his villa? Those are the ones I'm interested in. I want to try and identify this woman if possible."

"Okay, let me get on it. We've got an archive of all photos taken on our flights. I'll have Dallas cull the last four months' worth and send them to you via secure computer line. You can look through them yourself. Most will be irrelevant — a lot of hikers trek through the jungle around Machu Picchu."

"That's okay. Just send what you've got my way."

★ ★ ★

"Find out anything concrete?" Mike asked as his boss walked into his office. Morgan seemed deep in thought, his hand clasping his chin.

"Not yet." Morgan elaborated on his conversations with Mort Houseman and Maya Stevenson.

Mike sat back in his chair. "So this mole is Canadian? You know, this might be a Canadian-backed ops. Have you thought of calling your friends up north and finding out?"

"Doing that right now."

"Why are you pursuing this so intently?"

Morgan sighed. "I'm worried about Kathy. She said her undercover op was in South America."

"That's what I thought." Mike nodded, understanding. Morgan didn't like being shut out of an ops and he'd had the door slammed in his face on this one by the Pentagon. Usually, the feds were more than willing to share intelligence because Perseus was so heavily involved with them in mutual operations around the world. Not on this one, and Mike couldn't figure out why.

Jenny Wright came into Mike's office. "Morgan, no one among the bureaus in

317

Canada have such an agent or operation with Garcia."

"Hmm," Morgan muttered.

"Jenny, have you contacted the DEA yet?" Mike asked.

Morgan turned. "That's our next step. Check it out and let us know, Jenny?"

The blonde smiled. "Of course." She turned and went back out to her cubicle, which sat between their offices.

"Well," Mike said, "if we come up empty-handed with the DEA, that makes this really interesting. You know the CIA doesn't have anyone down there. We have all their need-to-know mission info."

"Right." Morgan scratched his head and looked around. "And if the DEA is out of this loop on Garcia —"

"Then who is the mystery woman? Apparently the ATF agent fingered her."

Morgan shrugged and said, "Agents in the field are paranoid by nature. This woman is working as a nanny, a babysitter for Garcia's daughter, and that's all she may be. The agent could be knee-jerking and hyping the situation. He could be wrong about her."

Nodding, Mike said, "Yeah, that's possible, too."

"Well, I've got work yelling at me, and

other stuff in motion," Morgan said with a twisted smile. "If I put this together, you'll be the first to know."

"Brightens up my normally dull days," Mike chuckled, lifting his hand in farewell. His days were anything but dull. Mike loved being the head of mission planning, which was his forte.

It was near quitting time, 1700, when Morgan started receiving the first of many black-and-white JPEGs from the Black Jaguar Squadron headquarters. He called his wife and told her he would be late for dinner. Something was driving Morgan to find out this woman's identity. When his gut sounded an alarm, he'd learned decades ago not to ignore it, but to follow it to the very end.

"This woman is not one of our ATF agents," Rosalia Fuentes told Mac Coulter. It was early afternoon and they sat sipping coffee in a restaurant in the wealthy Mira Flores district of Lima. Dressed in a light tan linen suit, Rosalia blended in with the usual clientele. She had been Mac's handler since he'd come to Peru.

"They're *sure?*"

Rosalia nodded and moved her sable-framed glasses up on her nose. "Completely. One hundred percent sure." She kept her voice down. They sat in the back of the restaurant, near a wall and the kitchen so they could watch the traffic. It was siesta and this was one of the few restaurants to remain open during this time of day. Outside, the sun was shining brightly, and making the petunias and marigolds in the window boxes a splash of rainbow colors.

"And they checked with all the other agencies?" Mac asked, stirring his espresso.

"*Sí, compadre.*" Rosalia daintily took a bite of her pastry, then set it back on her plate.

"How about Canadian agencies?"

"There is nothing, my friend."

"So, she's either not an agent and I'm crazy and paranoid, or she's a freelancer."

"*Sí,* any of the above," Rosalia said, smiling over her own white china cup.

"I'll tell you this, if she's an agent, she's a bad one. That slip at the penthouse sent off warning bells in me." He looked at the young Peruvian woman, a marketing expert for a major advertising company in Lima. "The way she looked at me with those eyes of hers when she asked if I knew who I was working for. She knows Garcia is a drug lord. I'd stake my life on it."

"*Sí,* but many know Garcia for what he is. It isn't a big secret."

Mac nodded. "Yeah, I know that, too. Still, it's little things, maybe not what she says, but what she does . . ."

"Give me an example, *amigo?*"

"She's insinuated herself with Garcia's lover, Therese. She's a Mac geek, and you know how many problems there are with computers out in that jungle. There is always a bad connection out of Agua Caliente, phone lines going down. . . . They can't get a satellite feed in, either. Kathy Lincoln works in Therese's office almost every day on that computer, the same one I've been trying to access."

"The one that has all the names and files we need?"

"Yes." Mac sighed. "I mean, why would a nanny volunteer as a part-time secretary to Therese unless she had an ulterior motive?"

"Perhaps she is just bored? Taking care of a child all the time isn't exactly intellectually stimulating," Rosalia said sourly.

Mac shrugged and looked out the window at the world passing by. Four days ago he'd kissed Kathy and *his* world had gone on tilt. It was still tilted. And he didn't like his response to her or the fact that his traitorous heart refused to give her up even if she might be an agent.

"What if she's undercover and working for another drug lord? Worming her way into Garcia's organization to bring him down?" he asked.

"That is possible," Rosalia said, sipping her espresso. "And that would explain why none of the Canadian or American agencies know of her."

"They are running a background check on her, aren't they?"

"*Sí,* as we speak. I won't have that info for you for another week or two, though. You know how slow they work on things like this. It is not considered a priority."

Yeah, he knew. This wasn't a class A emergency. "I'll be lucky to hear on it in a month's time," he griped.

Chuckling, she patted his hand. "Has she threatened you, *amigo?*"

"No." *Just the opposite.* Mac couldn't sit here and spill out his guts — and heart — to Rosalia, although that's exactly what he wanted to do. She had been a very good handler for him — sympathetic, a good listener, astute. She had been in the spy business for over a decade and he trusted this diminutive woman with his life.

"There are other things we must discuss,

Mac," she told him, looking around to make sure no waiters were near enough to overhear them. "There's a lot of pressure building on Garcia. You may not see it or be aware of it, but we have moles in several other drug cartels and the word is going out."

"Going out? On Garcia?"

"Yes. You know of Javier Rojas in Sacred Valley. The little guy who's muscled his way into the big leagues?"

"Yeah, he's a royal bastard, too."

"No argument from me." She bowed her head, her lips barely moving. "Arturo Molinos from Ecuador is Garcia's main enemy. Standing in line right behind him is Manuel Navarro from the Colombian cartel. We hear rumblings that either of these men may attack Garcia in the near future."

Lifting his brows, Mac asked, "Attack?" Panic struck him. He had been in one drug war shortly after joining Garcia's forces, as his personal helicopter pilot. Last time, it had been Molinos who had sent in two loads of mercenaries, dropping them by helicopter on Garcia's estate in northern Peru. Blood had flowed. Mac had saved Garcia's family from harm by thinking fast, getting them into their own helo and lifting off — just in time.

"Listen, we know that Navarro has four Russian Ka-50 Black Shark combat helicopters."

"The Black Jaguar Squadron, that U.S. Army black ops outfit fifty miles from Machu Picchu, has run into them," Mac agreed. "But I thought that Garcia had leased those Ka-50s from Navarro." The Black Shark helicopter was a one-man lethal machine with the capability of firing off rockets, missiles and cannon ordnance just like the Apache. But the Black Shark had one up on the American-built aircraft: its telltale heat signature was invisible to the Apache's sophisticated sensors. One could sneak up on an Apache without the crew ever knowing it was there — until it was too late. No, Mac was well aware of the capabilities of the Black Shark. Plus, Navarro paid Russian pilots to fly them, and those men, hardened veterans of the Chechnya war, could wreak hell on earth in a matter of seconds.

In fact, one or two Black Sharks could level any one of Garcia's compounds in a matter of fifteen minutes. This combat helicopter took no prisoners. And it had state-of-the-art look down–shoot down capability. It even had infrared that allowed the pilot to spot a human heat signature anywhere — jungle, villa, it didn't matter where the person was hiding. Once spotted, a target could be killed quickly with the Black Shark's amazing arsenal.

"*Sí*, that is correct, *compadre*. Garcia has leased them from Navarro. But who says that Navarro, instead of delivering them peacefully, can't order those Russian mercenaries to fly to Garcia's villa and wipe him and his family in one attack?"

Mac knew that could happen. Drug lords pretended to be the best of friends, but were enemies at heart. "So, Garcia's vulnerable?"

"*Sí*, because of the Black Jaguar Squadron continuing to stop his flights of coke out of the country. He's not getting the job done, so that leaves him vulnerable. We hear rumblings that Navarro wants to blow Garcia away and take over his territory. Get those cocaine flights out of here and into Bolivian airspace, where the Black Jaguar Squadron does not have permission to fly."

Mac rolled his eyes. "And I came down here to talk to you about a possible agent working as a nanny."

Fuentes smiled, but it was strained. "You have many challenges on this mission. And I know you want to rescue that little American girl, Sophie, and get her out of there. I wish I had more promising news, *amigo*, but my hands are tied. I tried to talk to the head of the ATF, but he didn't take my call."

"Thanks for continuing to try," Mac said heavily. "I haven't found a way to spring her without blowing my cover. And dammit, I want to. It's just such a precarious situation, and now, with the possibility of Navarro bringing in Black Sharks to waste Garcia . . ."

"*Sí, sí,* I understand." Shaking her head, Rosalia whispered, "That is so sad. I feel so deeply for the parents of this little girl. They do not know anything, where she is or if she is even alive. We cannot contact them because if we do, and word gets out, Garcia might kill her. And he would also know there's a spy in his midst. You."

Mac felt frustrated. "The only good thing there is Katherine Lincoln. She's taken Sophie under her wing and the little girl is coping a lot better."

"That is good. That is what a nanny does best," Rosalia stated.

"You think she really is a nanny, and I'm just spooked?"

"*Sí, amigo.* She does not fit the profile of an agent. No one knows of her. I think she simply does not like the idea of Garcia being a drug lord. I am sure that came as a shock to her. Perhaps it rides rough on her conscience, eh?"

"Then why would she hang around?" Mac demanded, opening his hands. "*That* is what doesn't make sense in this equation."

Giving a slight shrug, Rosalia finished her espresso and set the cup back on the saucer. "Money. Garcia is paying her well. Perhaps she has a sick parent who needs much money for medical help. Many people take jobs they don't like because the pay is good."

Shaking his head, Mac said, "Hell, she refused to take his cash. She was okay spending it on the kids at the orphanage, though."

Rosalia smiled brightly. "Well! She is a woman with a golden heart then, *compadre.* Perhaps you like her, eh? Every time you speak her name, your voice changes ever so slightly. Did you know that?"

Glumly, Mac finished his espresso. "I don't want to hear that, Rosalia." She chuckled indulgently and he smarted beneath the scrutiny of her knowing eyes. Kathy's kiss . . . She'd tasted so good to him, been so warm, open, inviting. And then he wondered if her kiss, her unexpected advance, had been in fact a deliberate distraction for her spontaneous words. It hurt him to think that, but Mac couldn't afford to be naive.

"Listen," Rosalia counseled him, patting his arm as if he were a little boy, "you have other priorities right now. Navarro, we believe, is on the hunt. Our agent isn't so close that he knows when, but the word is circulating among his soldiers to get ready for some action. Everyone at our agency firmly believes that Navarro will attack Garcia. Soon. So you must stay on guard, my friend. Try to maintain your cover, but do not get killed, okay?"

Nodding, Mac turned his thoughts to Kathy once again. If hell happened, he wanted to be there to get her and Sophie to safety. But he was gone so much of the time. Could he warn her?

Should he?

Chapter Seventeen

Kathy couldn't do it. She just couldn't kidnap Tiki after all. . . . Standing restively at the barred window of her bedroom, staring out across the dark, silent jungle, she folded her arms across her chest. She was exhausted and hadn't been able to sleep since coming back from Cuzco with Mac. The last week had been a special hell as far as she was concerned.

Garcia had had a surprise waiting for her and Tiki when Mac brought her back the next day: horses! A shetland palomino and two beautiful Andalusians. Because of Tiki's love of horses, Kathy had approached Therese about buying the child a small pony. Kathy thought it would be fun to take the little girl on rides along the wide, well-trodden paths around the compound. Down the slope and beyond the gate of the walled complex was a wonderful meadow, about a mile away and a thousand feet below the villa. It would be a perfect place to teach Tiki some basic riding habits.

Garcia hadn't just purchased a pony. With typical extravagance, he'd procured the Andalusians as well, so that adults could ride with her.

Carlos had had his little girl in his arms as he proudly walked her to the rear of the villa, where he'd had a new corral built overnight. The Andalusians, one white and one a dappled gray, were an expensive breed brought directly from Spain. Tiki loved her new Shetland palomino, which was one-third the size of the powerful, well-muscled Andalusians.

Kathy had been delighted by Garcia's gesture. Tiki had wriggled out of her father's arms so that she could pet her new pony. A stable hand stood nearby to supervise. After witnessing his daughter's joy, Garcia had profusely thanked Kathy for her influence and ideas regarding Tiki. When he'd turned to her, Kathy saw that his eyes were glazed with tears. His display of emotion had shocked her and confirmed once again that the murdering drug lord had a heart.

"Dammit . . ." she'd muttered softly as Garcia went to his daughter's side. The look on Tiki's shining face as she sat on the patient pony was one Kathy would never forget. The whole scene broke her heart — Garcia as a proud parent, tears glimmering in his eyes, his hands gentle and protective around his daughter's tiny waist as she sat there on the pony, all smiles.

How could Kathy kidnap Tiki? *How?* She would have to permanently wound Tiki in order to get even with Garcia. This was no surgical strike, that was for sure. In this plan everyone got hurt and no one walked away unscathed. Kathy couldn't bring herself to hurt Tiki to get even with her father. No innocent child should suffer that way.

Hurt, anger and the desire to get even with Garcia warred with the knowledge that what she had planned was wrong. Kathy's stomach knotted even more. The need for revenge had eroded away during the months she'd spent with the little girl. No, she would not lower herself to the drug lord's level by taking Tiki. Her family had raised her to be better than that.

And then, hell, there was that kiss with Mac Coulter. He curled her toes and made her go weak at the knees. Mac was the man of her dreams and she'd thought she'd never meet anyone like him. Yet there he was. And she'd been in his arms, with his mouth caressing her lips, his hands grazing her body as if she was a priceless gift to him. At the orphanage, in his work with the nuns and the way the children loved him, he'd shown himself to be a decent and loving man. Whether she wanted to admit it or not, Mac Coulter had somehow stolen her heart. But of course, it just wouldn't work. No way in hell could she fall in love with a drug dealer!

She was learning the hard lesson that nothing was as it seemed. There were no clear black-and-white situations anymore, but rather varying shades of gray. Rubbing her eyes with her hands, Kathy turned and bleakly shuffled back to her queen-size bed. The covers were tangled from her restless tossing and turning. She sat down, closed her eyes and gripped her hands together between her thighs, the coolness of her soft silk nightgown brushing against them.

To add salt to her wounds, Garcia had said he was very moved that she'd spent the money he'd given her not on herself, but on the poor. He'd informed her that every month he would see that the orphanage was supplied with whatever it needed, because she had been so thoughtful and generous.

So much for him being a bad guy.

Dammit, he was! A murdering bastard from a line of murdering bastards! Hands tightening, Kathy tried to deal with the inner clash of right and wrong. For months she'd fought the feeling that kidnapping Tiki would be morally wrong. Who then was going to make Garcia pay? His family deserved to be hurt just as much as he had hurt hers. Grinding her teeth with frustration, Kathy opened her eyes and lifted her head.

At that moment the moon rose above the jungle canopy. The silvery beams flowed brightly into her room and across her body. Kathy wasn't one for magical happenings, nor did she believe in miracles. But as the light silently touched her, she suddenly knew what she had to do. Maybe there was another way to even the score with Garcia other than making his innocent daughter pay the price.

Kathy's mind raced wildly. She knew that Therese's computer held all the information on the drug movements — the names of street dealers all over the world, the middle men who distributed, the drug lords Garcia consorted with globally. Therese already gave her daily access to the desktop computer. They were due for a software upgrade this week, one Kathy would be installing. Could she use that time to continue hunting for the password? She knew where the file was. And she knew now that Therese hated computers and she didn't try very hard to learn the more intricate operations. All Kathy needed was the password and she could open that file, make a copy of it and then leave.

Yeah, she had to leave, that was for sure. But not without little Sophie in tow. That was the other epiphany: she'd decided to turn mud into mud pies. Don't kidnap innocent little Tiki, but steal back Sophie, blow this joint and get the child to her home in Lima. Kathy knew Sophie's parents were aching from her loss. Kathy had seen what it had done to her own parents to have Jason kidnapped.

Yes, this was a better plan. Steal the information from the computer and then work out an escape route for Sophie and herself. That seemed daunting to Kathy. Stealing the computer file was nothing in comparison to an escape. There were only two reliable ways to get out of Agua Caliente: by train or helicopter. Even if she made it to Cuzco, she knew Garcia would be alerted, and he had a lot of men there who would cover the airport, which was the only way practical to get out of the Andean city and back down to Lima. No, it was a terrifying task, and Kathy knew she had to plan very carefully or her life would be forfeit.

First she had to sleep, so she'd be rested. Lying down, Kathy was glad for the overhead fan that moved the sluggish, heavy air around in the room. Even though the window was open, it was still muggy. As she closed her eyes she heard the far-off sound of thunder rumbling. That was the one thing she loved about the jungle — dramatic thunderstorms that would roll across the area at any time, day or night.

With that last thought, Kathy fell asleep deeply for the first time since she'd arrived at the villa.

Mac Coulter couldn't help but chuckle as he stood at the gate. Inside the corral, Kathy led Tiki around on her pony, Harry Potter, named after the famous child magician. Sophie sat on the white Andalusian gelding called General. The little girl had a small smile on her face, which warmed his heart. Kathy had the reins from each horse in her hands as she led them around the large corral at a sedate walk. The early morning air was cool, with gray clouds hanging, as usual, about a thousand feet above the jungle canopy. Resting his arms on the top rail, Mac grinned as Kathy rounded the corral and spotted him.

"Looks like fun," he called. He saw her eyes narrow slightly. Was something wrong? Mac hadn't seen her in a week, since returning from Cuzco. Not that he didn't want to see her after that life-altering kiss, but Garcia kept him plenty busy flying the chopper.

Tiki waved gaily. "Look! I'm riding, Señor Coulter!"

"So you are," Mac laughed. "You look like a real cowgirl, Tiki." And she did. Garcia had bought her a cowboy hat, a set of bright red leather chaps and black boots. The little girl laughed and waved one hand, while she gripped the horn of the western saddle with the other.

Mac shifted his gaze to the white gelding Kathy led. Sophie seemed happy — or as happy as she could be under the circumstances. He could tell she loved this outing. His gaze moved back to Kathy, who smiled at him. She brought the horses to a stop where he stood.

"You ride much?" she asked. Kathy had seen so little of Mac since their heated kiss. She ached for him. For his company. As she searched his twinkling gray eyes, she found herself snared by his maleness, no matter if he was a drug dealer or not. It was a bittersweet moment.

"Me? Yeah, I've thrown a leg over a horse now and then. Why?"

"Well, I need a riding partner for about an hour. Interested?"

Grinning, Mac shrugged. "Sure." Any time spent with Kathy was valuable. He met her clear blue eyes and felt helpless. Her smile reached her eyes, and that made him feel good and strong as a man. "What's the plan?"

"Well, these two ladies are doing so well that I thought I'd ride General, the white Andalusian here, and put Tiki's pony on a longe line so that she could walk next to me. I'd like to ride down to the meadow below the villa here. But I need help. If you could ride the gray Andalusian, Hector, with Sophie behind you on the saddle, we could go. What do you think? Are you game?"

Any time spent with you is worth it. Mac didn't say the words. He climbed between the wooden rails. "Sure. Is Hector saddled?"

"No, but the tack is in the room next to his box stall." Kathy didn't want to watch

Mac as he moved, but she did, anyway. He had on a pair of jeans this morning, his tennis shoes and a form-fitting polo shirt of navy blue that outlined his magnificent chest and proud shoulders. Trying not to remember how her hands had explored his body, or the pulverizing kiss he'd given her, she managed a twisted smile. "This will take an hour. Do you have it to spare?" She knew he was doing a lot more flying of late. Something must be up with Garcia's drug ties, but she didn't know what.

"Sure. I've got a flight in two hours, no prob," Mac called over his shoulder, heading across the deep sand of the arena to the tack room. "You get the girls ready and I'll be out to meet you in no time at all."

So, he was a cowboy, too. Was there anything Mac didn't do well? Kathy wondered as she opened the gate and led the horses out, with her charges on them. She tinkered with the girth on Tiki's saddle and made sure the little girl traded in her cowboy hat for a safety helmet. She handed one up to Sophie and asked her to put it on.

The morning was brisk, the sky still gray, and birds were singing in the jungle. Kathy stood between the horses, waiting patiently for Mac to reappear. She loved to ride and this was a chance to get away from the villa and nose around. The outing for the girls was a good excuse to scout the surrounding terrain to see if there was an escape route for her and Sophie later on.

Mac Coulter reappeared astride Hector, and rode as if he'd been married to the horse forever. Sitting straight and tall, one hand on the reins, he pulled a baseball cap from his back pocket and settled it on his head. Hector was sixteen hands tall, a gunmetal-gray color with silvery dapples across his body. The horse had a lot of fire and spirit, which was why Kathy wouldn't allow Sophie to ride him. The gelding was a handful and not for a beginning rider. Beneath Mac's capable hands, however, the horse was collected, lifting his feet high as he danced toward them, and arching his neck.

"Do I look like a knight in shining armor?" Mac teased as he guided Hector up to them. He saw Kathy grin sourly. "Well, maybe a knight without armor?" he added.

Laughing softly, Kathy tied General's reins around the railing and then lifted Sophie out of the saddle. "I suppose you want me to call you Sir Coulter?" She carried the girl over to Mac, who leaned down and settled Sophie behind him. Kathy watched him make sure that she was comfortable, her legs situated properly across Hector's broad back and her arms around Mac's narrow waist.

He looked across his shoulder at Sophie. "You okay back there, honey? You can hold on to me so that you don't fall off. Hector seems a little frisky today."

Sophie looked up and said, "I'm fine, Mr. Coulter. I rode every day at home. I have my own horse, Jelly Bean. Before that I always rode with my dad on his horse, and I'd sit like this behind him."

The sadness in her shadowed eyes tore at Mac. He kept the smile pasted on his face, but he felt like crying for the child. "Sophie, we're good to go, then. And you can call me Mac, okay? All my friends do."

"Okay, Mr. Mac."

Chuckling, Mac looked over to see Kathy mounting the smaller gelding, General. She did it like a pro and was obviously no stranger to the saddle. Her jeans and white cotton blouse showed off her body to advantage. And he couldn't stop admiring the glow in her expression. She was beautiful to him.

Tiki shrieked with delight as she steered

her pony alongside General. The movement brought Mac's thoughts back to earth.

"I think we're ready, Sir Mac," Kathy called to him.

Grinning, he said, "I'll lead the way, my ladies." He turned the eager Hector toward the rear gate. The two guards stationed there quickly opened it so they could ride through.

As they left the villa behind, Kathy began to feel lighter and lighter. Mac had his hands full with Hector, who was dancing, his legs lifting high as they went down the gently sloping trail. Sophie rode behind him like a pro, her face alight with joy. Tiki was all smiles, her hands clinging to the saddle horn. Fortunately, General was a quiet horse in comparison to the hot-blooded Hector. Mac was a damn good rider. And Sophie, bless her heart, seemed to be enjoying Hector's dancing antics. Yes, it was turning out to be a wonderful morning in the most unexpected of ways.

The oval meadow was two miles long, with jungle on all sides. Kathy noted many animal paths branching off the main trail that ran down the center of the field. Were they paths to freedom? Maybe one would lead her and Sophie out of here.

Hector finally settled down, and Mac pulled him to a walk next to General. "Nice area, isn't it?" He saw how light Kathy's eyes had become. She looked utterly relaxed for the first time.

"It's beautiful! I'm so glad we have this meadow to ride in."

"Oh, you haven't seen it all yet," Mac said, gesturing to the far end. "There's more beyond this."

"Oh?"

"Yeah, come on, I'll show you."

The clouds were lifting higher and higher as the sun burned them off. When the riders approached the end of the meadow, Mac took the lead.

"Follow us," he called over his shoulder as he urged Hector down a narrow path through the thick jungle.

Frowning, Kathy positioned Tiki and her pony behind General. The little girl was having the time of her life and, lucky for her, the pony knew to follow nose-to-tail on the narrow trail.

They walked down a steep embankment, after which the trail curved sharply. The horses dug in their hooves and shifted their weight to their rear legs to keep from falling on their noses. Alarmed at the steepness, Kathy twisted around in the saddle to make sure that Tiki was all right. The little girl was a natural rider and seemed overjoyed at the challenge.

Suddenly, the trail reached another meadow. As Kathy emerged from the tree line, her attention was fixed on Tiki and her pony. She didn't see what was parked there until she lifted her head, and then she gasped. A dark green, U.S.-made Blackhawk helicopter sat on a concrete pad right in front of them. Obviously, this meadow had been hacked out of the jungle with a lot of machete work, to make room for this bird. A Blackhawk! Her heart pounded. She knew how to fly it!

"You recognize it?" Mac asked, staring so deep into her soul that she had to glance away.

"It's a Blackhawk, isn't it?"

"Bingo."

"What's it doing here? It's not a commercial helicopter, is it?" Kathy couldn't believe her eyes. Her heart pounded with excitement. This was her escape vehicle!

Chuckling, Mac said, "It's the *patrón*'s secret escape helicopter. He bought it from a foreign country, uh, sort of on the sly, so to speak."

There were no markings on the helo, and Kathy saw it had weapons on board. "Wow," she muttered. "This is a real surprise." And it was. The best kind of surprise. She stilled her desire to kick General forward, dismount and check out the bird more closely. No one could know that she was trained to fly a Blackhawk. No one. Yet her hands itched to climb in and refamiliarize herself with the controls. How she missed flying.

"Yeah, it's impressive, isn't it?" Mac had witnessed the look on Kathy's face when she'd first seen the helo. *Shock* would be the word he'd use to describe it. And then her face had flushed, her cheeks becoming a bright pink. There was a new, intense interest in her eyes as she examined the chopper, and she couldn't seem to tear her gaze away.

"More than impressive." Kathy gulped. "Do you fly it?"

"Yeah, I can and do. It doesn't lift off often for a lot of reasons, but I do maintenance flights to keep everything on-line and up to speed."

"Does anyone else at the villa know how to fly it?"

Mac shook his head.

"You must have gotten your training in the military to know how to pilot it?" Kathy tried to keep her tone light, but she was dying to know. She saw Mac give her a slight smile.

"I was in the U.S. Army for a while." Well, that was a lie, but that was his cover story.

"And you flew Blackhawks. . . ." Kathy said, awed. Oh, this was too good to be true. She had a way to escape now! If Mac was the only one who could fly the bird, then she only had him to worry about when she made her escape attempt with Sophie. And the helo was armed. That was even better, for the Bell helicopter was a standard commercial type and had no armaments. It couldn't be used to shoot the Blackhawk down.

"Yes, well, you know why the *patrón* bought one with rockets, missiles and a cannon on it?"

"No," Kathy said. "I don't." She stopped and let Tiki ride around her. The little girl smiled and guided the pony with ease.

"Remember you asked me about that black, unmarked Apache helicopter you saw on the trail during your test?"

"Yes?"

Mac decided to level with her. "There's a U.S. Army black ops group that flies around this area." He halted Hector and Sophie seemed content to sit quietly be-

345

hind him and watch Tiki ride her pony.

She frowned. "Oh?" A U.S. black ops? Here? She hadn't known about it. So many operations were compartmentalized on a need-to-know basis. Kathy figured that was why Patrick hadn't known about it before she initiated this mission.

"Yeah," Mac said, "they're stationed about fifty miles from here. They use a cave inside a mountain as their base. Everyone knows about them, but no one challenges them. The Peruvian government knows they're here, too."

"But why are they here?"

"They interdict drug flights that originate in Peru, and stop them from flying out of the country." He saw the surprise in her eyes.

Mac didn't want to say much more. "Anyway, the reason I'm telling you this is that it's also known that, to counter their presence, some drug lords have bought Russian made Ka-50 Black Shark combat helicopters, and hired mercenary pilots who know how to use them. They even the odds against the Apache gunships."

All this was news to her. Gulping, Kathy said, "I've never seen any of them around here except on that trail."

"You probably never will." Mac pointed

behind them, in the direction of Agua Caliente. "No one plays out their stealth and dagger games around a global tourist spot like Machu Picchu. All the war games go on down below, about thirty miles from here. No one wants tourists going home and telling the newspapers they saw armed helicopters from the U.S. or unmarked Russian ones flying near the temple complex." He grinned wryly. "Wouldn't be good press for either side, you know?"

Swallowing her surprise, Kathy couldn't tear her gaze from the Blackhawk. "That makes sense, I guess. But I had no idea . . ." She waved helplessly toward the bird.

In truth, she wanted to yell, to jump up and down for joy, but she didn't dare. Mac Coulter was her enemy, whether she wanted to remember that or not. If she tried to make a break and escape, he would be the only person who could stop her.

Chapter Eighteen

It was time. Dressed all in black, Kathy tiptoed along the hallway toward Therese's office. It was 0200, deep in the night. The villa and its inhabitants, save for the guards on the perimeter walls, were asleep. The guards that hung around during the day didn't stay in the building at night. That made it easier for Kathy to sneak into Therese's office.

Heart thumping hard, adrenaline pouring into her veins, she slowed as she came to the closed door at the end of the hall. Yesterday, Therese had left a small notebook open on her desk. Kathy had seen the words *Computer Codes* written at the top of the page. In the woman's absence, Kathy had memorized the five passwords scrawled inside. One of them had to open that file she wanted. It had to!

Two weeks had flown by since her stay in Cuzco. Life was settling down into a happy routine for everyone. Buying the horses had been a stroke of genius, Kathy thought as she flattened her back against the wall and waited. Garcia was spending more time with his daughter as she practiced on her pony. Even more surprising, he was riding General from time to time, with Tiki in front of him on the saddle. Father and daughter had never laughed so much or been so happy. It further eroded Kathy's determination to get even. Looking into that child's happy eyes, how could she want to hurt her? She didn't. And she couldn't.

Kathy had resolved to avenge her family another way: by getting that file with the drug dealers' names and handing it over to the DEA or the CIA. Maybe it wasn't the revenge she'd envisioned originally, but it was a way to take Garcia down.

Keying her hearing, she heard no sounds out of place. She pulled the key out of her pocket and hesitated. Was she hearing things? A muffled sound, nothing sharp or noisy. Just . . . Frowning, she continued to listen. Had the noise come from within Therese's office? It was windy outside and thunderstorms were marching across the jungle tonight.

Wiping her mouth, Kathy glanced back down the hall. No sign of movement. No guards . . . *Good.* She eased the key into the lock and gently twisted it. Holding her breath, she reached out with her other hand and grasped the cool brass doorknob. Very slowly she turned it. Releasing a slow breath, Kathy slipped into the room and shut the door behind her.

"Hold it. . . ."

Kathy gasped and whirled around. Her eyes widened.

"Mac!" she whispered. "What are *you* doing here?" He was dressed in a black, form-fitting suit. Though he wore a balaclava over his head, she recognized him from his eyes, the only part of his face that was visible. He was holding a pistol — pointed at her. Pulse pounding, she pressed herself against the door. Kathy had no weapon. Her heart thudded heavily in her chest. Mouth dry, she repeated, "What are you doing here?"

Mac eyed her. She was frightened, no doubt. He saw no weapons on her. Pushing back the balaclava so that it fell behind his neck, he kept the pistol trained on her. "I should ask you the same thing."

Kathy saw that the laptop on the desk was open and running. Her gaze flicked to it and then to his grim features. There was a night-light that barely broke the darkness. The light from the laptop made his glistening features look hard and ghostlike.

"You're breaking into Therese's laptop." Why? Who *was* he? She saw his eyes narrow, and the gun didn't waver. Would he shoot her? She saw a silencer on the weapon. He could shoot her and no one would hear the bullet being fired. *Oh, God . . .*

"And you were coming here to do what? Some late-night typing for Therese? At 2:00 a.m.?"

She didn't like the lopsided grin on his face or the innuendo in his voice. Frowning, she growled in a hushed tone, "I'm not saying anything until I know who you really are!"

Mac nodded. "Okay, you first."

Her breathing shallow and hard, Kathy glared at him. "No way! You're working for a drug lord and I know you know that! You're in cahoots with him!" His smile didn't change. Right now, Mac Coulter was a hellish adversary.

Kathy rapidly considered her options. He was too far away for a karate punch. He had a gun and she didn't. Dammit, why hadn't she thought of that? She had two in her bedroom. Why didn't she wear one? The guards would think nothing of it. After all, she was Tiki's bodyguard, and it would be expected. She'd screwed up, royally. She'd gotten too complacent over time.

"Who are you working for?" Mac demanded. He didn't like aiming the pistol at her, but there was nothing else he could do. Seeing the rage and then the frustration in her deeply shadowed face, he wondered if she was his enemy. If so, he was going to have to get rid of her — permanently — or his cover was blown. This was messy. Mac hadn't expected anyone to be in the office. From time to time, he'd sneak in, jimmy the lock and try to find out where Therese kept the information on the drug lords and shipping routes. He knew it was in her laptop. Finding the password had been a slow process over the last year, because Mac obviously couldn't be caught in here. Tonight he'd located the file — finally — and then Kathy had come into the office. He still didn't have the password, however. Grimly, he held her belligerent stare.

"I don't have to tell you a damn thing, Coulter. If that's who you really are," she spat out. Again, she saw that one-cornered smile. It didn't quite reach his glittering gray eyes. That pistol didn't waver, a fierce reminder that she was in way over her head. What had made her think she could ever pull off this mission? And look who had stopped her! The man she'd least suspected.

"You'd better tell me or you aren't going to live to see the dawn," he drawled. Her eyes widened, and he saw her tremble.

"You're the enemy!"

"How the hell do you know that?"

"Dammit, you work for *him!*" Kathy stabbed her finger toward the villa, where Garcia was sleeping.

"Keep your voice down," Mac ordered her harshly. She was shaking now. From fear? He wasn't sure. Standing tensely, her fists at her side, he clearly saw the rage and frustration in Kathy's expression. Even hatred. Toward him? Garcia?

"Why the hell should I trust you, Coulter? You fly for that son of a bitch!"

Lifting his chin, he asked, "Is that why you're here? To get even with him?"

Stunned by his insight, Kathy gulped. She wiped the perspiration from her face. "I'm saying nothing."

"You're an American spy."

His accusation felt like a slap in the face. And he'd said it like a statement of fact. Should she trust him? Heart racing, feeling shaky with the surge of adrenaline, Kathy stood there, uncertain. She wanted to trust him. Her mind raced over all the times Mac had been kind and thoughtful to her and the children. Especially the children.

Tilting her head, she looked deep into his hardened gray eyes. "I can't believe *you're* not an American agent."

"What would make you think that?" Mac saw every fleeting expression on her pale face.

"You're good with the kids."

The corners of his mouth lifted. "That's a helluva way to decide if someone is your friend or not."

"Women's intuition, dammit!" she flared. "Who are you?"

"Like I said — you go first. Are you an American agent or not?" Her life depended upon her answer. Mac listened for other sounds. They were in a highly delicate position here in this office — two spies tripping over one another unexpectedly. "How do I know you're not a mole Garcia planted?" he demanded darkly.

"Oh, give me a break, Coulter! I wouldn't work with that bastard if my life depended on it!"

"Well, your life *does* depend on it."

Glaring at him, Kathy snarled, "Okay, I'm here on a mission. I'm here to bring the bastard down."

Relief sheeted through Mac. He was damn glad this room was not bugged. "What agency are you working with?"

"None," Kathy barked. "I did this on my own."

Surprised, Mac kept the pistol trained on her. Her eyes were round with righteous anger. "That's impossible. No one gets this far up into this drug ring without outside help."

"Okay, so I had a little help from a SEAL buddy of mine. They had the intel I needed to break into Garcia's little world."

Stymied, Mac stared at her. "You're military?"

"Yeah, I'm a U.S. Marine, mister."

"I'll be damned." Mac grinned tightly and lowered the pistol. He saw her visibly sag against the door. "A Marine, of all things. Well, you certainly tripped me up on that one. I thought you might be a spy, but I never suspected the angle you were coming from."

"Now tell me who you are."

"I'm on your side," Mac said briskly.

"You aren't telling me?" Kathy demanded, stunned.

"No. Need-to-know basis only." He slid the pistol back into the shoulder holster beneath his left rib cage. "We're friendlies. That's all I'll give you. If Garcia tortures you, you can't tell him a thing about me."

That made sense. Easing away from the

door, Kathy walked toward the desk he stood behind. "Okay, I'll buy it for now." She pointed to the laptop. "What were you doing?"

Mac sat down and pulled the computer toward him. "I've just located the file I've been looking for."

Kathy came to the side of the desk. She wasn't sure about Mac Coulter. She wanted to believe that he was the good guy he said he was. Yet she had no proof except that he'd put his pistol away. Was it a ruse? When she wasn't looking, would he put the silencer to her head and pull the trigger? She didn't want to get any closer to him. "I have five passwords you can try to open it with. That's why I came here tonight. Therese has a little black book that she keeps in a safe. She was in a hurry and left it on her desk today after she asked me to do some filing." Grinning, Kathy said, "I peeked into it."

Mac smiled back. "Good thinking. Give them to me and I'll try each one. Maybe we'll get lucky."

He looked up at her. Her heartbeat was beginning to slow, the danger past. Strands of his dark hair lay across his perspiring brow. "Okay. But what will you do with the intel if you get it?"

Pulling a CD from his pocket, Mac put it into the laptop. "When I fly to Cuzco tomorrow around 1000, I'll pass it to my handler. From there, the intel will be sent back to Washington, D.C., for reconstruction."

It all sounded good. "What if you're working for another drug lord?"

Mac barely smiled. "Not my style."

Stubbornly, Kathy whispered, "You have shown me no identification, no proof that you really work for a U.S. agency. Why should I trust you?"

"Because I put the pistol away instead of shooting you."

Staring down at him, at that crooked smile on his mouth, Kathy snorted in frustration. "All right, all right." She gave him the first password.

As Mac typed it in, he held his breath. "The first one doesn't work. What's the second one?"

Kathy gave him the next password. She watched his rugged profile, the light making his face look harsh and strong. Her gaze fell to that pursed mouth of his as he intently typed in the word.

"Bingo!"

Heart leaping, Kathy eased around the desk and looked over his shoulder. Sure enough, the file opened. Her eyes widened as the information popped up on the screen. "Wow. Look at that. . . ." She pointed to the monitor.

Mac nodded and perused the information. "This is a gold mine," he rasped. Once he quickly copied the file, he moved it to the CD to burn. The machine whirred to life. Sitting back, he angled a glance up at her. "Nice work."

She was so beautiful. He had a thousand questions for her, but this wasn't the time or place to ask any of them. They were both in grave danger, being here. If discovered, their lives would be over in seconds.

"Why don't you go now?" Mac suggested. "We can't leave together."

Kathy straightened. Here came the next test. If Coulter was a foreign agent and not one from the U.S., he'd put a bullet into her. Wiping her brow, she stepped away from him. There was no way to get to his pistol, which was tucked beneath his left arm. "You just want me to go back to my villa?"

"That's right. Go back and go to sleep. Tomorrow, act as if nothing happened here tonight. Talk to no one, Kathy." And then he smiled again. "Is that your *real* name?"

"Need-to-know basis only, Mr. Coulter.

Right now, I trust you about as far as I can throw you."

Chuckling, Mac said, "That isn't far." He couldn't blame her. He saw the suspicion and questions in her eyes.

"No, it isn't."

"Now that you have the file, does this mean you're gone?" She gestured toward the laptop. Out of her life forever?

"No," Mac said, shaking his head.

"So, you'll be around after this?"

"Yeah."

"My own mission is complete with that file going to the Pentagon."

"Okay, I understand."

"We need to get Sophie out of here. That's the last thing I've got to do before I leave." She searched his sweaty features. The tension between them was palpable. "Can you help me do that? Get Sophie back to her parents?"

"Maybe," Mac said heavily. "Let me think on it. I'll contact you in about a week with some possibilities. No promises, though."

Relief flowed through her. She moved toward the door, listening for the snap of his shoulder harness. She walked lightly, waiting for him to pull out his pistol. As Kathy reached the door, she saw him stand, take the CD, slide it back into his thigh pocket, then shut off the laptop. He wore latex gloves so as not to leave prints. She hadn't worn gloves, she realized. But then, her fingerprints were on that laptop daily, so no one would suspect her. If they found Mac's prints on it, he'd be in trouble for sure.

Hand on the knob, Kathy gave him one last look. The expression on his face was one of pure satisfaction. "When will I see you?" she demanded in a whisper. "For Sophie's sake?"

Mac lowered the lid of the laptop. Looking over at her in the shadows, he said, "As soon as I can make things happen. Now, get out of here. . . ."

Sleep never came. Kathy lay in her bed, tossing and turning, her mind churning with thousands of questions. Mac Coulter was an American agent of some kind! Who did he work for? Could he really help her get Sophie out of here and back to her parents' arms? At this point, Kathy wanted nothing else but that.

She couldn't be sure that the file would make it to D.C., either. What proof would she get? And what would Mac do with the information that she was a U.S. Marine, working undercover? Terror ate at her. And panic. What if he told Garcia? What if he really wasn't a U.S. agent, but one in the employ of another drug lord, who wanted to topple the Garcia empire?

Scrunching her eyes shut, Kathy rolled onto her side and punched the feather pillow into a comfortable position. The windows were open, the breeze humid and sluggish. It was dawn, judging from the hint of gray along the horizon. She had to sleep!

But was Mac her enemy or her friend? Again she felt a wave of relief that the CD was on its way to the authorities — if she could believe Coulter. How badly she wanted to! Her whole being was now oriented to getting sad little Sophie out of this hellhole and back home.

Her thoughts swung to her own parents. Kathy missed her mother and father. In the past, she'd called them regularly, no matter where she was. Even on deep undercover missions as a Seahawk pilot, dropping off SEALs or Marine Recons in other South American countries, she'd been able to call them from time to time. It had been five months since she'd last made contact. She knew they were worried — especially her father, who didn't like being shut out of the loop involving any of his children.

"Mike? I want you to look at this photo and tell me what you think." Morgan Trayhern handed his second-in-command a black-and-white photo made from a JPEG off the computer. He had spent five days going over the hundreds of photos shot by Black Jaguar Squadron pilots on their flights to detour drug shipments. They filmed everyone they came across, most of them tourists from the Machu Picchu area. Others were archeologists, amateur and professional, going to sites within a hundred mile radius of Machu Picchu. That was BJS territory, and anyone in it was filmed for future reference.

Mike frowned and took the photo. It was barely 0900, and he hadn't had his first cup of coffee yet. "Find something from the BJS photo archives?" he asked, holding up the picture and squinting at it.

"I think so," Morgan growled impatiently. "What do *you* see? Remind you of anyone we know?"

Mike saw a female hiker with a knapsack on her back. The photo had been taken from about one thousand feet, and it was a side view, a profile. The woman had blond hair, and she'd been looking up at the helo when the photo was snapped. "Kathy?" he asked, disbelief in his voice as he looked over at Morgan's dark countenance.

"That's what I think. I'm having our computer section enhance the photo and match it with Kathy's facial features." Stabbing a finger at the photo, he snapped, "But I know what my daughter looks like no matter how far away. It's her."

Turning the photo over, Mike asked, "Where was this taken?"

"Fifty miles from Machu Picchu. According to Major Stevenson, that particular spot is a jaguar trail that leads from the Urubamba River straight to Garcia's villa, near Agua Caliente."

Mike was familiar with all the trails and turf of the area. He'd spent many years fighting in Peru, a U.S. Army combat trainer who had taken his gung ho soldiers into repeated head-on frays with the drug lords there. Locals had called him the Jaguar God, because he seemed to have nine lives, just like the fabled cat that was worshipped by the Incas.

"Yeah, Garcia has a 'test' for his nannies," Mike murmured as he studied the photo intently. "Did you know about that?"

"No, tell me," Morgan demanded gruffly.

"Garcia likes a nanny to be able to guard his only daughter, Tiki. His wife is a heroin addict and is 'gone' most of the time. Last I heard, he had a live-in mistress by the name of Therese. She runs his day-to-day operations for him, plus warms his bed at night." Mike gave Morgan a cutting smile. "Being the good Catholic boy he is, Garcia isn't about to divorce his drug-addict wife for this other woman. But he loves his daughter and wants to protect her. To that end he's been known to put the nanny applicants through a series of tests."

Mike pointed to the photo. "The last test, the most dangerous one, is that the nanny is dropped in the jungle with no food, no water and no pistol. There was gossip from time to time down in Lima when I was there that the remains of another applicant had been found, mostly eaten by the jaguar." He raised an eyebrow as Morgan looked more grim. "But if this is Kathy, and it sure looks like her from this angle, she's got a backpack on, so she wasn't left without supplies."

"So the real question is what was she doing on that particular trail?"

Scratching his head, Mike handed the photo back to his boss. "She's undercover, right?"

"Yes, and they won't let me in on the black ops. They've shut me out."

"Okay," Mike said slowly, thinking out loud. "Who kidnapped Jason, you and Laura? Guillermo Garcia. Carlos is his son."

Stunned, Morgan stared at Houston. "What are you saying?"

"That maybe Kathy has gone undercover to right a wrong. She's on a well-known trail that Garcia uses to test his nannies. There's only one end to this trail — his villa. Is she working there? And if so, why? Revenge, maybe?"

"Dammit!" Morgan snarled. He tightened his hands into fists as his mind raced with possibilities. There was no way he wanted his eldest daughter *there*. *Good God.* Swinging a sharp glance toward Houston he rasped, "Revenge? What kind?"

"Garcia has a daughter. Would Kathy do an 'eye for an eye' thing? Kidnap Garcia's daughter just as the three of you were kidnapped by his father?"

Bludgeoned by the possibility, Morgan grabbed a chair and sat down. "She couldn't. . . . No, that's foolish. Dangerous . . ."

"Deadly," Houston said sympathetically.

365

"Look, Morgan, don't dive down that hole just yet. It's only a theory. Why don't you get someone on the phone back in D.C. who can blow the cover off this black ops? That way you'll know for sure what's going down." He pointed to the photo on his desk. "For all we know, Kathy may be hiking and nothing more. We can't go ballistic just yet." He drilled Morgan with a hard look. "Get ahold of some key players in Washington. Find out what's goin' down. Then panic, if you don't like what they say."

Gripping the desk, Morgan stood up. His feet felt like thousand-pound lead weights. His heart hurt as he thought of Laura. If this was true, it would tear his wife apart. Hell, it would tear the family apart — again. In a new and different way. "What if she's down there, Mike? What if Garcia has found her out?"

"Boss, don't go there. Not yet, at least. Find out where she is, first." Mike gave him a sympathetic smile, noting the suffering clearly etched on Morgan's face. "Make some calls?"

Chapter Nineteen

It was hell on earth as far as Kathy was concerned. Two days had gone by since her unexpected meeting with Mac in Therese's office. She'd barely seen him, since he was flying much more than usual for Garcia. She felt jittery and wondered if she should just leave now without Sophie. No, she couldn't do that. She would *never* leave that little girl in the lurch, as Jason had been left.

Kathy grimaced and tightened the saddle girth on Hector. She watched as Sophie stood in the box stall with General, brushing him even though his saddle was on. Kathy had just delivered Tiki to Garcia, who was going over to see his wife at her caseta. He visited Paloma regularly. Kathy wondered if the drug addict was even coherent enough to know that Tiki was her child. Shaking her head, Kathy tried to focus on something positive in her murky, sordid little world.

At least there was a clear blue sky this morning, which was highly unusual in the jungle. With her nerves raw and screaming, Kathy wanted to escape the villa for just a little while and take Sophie for a ride down in the meadow.

She heard a helicopter returning, and could tell by the sound of the engine that it was Mac. He was approaching at a very high rate of speed, which was unusual. The stable was located down below the landing pad, but she could feel the buffeted air from the helicopter blades vibrating around her as he brought the bird in for a landing within the walls of the villa complex.

Pulling down the stirrup, she took Hector's reins and turned him around in his cushy box stall, filled with dry, sweet yellow oat straw for bedding.

"How are you coming along?" she called to Sophie over the thick wooden wall.

"Fine, Kathy. I think General likes me to brush his legs. He keeps moving his lips all over me." She laughed shortly. "He's giving me horsey kisses."

It felt good to hear Sophie laugh. Only since the horses had come into her life had the little girl emerged from her cocoon of depression. "Okay, squirt, hold on. We'll get you mounted up in just a second," Kathy said, her heart bleeding for the little girl. She'd marveled over Sophie's riding abilities, then learned she had been taking riding lessons since she was four years old.

As the helicopter landed, Kathy's mind drifted back to Mac. Her paranoia returned despite the fact that he had had every chance to turn her in and hadn't. *Was* he a friendly agent? Who did he work for? She'd barely slept the last few nights. Had he delivered the CD to his handler in Cuzco? He'd been gone most of the time since the night they'd accidentally met in the office. And when she had seen him, he'd looked grim. Very grim. More so than ever before.

Something was going on. She could feel it in the air. The last two days the horses had been more fretful and restive than usual. And Tiki seemed to psychically pick up on everyone's restlessness. She was crabby most of the time.

Only once had Kathy seen Garcia, and he, too, seemed tense. The guards were always on alert. The gate sentries had added ammunition, heavy belts of bullets that crisscrossed their chests. These weapons complemented the two pistols on their hips, not to mention the M-4 rifles. So much protection and anxiety. Why? What was going on? She wished someone would tell her.

As Kathy opened the box stall, she heard heavy footfalls; someone was running full speed toward her. Mac Coulter! His mouth was set and his eyes narrowed on her. Kathy started toward him then hesitated when she heard a sound — like a squadron of droning helicopters flying toward them.

The guards at the gates shouted orders and started scurrying about. Hector whinnied and moved around nervously in his stall. As Kathy tried to ascertain the cause of this commotion, Mac barreled down the hill toward the stable. Something was wrong. Badly wrong.

Tensing, she saw him run to the gate and jerk it open. Sweat beaded on his face, and his brow was furrowed. "Get those horses out!" he yelled. "Where's Sophie?"

"She's in there." Kathy pointed. "What's going on?" she demanded, opening the stall door and grabbing Hector's reins.

"We've got Russian Ka-50s, Black Sharks, four of them, coming down on us right now," he yelled. "A drug dealer named Navarro is making an attack on Garcia. He intends to wipe this place off the face of the earth!" Throwing a glance over his shoulder, he rasped, "Take the white horse! Take Sophie with you." He grabbed Hector's reins. "I'll ride this one."

"What — ?"

"We're going for the Blackhawk. It's our only escape, Kathy." He opened the door to General's stall. "Come on. Hurry! There isn't time to chat. We got about five minutes before those bastards hit this villa with enough firepower to destroy the whole damn thing!"

"Wait! What about Tiki? We can't just leave her!" Kathy cried.

Mac hesitated, obviously torn. "Where is she?"

"Oh, God, Mac, she's down at her mother's caseta with her father!"

"That's too far away! We'll never make it in time!" Mac turned and looked skyward. Black dots were coming their way, the blades already starting to buffet the air. He heard Kathy cry out in frustration. Turning, he saw her start toward the gate.

"No!" he yelled. "You'll never reach them in time!"

Tears flooded Kathy's eyes. "We can't leave her! We just can't!"

Grimly, Mac pulled her to a halt. "Listen to me, will you? You either save three lives here or *all* of us are going to die in a very few minutes, including Tiki and her family. Which will it be, Kathy?"

Fighting back a sob, she stared into his burning gray eyes. "Tiki . . ."

"I know, I know . . . I'm sorry, but she's gonna have to take her chances here. Come on! Let's get going!"

Gasping, Kathy grabbed Sophie. "Honey, can you ride behind me? Hold on real tight around my waist?" She saw Sophie's eyes go wide.

The puncturing beat of the double axial blades of the Black Sharks drew closer and closer. The entire villa vibrated with the power of the approaching enemy helicopters.

"Well — sure. That's easy!" Sophie frowned, looking up at the sky.

"Climb aboard," Mac ordered Kathy tightly, and he held out his hand to grasp her bended knee and lift her onto General.

Mounting quickly, she watched as he easily lifted Sophie, settling the child solidly behind her on the saddle.

"Now, you hold on," Mac told her. "Don't let go, Sophie! We have to get out of here."

The little girl nodded and wrapped her arms tightly around Kathy's waist.

General snorted, his eyes rolling as the puncturing noise thundered above them. As Kathy turned the Andalusian around, Mac leaped into Hector's saddle like a born cowboy. "Follow me!" he yelled over the gathering din.

Everywhere Kathy looked, soldiers were running like rats escaping a sinking ship. As she reined the jumpy gelding around, Sophie stuck to her like glue. *Good!*

Mac galloped down toward the gate leading to the meadow. He made a flying dive from the horse as it skidded to a stop, sending up clouds of dust. Mac swung the white gate open and quickly leaped back onto Hector's saddle.

Kathy galloped up to him. "Then we're escaping to the Blackhawk?"

He gave her a tight smile and a short nod. "Damn straight. This is our chance! Let's ride like hell." He dug his heels into Hector's heaving sides. The gelding snorted, leaped upward, landed on his front feet and galloped heavily down the narrow trail.

"Hold on to me," Kathy told Sophie urgently, then leaned forward and sunk her heels in General's sides. Instantly, their mount jumped forward.

Oh no! Kathy caught her first glimpse of a lethal Black Shark as it appeared over the villa. Real terror raced through her, the Black Shark was a flying arsenal. They were in *big* trouble! Leaning forward, the wind whipping around her, she urged the gelding faster.

As they flew down the winding trail, leaves hanging out in the narrow path swatted at her arms, legs and face. Kathy kept dodging and ducking, to avoid the larger ones.

The sucking sound of General's hoof-beats as he slowed for the curves and corners made her sit up. The soil was red clay and always damp — dangerous conditions for a galloping horse. If the animal slipped, they could all go tumbling.

Kathy heard the hiss of a rocket, then an explosion at the villa. A booming sound rolled over them like a violent storm. They were too close! Slapping the reins hard against General's withers, she coaxed him to a dizzying speed. More explosions erupted behind them.

Sophie screamed in reaction to the attack. She clung to Kathy's waist, her arms so tight that Kathy could barely breathe. A fireball rolled across the tree canopy overhead, then the stench of smoke assailed Kathy's flared nostrils. The heat hit next, and General panicked. Kathy fought him, hauling back on the bit. The horse's mouth gaped open as he reared crazily, slipping and sliding down the winding trail.

Kathy wrestled with the Andalusian, knowing that in a quarter of a mile they'd reach the meadow. Then it would be a straight run to the Blackhawk. What if the Black Sharks found their helicopter? They'd sure as hell destroy it!

"Come on," Kathy crooned. "General! Settle down, dammit!" She took command of the careening horse, until he was once more under her control. She reined him in as they came to another sharp bend in the path. It was steeper now, and more slippery. Wrenching back on the reins, her legs pressed against his sweaty barrel, she used all her strength to control the panicked horse. Instantly, General sat back on his haunches, his rear hooves skidding beneath him along the red mud trail.

"Hang on!" Kathy cried to Sophie. Ahead, she caught a glimpse of Mac on Hector. The gray gelding, too, was sliding and scrambling, red mud splattering up his legs and across his underbelly.

This was the dangerous part! The trail became exceedingly steep. Everywhere, tree roots jutted out, and if a horse hit one the wrong way, they could flip end over end.

"Slow!" Kathy yelled at General.

The horse snorted loudly, his ears

twitching back and forth. His sides were heaving and sweat made his white body shine. Behind her, Kathy heard another explosion, then another. The Black Sharks were wreaking hell at Garcia's villa. Kathy worried for Tiki's safety, but there was nothing she could do. Tears flooded her eyes and she sobbed. Oh, poor Tiki! She didn't deserve this! She was an innocent!

Finally General reached the bottom of the slope and the jungle opened up to reveal the meadow. Kathy leaned forward and again whipped the reins across his withers. The Andalusian strained forward, his neck straight out, ears laid back. Ahead, Mac rode Hector hard, bent over the horse's gleaming, steel-colored neck. The gelding's black mane and tail flew like flags in a strong wind, and clouds of dust rose as Hector raced toward the end of the meadow.

Suddenly, Kathy heard an ominous sound behind her. Jerking a quick look across her shoulder, she felt her heart freeze. *Oh, no!* A Black Shark hoved into view, flying about a thousand feet above them — and straight at them!

"Mac!" she cried.

He didn't hear her! Kathy knew she had to take evasive action. If they stayed on the trail, the Black Shark could target the Blackhawk and destroy it before they had a chance to escape.

"Hang on, Sophie!" Kathy knew she had to become a decoy so that, at least, Mac could get to the Blackhawk. As she glanced back, she saw six different fireballs mushrooming skyward from the villa. Two other Black Sharks hovered there, firing repeatedly into the place.

Jerking General to the right, Kathy veered off the trail. The horse leaped through the knee-high grass and jumped over small bushes. She steered him toward the jungle, a half mile away. After hearing the Black Shark change course, she realized it was now following and targeting them. Could she outmaneuver the pilot?

One thing Mac had told her was that only one pilot was on board the lethal monster. He had all the work of flying as well as targeting, whereas the Apache held two pilots — one to fly and one to fire. Was this pilot too busy flying to aim at them? Kathy prayed it was so.

She leaned low over the horse's neck. Wind whipped them, making her eyes water, and General's mane repeatedly slapped her face. Sophie was hanging on, thank God, her face pressed hard against Kathy's back.

Seeing a small opening in the jungle wall, Kathy aimed for it. But then the helicopter stopped and hovered. It was drawing a bead on her.

At the last possible second, she wrenched General to the left — back across the meadow. The horse grunted, flexed his rear legs and leaped like a startled jackrabbit. Kathy dug her heels into his sweaty flanks, asking everything of him.

She heard the pop of a rocket. Gritting her teeth, she kept General swinging to the left.

Seconds later, the rocket exploded behind them.

General whinnied hysterically and ran even harder. Heat rolled by them. Rocks and dirt pelted them.

"Come on!" Kathy cried to the gelding. She lay low on the horse, urging him on with her hands, her legs and her pleading voice.

The Black Shark shifted. She could hear it. Was it stalking her again? Fear gutted her. Risking another look over her shoulder, Kathy saw to her surprise that it was turning around and flying back to the villa! The pilot must have thought they were poor pickings compared to the damage he could do at the villa.

The end of the meadow was coming up fast. As she guided the wild-eyed General to the jungle trail that would lead to the second, smaller meadow, Kathy gripped the horse with her legs to keep from being pitched off. Sophie continued to cling to her.

As they broke out of the jungle, she saw Hector running away from the Blackhawk, riderless. Mac was in the helo and had it started up, with the rotor turning! *Good!!* Kathy brought General to a sliding halt two hundred feet away from the whirling blades. The horse was wild, obviously scared of the noisy helicopter. Wrestling with him, Kathy gripped Sophie with one arm and lifted her off, setting her safely on the ground. Then she leaped off in turn. Hooking the reins over the saddle horn, Kathy spooked General by throwing up her hands. The horse took off at a gallop back up the trail, following the fleeing, panicked Hector.

Reaching down, Kathy gripped the child's hand. "Come on, Sophie, we're taking you home!" Kathy raced forward, her head down as she pulled the little girl toward the open door behind the cockpit. The wind punched at them, and Kathy held up her hand to protect her eyes. The little girl was close at her side as they struggled forward. Mac sat in the right-hand seat — the pilot's seat — and had on a military helmet. As Kathy lifted Sophie aboard, she saw two flak vests, one small and one large, lying on the metal deck in front of them.

Diving inside, she quickly slid the door shut and locked it. The cabin wasn't large, and she was on her knees. She hooked her thumb between the two seats in the cockpit to let Mac know he could take off.

First things first. Gasping for breath, with sweat dribbling into her eyes, Kathy shakily pulled the smaller flak vest off the deck and put it around Sophie. There was a net cargo seat against the armored wall at the rear of the bird. She hoisted Sophie into it and pulled the nylon straps across her small body, buckling her in as tightly as possible. Kathy's hands shook so badly she could barely get the closures fastened and locked.

Leaning forward, her mouth near Sophie's ear, she yelled, "No matter what happens, Sophie, stay in this harness, okay? It's going to be a rough ride. Just hang on, okay?" She patted the girl's shoulder. Sophie's eyes were huge, but she had a fearless look in them as she nodded her head in understanding.

Kathy grinned and turned. She grabbed the other flak vest and quickly put it on with trembling fingers. Adrenaline was running full bore through her now. Giving Sophie a last reassuring pat on the knee, Kathy pivoted just as Mac powered up for takeoff. The noise was deafening, and the bird shook. The Blackhawk broke contact with the earth, throwing Kathy backward.

As he brought the chopper at a steep climb out of the jungle, Kathy scrambled to her hands and knees and made her way forward into the cockpit. She saw a second military helmet sitting on the copilot's seat. After grabbing it, she crouched between the seats so she wouldn't continue to be thrown around. Mac made several sharp, banking maneuvers to try and escape the sights of the Black Sharks no more than three miles away.

Once she'd climbed into the left seat, Kathy donned the helmet, strapped it on and positioned the mike close to her lips. She plugged in the connection.

"You hear me?" she demanded as her hands flew with familiar ease over the nylon harness system. She was soon strapped in tightly to her seat. They were on a rough ride and she knew it.

"Roger, I hear you loud and clear."

"I'm Blackhawk qualified, Coulter."

He glanced over at her in surprise, then grinned. "You're just a bundle of surprises, you know that? Then be my copilot. I need a weapons officer. Can you handle that?"

"Shoot fast. Shoot straight. Load often. In my sleep, Coulter," Kathy said, smiling wryly. The Blackhawk rapidly gained altitude as the jungle fell away. Altitude was their safe haven, in one respect. The more height they gained, the more room they had to maneuver if they were chased or cornered. Her hands flew across the console in front of her as she switched on the bird's array of weapons.

"Watch our six," Mac warned, his gaze pinned to the horizon ahead of them. "We're making a run for Dodge. The moment the Black Sharks see us, they're gonna come after us."

"I'm on it," Kathy said, intently studying the headsup display. The green HUD screen was five inches by five inches and resembled a television.

The helo was shaking and straining. The blades beat heavily to gain precious altitude in the turgid, humid air. Helos never climbed fast in high humidity like this. Kathy wished it was drier since it would mean a faster climb. She also wished she had a pair of aviator glasses like Mac wore to combat the bright sun.

"You got another pair of glasses around, Coulter?" she demanded.

"Yeah, side pocket."

"You've thought of everything." Kathy reached down into the nylon net pocket on the right side of her seat. There they were. She quickly took them out of the case and slipped them on; it was better than pulling down the half-face black shield of the helmet. The heat of the sunlight coming through the cockpit windows made her feel like a sponge. She quickly saw that Mac hadn't turned on the air-conditioning yet. Normal checklists were thrown out the door on an emergency liftoff like this. Usually a copilot took care of such details.

"Mind if I cool us down?" she asked, reaching across and flipping on the switch.

"Not at all. Thanks . . ."

Kathy studied the HUD and switched it to radar mode. So far, the Black Sharks were otherwise engaged. Twisting around, she checked on Sophie. The flak jacket was huge for her and she looked tiny in it. After giving her a smile and a thumbs-up, she saw Sophie smile and return the gesture.

Kathy turned back and looked at Mac. His jaw was hard, his expression harsh and focused. "Where's Dodge?" she asked him. "You got a plan where you're taking us?" He was headed away from Cuzco, and Kathy knew there were no major airports in the direction they were flying. Her heart pounded hard in her chest. She gulped and tried to steady her breathing.

"Yeah, I got a plan. We're heading straight for the safest place in this region — the Black Jaguar Squadron. I want you to set the radio to a special frequency that lets them know we're friend, not foe." He pointed to the radio console.

"Roger, give me the frequency," Kathy ordered. When he did so, she turned the radio to that frequency. Instantly, Mac began the call to them.

"Black Jaguar. Black Jaguar, this is King's Ace. Over. Do you read? This is King's Ace. I am initiating Operation Emerald. Repeat — Operation Emerald. Confirm you have received this request. We are heading in your direction and we need any help you can throw our way. We have four Black Sharks, repeat, four Black Sharks at the Garcia villa and they are going to be coming after us. This is a mayday. Mayday. We need your help and protection. Over."

"Oh, shit! Here they come!" Kathy cried as four specks suddenly appeared on her radar screen. They had been spotted! Her heart rate soared.

"Roger, just keep the chaff handy. We're gonna need it," Mac growled.

Kathy frowned and checked out the chaff dispensers, devices designed to confuse incoming missiles. Normally a Seahawk had two, but on this one there were six, which was fine with her. Chaff could make the difference between them surviving a missile attack or not.

Mac went back to making the emergency call to the BJS. Operation Emerald was a secret code for help. It meant we are a friendly in your territory and we need your Apaches to fight for us so we can reach your base safely.

Mac held his breath. He saw Kathy's hands flying across the console, preparing and activating their array of weapons. But they were no match for a Black Shark. Not in the least.

Come on, answer me! Answer me! His nostrils flared as he waited to hear a response from the supersecret base located inside one of these conical mountains. Mac had the exact coordinates of their location in his head. It was his only safe place if everything went to hell in a handbasket. Well, today it had gone there.

Every second felt like years. He compressed his lips and felt the trickle of sweat down his temples beneath the helmet he wore. Glancing to his left, he saw Kathy continue to work the weapons systems like a pro. What a surprise she was! A U.S. Marine Seahawk pilot! Any other time he'd have laughed over the absurdity of it all; how well she'd cloaked her true identity from him. Never in a million years would he have guessed her to be a Marine Corps pilot!

"King's Ace, this is Black Jaguar Base, we read you loud and clear. We are initiating Operation Emerald. Can you give us your location once more?"

Relief tunneled through Mac. He saw that the Black Sharks were speeding rapidly toward them. They were faster because of their double axial blades. Quickly, he gave the latest flight coordinates. "Black Jaguar, I say again — we are in trouble. The four Black Sharks are less than ten miles away and rapidly gaining on us."

"Roger, King's Ace. We are in emergency mode here and getting every available Apache into the air to come and meet you. Be aware that Cobra Two is only ten miles from you in the direction you need to go. We've already let them know and they are heading your way. Over."

"Roger, that's good news." But it wasn't near enough. The Apache and Black Shark combat helicopters were basically the two biggest junkyard dogs in the world and an even match for one another. There were four enemy Sharks pitched against one Apache coming to their rescue, and the firepower wasn't sufficient to turn the tide in their favor.

"Please switch your radio to Cobra Two's frequency. We'll be on it, as well, and keep you updated on the other Apaches coming to your aid, King's Ace. Over."

"Roger and thanks." Mac dialed in the new frequency. "Cobra Two, this is King's Ace. Do you read me?"

One Apache was flying at top speed to intercept and try to protect them. Mac was afraid. He tried not to let it show in his voice. More than anything, he wanted to take Sophie home to her family — alive. And dammit, he wanted to meet Kathy Lincoln, or whoever she really was, in a place where they could finally reveal their true identities to one another — because he had fallen in love with her.

Chapter Twenty

"Hey!" Wild woman crowed in her best Montana drawl, "We are *finally* gonna get four of those Black Sharks all in one place, at one time. Hell's bells! It's time to do 'em all in! Yippee!" She flew the Apache at hightailin' speed toward the escaping Blackhawk known as King's Ace.

Snake, who was in the upper seat behind her pilot friend, hurriedly typed in the data commands to her weapons computer. Her dark brown brows fell. "Dude, it's one of us against all them, in case you're ignoring that minuscule piece of info. One Apache against four of those bastards."

Chortling, Wild Woman pulled the dark visor down over her eyes and continued to scan the clear blue skies around them. "One Apache can take four of 'em on and win!" She reached out and patted the console in front of her. "This dog'll hunt, sister."

"Your cinch is loose, girlfriend," Snake muttered. "I got 'em painted on the HUD. See 'em? See that Black-hawk? He's redlining it for all he's worth."

"What's that favorite saying of yours? Don't drop your gun to hug a grizzly bear? A Blackhawk, even armed, isn't able to go up successfully against a Shark. Yeah, I got 'em painted on my screen. Arm our missiles. I want to put a few of them up those good ol' Russki boys' asses."

"Humph. Before they put one up ours . . ." Snake quickly flipped several switches to arm the missiles and rockets. The Apache screamed toward the fray, flying at ten thousand feet. "You gonna climb, Wild Woman? Let's get some more air between us and those dudes. They're all low level, running at about five angels, five thousand feet. Arrogant enough to think no one else is around to stop them from doing what they're doin', so they aren't looking for us. Best to come at 'em high and from out of the sun."

"Good plannin', Snake. We're gonna make their day."

Grimly, Snake looked up, her eyes narrowed. "If you take all of 'em on, you'll think you've been in a sack with a couple of bobcats."

"Bring 'em on," Wild Woman said. "We can whip our weight in wolves *and* bobcats."

"I hate it when you get into this kind of mood."

Giving a wicked cackle, Wild Woman said, "PMS is a wonderful thing." She laughed loudly.

A grudging grin pulled at Snake's mouth. "You'll get no argument outta me. Put a bunch of PMS women into combat and they will annihilate the enemy in the blink of an eye. It's our secret weapon."

"Roger that, Snake." Wild Woman took the Apache in a steep ascent, the blades cutting aggressively through the air. The vibration shook the cockpit. Grinning evilly, Wild Woman said, "Dude, I have waited years for this little window of opportunity to show up! Those Sharks are always hangin' around between the mountains to jump us, because they know we can't detect their signature on our radar. This is one time they're in the open. Yessiree, this is gonna be an old-fashioned Montana turkey shoot, and I can hardly wait to get 'em!"

"Cowboys and Indians," Snake grunted, her gaze on the HUD and their targets. "And I'm an Indian."

"Half Navajo and half German. Hell, I'm half Cheyenne. My gawd, what a Heinz variety mix!" Wild Woman yelled.

"But I like you, anyway, Snake."

"Thanks — I think." A sliver of a grin curved the corners of Snake's mouth.

"Just think, Snake, it's usually the cowboys showin' up to protect the settlers from the evil ol' Indians. Now it's reversed — we Indians are gonna save the day for that poor settler being chased by the bad guys."

"Hey, that Blackhawk's really clawin' at the sky."

"The dude flying it is an ATF agent, according to intel I just received," Wild Woman noted. "But I'm sure he's ex–U.S. Army by the way he's haulin' ass with that bird. Those are combat maneuvers."

"Yeah, well, he'd better put extra fire under that bird's butt because the Sharks are closin' in on him like vultures on a carcass." Wild Woman frowned. "When are the other three Apaches coming, Snake? You heard from base yet?"

Shaking her head, her friend said, "They're rollin' them out to the lip right now." The base was forty miles away from the air-to-air combat about to take place. Snake could imagine the claxon bell clanging harshly throughout the cave complex, the race of the crews and pilots toward the Apaches that were being pushed out on the lip of the cave for takeoff.

"Then it really is us against them."

Snake rolled her eyes. "Has reality just landed on you with both feet?"

Wild Woman snorted. "Feathers are gonna fly shortly and it sure as hell isn't gonna be off *our* bird."

"Yeah, right. Well, we'll do what we can. Our first priority is to keep that Blackhawk from getting blown out of the sky. They're VIPs."

"Roger, I hear you." The growl of the Apache engine deepened as the blades seized the air and found purchase. At twenty thousand feet Wild Woman leveled the bird off and, redlining the screaming engines, sent it hurtling forward.

"Cobra Two, this is King's Ace, over."

Wild Woman's blond brows shot up. "Damned if that ain't a woman's voice, Snake. Or am I hearin' things?"

"You're not hearin' things. You fly, I'll take the coms." Snake switched to the channel. "King's Ace, this is Cobra Two, over."

Kathy tried to keep her voice low and modulated even though her heart thundered like a freight train. Mac was forcing the Blackhawk as high as it could go without draining away too much forward speed. Climbing was a delicate balancing act, one Mac accomplished with great skill as the Sharks came up fast behind them. Just hearing the calm, soothing tone of another woman's voice at the other end of the radio helped Kathy think they might have a chance of living through this.

"Cobra Two, we're heading toward the BJS coordinates. Right now we need some help. The Sharks are almost within missile range of us."

"Roger, King's Ace, we understand. We're at twenty angels and redlining it. We will be within range of you in . . . five minutes. Over."

Five minutes was a lifetime to her. "Roger that." Kathy gulped and twisted around to peer out of the cockpit. She saw four black dots on the horizon, coming closer and closer. "Tell us you have more than one Apache coming?"

Kathy heard the woman pilot give a husky laugh. "That's a roger, King's Ace. Three more rolling out as we speak. For a little while, though, it's just little ol' us against the four of them. We consider that an even fight. We want you, however, to take whatever evasive action you need to. Does the pilot know this area at all?"

"Roger, he does. Over."

"Good. Tell him to play hide 'n seek around the mountains ahead of him. Sharks have damn good radar but they cannot penetrate mountains to see where you're hiding. So tell him to head for the hills slightly east of where you are presently. BJS is in that direction, anyway. If you can get behind a mountain, they can't shoot at you. Do you copy? Over."

"Roger, I copy. Good advice, Cobra Two, thanks. I'll tell him. Out."

Kathy turned to Mac, who had heard the entire conversation, she knew. "Well?"

"Yeah, good idea in theory." Mac nodded his head toward the horizon. "Those are lava mountains. They're shaped like loaves of French bread standing on end, and are covered with orchids, bromeliads and other jungle brush. They're roughly one quarter to half a mile in circumference — not large, but big enough for us to hide behind if shot at. The problem is getting there before the Sharks do."

Looking around, Kathy said, "Well, heading for them beats the hell out of being a target in the middle of this blue sky."

A sour smile pulled at Mac's mouth. Sweat trickled nonstop beneath his arms as he tensely held the controls and mentally urged the Blackhawk to move faster. "Yeah, I roger that. Is Sophie harnessed in?"

"Yes, she's good to go."

"Flak jacket on, right?" Mac couldn't risk turning to look.

"Roger."

"Okay, we're gonna have to start jinxing around when they start throwing lead at us. Hang on. . . ."

"I know that." Kathy watched the HUD intently. The Sharks were now within range. "They will throw missiles at us." She got ready to pop the trigger on the first chaff dispenser.

"How did this Blackhawk end up with six dispensers of chaff and not the standard two?" she asked Mac.

Chuckling, he answered, "Garcia wanted more insurance. He had them built in."

"Damn insightful of him."

"Roger that."

Most missiles and rockets were heat seekers. They would follow anything that was hot, like an engine. Chaff, when released from the fuselage of a helo, would act as a heat decoy, drawing the weapons after them instead of the bird. At least, that was the theory. Throat dry, her eyes slits, Kathy watched and waited.

There was a sudden beeping sound in

her helmet. "One of 'em has acquired us as a target," Kathy rasped, her finger hovering over the chaff switch.

"Roger." Instantly, Mac banked the helo to one side, then the other. He didn't want to lose much altitude. If the Sharks ever worked him down to the level of the forest canopy, there'd be no more maneuvering room. Even here they'd be an easy target to knock out of the sky, like shooting ducks in a barrel. No, he had to not only maintain altitude, but try to inch upward.

Every time Mac banked the Blackhawk, though, it slowed his forward speed, which meant the pursuing Sharks would get closer that much faster. *Damn!* If only that Apache would get here! Mac knew that, for the next five minutes, it was their game to win or lose.

"Missile fired!" Kathy snapped.

"Chaff!"

"Fired!" She flipped the switch. Jerking her head to the left, craning her neck, she stared out the cockpit window, watching two arcing smoke trails leave the Blackhawk. The brightly lit chaff glowed more brilliantly than the sun. Would the missile follow it and not them? The straps of the harness bit deeply into her shoulders as Mac banked the bird again. The beeping in her helmet got louder and louder as the stalking missile approached. Tearing her gaze from the sky and the glowing chaff now arching below them, she watched the green HUD screen, her eyes wide with fear.

The air turbulence was rough. As the sun warmed the jungle, creating updrafts of hot air, the ride became brutal. Mac swung the bird violently into a left bank, and the engines whined from the strain. An explosion erupted a hundred feet below them, and Kathy gripped the seat. A shock wave from the explosion hit them, and the Blackhawk shuddered.

Mac rode out the explosion as the bird was thrust upward fifty feet. He quickly moved the rudders and controls to stabilize the floundering helo. The missile had hit the chaff! But he didn't have time to cheer, for another beep sounded in his helmet. A second missile was being fired at them!

"Number two on the way," Kathy told him grimly. They had six rounds of chaff to release, and that was it. She knew the Sharks probably carried four or six missiles apiece — way more than they could evade this way. The pounding of the blades thumped through her. Mac wrestled with the bird. They'd lost five hundred feet in altitude. Again he swung the helo in a side-to-side motion to try and evade their pursuers.

"Chaff!" Mac said.

"Fired!" Kathy flipped the switch. There was a timing element to releasing chaff. Too soon and it wouldn't catch the attention of the speeding, heat-seeking missile. Too late and the missile would pass it up for the engine heat of their helo. Up ahead, Kathy could see the loaf-shaped mountains drawing closer and closer. Oh, if only they could reach them!

Another explosion. Again, below them. The Black-hawk was thrown upward by the blast.

"Shit!" Kathy yelled as she was slammed hard against the left side of the fuselage. The Blackhawk bobbled, out of control. That explosion had been close! Too close! They'd be lucky not to get hit by shrapnel.

Kathy watched the HUD, heard yet another beep in her helmet. Dread filled her. "They're throwing another missile at us."

"Cobra Two, this is King's Ace. Where the hell are you?" Mac snarled into the radio.

"We're one minute from joining your dance, King's Ace. You're doing fine. We're stalking them from above. Just keep doing what you're doing. Over."

One minute. One friggin'minute! "Yeah, roger that," Mac growled, frustration etched in his voice.

Kathy quickly flipped the switch for the third round of chaff. "Chaff fired!"

The beep became faster and louder. The third missile was hunting them in earnest! She glanced at the altitude indicator, they had lost another thousand feet. *Damn!* Mac was doing what he could, but there was only so much to work with. . . .

Another beep. "Damn, they're throwing a fourth missile at us!" Kathy cried.

Mac nodded and kept his focus on their escape. All he wanted to do was get to the mountains, which he could use as a safety net of sorts. Air turbulence jarred them like a dog shaking to get rid of fleas. Grinding his teeth, Mac gripped the controls and tried to ride out the huge air pockets. But every time they hit one, it slowed their forward speed a little more. And in this run for safety, every mile per hour counted.

"Chaff fired!" Kathy flipped the switch. Two missiles came at them. She saw them streaking toward them on the HUD. Her eyes widened as the chaff arced away from the Blackhawk. Would both missiles follow it? Oh, God, if they didn't . . . She touched her parched throat in a nervous motion.

Two explosions rent the air. The Blackhawk groaned, flailed and shuddered as the blast waves, one right after the other, hit them. Cursing softly, Mac worked the controls. The harness kept him from being slammed around. He heard Kathy give a cry, her hand going up against her drawn visor to protect her eyes. Seeing the red welts of fire and the black smoke venting upward past the chopper, he realized just how close they'd come to dying.

Another beep began.

"Next to the last chaff," Kathy announced. Sweat trickled down the sides of her face, and her breath came shallow and fast. The mountains loomed ahead. Gaze glued to the HUD, she saw the missile approaching.

"Chaff fired!" she cried, trying to prepare for the blast.

It came so close this time that the fiery red clouds and yellow tongues of flame belched upward toward Kathy's side of the cockpit.

Another beep began.

"We're almost outta chaff," she told Mac tensely, and glanced over at him.

"I know. We need to save the last of it for when we really need it. Hold on." He hauled the scrambling Blackhawk into a nearly vertical climb. The metal craft groaned, and the blades thumped hard. As vibrations shook the helicopter, the engines screamed in protest. Blades whirled, trying to find enough air to gain altitude.

What was he doing? There was no place to go! Kathy hung on, slammed back into her seat, pinned by the sudden pull of gravity. Her gaze was on the missile now stalking them. They were almost out of chaff! Oh, God, were they going to die? Giving Mac one last glance, Kathy realized that she might never get to know him, never get to kiss him again, never get to love him as she wanted to. Her hands curled into the seat and she held on.

Wrenching the Blackhawk out of the climb, the engines shrieking in protest, Mac banked the bird hard right. For an instant, the craft hung suspended in the air. Then the blades beat hard and it flipped onto its side, plummeting toward the green carpet of jungle below. It was a ruse to fool the incoming projectile. Mac knew missiles couldn't make fast turns, and he was jinxing the bird so that the device lost track of them. *Hurry! Hurry!* The bird fell like a rock. The land raced up at them. His breath jammed in his throat, his eyes on the jungle below, he started to pray.

Suddenly, there was an explosion.

Kathy gave a cry.

Mac blinked. What had happened? Did the missile blow up before it had reached them? *No, impossible.* After leveling out the Blackhawk at five thousand feet, he jerked a look toward Kathy.

"What happened?"

"The Apache took out the missile meant for us!" Kathy crowed, lifting her fist in victory. She smiled triumphantly. "Damn, those sisters are *good!*"

Relief sheeted through Mac. He again redlined the Blackhawk. "Let's make a run for it," he muttered darkly, aiming for the mountains, now ten miles away.

"King's Acc, this is Cobra Two. Over."

"King's Ace, Cobra Two. Thanks for saving our ass. Over."

"Roger that," Snake chuckled. "Listen, we see that these good ole boys are outta rockets and missiles. They musta expended them elsewhere?"

"Roger," Mac declared. "They fired on the drug dealer Carlos Garcia's villa and blew it to hell earlier. That would be my guess why they're low on ammo. Over."

"Okay," Snake said. "Then we'll see what we girls can do to get them with *our* rockets and missiles. In the meantime, head for the fortress as fast as you can. Over."

"Roger," Kathy said, giving Mac a tense smile. He grinned back, but she could see the worry in his eyes. "Out."

She gulped and tried to slow her erratic breathing as she watched the HUD screen. She saw the Apache, which was ten thousand feet higher than the Sharks, loose three missiles at the pursuing enemies on their tail. Clenching her hands, she whispered, "Get those sons of bitches!"

Within moments, she saw chaff spewing from the Sharks that had been targeted. One got hit.

"Bingo!" Kathy yelled triumphantly. "Cobra Two bagged one!"

"Three more to go," Mac reminded her sternly. "Don't ever underestimate those guys. They're damn good hunters."

Even as he said it, Kathy gulped. The three remaining Sharks spread out in a fan, at least three miles apart. "Hey, Mac . . ."

"I see. They're coming after us." And they were only two miles behind.

"They have no rockets. No missiles."

"But we do. We're going to turn around

and make a stand. Get ready to fire those AGM-114s."

Revenge soared through Kathy as she quickly punched in the instructions. "Hellfire missiles hot."

"Roger that. Hang on, I'm coming around." He brought the shrieking Blackhawk into as tight a turn as it could make. The first Shark was less than two miles away, its double axial blades whirling like a meat chopper ready to slice and dice them.

Mac didn't have to tell Kathy to fire. She knew what she was doing. As soon as he got the nose of the Black-hawk turned so they were staring at the Shark screaming toward them, she went into action. The Blackhawk shuddered as the Hellfire missiles, two of them, flew from beneath the bird. Mac watched with satisfaction as both zoomed toward the Shark. The enemy pilot instantly threw out chaff and tried to evade the incoming missiles.

One went for the chaff. The other went for the Shark.

Kathy whooped and threw her hands upward in triumph. The Hellfire found its intended target, and the sky suddenly became a red-orange fireball in front of them. The Blackhawk rode out the blast wave.

"Let's get outta here," Mac said, turning the helo toward the mountains.

"Look out!" Kathy yelled. "Enemy at six o'clock!" That meant another Shark was on their tail. Somehow, it had made its move while their attention was on the other target. "Firing! He's firing his machine guns!"

The first 30 mm rounds tore into the Blackhawk. Metal ripped, and the helo staggered.

Mac wrenched the bird downward, toward the jungle. The Black Shark's guns continued to spew hot lead into them. His breath jammed in his throat, he concentrated on not getting knocked out of the sky by the cannons, which had the capability of doing just that. The air turbulence was rough, and the harness cut into his shoulders. Would Sophie be all right? Lucky for her, she had a protective armored wall behind her seat.

"Get our guns on-line!" he yelled to Kathy. "Hang on!"

"I'm on it! Give me a target, dammit!!"

They were flying at two thousand feet. The canopy below was a flowing green carpet. There was nowhere to hide!

The bird was being jerked around so hard that Kathy had problems flipping the switches. "Armed and hot!" she cried. The Blackhawk groaned as Mac brought it around in a turn so tight that she held her breath. Her eyes widened. The Shark loomed in their cockpit window. *Oh, God!* Without thinking, Kathy fired continuously and watched the red tracers arc toward the oncoming aircraft.

They were so close to a head-on collision that she could clearly see the pilot sitting at the controls, the helmet on his head, the olive-green color of his flight suit. This was a game of sky chicken! Who was going to blink first?

The tracers slammed into the Shark, and smoke immediately began to curl from the engines.

Mac wrenched the Blackhawk to the left. The blades of the helicopters came within inches of colliding as he banked the craft one way, while the Shark went the other.

Kathy gulped and held on for dear life. Mac straightened out the chopper just above the treetops. The tricycle gear beneath the fuselage was slapping against some of the higher limbs. *Christ!* Kathy jerked her head to look around. The smoking Shark was turning toward them.

"He's pursuing!" she warned.

"Okay, hang on. . . ."

Kathy prepared herself, her hand hovering over the gun switch. They had nowhere to go. The Blackhawk labored mightily to gain forward speed as well as climb. If they stayed on the deck, they were dead! After giving Mac a quick glance, she watched her HUD once more. Her whole body was soaked in sweat. They were fighting for their lives. Anxiously, she studied the HUD, and saw two dots. One was an Apache and the other a Shark.

Just as Mac was getting ready to turn the Blackhawk for another salvo, there was a huge explosion.

"What the hell!" he yelled, grappling with the controls as the blast wave hit them. The bird skidded sideways, losing two hundred feet of altitude. The landing gear began clipping the tops of the trees and branches flew up. Green leaves exploded around them as if they'd been chopped up in a huge blender. Wrenching back on the controls, Mac urged the bird skyward.

"What happened?" he demanded, his voice tight with strain.

Kathy shook her head, looking at the HUD. "I don't know . . . I don't know. The Shark's gone. Blown away . . ."

"King's Ace, this is Cobra One. Over."

Kathy gulped. The voice was a woman's. She sounded cool, under control, and that served to soothe Kathy's frayed nerves. "Cobra One, this is King's Ace. Over."

"We just took out your friend for you. This is Major Stevenson. I'm ordering you to our fortress. We have four Apaches in the air now. We'll mop up here so you can land without further problems at our base. Over."

Shutting her eyes for a moment, Kathy reopened them and turned to Mac. He was pale, his face glistening with sweat, his mouth a thin line. "Roger that, Cobra One. Thanks for saving our bacon. We owe you. Over and out."

Mac took in a deep, shaky breath as he eased the Blackhawk upward. It was only then that he saw several bullet holes on his side of the fuselage, near his legs. They'd come so close to dying. So close. Above them, he saw the Apache called Cobra One flash overhead, flying into the fray to finish off the last Black Shark. Mac saw two other friendlies nearby, as well. The Apaches owned the sky.

"We're safe. . . ." he stated wearily. To hell with it. He put the Blackhawk on autopilot and reached out and gripped Kathy's right hand, which was still curled in a fist on her thigh. "We made it. Thanks to you . . ." He stared into those wide blue eyes that were so incredibly beautiful to him.

Her lips parting, Kathy felt the tension begin to bleed out of her. She gripped Mac's hand and then looked over her shoulder to make sure Sophie was okay. The little girl was pale but smiling. Kathy smiled back at her and gave her a thumbs-up.

And as she glanced behind, she noticed a huge column of black smoke rising high in the air over the jungle. It was Carlos Garcia's estate. Tiki? What about her? Kathy wanted to cry. And as she sat there, twisted in the cockpit seat, watching the rolling black smoke spread outward, she thought of Garcia. Tiki loved her father. . . . Kathy's thirst for revenge began to dissolve.

No, he was an evil man even if he did love his daughter. One good turn out of a hundred bad ones didn't make him a good guy. Kathy would cry later for the loss of Tiki, but not her father.

Then, she turned her attention back to Mac. "I think we have a lot of talking to do once we get to this secret base, don't you?"

Nodding, Mac squeezed her fingers gently and then released them. "Yeah, I do, bright angel. I really do. . . ."

Chapter Twenty-One

"Mommy, Mommy, I'm coming home! I'm coming home!" Sophie sobbed as she gripped the red security phone to her ear.

Kathy smiled gently and held Sophie on her lap. They were in the office of Lieutenant Dallas Klein, executive officer of the Black Jaguar Squadron. Anyone and everyone who had seen Kathy carry little blond Sophie out of the Blackhawk after they'd landed had cheered at their return to freedom.

As Kathy soothed her, she glanced at her surroundings. She was amazed by how many women were here. All the crews, with few exceptions, were female.

And now Kathy sat in the chair behind Dallas's desk, and the small office was crowded with happy faces of the crew, as well as some of the returning pilots. Mac stood off to one side, his arms across his chest, grinning.

While the little girl spoke with her parents, Dallas Klein smiled with tears in her eyes. It had been her idea to contact

Sophie's parents directly over a secure satellite phone connection. As Sophie talked animatedly with her mother and father, Kathy continued to gently run her hand across the child's back in soothing motions. She could still feel Sophie trembling from their experience in the Blackhawk. But getting to hear her parents' voices was working wonders on the child.

When Sophie was done talking, she held out the phone toward Mac, the agent in charge of the mission. He playfully ruffled her hair and took it.

Kathy got up, and Sophie wrapped her thin legs about her right hip. Mac sat down to fill in the parents on what had happened and to assure them that Sophie was indeed safe and well.

As Mac gave his update, Dallas Klein came over to Kathy. "We need to get you and Sophie to the dispensary at the back of the cave. A doctor will check you out. Mac will go over later."

Nodding, Kathy saw the crowd part so they could leave the office. A number of the women murmured their heartfelt congratulations, and Kathy thanked them all. Then she followed Dallas down the hall, down the stairs and out of the building. They were once again on the floor of the magnificent lava cave, which hummed with constant activity. The noise became unbearable when an Apache came in for a landing. Sophie clapped her hands over her ears as Kathy carried her on her hip toward the rear of the cave.

They passed Mess, where they served food, a dispensary and a revetment area where two civilian helos were parked. Kathy looked toward the opening and saw a second Apache heading in. The puncturing reverberations hurt her ears, too. Finally, both birds were down and the engines shut off. The noise lessened quickly, much to her and Sophie's relief.

In her heart, Kathy wanted quality time with Mac, but right now she knew that was impossible. The military's need for doing things by S.O.P., standard operating procedure, would delay any reunion. The three of them would be put through their paces now that they were at the black ops base. Kathy glanced down at Sophie, who had uncovered her ears. The child grinned fully and her features relaxed, probably for the first time since her capture. Inwardly, Kathy cried over Tiki. Could she have survived that terrible attack? Remembering that towering column of black smoke, she thought it impossible. But she suppressed her tears over Garcia's daughter because Sophie needed her now.

"You're going home, sweetheart," she told her.

Nodding, Sophie placed her arm around Kathy's neck and began to look around. "Mommy was crying. So was Daddy."

"You were, too, but that's okay, Sophie. They're happy you're coming home to them."

"When can I go home, Kathy?"

"Soon," she said. "But first we have to get checked over by Dr. Elizabeth Cornell to make sure we're okay."

Sophie rubbed her damp eyes. "I miss my mommy and daddy. All I want to do is go home."

"I know, Sophie, I know. And I'm sure Mac will work hard to see that you go home just as soon as you can." Kathy stepped into the air-conditioned dispensary and met Sergeant Angel Paredes, and a Special Forces sergeant, Burke Gifford, who would examine them. They would do the initial exam and then Dr. Cornell would come in later.

As the paramedics looked them over, Kathy's thoughts turned to her own family. God, how she missed them! And she was going home to them, when she had thought all along she'd never see them again. That realization brought tears to her eyes as she set Sophie gently on a gurney.

Wait until her parents found out what she'd tried to do. Her father would raise holy hell over her self-planned mission. And her mother? Kathy didn't even want to think about how she would react. . . .

"Morgan?" Mike Houston called from the door to Morgan's office. It was 1900 and past quitting time.

"Yeah, Mike?" He lifted his head.

"I just got some news from an old friend of mine in Lima."

Heart racing, Morgan set down the report he was reading. Mike had spent seven years in Peru, chasing down drug dealers, and still had an extensive network of contacts there. When sources confirmed that Kathy had been the one on that trail to Garcia's villa, Morgan's life had exploded with terror. And he'd quickly put together *why* she was there. How he'd wanted to deny it! Deny all of it. Because that meant Kathy was going after the son of the drug lord who had made their lives so horrifying.

He watched Mike close the door and walk across the carpet to his desk. "Well? What did you find out? Did one of your sources come through for us?"

"Yeah," Mike said, "one did. My source is out of Cuzco and her general region is Agua Caliente. She just heard over the radio that Carlos Garcia's country villa near there was attacked by combat helicopters — four of them. Apparently Manuel Navarro, from Colombia, set up the hit on him."

Scowling, Morgan muttered, "Just deserts. It does my heart good when one drug kingpin takes out another one. Any more info on the strike?"

"Apparently several tourists were hiking near the villa when it was hit. They took digital pictures of the whole thing."

"There's one way to find out who was there, then." He hit the button on his intercom. "Jenny? Will you get Major Maya Stevenson on the scramble phone for me?"

"Of course, Morgan."

Frowning, he scratched his jaw. "You had said there was discontent among the other drug lords because Garcia's shipments were being stopped at the border by the Black Jaguar Squadron."

Mike perched one hip on a corner of Morgan's messy desk. "That's right. And we know that drug lords in Ecuador and Colombia own some Russian Black Sharks."

"Four of them?"

Shrugging, Mike said, "BJS has reported four in the area and they ought to know. They're the ones who play cat and mouse with these mercenaries, who would just as soon shoot them out of the sky."

Morgan nodded slowly as terror ate away at him. If Kathy was at that villa, she could be dead. He didn't want to go there. He just didn't, but the military strategist in him had to. The fear that she could have died in that attack shattered him. Wiping his mouth, he avoided Mike's hooded gaze. Mike knew. He knew exactly what Morgan was thinking.

"I'm trying to get an eyewitness snitch of mine that lives in Agua Caliente to call me," Houston said sympathetically. "Right now, we have no satellite reconnaissance of the attack. I've asked the U.S. Air Force for a fly-by on one of their spy satellites so we can get pictures, but they aren't going to be able to position it for another two hours."

"Jesus, Mike. I'm worried. My daughter . . ."

"I know." He grimaced.

"I haven't told Laura what we suspect. I just couldn't do that to her. She's been through so much, with the kidnapping and the rapes. If she realized Kathy was down there trying to get even with Garcia . . ."

Mike reached out and patted Morgan's slumped shoulder. "You said yourself you had no idea Kathy was going on such a mission."

"No." He sighed and looked up at the ceiling, tears burning in his eyes. "I mean, she came home unexpectedly, but that was all. I should have suspected something, dammit. I just should have, but I didn't."

"She normally comes home after completing a black ops assignment," Mike pointed out. "And she gave nothing away on what she was going to do when she left again."

Rubbing his eyes, Morgan sat up. "She came home to say goodbye to us. I realize that now." His voice broke. Oh, God, his daughter was trying to settle a family score with the drug lords! Missions just didn't work that way, but his daughter must not have realized it. Kathy had very likely bitten off more than she could chew. The fact that the U.S. Navy had stonewalled him and not given him any info on her mission enraged him.

Luckily, Mike's contacts and his own combined had found a way around the red tape. They'd learned that Kathy had gone on a revenge mission, pure and simple, and now she could be dead, a victim of the attack on Garcia. What hellish irony.

Clenching his hands into fists, Morgan stood up. What was taking so long? Generally, a scramble connection with BJS happened in minutes.

"Take it easy," Mike said as Morgan began to pace the office. His boss's face was pale, his eyes narrowed with pain and grief. "There's been a lot of satellite traffic today, so Jenny may be having trouble getting a connection."

The phone rang. Morgan hurried back to his desk and snapped it up.

"Morgan here. Maya?"

"Hi, Morgan."

She sounded sleepy, and he realized there was a five-hour difference between them. "I'm sorry to wake you, but this is urgent."

"No problem." She laughed huskily. "I've got Dane making me coffee as we speak."

U.S. Army Major Dane York was Maya's husband. He helped her run the squadron, although she was the commanding officer and creator of the black ops.

"Great. Listen, I need to know if my daughter, Kathy Trayhern, is with you." He held his breath, his heart bursting with anguish. What if Maya said no? What if she knew nothing about Garcia's villa being leveled?

"Yes, she is. I thought you knew she was down here."

Groaning, Morgan covered his eyes with his hand for a moment and sat down in the chair. Looking up, he gave Mike a thumbs-up. Houston grinned. "No, I didn't. That's why we asked for those photos from your pilots. Is she okay? Unharmed?"

"She's fine. We just rescued them — around 1100 today, our time. They escaped Garcia's villa just as four of Manuel Navarro's Black Sharks attacked it. From what we can piece together, there were two other drug lords, one from Ecuador and one from Colombia, who conspired to destroy Garcia and get him out of the picture. Navarro made the attack for all of them."

Relief, sharp and deep, sheered through Morgan. "Thank God she's okay. My daughter's really all right? No wounds? Any problems?"

Laughing, Maya said, "Right now, she's at the barracks sleeping like a rock, Morgan. The doctor checked her over earlier and she's in excellent shape. A little thin, but that's all. They rescued little Sophie. You remember her?"

"Yeah, I do. That's great news!" Morgan felt shaky inside. "Maya, what's the drill on this one? When is Kathy coming home and where will she be?"

"I don't know, Morgan. An ATF agent who was working undercover at Garcia's is calling the shots now. It's his assignment to clean up. I'll know more tomorrow morning."

"Okay, I'm flying down to your base, Maya. I don't care what this ATF agent has in mind, I want Kathy to stay there until I arrive. Okay?"

"Sure. I don't think it will cause a problem. You want me to tell her you're coming?"

Grimly, Morgan said, "No, I don't."

"She's lucky to be alive. The ATF agent and she stole a Blackhawk and managed to evade the Sharks that chased them as they headed our way." Satisfaction filled her voice. "I know you'll be happy to hear that there are four less Black Sharks in the skies around here. For a little while my pilots are going to be safe."

"That's good news," Morgan declared. "But you know the drug lords will buy more."

Sighing, Maya said, "Yeah, we're aware of that. At least for a couple of weeks, though, the skies over Peru will be more friendly as we continue to interdict drug shipments. Give my women a breather of sorts. Okay, listen, send me an e-mail on your arrival time. I'll have one of my pilots fly into Cuzco with our civilian helo to pick you up at the airport and bring you back here."

"Sounds good, Maya. Thanks for letting me know that Kathy's okay. . . ."

"Have you heard anything about Tiki from your handler?" Kathy sat with Mac in the busy mess hall the next morning. All around them, crews coming on for the day shift and the others coming off the night shift milled about, hunting up breakfast. Her heart twinged at the sight of Mac. He had showered and shaved recently, and his damp dark hair gleamed beneath the fluorescent lights. How handsome he looked in his army-green trousers and a T-shirt that showed off the expanse of his chest and broadness of his shoulders.

"No, I haven't heard anything. My handler's in Lima. I was on the phone with her after I got up this morning and she's flying here. Until she arrives at Garcia's villa, we won't know anything." He saw the grief in Kathy's eyes. "I'm sorry, Kathy. I'm sick about this, too. Tiki was an innocent."

Nodding, Kathy muttered, "I tossed and turned all night. I kept dreaming about her, Mac. Hearing her scream. I wanted her to survive that attack but I don't see how she could have."

He reached over and squeezed her hand. "Have a little faith. She's not on the latest DOA list." Mac gave her a slight, lazy smile meant to distract her from her worry.

He was trying to make her feel better.

"Okay, you're right. You're the spy, I'm not. I have no idea how things like this are handled."

"While we're waiting, you might want to ask me some questions?"

"Okay, dude, it's twenty questions time. Who are you, really?" Kathy demanded, smiling back at him.

"I thought you'd never ask." Slathering strawberry jam on his toast, he said, "My real name is McKinley Chandler. My friends have always called me Mac." He gazed into her soft blue eyes, which had lost all that darkness. Mac wished he could have shared her bed last night, but it was impossible under the circumstances. His heart wanted to be with her, body and soul. His head knew different. "How about you? I've heard tell that you're Kathy

422

Trayhern, daughter of the famous Morgan Trayhern. Is that true?"

Kathy felt heat flood her cheeks. Her time with Mac was drawing to an end, and they hadn't had any privacy since coming to the busy squadron. She had nothing to lose by telling the truth. "Yes, that's right." Tilting her head, she asked, "How did you learn *that* bit of information?"

Mac set the knife aside. "I have ears, Ms. Trayhern. That's what spies do — keep their ear close to the ground."

Her heart thumped once, hard, in response to the smoky look he gave her. Kathy knew Mac wanted her. And she wanted him. But how could they ever get together, in this impossible situation? Kathy wasn't sure. She *was* surprised to realize that, in the turmoil of the past months, she had quietly laid Curt's memory and their love to rest. Kathy felt the need to move on. Mac was responsible for that desire in her.

She nervously fingered the flatware on her aluminum tray. "You're a good spy, no argument from me." When his mouth curved deeply in response, Kathy ached to be in his arms. Throughout the last day and night Mac had been a solid, stable rock in a horrific storm. He didn't get rattled by anything, not even Black Sharks breathing down his neck, trying to take him out of the sky. The guy was incredible, in her opinion.

"I hope you're my friend, Kathy," he said, putting the toast aside. "And yes, call me Mac. Can I still call you Kathy?"

"Yes, we're friends." And more, she wanted to add.

Mac looked around the bustling, noisy mess hall. People were coming and going, their laughter and joking filling the air. He turned back to Kathy and said, "Look, we need some quality time to sit down and talk, some place quiet."

"Tell me about it." Her body responded hotly to the stormy look in his gray eyes.

"Do you want time alone with me?" Mac wasn't sure. He could tell Kathy was nervous. Or maybe because she was no longer undercover, he was seeing the real Kathy and not the nanny, Ms. Lincoln. In his heart, he wanted time with her more than anything in the world.

"Yeah, I'd like that, Mac." Kathy wasn't sure where their friendship was going. What she wanted and what she got could be two different things, and she tried to prepare emotionally for that reality.

Mac toyed with his knife and frowned. "For the next three days I'm going to be busier than hell. I have a lot of stuff to co-ordinate with the ATF from here. I have to go back to Garcia's villa, or what's left of it. The Peruvian police are already on site and so are a couple of CIA operatives from Lima. I've put a call in to one of them and I'm hoping to get info on Tiki if they find her. But cell phones don't work there, and getting time on an Iridium satellite phone is like trying to move fast in Los Angeles freeway traffic. But, I keep trying to get through." He looked directly into her eyes. "You've got pertinent info, too. You helped me get that CD of files from Therese's computer. The ATF will be wanting to de-brief you back in Washington as soon as I can wrap up things at Garcia's villa. I don't know who you're working for, and I need to query them on this and get permission to take you back to D.C. with me once we're done down here."

Nodding, Kathy said, "This was done under a U.S. Navy SEAL mission. I'm sure the commander who helped me will give me TDY orders to follow you to Wash-ington with no problem."

"A SEAL ops?" That didn't make sense. He saw Kathy raise her brows and give him a one-cornered smile.

"It's a long story, Mac. Something I'd

like to save for a quieter time." If there was going to be one. Her stomach knotted even more over that thought. Nothing was for certain here — not him, not her. Right now, Kathy felt as if she'd been tossed upside down and wasn't sure where the hell she was going to land.

Mac turned and looked toward the door of the mess. The X.O., Lieutenant Dallas Klein, was standing there.

"I think Dallas is looking for you." He tipped his head in her direction.

Kathy saw Dallas beckon to her. "Gotta go, Mac." She rose from the picnic table. "See you later?"

"That's a promise, bright angel." He saw her lips curve in a brilliant smile. "I'll find you. . . ."

"I bet you will. You're a spy, after all." Kathy laughed as she picked up her tray. After handing it to a server, she joined the lieutenant.

"Is Sophie okay?" The little girl had slept in a cozy room in the barracks, and one of the women had given her an old, well-loved teddy bear to sleep with last night. When Kathy looked in on her earlier, Sophie was sleeping deeply and soundly, her arms wrapped around that old, nearly hairless bear.

"She's fine. Still sleeping, probably. Don't worry about her for now. I have Angel, our paramedic, keeping an eye on her. When she wakes, Angel will bring her over here for a meal."

"I thought you might be here because Sophie needed me. Or because you had word of Tiki."

Shaking her head, Dallas said, "No, sorry. I've got my communications people on top of any info that might come to us about Garcia's daughter. You'll be the first to know, I promise."

Relief ate at the knots in Kathy's stomach. "Thanks, Dallas. That means a lot to me and Mac. We both really love that little tyke."

Kathy followed the officer out onto the smooth, black lava floor of the cave. The place was busy as crews performed routine maintenance on the huge Apaches.

Electric cars zoomed quietly back and forth, in and out of the tunnel at the back, which Kathy learned led to a mining operation on the other side of the mountain. It used to be a mine, anyway, so it made a good cover. When Maya Stevenson had been hunting for a place to put an Apache squadron she'd seen this huge cave and the defunct mining operation and figured all they needed was a tunnel connecting the two.

To outsiders and tourists, the mining operation appeared to be up and running. There was machinery and equipment, plus many company houses on the other side of the mountain. The two civilian helicopters had the name of the mine, Condor Mining Company, on their fuselage, and via them BJS was able to ferry in personnel, supplies and ammunition without raising suspicion. Yes, Maya Stevenson had been an incredible visionary. She'd brought an all-woman U.S. Army Apache helicopter team down here and built the cave complex from scratch.

As they walked toward H.Q., which was positioned on the left side of the mouth of the wide, deep cavern, Kathy was overwhelmed with how Maya's vision had come to fruition. Dallas had explained to her that at first the U.S. Army was glad to get rid of Maya because she wasn't about to be relegated to second-class citizen status. She'd been one of the first women to train and graduate as an Apache helicopter pilot but they'd refused to give her a combat slot. Maya said to hell with that.

Her father, a U.S. Army general, had pushed through her plan. Everyone said it wouldn't work, Dallas had told Kathy. Everyone expected Maya to fail, and wanted her to, this upstart woman in the U.S. military. But she was a combat pilot and, by God, she was going to fly combat or else.

Dallas had chuckled and explained how Maya recruited women from other foreign services to fly with her. Dallas was from the Israeli Air Force, and there were three Peruvian women helicopter pilots on their team. The rest came from the U.S. Army. And in five years the Black Jaguar Squadron had taken a sixty percent bite out of all drug running in Peru. Half of all the cocaine shipments hadn't made it across the border.

No one was laughing at Maya Stevenson's ideas now. Instead, they were trying to duplicate them in other South American countries. She had gone from being a troublesome bitch to being hailed as a visionary woman who had the moxie to carry out her goal. At some point, Kathy wanted to meet Maya. After all, it had been Maya and her copilot who had saved them from being killed by that last Black Shark.

"What's up, then?" Kathy asked as she walked at Dallas's shoulder. "Why did you come get me?" Perhaps to meet some of the women officers?

"You've got a visitor," Dallas said.

"A visitor?" She arched her brows in surprise. Who could know she was here?

"Yes. Your father."

Chapter Twenty~Two

Kathy tried to prepare herself to meet her father. What was he doing here? She hurried down the busy hall on the second floor, her heart pounding with dread. How had he found out about her mission? Frowning, she headed for room 202 and tried to gird herself for the coming confrontation. What she really wanted to do was throw her arms around his neck and be held by him. Her father had always been a bulwark of strength for her. Not protection — no, not that. But strength. She opened the wooden door and entered.

Nothing could have prepared Kathy for what she saw. Her dad, the legendary head of the Trayhern dynasty had red, swollen eyes, was unshaved and wore a severely rumpled dark gray suit. Stunned, Kathy quietly shut the door, a lump forming in her throat.

"Dad?" Her voice was low and trembling as she hesitated by the door, hands at her sides. A desk separated them.

Morgan tried to smile but failed. His

daughter looked incredibly well. Fit. Confident. She looked fine. Such relief flowed through him that he thought he was going to faint. Instead, he gripped the back of the chair he stood behind.

"I found out," he said.

"I can see that."

"Are you okay?"

"Yeah, I'm fine, fine." She felt torn inwardly. Her father looked like hell, and Kathy realized the suffering he'd gone through was because of her. That stung. "Dad," she said haltingly, lifting her hand, "I didn't mean to get you involved for this very reason. Look at you. Look at the hell you went through."

"When you have children, you go through hell, Kathy." Morgan saw the suffering, the guilt, in her huge blue eyes. Her lower lip trembled. "I know you didn't mean to hurt me like this, but I had to know what was going on," he said. Running a hand through his hair, Morgan gave his daughter a pained smile. "You know me. I love my kids and I have more than a little vested interest in wanting to keep them safe. I can't help it, I love you. . . ."

The words, so sweet and poignant, so filled with emotion broke Kathy up. "Oh, Dad, I never thought I'd see you again. I thought I would die on this mission." She rushed forward and launched herself into her father's arms. Morgan Trayhern was a giant in her eyes, no matter what he'd done to hurt her and the family. When she felt his arms sweep around her, hold her tightly against him, she buried her cheek against his broad, solid shoulder and shut her eyes. A sob escaped her as she clung to him.

"I love you so much," Morgan whispered roughly, kissing her hair. Patting her shoulder, he added, "And I'm sorry, so sorry about this, Kathy. It wasn't right that you had to try and even the scales with the Garcias." He choked and buried his face against her.

Morgan didn't know how long he held his tall, stalwart daughter, but he felt her crying, her body shaking in convulsions of pain. All he could do was hold her and gently rock her in his arms as he had when she was a baby.

"I'm sorry," Morgan soothed, "so sorry that I did this to all of you. It's my fault, not yours, Pet. The score was settled with Guillermo dying." He ran his trembling hand across her soft, silky hair. Her sobs deepened and Morgan bore the brunt of her anguish. How long had Kathy held on to this vengeance? Probably since the kid-napping so many years ago. Why hadn't he seen it in her? Probably because he felt with Guillermo dying, the score had been settled.

Why hadn't he recognized that while she hadn't been kidnapped, she had been as adversely affected as her loved ones who had been? And even more importantly, why hadn't he established a deep communication with his daughter, so that he'd know what was eating away at her like some shadowy monster? Hot tears flooded into his tightly shut eyes. Oh, God, he'd failed again as a father, as a parent. Was he ever going to get this right? Parenting was the hardest job in the world as far as Morgan was concerned.

As Kathy's sobs lessened, Morgan eased her away from him. The tears streaming down her reddened face, the inconsolable grief in her eyes, ripped him apart even more. He lifted his hand and pulled a white linen handkerchief from the breast pocket of his suit coat, awkwardly dabbing at his daughter's damp face.

"I'm sorry, so sorry, Kathy. I failed you — again. I should have talked to you about this. I should have known what was going on inside your head a long time ago."

Feeling utterly helpless, Morgan blotted his own eyes. He felt Kathy's hands on his upper arms and saw her smile brokenly through her pain.

"Dad, it's okay. How could you know?"

"I could have asked. And I didn't."

Shaking her head, Kathy murmured softly, "Dad, everyone was so wounded after that kidnapping. They tortured you for months! You were so close to dying when they rescued you. All I could do was cry a lot and pray you wouldn't leave me."

After he stuffed the handkerchief back in his pocket, Morgan gripped his daughter's cool hands. "Listen to me. I failed you terribly. Once I recovered, I should have started understanding how the kidnapping had affected you, too. I just didn't think it had, Pet. Looking back on all of this now, I realize how stupid that was on my part. How could you *not* have been affected?"

Kathy cherished this moment of brutal honesty with him. "For so long, I wanted to tell you how I felt, but I was afraid to, Dad. I knew Guillermo was dead but I didn't feel they'd suffered enough. It was like a monster growing inside me, pushing me, and by the time I entered the Naval Academy, that's all I could think about." Kathy saw the suffering in Morgan's eyes

435

as she admitted the truth. But it was time to get it all out on the table.

"In the academy I used all my knowledge, information and networking contacts to build this mission. I'd had the idea for a long, long time. The SEAL commander is a good friend of mine."

"And he still is," Morgan told her. "He didn't tell me a thing."

Tilting her head, she asked, "Then how did you find out?"

"Mike Houston figured it out."

Quirking her lips, Kathy said, "That was the one door I couldn't nail shut. I feared that Houston might figure it out."

"I'm glad he did, Pet. Come on, sit down," Morgan said, guiding her to the chair behind the desk. He perched his hip on the desktop and faced his daughter. "There are some things you need to know, Kathy. I decided a long time ago not to try and get even with the Garcias."

"Why not, Dad? That's something I could never understand. They hurt us so badly. It wasn't right."

"I know, I know. But Kathy, maybe as you get older you'll understand what I'm going to say. When the kidnapping occurred, I was at fault for not protecting my family well enough. I was arrogant. I thought they'd never have the guts to come after my family in Washington, D.C. But they did.

"After being rescued, I spent my recuperation figuring out a way to keep all of you safe and protected. That's why we moved to Montana and I created that fictitious tourist business as a front for Perseus. I felt all of us had suffered enough. Too much."

Morgan sighed, looking more deeply into his daughter's eyes. She had to understand why he'd done what he had. "Did I want to get even with the Garcias? Yes, I did. We mounted a mission and Guillermo was killed. I felt the score was evened. What I learned from all that was to put my family first, Kathy. I knew if I tried to continue retaliation, they'd come after my loved ones again. And that's something I couldn't bear to have happen twice."

"Oh, God, Dad." Kathy looked down at her tightly knit hands. "Have I just put all of us at risk again?" She'd never thought of this angle. Shaken to the core, she realized that she was just as much of an extremist as the drug lords. Looking up, tears welling in her eyes, she whispered brokenly, "Oh, don't tell me I've screwed it up for the family."

Shrugging, he said, "I don't know yet.

That ATF agent you worked with is supposed to go back sometime today to Garcia's villa and see who survived." Morgan grimaced. "I'm going with him."

"So am I."

Morgan hesitated. He saw the rigid set of Kathy's jaw and the look of stubbornness burning in her eyes. "Why?"

"Because of Tiki, Garcia's daughter. That little girl is innocent, Dad. I got to take care of her for many months and she's the sweetest child. I woke up this morning worrying about her. Is she alive? Dead? Wounded? I can barely stand not knowing. I'm going back there to find out. I have to."

"And yet your focus was to do what? Kidnap her to get even with Garcia?"

Hanging her head, Kathy muttered, "Yeah, that was the plan."

"But it changed," Morgan said, watching fresh tears track down his daughter's cheeks.

Sniffing, Kathy rubbed her nose with the back of her hand. "Yeah, it did. When it came time to do it, I couldn't. I realized I wouldn't put another child through what Jason went through. I've seen the result of his kidnapping. Tiki was another innocent victim and I didn't want to do that to her."

Kathy wiped the tears from her face with trembling fingers. "I wanted Garcia to suffer, Dad. I wanted it so badly."

He reached out and settled his hand on her shoulder. "I know. But you didn't take his child. You didn't go that route and I'm proud you didn't. You're better than they are, Kathy."

She met her father's dark, burning gaze and felt a wave of love for him. "You mean that?"

"Every word of it, Pet."

"Well," Kathy whispered, gazing around the small office, "I guess fate intervened, anyway. Garcia got hit by some other drug lords."

"Sometimes fate manages to set the scales of right and wrong back into balance," Morgan answered. He gave her a slight, strained smile. "I have something for you." He dug into the inner pocket of his suit coat.

Kathy gasped as he produced a thick batch of white envelopes. "My letters!" They were the goodbye letters she'd written to each member of her family. Her gaze flew to her father's face. His expression was grim as he held them out to her. "But how . . . ?"

"Kamaria lost her pet gecko. Apparently, it ran into your bedroom."

"Oh, God," Kathy said. She looked down at the envelopes in her damp hands. The one with Morgan's name had been opened, and her heart banged in her chest. He'd read it. A lump grew in her throat. Nervously, she fingered the well-worn envelope.

"I was digging around in your rolltop desk, looking for the damn lizard. Kammie swore it had ran up under the hood." He saw Kathy's eyes shimmer with tears. "I found your letters by accident the evening before I left to come down here. I only opened mine and read it." He choked. "I read it many times. . . ." His voice grew hoarse. "I had a lot of hours on that plane coming down here to read the goodbye you wrote to me, Pet. I just sat there in my seat and cried. I realized then what I had done to you."

"Oh, God, Dad, I'm so sorry." Kathy wiped her own eyes. "I didn't mean to hurt you like this."

"I had it coming. I should have been more unselfish and looked to my children to see how much they were hurting," Morgan rasped. He gave her a soft smile as she pressed the letters to her breast. "The rest are unopened. Do whatever you want with them."

Sniffing, Kathy nodded. She looked down at them and whispered, "I'm glad no one had to read them. I'm glad to be alive."

Taking a deep breath, she asked, "What about Mom? Does she know about any of this?"

Morgan shook his head. "No, none of it. I wanted to save her from the worry. She's gone through enough, Pet. But when you get home it would be good to sit down with her and tell her everything."

Kathy agreed. "Thanks for sparing her. She didn't need this. Just as soon as I can work out some leave after this mission is wrapped up, I'll come home. I'll tell her everything then."

"I think she'd appreciate a heart-to-heart talk with you, Pet."

"I'll do it." She brushed the last of her tears from her cheeks.

Morgan looked at his watch. "Listen, I'm going to get a hot shower, shave, climb into some casual clothes. Then we're taking one of the commercial helicopters to Garcia's villa. Meet me at the helo in an hour?"

The helicopter landed beside Garcia's villa. Kathy couldn't hold back her anxiety any longer. She couldn't choke down her fear, since every building lay in ruin, most still smoking from the fire that had swept throughout them. There were police and emergency workers sifting through the wreckage. She guessed they were searching for bodies. A number of locally owned cars were lined up in the driveway, along with two ambulances from the nearest village.

She was the first out the door, before the rotor stopped turning. As she jogged up the brick path, she felt Mac hard on her heels, despite the fierce buffeting from the helicopter blades.

Kathy knew her father would understand why she had to return to the villa. Tiki deserved more in life than to be a pawn. She was a child, someone Kathy had grown to love.

As she hurried through the complex, she tried to avoid the worst of the smoke. The air had the combined scent of burning wood and a horrendous odor that she knew was burned flesh.

Please, God, don't let it be Tiki. . . . Please . . .

Kathy swallowed and remembered that Tiki had last gone down the other side of the hill, to the caseta where her mother stayed. As she leaped over debris in the path, Kathy noted that, with all the palm trees and vegetation gone, the once lush estate resembled the moon, full of craters and lifeless.

The main buildings were completely leveled. When she topped the knoll and looked anxiously downward, she saw that half of Paloma's caseta was still standing. Kathy's heart jolted. Two stretchers held covered bodies. *Oh, no!* Hand at her throat, holding back a flood of emotion, she lurched forward again. The emergency workers had found two bodies so far, but there had to be three. Carlos had taken Tiki to see her mother.

Wiping her eyes, Kathy raced down the hill toward the men, whose faces were grave.

"Where's Tiki? There was a little girl in this building! Where is she?" Kathy cried out as she slid to a halt. Looking at the body bags on the stretchers, she realized that the still forms were too large to belong to a child.

"Señorita?"

Kathy whirled around. A short, thin man with black eyes stood nearby. He wore the same blue uniform as the other workers. "Y-yes?"

"The little girl?"

Her heart plummeted. "Yes, there was a

little girl in there. Her name is Tiki. H-have you found her?" *No! Oh, God, please, no. Don't tell me she's dead. . . .*

"*Señorita*, she was found first." He motioned to the larger of the body bags. "We found her alive beneath her father, who was dead." Shaking his head, he added, "And the mother, well, she is dead, too."

"Tiki — she's *alive?*" Kathy's voice was trembling. "Where is she?"

He smiled through his weariness. Leaning on the shovel he held, he pointed back up the hill. "There were only two survivors from this caseta. Pablo, here, heard the little girl crying, so she was the first to be found. A paramedic took her by helicopter to Cuzco. I think she had some burns on her hands. Her hair was singed. But she looked okay to me."

Mac came up behind Kathy, hearing the explanation. Seeing the tears running freely down her face, he wrapped his arm around her shoulders. Without a word, she leaned against him and pressed her face into his neck. "And the other person who survived, *amigo?*" Mac asked.

"The gardener. I do not know his name. He had a broken leg. They took him to Agua Caliente. The doctor at the medical clinic there is taking care of him." Looking around, the man said, "I know others who survived but I do not have a list of names yet."

"Thank you," Mac murmured, holding Kathy tightly in his arms. "We're glad the little girl survived." He closed his eyes and pressed his cheek against Kathy's hair. For the longest time, the world stopped for Mac. She was in his arms and leaning on him. They needed each other in that moment. For all the hell he'd gone through as a mole, it had had a damn good outcome. Tiki was alive. He was glad, too, for the gardener, a sweet old man who dearly loved the plants he tended. Good people shouldn't die in such a situation, and too often, they did. This time, they'd had some luck.

He gave Kathy a gentle squeeze and lifted his head to whisper, "Come on, I'll take you for an early dinner in Agua Caliente. We'll hitch a helo flight into town. I'll let your father know about Tiki and where we're going."

Kathy lifted her hands and with trembling fingers wiped the tears from her face. Sniffing, she said, "Yeah, fine. I — I just want to get out of here." Looking around, she stated, "This place looks like how I feel — devastated."

"A normal reaction," Mac assured her. "I'll meet you back where those jeeps are parked. We'll get someone to drive us into town. You okay while I hunt your father down and give him the news?"

She nodded and said, "I'll be fine, Mac. Thanks."

"I'm so glad Tiki survived," Kathy confided wearily to Mac. They sat at the India Felize Restaurant in the heart of Agua Caliente. It was 1900 and they'd hitched a flight down the mountain to town.

"Yeah," he murmured, cutting into his medium rare steak. "If anyone should have survived, she and that old gardener deserved to."

Kathy dipped the spoon into her sopa criolla, a Peruvian style vegetable beef soup. "I'm so relieved. And thanks for making a call to the Cuzco hospital to see how she was doing. First degree burns on her arms and hands is getting off easy. I can't believe she wasn't hurt more than that, Mac."

"It was my pleasure to get the info," Mac said. "We'll both sleep better tonight knowing she's safe."

"I know Tiki has relatives in Lima. Have they been contacted?"

"Yes. Her uncle is flying up as we speak. I'm sure Tiki will be absorbed into his family. It's a big one and the man is honest as the day is long. Tiki will finally have a real family. In time, I think, she'll deal with this loss, and with the steadying influence of her uncle and aunt, she'll grow up to be a pretty nice kid."

He and Kathy sat up on the second floor, whereas most of the guests of the highly popular restaurant were dining on the ground floor. The owners sensed that they wanted privacy and so had given them the second floor all to themselves. Mac was grateful for that courtesy.

Kathy seemed exhausted. Her hair was crinkled from the high humidity and she wore a simple white blouse, jeans and hiking boots someone had given her at the BJS base. She filled it out in the most provocative of ways.

"I wonder if Tiki saw much?" Kathy murmured, losing her appetite at that thought. She set the spoon back into the large bowl of delicious soup. "She has to be completely traumatized by it all."

Perhaps the only good news — other than Tiki's survival — was that Paloma had now been released forever from her heroin habit. As they'd left the caseta,

Kathy spotted an important find. To her surprise, the laptop bearing all the vital information on Garcia's operation was intact when she pulled it out from between two pieces of drywall that had fallen over it. Therese had been found earlier in the smoldering debris, one of the workers told them later. They'd also learned that Adelino, Tiki's British schoolteacher, had been in Cuzco at the time and was spared. Most of the kitchen crew had survived because they'd run out the back door and into the jungle to escape. Kathy had been thrilled to hear the news. The people she'd grown fond of had been saved, much to her relief. And she silently admitted she was glad Garcia was dead.

"I hope Tiki didn't see much at all, but we'll never know," Mac said. He saw the pained look on Kathy's face and gripped her hand for a moment. "Listen, you did what you could. Tiki will now be fine in Lima, surrounded by her relatives. She'll be okay there, raised by her uncle."

Kathy savored the warmth of his hand and squeezed his strong fingers. "I guess you're right," she whispered, rallying beneath his searching look.

In an effort to cheer her up, Mac brightened his expression. "I got a message late this afternoon from ATF headquarters. They want us to fly back in a few days and start the debrief on this mission. Want to spend a little more time with me?" he asked in a teasing tone. Watching Kathy recover sent his heart skittering in his chest. He'd never forgotten that one, heart-stealing kiss they'd shared, and he wanted more. Much more. As she lifted her thick blond lashes and looked across the table at him, Mac felt his heart expand with joy. Her blue eyes were large, trusting and filled with an undeniable emotion aimed directly at him. Mac was afraid to call it love even though that's what he wanted to do. Kathy had never said she loved him.

"I'd like that. . . ."

He cut another piece of his steak and asked, "Yeah? You can stand being around me for a little longer?"

"You tend to grow on people."

Chuckling, Mac popped the meat into his mouth, chewed and swallowed. "We don't know much about each other. I'd like to spend the time in D.C. changing that. The debrief will take at least a week." He lifted his brows and grinned. "I've talked to your squadron commander and he's granting you thirty days leave, which is appropriate in this case. You've been through a lot. And you've done a lot to help curtail global drug movements."

Thirty days. That was news to Kathy. She gave Mac a suspicious glance. "Now, you wouldn't have had a hand in that thirty-day leave, would you?"

Mac had the good grace to blush. He busied himself with cutting another piece of steak as Peruvian music, consisting of drums, accordion and throaty panpipes, drifted up the stairwell. He smiled briefly. "Can I plead the Fifth?"

"Not anymore you can't," Kathy insisted. Suddenly, her appetite was back. She took a piece of the warm, grainy dark bread and slathered it with butter. Her heart swelled with happiness as she stared at Mac.

Dressed in civilian clothes, a simple white, short-sleeved shirt, jeans and hiking boots, he looked like any other tourist coming to see Machu Picchu. But the curve of that delicious male mouth of his made her hot and hungry for him on a whole new level of her being. "I'm through being a spy. I was lousy at it, anyway. I blew it with you at the hotel. I knew it the moment those words flew out of my mouth."

Chuckling yet again, Mac shook his

head. "Yes, you did. Lucky for you, I was on your side. If I'd been a drug dealer or a snitch, you'd have been marked and dead within twelve hours."

"I know that," Kathy said defiantly. "That's why later, when I found you in Therese's office, I decided at the last minute to trust you. I knew deep in my heart that if you were an enemy, I wouldn't have lasted two days after returning from Cuzco."

"You're right about that. I think you should stick to being a Seahawk driver, doing your thing down here behind the scenes and working with Navy SEALs and Marine Recons." He gazed at her. "I hear from your SEAL commander you're damn good at what you do. You're not afraid of returning fire when you go into a hot zone to pick up a team."

After sipping the well-spiced tomato-based soup, she said, "I like to be where the action is."

"No joke." Mac gave her a look filled with pride. Kathy Trayhern was a modern-day heroine in his eyes. She was cool under fire. She could think during a crisis and plan what had to be done next. "Well," he said huskily, setting his flatware down on either side of the white platter, "you showed your stuff the other day when we stole that Blackhawk and made a run for the BJS base."

"And just where did *you* learn to fly like that?"

Grinning more widely, Mac said, "Where do you think? I was in the Marine Corps just like you at one time. I flew Seahawks and inserted black ops teams just like you're doing. After my six years as an officer were up, the ATF courted me. So I left the service and decided to try my hand at undercover work. And here we are."

Eyes wide with awe, Kathy sat back. There was so little she knew about Mac. "You're one of us! You're a Marine no matter where you go in life or what you do after you leave the Corps."

"Yep, Marines stick together," Mac said, chuckling. He liked the soft smile that graced her lips. Kathy wore no makeup, but she didn't have to. She was beautiful au naturel.

"So what are you going to do after this mission?" Her brows dipped. "Go undercover again?" She began to realize that Mac had been a mole for nearly a year and a half in the Garcia organization. If she allowed herself to have a relationship with him, she wouldn't see him for long stretches at a time. That didn't sit well with her. Having gotten a taste of spy ops, she understood only too clearly how one slip could put his life into complete jeopardy. Having Mac die was not something she even wanted to entertain. She'd just found him.

"I don't really know yet," Mac admitted. "It depends."

"On what?"

"Brazen woman, aren't you?"

"It's my nature to confront." Kathy grinned like a wolf, holding his laughter-filled gaze.

"Okay, it depends upon you and me."

"Go on . . ." Her heart skittered. She saw Mac sit back as if considering what he was going to say next. Her palms got damp.

"I want to think that there's more than a fleeting attraction between us, Kathy." Mac took a deep, shaky breath, because he was scared to death that she might not feel the same. "And I'd like the time to explore what we have or don't have. Being down here for nearly five months, working together, wasn't a fair test. We were undercover and we sure as hell didn't give anything of our real selves away."

"What about that kiss? Was that fake, too?"

He saw the fire in her eyes and the obstinate set of her lips, and had a tough time not smiling. Mac reached out and gripped her hand in his. "No, that was real. That was *me*. And that's how I felt about you. Nothing fake about it. Okay?" He searched her eyes deeply.

Her fingers tightened around his. "Okay."

"Were *you* faking it?"

Kathy sat up, stunned. "Me? No way, dude! Did you think I was?"

Releasing her hand, Mac smiled. He lifted the white linen napkin and wiped his mouth. "You could have. You had reason to. You'd just blown your cover with me. I thought you were angling to lure me into some kind of a relationship so I wouldn't squeal to Garcia about you."

"Humph! No way! I would *never* do that." Her expression was indignant.

"Do me a favor, bright angel? Don't apply for another undercover job because, trust me, you won't be able to carry it off. You just don't have it in that heart of yours to be a first-class liar," Mac said, winking at her. How he would love spending time with her. And in the end, he hoped his instincts were on target — that Kathy Trayhern could very well be the person to change his life forever.

Chapter Twenty-Three

Mac could see the closeness between Kathy and her father. He'd seen it often in the last four days. Each morning they'd fly out to the destroyed villa, searching for anything to help them with the drug war. Every night they'd sit in the conference room of the BJS base, huddled together with Major Maya Stevenson, her husband, second-in-command Major Dane York, himself and a secretary who typed up their findings.

Mac was moved whenever Morgan gazed across the table at his daughter. The man's eyes radiated love. It made Mac feel lonely and wish he'd had such a family. But he hadn't been so lucky.

"Well," Morgan said on the fourth night, tapping his watch and then looking up at the convened group, "it's 2300. Are we ready to wrap this up? Anything more?" He gazed at each individual in the cramped room.

"Sir, from my vantage point as Agent in Charge of the scene, we've sifted through that villa with a fine-tooth comb. I'm satisfied that we've found what's important," Mac said. He then looked at Kathy, who sat on his right. "And you had the biggest find of all — Therese's laptop. That alone, I think, is going to help us more than we know."

Kathy felt heat rising in her cheeks as she saw the pride burning in Mac's gray eyes. "A lucky find," she said. Across the table from her sat the legendary Maya Stevenson, who nodded and smiled at her. Kathy had already thanked her and her copilot for saving their lives out there that day they'd nearly died.

Kathy had the utmost admiration for the black-haired woman with the amazing emerald-green eyes. Maya was powerful and empowered. The whole squadron revolved around her, for her charisma as a leader was palpable. Kathy had found no one who disliked the major, and the whole unit almost idolized her. There were many rumors about her, one of them being that she was a trained medicine woman in some sort of metaphysical craft. Kathy hadn't found out more than that, for her people were highly protective of her.

In Kathy's mind, it didn't matter. Maya was one hell of a kick-ass leader. She had created this amazing black ops out of nothing more than a desire to help free her world of drugs. That in itself made her larger than life. Kathy had enjoyed being around Maya, for she was learning a lot from her being a good officer and leader.

"Let's wrap this up, then," Mac said with a smile. "I want to thank everyone here for your cooperation."

As they filed out of the room, Kathy noticed that Morgan pulled Mac aside. Curious, but realizing her father wanted to talk to him in private, she ambled down the hall, heading toward her barracks cubicle, located on the second floor. It was near midnight and most of the cave was dim, except for strategic lighting here and there. In the rear of the cavern the routine maintenance on the Apaches continued, as it did twenty-four–seven. She could hear the clink of tools, the soft murmuring of the crews on duty. It soothed her. She loved the military.

After showering and slipping into a dark blue cotton gown that fell to her knees, Kathy was heading for bed when there was a soft knock on her cubicle door. Frowning, she padded over in her bare feet and opened it. Mac was standing there.

"What are you doing here?"

He grinned sheepishly. "My room is

down on the first floor, I know. Men on level one and women on level two."

She returned his smile. "I don't think you're lost, Mac. Come on in. I'm about ready to call it a night." Kathy stepped aside. Her heart beat a little faster as Mac sauntered into her cubical, which held nothing more than a bed, a dresser and clothes closet. It was spare and simple.

Mac closed the door but remained near it. Kathy looked beautiful with her hair damp from a recent shower, her skin glowing in the low light. The loose gown could not hide her full breasts, or the luscious curve of her hips — attributes that had teased him mercilessly since he'd met her.

"It's late," Mac said apologetically, "but I wanted to let you know something."

Kathy sat down on the edge of her bed. Mac was so easy on the eyes. Folding her hands in her lap, she said, "Shoot."

"Your father invited me to come for a visit."

Her brows shot up. "Oh?"

"Yeah," Mac muttered. "After we're done with the debrief in D.C., he wants to fly us to Montana together on one of his Perseus jets."

She gave him a guarded look and wondered if her dad was matchmaking. Her mother was well known for it. Now her father? Gulping, she said, "Why?"

"He wants to offer me a job working for Perseus. I'd be flying Blackhawks again, inserting and extracting merc teams this time around instead of Navy SEALs."

Tilting her head, she smiled. "My dad knows good people when he sees them, so I'm not surprised." Just the thought that Mac might work for Perseus, might not be undercover anymore, lifted a load off Kathy's shoulders. "How do you feel about that?"

"I don't know. I just want to make sure you're okay with me going home with you, that's all. I'll listen to what he has to say, talk to his strat and tact people and then make up my mind."

"You're a great pilot," Kathy said, meaning it. She saw Mac puff up a little bit with pride at her praise. The man deserved to. "Won't you miss the adrenaline rush of combat flying?" She grinned knowingly.

"Well," he hedged, keeping his voice down because the walls of the cubicles were paper thin and he was sure other officers were sleeping on either side of them at this hour. "Being undercover is a constant adrenaline rush."

Nodding, Kathy said, "Yeah, tell me about it. Not any fun, either."

"Right on. Listen, I'm going to take off. So you're okay with that? Me hopping a flight with you to Montana in about a week?"

"I think it's great, Mac." Her heart was pounding. As much as she wanted to reach out and pull him to her bed, it was still the wrong place and wrong time. This was a U.S. Army barracks and such things were forbidden.

She saw hope burning in his eyes, maybe hope for a future together. Meeting his hooded gaze, she touched his hand. "Let me show you the fine points of fly-fishing."

"Bring it on."

Kathy was trout fishing in a deep pool of a snow-fed river that lazily wound through the dense pines above her parents' home. The day was cool, the sky a muddy gray, promising snow by late afternoon or early evening. It was late November, near Thanksgiving, and she inhaled the crisp air, savoring the scent of pine. As she stood in thigh-deep water in her rubber waders, she moved her rod back and forth in slow, graceful sweeps.

Mac was spreading out a red-and-white-checked wool picnic blanket on shore. On the flight out from D.C., they had agreed to spend this special time together. For three days he'd been shown how Perseus worked by Mike Houston. Mac stayed at one of the condos in town reserved for mercs coming and going on missions, while Kathy remained at her parents' home. It had given her the opportunity to talk to her mother — about everything. Kathy was relieved that Laura understood. It had been a tearful time with a very positive outcome.

Not a night went by when Kathy didn't lie awake thinking about Mac. About them. Glancing over her shoulder now, she saw that Mac had a nice fire going. It was time to quit fishing and fry up the four trout she'd already caught. She shifted her creel of woven willow to her left side, reeled in the line and then waded slowly back to shore. The temperature was hovering in the forties, the wind making the pines sing off and on above them. A storm front was moving in.

"I'm ready to fry those trout," he told her, getting up and taking her rod and reel.

"Great. I'm starving!" *For you.* But Kathy didn't say that. She handed him the creel, and Mac opened it and took out the fish. Kathy quickly peeled off the rubber waders and joined him as he knelt on the ground with the trout. Together, they gutted them and prepared them for frying in a big black skillet over the fire. Kathy tossed in a hunk of butter and knelt nearby as the filleted trout were thoroughly washed in the river by Mac. He then came back and placed them in the hot skillet.

"Mmm, they smell good," Kathy sighed as she quickly flipped the sizzling fillets over with an aluminum spatula.

"Yeah, I can hardly wait to eat them. I loved the fresh trout we always had down in Peru." Mac quickly brought over two red plastic plates. The night before he'd made potato salad and three-bean salad — about the extent of his skills when it came to cooking, he'd confessed with a laugh. Setting out the containers of salad, he sat and waited for Kathy to scoop the trout out of the pan onto the plates.

"Fresh trout. Yum," he murmured.

Kathy smiled, enjoying his closeness. "Did your dad ever take you fishing?" She was dying to find out more about Mac, but the time simply hadn't been available until now. She saw his smile fade. Turning the trout over in the skillet, she noted the meat was white, which meant the fish were ready to eat. After scooping up two of them, she placed them on the plate Mac held forward.

"No, my foster father was an accountant and a city guy, so I really didn't get out into the country until after I left for college."

He'd been orphaned? Kathy stared at him for a second and then scooped the remaining trout onto the second plate. She took the skillet off the grate and put a tin coffeepot in its place. They would have hot perked coffee by the end of their meal. Mac handed her cutlery and got out the salt and pepper. As she sat there, their elbows pleasantly brushing now and then, she murmured, "Your foster father? You were orphaned, Mac?"

Salting his trout, he said, "I was taken from my parents by the child protective custody people when I was very young. I don't remember most of it." He handed her the salt, their fingertips touching. He liked touching Kathy. When he saw the angst in her wide, beautiful eyes, he gave her a lopsided smile. "Hey, it's not the end of the world, you know?" He cut into his trout, finding the flaky fish incredibly tasty. Between bites he said, "I was three years old when a family adopted me. My foster dad was an accountant and my foster mom a teacher."

Her heart ached for him. Kathy ate slowly, milling over this surprising news. No wonder Mac seemed fascinated with her and her family. One night he'd been invited to dinner and had met Jason, Annie and their young baby. Kathy had seen him watching almost hungrily the interaction between her brother and his wife, as well as those between her and her parents. Now his interest made a lot more sense.

"What about your real parents? Do you know them?"

Mac spooned up a bite of potato salad. "My mother was a drug addict. She died a year after I was taken from her."

"I'm sorry," Kathy murmured. She reached out and squeezed his arm. His face lost some of its tenseness when she touched him. It felt good to know that she could make him feel better. "And your father?"

"I never knew him. From what I've been told, my mother was a prostitute making money to feed her drug habits."

"That's terrible," Kathy said sympathetically.

"Don't feel sorry for me," Mac replied, relishing the trout as if it was the best meal he'd ever had. "I love my foster family. They're proud of me and they love me. And I love them."

"That's good. . . . Were you the only child?"

Chuckling, Mac said, "Yeah. Does it show?"

"No, it doesn't. I was watching you with Kammie after dinner the other night and you were playing on the floor with her as if you'd always played with siblings."

"Maybe it comes naturally." He shrugged and slanted a glance at Kathy, who was looking at him in a new way. "I don't know."

"I'm lucky and I know it," Kathy said, picking up flakes of the trout with her fingers. "I've got a great family. It's not perfect and, yeah, we fight sometimes. But when it comes right down to it, we're tight and we love one another. I've seen enough dysfunctional families to know that mine isn't that bad."

After finishing off the trout, Mac said, "You're right. You have a healthy family. And knowing what I know now, I think you all survived the kidnapping pretty well."

"Except me. I had to go out half-cocked and try to get revenge for my family. I wonder if I have Mafia blood in me and don't know it?" She grinned at him as he laughed.

"I think you were the child that fell through the cracks on this," Mac told her, his tone serious. "Maybe because you weren't kidnapped, your parents thought you weren't wounded by what happened, but you were. They just didn't realize it, and you didn't communicate it, either." He sized her up, raising one eyebrow. "And that's taught me a lot about you. You hide what you really feel."

"Men do, too." She dug into the potato salad. Mac had done a nice job with it, adding chunks of red pepper to make it look pretty.

"Guilty as charged."

Kathy set her empty plate aside. She took a pot holder and moved the perking coffee to the edge of the grate, where it would stay warm, then got up to retrieve two tin mugs from their picnic basket. She sat back down on the log and, taking a deep breath, asked the questions that had been eating at her since they'd arrived in Montana.

"What do you think about my dad's business? Do you like what you see? Has he courted you enough to make you quit the ATF and come work with him?"

Kathy wrapped the pot holder around the coffeepot handle and poured the steaming brew into the mugs sitting at her feet.

"It's tempting," Mac admitted slowly. He placed his own empty plate behind the log where he sat. Picking up his mug, he watched the rising steam twist into the air. It was getting colder. Snow was on the way.

"My dad has a phenomenal record of sweet-talking the people he wants to come and work for him, and they all say yes." She sipped the hot coffee carefully and then looked in his direction.

"What about you?" Mac asked. "You graduated from the Naval Academy at age twenty-two and you're twenty-seven now. You have a six-year commitment with the military and two years to go. Are you going to re-up at that time or come back here and work for Perseus? I noticed Jason works with your dad. And Annie, his wife, is their corporate helicopter pilot. Morgan seems to want to keep Perseus a family affair."

Nodding, Kathy sat there, her knees spread, elbows resting on them. The mug warmed her cool hands and fingers. Frowning, she said, "I know he wants me to come and work for Perseus after my six-year hitch is up."

"So what's stopping you?"

Mouth compressed, Kathy answered, "Nothing, really."

"Maybe I need to be more straight with you," Mac said, noting her surprised look. "Ever since I set eyes on you down there at the villa, I wanted to know you a helluva lot better than I could at that time. When this ops blew up under us and I found out who you really were, I got hopeful." Opening his free hand, Mac felt fear moving through him. He had to get the truth out or it was going to eat him alive. "Kathy, if I take this job with Perseus it's because I want to have time to develop a relationship with you. If I stayed undercover with the ATF, we might as well say goodbye. I don't think any relationship could survive if I'm undercover for a year at a time. It would be impossible."

"I see." Her heart pounded as she stared down at her coffee cup.

"If I took this job with Perseus, I'd be available." Mac laughed sheepishly, giving her a shy look. "I'm coming clean with you. And that's why I was hedging about taking a job with your father. If you don't think there's anything between us, then I'm not quitting the ATF." He gazed into her warm blue eyes, which were so soft and inviting. At that moment, her full lips parted, and he groaned inwardly. "If there is, then I want to court you right and proper. I know the next two years are going to be rough because I'm sure you'll continue the South American assignments you were handling before. But at least we could see each other off and on."

"Yeah, I talked to my C.O. about that already. He's agreed to let me take assignments that are a month to three months long. I can take a week off between them and come home . . . here." She waved her hand, indicating the pristine beauty of the woods surrounding them.

"How do you feel about that? About us?" His heart thundered in his chest. Mac had never been so scared. Not even while staring a Black Shark in the face. If Kathy said no, all the dreams he'd built over the last five months were his alone and not hers. He could barely stand that possibility. As he studied her confident profile, he wasn't at all sure what her answer might be.

"You never mentioned having a man in your life," he added, his voice husky. "Not that we've had a lot of time together to discuss our private lives until now."

Kathy shifted, resting one knee on the

log, touching his hip. Cup in hand, she said gently, "I'm not in a relationship right now, Mac. I haven't been for about a year and a half. The guy I loved, Lieutenant Curt Shields, got killed in a firefight in Colombia. He was a Navy SEAL."

"I'm sorry. . . ." Mac felt his own chest constrict as darkness momentarily shadowed her magnificent azure eyes. "He must have been something." Kathy was the kind of woman that only a man very comfortable with his own identity would be able to appreciate and desire. Men of weaker caliber would be highly threatened by her composure, confidence and leadership abilities. All that did was make him want her even more. To Mac, she was like sunlight, and he wanted to hold her, love her and share in that brilliant part of her.

Looking down at the cup, Kathy whispered, "Yeah, Curt was one of a kind."

Mac's heart dropped a mile. How could he possibly measure up to her lost love? "Maybe you aren't ready for a relationship yet?"

Kathy lifted her head. "I really admire your guts, talking about how you feel. You're braver than I am. At heart, I'm a coward." She touched her chest for a moment. "I went through a lot of grieving after Curt was killed. It was after that that I decided to get even with Garcia. Drug dealers had wounded my family. They'd taken the man I loved."

"You funneled your grief into revenge?"

"Exactly." Kathy grimaced and sipped her coffee. As she looked up she could see that the clouds were getting lower, a solid, dark gray ceiling forming above them. In another couple of hours it would snow, she was sure. They were at a nine thousand foot elevation and the road was unpaved. When it got wet, it could quickly become impassable. Soon they'd have to leave, but she didn't want to. Talking with Mac was like breathing air — essential to her life.

His brows were drawn, his eyes thoughtful. She knew he was listening to her with his head and with his heart. When he reached out, captured her hand and rested it on her knee, she felt a lot of old walls she'd hidden behind for a long time begin to dissolve. Mac had magic for her. And that gave her the courage to go on.

"When I saw you for the first time, I felt so safe with you, Mac."

"You had no reason to," he said, moving his fingers gently across hers. She had such beautiful hands. Flight hands.

"I know, but I did. Call it gut intuition,

maybe." She smiled awkwardly. "Anyway, it got so that I waited for the day I could see you. You flew a lot and we really didn't get much quality time together, but I want to tell you, I hungered for your company. I loved having you nearby. I liked talking with you even though I couldn't really be me."

"So," Mac whispered, taking a firm hold of her hand, "where does that leave us now?" He searched Kathy's flushed face, noting that her eyes were bright with un-shed tears. When he saw her lower lip tremble he gently removed the cup from her hand and set it on the ground beside them. Without speaking, he brought Kathy close to him and placed his arm around her waist. The first tears trailed down her cheeks as he slid his fingers across the warm, firm flesh of her jaw.

"I'm afraid, Mac. So damn afraid," she confessed, closing her eyes as his fingers trailed across her jaw and cheek. "I'm afraid if I admit I'm falling in love with you that I'll lose you, too." There. It was out. Opening her eyes, she looked up, to find Mac's face blurred momentarily by her tears.

"Oh, bright angel," he murmured, framing her face with his hands, "nothing

472

in life is safe. You've got to know that by now. . . ."

"I — I know. My heart's scared, Mac." *So damn scared I feel like running away from you. . . .*

Mac smiled gently into her sparkling blue eyes. "You know, life is a game of chance, Kathy. I can't stop you from feeling scared. What I can do is love you, like you, learn how to be your best friend and be at your side as much as I can." As he searched her face, he saw a deep fear in her eyes. Mac understood where it came from: the kidnapping ordeal her family had undergone. At such a young, tender age, Kathy had had her family stripped from her. A very old tape played in her, one that told her no one she loved would be there for long; loved ones would be snatched away from her, as they had been before.

Mac gave her a broken smile and brushed the tears from her cheeks. "Listen to me. I'm not going to abandon you, Kathy. Yes, we'll be separated a lot in the next two years, but that will change with time. We can make our relationship work. We can take this time and build it one solid brick at a time. No relationship worth keeping was ever built overnight, anyway."

Just the gentle movement of his fingers

against her damp face soothed some of the demons still clamoring inside her. "You're like a dream come true, Mac. You always say the right things . . . to make me feel like this can work." Kathy saw his mouth curve into a rueful smile.

"I just got lucky. I'm not always going to have the right words, Kathy. I'll flounder around and make mistakes with you, with us. And so will you. But that doesn't mean I won't love you, because I always will." His hands framed her face and he added in a hushed tone, "When we were escaping in the Blackhawk I knew without a doubt that I loved you, Kathy Trayhern." He let his huskily spoken words sink into her. "I *love* you. I want you in my life now and in the future. I know it's going to be rough, but I'm willing to work at it because you're worth it. Frankly, I can't see a life without you in it." Mac smiled gently down at her. "Now, what do you say to that?"

Chapter Twenty-Four

Mac loved her. Kathy stared into his dark gray eyes. His black pupils were large and burning with tenderness as he held her bold stare. Mouth dry, her heart beating hard in her breast, she whispered, "I'm afraid, Mac."

Touching her cheek, he whispered, "So am I. Can we be afraid together? Just like gladiators in an arena, we can keep our backs together to protect ourselves from all outside threats."

Heat tunneled through Kathy as never before. The continued contact of his fingertips against her skin sent powerful waves of need through her. "I lost the only other man I loved to war."

"I understand that, sweetheart. But what are you going to do? Say no to love for the rest of your life because of that? Life's too short. How many times do we find the right person? Not often."

Kathy sighed as his fingers trailed down her neck. "Maybe I'm a bigger coward than I ever realized, Mac."

"We're all cowards at heart in some way. It's how we deal with our fear that really counts, Kathy. Are you going to let fear dictate your life? Or are you going to set it aside and grab on to something you really want?" Mac threaded his fingers through the gold strands of her hair. Her eyes turned that smoky-blue color telling him that she wanted him in all ways. "A coward would let the fear win. I don't see you as a coward. I see you as courageous in the face of overwhelming odds. Look at what we did together back at Garcia's place. To-gether, we took him down. Now if that isn't teamwork, nothing is." He chuckled.

The rumble of his laughter calmed her fear. "You're right. I know you're right."

"Listen," Mac said, becoming serious once again, "you're the one who's going back into black ops assignments in a few weeks. How do you think I'll feel? I'll worry for you every moment you're away from me. When you love someone, Kathy, you get the sweetness of their life with yours, as well as the things that might tear you apart. You work in danger. I work in danger. All we can do is try to be careful, stay safe and know that we have someone waiting at home for us when we come off an assignment."

His hand stroking her hair settled her down so that she could think through the haze of fear. Reaching up, Kathy grazed his strong, unyielding jaw. Mac was solid and strong. He endured. He had come from a terrible childhood and grown tough because of it. Like her. "You're right," she whispered unsteadily, tears welling up in her eyes and blurring his face. "I'm being a wimp about this."

"Your reaction is based on your experience, Kathy. I don't call that being a wimp. You have good reason to react the way you do." Mac leaned down and brushed her mouth with his. He tasted the salt of her tears and absorbed them, as if to take the terror and the hurt away from her. "I love you," he said gently against her lips. "I always will. I had nearly five months to realize that and I'm not running away from it now." He moved his tongue across her lower lip. Feeling her tremble, he smiled, and felt her smile in turn. "I want to love you, Kathy. Love you until we melt into each other and become one."

His words, a low, guttural growl, reverberated through her. Around her the sky was a gunmetal gray. The wind had stopped, or so it seemed. She felt as if the very earth was still, waiting for her answer.

The soft gurgle of the wide, shallow river, the singing of the pines around them seemed to be urging her to take Mac into her body and into her terrified heart.

"Yes," Kathy breathed finally, and began to unbutton his vest with unsteady fingers. His mouth clung to hers as she felt Mac start on the buttons of her goose down coat. The temperature was in the forties but she didn't care. Her body was hot, feverish and yearning. As she eased off the vest and tackled his shirt, she continued to kiss him, clinging to his mouth.

Tugging the flannel shirt off his shoulders, she felt the smooth warmth of his skin beneath it, the powerful set of his shoulders, the tensing of his muscles wherever she grazed him. Mac got rid of his shirt, his massive chest exposed to her gaze and exploring hands. When her fingers curled in the dark mat of hair, she felt him groan.

Suddenly, her fear dissolved. In that moment her inhibitions seemed silly compared to the man who was now waging a passionate war to win her heart and her soul. Standing, Kathy held out her hand to him. "Let's go to the blanket."

Mac nodded and stood beside her. He squeezed her hand. "No regrets?"

Kathy led him to the blanket and sat down. As he knelt beside her, she said, "None." The look in his eyes told her of his love for her. Wordlessly, she moved into his arms.

His mouth was hungry, taking hers as he removed her blouse. Kathy never wore a bra, preferring a cotton camisole. When Mac leaned back for a moment to slip it off, she saw raw hunger burning in his hooded gray eyes.

"You are so beautiful," he murmured, sliding his hands around her breasts and cupping them reverently. "So extraordinarily beautiful." He leaned down, ravishing her awaiting mouth as he stroked the curves of her full, firm breasts. Her moan, soft and musical, filled Mac with a heated desire that nearly overwhelmed him. Easing away from her lips, Mac smiled into her luminous eyes. "Lie down."

The blanket was warm, the air cold on her heated body. Mac opened the button on her jeans and with both hands tugged the denim downward. She watched, mesmerized, as he scanned her lower body as if memorizing every inch. Mac pulled her jeans from her feet and tossed them aside. His hands settled on the dark blue wool socks she wore and she smiled at him.

He made taking socks off a whole new experience. Mac slid his fingers into the top of her first sock and drew it down with excruciating slowness. As he did, he used his tongue to create a wet spot on her ankle, then softly kissed the area. Pulling the wool farther down, he moved his tongue across the top of her foot, smiling to himself when she moaned again. He was going to love every brave inch of her before he was done.

Wanting to memorize Kathy's body, her sweet, womanly fragrance and taste, Mac eased the sock off her foot. He rested her heel on his thigh and took each of her toes into his mouth and suckled on them. Kathy's fists were opening and closing now. It made Mac feel good to know he could give her such pleasure. The look on her face was one of barely constrained hunger as he set that foot down and began a sweet assault on the second one.

Kathy was going crazy, feeling wild bolts of lightning moving up her legs and converging in her lower body. She ached for Mac! And after he had driven her to the edge by taking off her socks, he started sliding his hands provocatively up her legs, stopping to kiss her here and there, his tongue tracing hot, wet patterns upon her tense, screaming flesh.

Feeling helplessly aroused, Kathy wanted to sit up and grab him and press her mouth to his. But he wrapped his hand around her shoulder, holding her down. She saw him give her a feral smile, his eyes glittering.

"Hey," he whispered in a husky tone, "I've spent five months waiting to love you. You have no idea how many sleepless nights I've had, thinking about how I was going to do it."

She laughed softly and stopped fighting his hand, which kept her pinned to the blanket. "Okay, okay," she whispered breathlessly. "Don't ever stop."

Gliding his palms across her ribs, Mac placed a series of heated, lingering kisses on the right side of her torso. As he approached her breast, her taut nipple, he smiled. Kathy gripped his arm, silently begging him to touch her. He settled his mouth around that tight little peak and gently began to suckle. Instantly, she groaned and curved her body around his. He slid his arm beneath her neck, the other against her long, strong spine, holding her captive as he teased her with his tongue.

Mac saw the wild hunger in her blue eyes. He quickly eased out of his jeans, boxer shorts and socks. All that was left between them were her cotton panties, and when he grasped the elastic, she groaned and tipped her head back.

Smiling, Mac eased off the lingerie and ran his tongue across her abdomen. He then trailed a series of hot, lingering kisses downward until he could inhale the sweetness of the core of her femininity. He placed another exploratory kiss at the apex of her thighs, and a cry tore from her lips.

As he slowly coaxed her thighs apart, he used his tongue not only to taste her but to revere the sacred feminine in a way that would send pleasurable shocks through her body. He had to let her know just how much he worshipped her.

A groan rippled from Kathy's throat. Her body bowed, her back arching as his mouth wreaked havoc on her composure. Gripping his shoulders, she rasped, "Enough! Come here!" She hauled Mac toward her. He smiled knowingly and allowed her to pull him down on top of her.

"Had enough?" he growled, burying his fingers in her tangled blond hair. "Convinced yet that I love you?" He gave her a wicked look.

"You've done more than convince me! You're driving me crazy! Come here. I need you, Mac. *All* of you!" Kathy arched assertively, to meet and find his warm male hardness waiting for her.

It was so easy to thrust forward into her hot, wet body. Her strong thighs wrapped around his legs, and Mac's lips pulled away from his clenched teeth as she waged a new assault on him. Her mouth was hungry and bold as she kissed him. She used her hands to pin his hips against her as she moved with strong, sinuous undulations. It was his undoing.

Their mouths were wet as they clung together. Kathy moaned and felt the pressure in her body building and building as he thrust powerfully against her. She met each thrust with her own. *Oh yes!* She heard him groaning, a bull ready to charge recklessly ahead. With the taste of his sweat on her lips, the scent of his masculine fragrance saturating her flaring nostrils, she dug her fingers into his biceps. At that moment, Kathy felt her inner core explode in a white-hot heat that sent out tidal waves of pleasure within her. Squeezing her eyes shut, she froze against his hard, sweaty body. She pressed her cheek against his sandpapery jaw, her lips parted in a soundless scream of incredible gratification.

Feeling her grow taut, her body flexing

beneath him, Mac knew she was reaching her climax. He felt her tremble as if an earthquake were rushing through her. *Yes! This was it!* Thrusting deeply into her, he gripped her hip and held her in a position that he knew would accentuate and prolong the pleasure of her orgasm. And then his control snapped.

With a growl, Mac took her hard and relentlessly. Her body was soft, accommodating and glowing with her ecstasy. Within seconds, Mac felt his own explosive release. Groaning, he held her hard, burying his face in her tangled curls, his breath coming in savage bursts as the world went spinning.

To Mac, there was no greater communion than this — being with a woman who loved him, who shared her sacredness with him. A woman who allowed him to be within her, to participate in her dark inner mystery. Submerged within the white-hot pleasure flowing through him, all Mac could do was hold Kathy, his breath raspy as he strained against her. She held him in turn, strong and steady and loving. Moments spun into an eternity of light, starbursts of color and scalding satisfaction.

When it was over, he rolled to his side

and brought her against him, pulling up the wool blanket to protect them from the cool wind.

Cradling her head on his arm, Mac gazed down at Kathy. He felt a fierce kind of love he'd never felt before as he gently pushed the damp strands of her blond hair off her brow. And when she lifted those thick, long blond lashes, her blue eyes dazed with pleasure, he felt stronger as a man than he ever had before. His gaze moved to her lips, slightly pouty from his ravishment, wet and gleaming, still beckoning.

"What we have is one of a kind, bright angel," Mac began, his voice gravelly as he brushed her flushed cheek with his fingers. He trailed his hand down her slender neck and cupped her breast.

"Mmm," Kathy whispered. "I'm so weak, Mac. Weaker than a kitten. That was something else. . . ." Blissfully she looked up and met his stormy gray eyes.

"It was us. We're good together, Kathy. I knew we would be." Mac brought her fully against him, their damp bodies clinging. He slid his hand around her hip and held her close. Her head came to rest on his shoulder, her face pressed against the column of his neck. Nothing had ever felt more right to Mac than this precious instant in time.

"I love you, Kathy Trayhern. I'll live loving you and I'll die loving you." He pressed a kiss against her temple, her hair tickling his face. "I'm not afraid to love you a hundred and ten percent. You're my life."

His words were like raindrops in the parched desert of her heart. She smiled as she nuzzled him, kissing his throat and feeling the powerful pulse of blood through it.

"You've convinced me, darling."

Mac stayed very still. "Do you mean that, Kathy? Do we have a chance for a life together, no matter what it throws at us?"

Lifting her head, she met and drowned in his gaze. "I mean every word of it, Mac. I've never been so thoroughly loved, one inch at a time. . . ." Her mouth stretched into a smile of wonderment as she searched his eyes.

"We've got more than three weeks here together," Mac whispered, cupping her face and holding her gaze. "Let's use this time to seal what we have. Let's use it to really explore one another, to get to know one another like we should."

Nodding, she turned her head and

kissed his palm. "I'd like that, Mac." Kathy saw relief flood his face. "I love you, too. I was just afraid to admit it."

A self-satisfied smile curved his well-shaped mouth. "Really?"

"Yeah, really, flyboy." Laughing briefly, she said, "You don't know how many nights I tossed and turned, thinking about *you.*"

"It's good to know that I wasn't the only one losing sleep," he teased.

Giggling, Kathy gave him a fierce hug and kissed him deeply. As she eased away from his mouth and met his eyes again she said, "But remember, I thought you were a drug dealer, and there was no way I was going to fall for you no matter how attracted I was to you."

Preening a little, Mac said, "You *were* attracted to me all along? I thought so!"

"You're easy on the eyes, darling." She slid her hand over his shoulder and arm. "I had one helluva time trying not to think about your mouth, how you would kiss and whether I'd like it or not."

"Did you?"

"And if I tell you the truth will it go to your swelled head, flight jock?"

Chuckling, Mac said, "Oh, probably." He leaned over and brushed her smiling lips with his. "You're easy on the eyes all the time, dressed or undressed." He smiled into her shining gaze which was filled with love — for him. It was a euphoric and freeing discovery for him. Kathy was not going to let her fear stop her from reaching out and having a relationship with him. It couldn't get any better than this.

"I thought I saw a lascivious glint in your eyes every time you looked at me!" Kathy accused, laughing. She enjoyed his maleness, his strength and his gentleness.

Above them, the sky was darkening, and the temperature dropping even more. She shivered and shifted closer to him.

"Trust me, every time I saw you at the villa I had plenty of thoughts about what I'd do to you if I could get you off by ourselves somewhere."

"You had your chance when we were in Cuzco," she taunted with a laugh.

"Yes, and I damn near blew it after kissing you. I tried to resist you, Kathy, but I just couldn't. I didn't really want to, but I knew it could lead to my being discovered, my cover being blown." Mac gave her a devilish look. "And when you went after me, chased me, well, I couldn't say no."

"Nor did you want to!" she accused, ruffling his dark hair.

"Did you kiss me there because you'd blown *your* cover?" Mac had always wondered that.

The first snowflakes were twirling down around them. It was time to leave their place of love. Getting up, he tossed her clothes to her.

Kathy caught them and smiled. She stood up with his help, her knees still a little weak from his wonderful lovemaking. "Yes and no. I was afraid you'd seen through me. There was a part of me that panicked, Mac, and yet my dumb heart kept screaming at me to go ahead and trust you." Pulling on her jeans, she slipped the camisole over her head and then took the proffered blouse from Mac.

Buttoning his jeans, he looked at her. "So your trust in me won out? That's why you kissed me in Cuzco?"

Nodding, Kathy put on her jacket, then sat down and pulled on her socks. She'd keep these socks under glass forever when she got home. "Yes, I caved in. I fought my attraction to you for so long, Mac. I didn't want to fall in love with a drug dealer." She looked up with a twisted grin. "No matter how easy you were on my eyes, or how badly I wanted you."

Mac quickly pulled on his own socks and

boots. The snow was thickening. All around them, the forest had quieted, except for the happy gurgle of the river nearby. "I'm glad you didn't resist me, sweetheart." He stood up and held out his hand to Kathy, who had just finished tying her boots. "Come on, let's pack up and go home."

Kathy gripped it and straightened, then released his hand even though she didn't want to. Her body glowed with such pleasure even now that just looking at Mac, stalwart, strong and so devastatingly handsome, made her hungry for him all over again.

"I have an idea," she murmured.

"I'm listening." He saw the devilry in Kathy's eyes.

"I'm going home with you, to your condo. You got a problem with that? I'm not done with what we started here. I want more. A lot more."

Grinning broadly, Mac picked up the blanket and, between them, they quickly folded it up. "Fine with me. But is your father going to fire me before he hires me if his daughter is warming my bed?"

Clasping the blanket against her body, Kathy hesitated. "You're going to work for Perseus? You've decided?" She searched his face ruthlessly, her heart beating hard.

Looking around, Mac drawled, "A man would be crazy to go undercover when he could have all of this."

"What about us?"

"And us, too."

She knew Mac was teasing her. "And you're taking the job because . . ."

"Because of you and me," Mac told her seriously. He walked over and gripped her shoulders, his voice rough. "I told you before, Kathy, you're my life. I knew it the moment I saw you at the villa, and I know it now. Nothing's changed for me. What had to change was your belief in us having a chance." He squeezed her arms gently. "And I think I just convinced you of that. Didn't I?"

Matching his grin, Kathy said, "Yeah, you did."

"Are you sorry?" Mac studied her clear blue eyes, which were regarding him with such love and desire. He never wanted to read Kathy wrong. Oh, he knew he would. It was a matter of getting to know her, learning her expressions, her voice and her body language. But right now Mac knew how tentative their relationship was, how fragile, and he didn't want to do anything to undermine it.

Licking her lower lip, Kathy said huskily, "Sorry? No way, dude. When I commit, it's forever. I'm not a halfway kind of woman, as you'll find out."

Relief flowed through Mac's heart. Kathy was a treasure — and she was his. "So am I, bright angel. We've found each other, now let's find ways to keep what we have. I know we can . . . forever. . . ."

About the Author

A homeopathic educator, **Lindsay McKenna** teaches at the Desert Institute of Classical Homeopathy in Phoenix, Arizona. When she isn't teaching alternative medicine, she is writing books about love. She feels love is the single greatest healer in the world and hopes that her books touch her readers on those levels. Coming from an Eastern Cherokee medicine family, Lindsay was taught ceremony and healing ways from the time she was nine years old. She creates flower and gem essences in accordance with nature and remains closely in touch with her Native American roots and upbringing.

The employees of Thorndike Press hope you have enjoyed this Large Print book. All our Thorndike and Wheeler Large Print titles are designed for easy reading, and all our books are made to last. Other Thorndike Press Large Print books are available at your library, through selected bookstores, or directly from us.

For information about titles, please call:

(800) 223-1244

or visit our Web site at:

www.gale.com/thorndike
www.gale.com/wheeler

To share your comments, please write:

Publisher
Thorndike Press
295 Kennedy Memorial Drive
Waterville, ME   04901